Death of a Dear Friend

Death of a Dear Friend

Ann Quinton

PIATKUS

Copyright © 1990 by Ann Quinton

First published in Great Britain in 1990 by
Judy Piatkus (Publishers) Ltd of
5 Windmill Street, London W1

British Library Cataloguing in Publication Data
Quinton, Ann
   Death of a dear friend.
   I. Title
   823.914 [F]

   ISBN 0-7499-0038-5

Phototypeset in 11/12pt Compugraphic Times by
Action Typesetting Limited, Gloucester
Printed and bound in Great Britain by
Billing & Sons Ltd, Worcester.

Chapter One

The North Sea ferry lurched across the mouth of the estuary. As she edged past the sand spit that marked the convergence of sea and river, the comparatively sheltered water reduced the sickening pitch and roll to a more subdued judder. The tail end of March had roared out in a fury and All Fools' Day was heralded by a force 8 gale blowing from a northwesterly direction: the worst possible combination for a Channel crossing.

The battered ship nudged through the black, heaving water and came to rest with a final shudder at her berth. The journey had taken nearly an hour longer than the scheduled time. Now disembarkation was soon under way. The gangway was rolled into position and before long the first passengers tottered wearily down, clutching their bags of duty-free, their faces pinched and sickly in the early morning light. Almost immediately the mighty stern doors opened and the bowels of the ship reverberated as engines sprang to life and the first vehicle roared ashore.

At that moment a jagged tear rent the cloud formation overhead, revealing a pale turquoise triangle of sky through which a delicate shaft of sunlight touched the gantries and giant cranes looming over the quayside.

The red Volkswagen was locked and empty. Drivers attempting to leave the ferry, frustrated by the vehicle in their path, hooted futilely and grumbled at the stewards supervising the operation. A call went out over the tannoy system requesting the owner of the car to report immediately to the car deck because his vehicle was causing a hold-up. The plea went unanswered. Eventually the Volkswagen was manhandled and shunted sideways to allow all cars access to the ramp. Half an hour later the red car was still there, the solitary occupant of the vast deck, and the stewards were discussing the possibility of a man overboard.

Terry Hibbert, the duty steward on B Deck, bowled down the passageway between the row of cabins, flinging open the doors on either side. Phew! It didn't take much sea to get the landlubbers puking, and last night it had been heavy seas indeed. He had had to admit that even he had been affected; a nagging ache over his left hip paid witness to the way in which he had had to brace himself against the ship's movements.

The end cabin door resisted his efforts and he rattled the handle. It was locked and the key was not on the outside. He bent down and tried to peer through the keyhole, and his nostrils tightened as he caught a whiff both sour and nauseously sweet. Some poor bugger had sicked his guts up. He rapped on the door and called out:

'We've berthed, sir. Time to go ashore!'

Silence greeted him and he sighed. This was all he needed. Turn-around was late already; at this rate he'd still be working when the ship embarked at fourteen hundred hours, with no time for a break. He gave a final tap on the door and turned back to the purser's office where the master key was held.

Jack Paynter, the purser, looked up from his desk.

'Trouble?'

'Cabin 32 is locked and I can't make anyone hear. Reckon he's been throwing up all night and is now sleeping off the effects.'

'Or has laid himself out with too many pills. Let's see ...' He ran his finger down the list of cabin occupants. 'A Mr Hargreaves. I remember now, he booked both berths because he wanted privacy and refused to give one up although I had people begging me last night for a cabin. Well, let's go and give him his morning call.'

Jack Paynter was a large man with a bluff, hearty manner. In his years as an employee of the shipping company he had seen it all, or so he reckoned. Very little ruffled his calm.

He paused outside the cabin, hitched up his trousers over his generous paunch and knocked on the door.

'Good morning, sir. We've arrived at Felstone. Time to get up! Dead to the world,' he boomed to the steward beside him. 'Ah, well.' He shrugged, turned his key in the lock and swung open the door. The cabin was in darkness and the foetid air from inside enveloped them.

'What the – ?' The purser snapped on the light and stopped short. Behind him the steward poked his head round the bulk of his superior.

'Christ! He's done himself in!'

'Or been done for.'

The body lay half in, half out of the bottom bunk; a middle-aged man with gaping stab wounds in his chest and neck. There was blood everywhere – on the bedclothes, across the pillow, seeping across the floor, even the wall beside the bed was stained as if someone had thrown a bucket of red paint against it. The purser swallowed his gorge and slammed the door shut on the appalling scene.

'This is a case for the police. The Master must be told. Pull yourself together, man!' The steward was hugging himself with shaking arms and retching miserably. 'Stay here while I report it. Don't let anyone past that door and keep your mouth buttoned.'

He went towards the bridge in search of the Master. Behind him the steward huddled against the wall muttering, 'Gawd! Oh, Gawd!'

Detective Inspector James Roland was in the CID general office at Felstone police headquarters when the call came through. He looked across the desk at his sergeant, who was laboriously typing out a report with two fingers.

'There's a stiff turned up on the *Mercia* ferry. Uniformed branch are already there and they've sent for us.

'Unnatural causes?'

'He's been knifed apparently. Can you bear to tear yourself away from all this?' Roland gestured to the papers and files littering the work surface.

'You mean we actually get to do some real detecting?' Patrick Mansfield pushed aside the typewriter with alacrity and lumbered to his feet. He was a tall, thickset man with dark, close-cropped, greying hair and deep-set eyes, who was increasingly frustrated by the amount of paperwork thrown up by modern policing. At forty-five he was thirteen years older than his immediate superior, but what could have been an awkward situation had been turned into a good working relationship by the two men. James Roland, with his university degree, his dark romantic looks and his reputation as a hard, ambitious man who wasn't afraid to stick his neck out, needed an anchor and he had found it in his sergeant. The Suffolk-born, phlegmatic, dry-humoured Mansfield and the quick-witted, somewhat arrogant Roland complemented each other.

'Do we know any details yet?' Mansfield asked as Roland swung the car round the corner of the station yard and headed for the dock road.

'They think he's British. He was found inside his locked cabin after the ship berthed.'

'Drugs? Or could he tie in with this illegal immigration caper?'

'Could well do.'

Felstone was a thriving east-coast port with a healthy container traffic and a reputation as an up-and-coming British dock. As such it had seen its share of drug-running and only last month a large quantity of heroin had been seized in the course of being smuggled ashore. Felstone was also a target for illegal immigration and eighteen months earlier a container full of Pakistanis had been found in a lorry parked in one of the dock-company car parks. The dock authorities, Customs officials and local police worked in close liaison and Roland and Mansfield were no strangers to the dock complex.

'I'm surprised there's not more than one corpse after a night like last night,' said Mansfield. 'I wouldn't have liked to have made the crossing.'

'Me neither, and the ship must have been packed, it being Easter Monday. I should think it'll rank as one of the worst crossings on record.'

4

'It seems to have blown itself out now. The wind has dropped.'

A weak sun was chasing the ragged clouds across the sky. There would be rain later, but now the only reminder of the overnight storm was a fitful breeze tugging at the treetops and scattering drifts of torn, bruised blossoms across the pavements and road.

Roland parked the car and the two men hurried through the terminal building and were ushered aboard the *Mercia*. They were taken to the Master's cabin where Captain Bell-Jones awaited them. He was a short, rotund man with a brisk manner who did not welcome the presence of police officers aboard his vessel. Grudgingly he introduced the two men who were with him.

'My purser, Mr Paynter, and Mr Hibbert, the steward who was on duty on B Deck this morning.'

'Where the body was found?'

'Yes. I expect you want to see the, er ...'

'All in good time. I take it you're the two people who found the body?' Roland turned to the purser and steward. 'Just tell me in your own words exactly what happened — the sequence of events and what action you took.'

'Well, it was like this.' The steward swallowed and took a grip on himself. 'I was just doing my rounds.' At Roland's raised brows he hurried to explain. 'At the end of each trip, after all the passengers have disembarked, the cabins have to be cleaned and made ready for the next crossing.'

'Do outside cleaning staff come aboard?'

'No, it's all done by ship's personnel — whoever happens to be on the rota for that day. Anyway, I was just walking down the passageway throwing open the cabin doors prior to doing that and when I got to cabin 32 I couldn't. I mean, it was locked and the key wasn't in the door. There was this horrible smell, reminded me of a butcher's shop on a hot day,' he said with hindsight. 'I knew that something was wrong, I had this funny feeling.'

'Detective Inspector Roland is here to ascertain facts, not to listen to your premonitions,' the captain boomed.

'Yes, sir.'

'What did you do then?'

5

'Well, I banged on the door and called out as I thought he might have overslept, but nuffink, not a dicky-bird, so I went to find Mr Paynter. He has the master key.'

The purser took up the story. 'There was a bit of a swell last night and a lot of passengers were under the weather. I thought nothing of it, just imagined that he had been ill in the night and was sleeping it off or had doped himself with seasickness pills — it's surprising how many do. They think if one will help them, three or four will do miraculous things. So I also hailed him and knocked on the door and, when there was no reply, I unlocked and opened it.'

'There was this geezer lying there' the steward croaked, 'all covered with blood and these bleeding great ... great *holes* in his chest!'

'Was the light on?' Roland asked sharply.

'No,' said the purser firmly. 'I distinctly remember, when I pushed open the door the cabin was in darkness and there was this horrible smell, as Hibbert has mentioned. So I switched on the light, and there he was. He hadn't just been killed, Inspector. Someone had run amok!'

'Did you go inside the cabin? Touch the body?'

'No way. You could see he was as dead as a doornail. I just slammed the door on him, left Hibbert on guard and came for Captain Bell-Jones.'

'As soon as I had ascertained that he hadn't died from natural causes,' said the captain, causing Mansfield, who was taking discreet notes in the corner, to think that that must surely be the understatement of the year, 'I realised it was a case for the police and I rang through to shore. Two uniformed officers came aboard and they immediately recognised it was a case for you chappies.'

'We know the name of the dead man?'

'A Mr Hargreaves, sir,' said Paynter. 'Or, at least, that was the name given when he booked the cabin.'

'You remember him doing so?'

'No, I'm afraid not. We were very busy and we carried a full complement of passengers. I just have his name on my list but I do remember that he booked a double-berth cabin and I must have spoken to him later because he refused to share even though people were crying out for sleeping accommodation.

6

But as I say, I can't actually recall speaking to him though I must have done.'

'Do you have an address for him?' Mansfield put in.

'No, we just make a note of names.'

'And what about the other passengers, the ones who don't book cabins?'

'We have no record, I'm afraid, though, of course, people booking cars on board are registered.'

'Are you saying you have no manifest of passengers? You carried how many last night − six, seven hundred people? And you have no list of names and addresses? This is going to make our task considerably easier,' said Roland sarcastically. 'Was the victim a foot passenger or did he have a car, do we know?'

'There is a car unaccounted for,' said the captain cautiously. 'It was left unclaimed when we docked, a red Volkswagen Golf. It's still on the car deck, though it had to be moved as it was blocking the exit for two columns of vehicles.'

'Sounds as if it must belong to the dead man. We'll have a look at it as soon as we've finished with the body. Please take me to the scene of the crime.'

'Have you finished with Mr Paynter and Hibbert?' the captain enquired.

'For the time being. We'll need official statements later and I shall want to talk to you all again. For now, you can carry on with your duties as long as you're not planning to leave the ship. I shall want to interview the rest of the crew and ship's personnel who were on duty last night and this morning. Is the crime common knowledge?'

'We tried not to advertise it but these things get around, and I've had to put that section of the ship out of bounds.'

'Good thinking. Well, let's be on our way − and Captain, could we have the use of a cabin as an interview room?'

'Mr Paynter?'

'I'll see that it's arranged, sir.'

'As master of this ship *I* shall show the inspector and sergeant around.'

'Very good, sir,' said the purser stiffly.

'I hope that this is not going to take long,' said the captain, leading the way down the companionway. 'I'm due to sail in less than four hours.'

'Captain Bell-Jones, this is a murder inquiry; a particularly nasty murder has been committed and there's no way this ship is going to sail until I have completed my investigations this end. We shall be as quick as possible but I should think it extremely unlikely that we shall have finished by then. Is this B Deck?'

They were in a lounge area with long sections of upholstered seating divided by low tables. The floor was covered in mottled fawn carpeting and there were prints of old sailing ships on the walls and posters advertising the ship's activities. Alongside this lounge was a self-service cafeteria and beyond that the duty-free shop. Mansfield reflected that the standard of decor and trappings had considerably improved since he had last made a Channel crossing; the *Mercia* was a relatively new ship. They walked past a smart-looking boutique and entered a narrow passageway with doors on each side.

'This is the cabin accommodation,' said the captain. He indicated the doors at the head of the passage. 'There are the toilets and showers. Each cabin has a wash basin.'

'Are they all double-berthed?'

'Yes, but there are interconnecting doors between some of the cabins for family bookings; not number 32, though.'

'Are these the only passenger cabins on the ship?'

'There are cabins in the drivers' quarters astern but they are only used by the long-haul lorry drivers.'

They reached the far end of the passage, where a uniformed constable stood guard outside the end door. He straightened up and saluted as Roland identified himself and Mansfield.

'PC Crowther, sir,'

'Right, let's have a look.'

'Do you need me — er — inside?' Bell-Jones enquired cautiously.

'No, stay here with the constable. Has anything been disturbed?' he asked Crowther.

'No, sir. He was obviously beyond help so everything was left just as it was — untouched.'

The door was unlocked and the two men had their first view of the *mise-en-scène*.

8

'God! He's been butchered — it's the work of a maniac!' said Mansfield. The body was clothed in pyjamas but the jacket top had been torn open and partly off. The upper chest and neck had been stabbed repeatedly and the deep wounds had bled profusely. One hand clutched the bedclothes as if the victim had tried in vain to deflect his killer by drawing up the coverlet. Inured as he was to violence, Roland felt himself balk at the scene.

'Just one of those wounds would have been enough to kill him; his attacker went berserk.'

'Or was making sure he'd really finished him off.'

'No sign of the murder weapon?'

A cursory examination of the cabin revealed no knife or dagger. The body was lying on the lower bunk and nearby the man's underclothes were neatly folded on a seat, but his jacket, trousers and overcoat were strewn across the floor as if someone had made a hasty search of the pockets before discarding them. An overnight bag, gaping open, was lying on the top bunk. Roland donned rubber gloves and examined the contents. It contained a pair of pants and socks, a navy towelling dressing-gown, a toilet case holding shaving tackle, medication and washing gear, and a paperback copy of a popular actor's autobiography. There were no personal papers, no passport, chequebook, credit cards or keys, and an examination of the scattered clothing revealed only a handkerchief, a tube of cough sweets and some small change in English, Belgian and Dutch currency. Roland noted that the clothing was of good quality.

'His murderer seems to have removed everything to prevent identification. He may have been carrying a large amount of money or drugs for which he was killed. Well, let's get the team in and get down to work. I want Doc Brasnett here. As well as certifying death he may be able to give us some idea of how long he's been dead and what sort of knife was used. I want the sniffer dogs, too, to see if there are any traces of drugs around. With over six hundred itinerant suspects all now dispersed to the four winds, we're going to have our work cut out getting a lead.'

Celia Calder-Brown looked from her wristwatch to the clock

on the mantelpiece and tapped her fingers irritably on the bureau flap. It really was too bad of the wretched man; all the fuss about an early appointment and now he hadn't bothered to turn up. She had given up a session at the hairdresser to accommodate him. The least he could have done was to phone and let her know he couldn't make it. After all, she was doing *him* a favour; he had been the one to approach her about the possibility of borrowing the painting for the exhibition.

She got to her feet and walked over to the window, a fine oriel casement that jutted out over the moat and gave a splendid view of the parkland that rolled down to meet the boundry with Barndon churchyard. The overnight gale had savaged the sheets of daffodils and narcissi that clothed the slopes beneath the trees and had broken off hefty branches of the ancient oaks that lined the driveway, but even this failed to stem her pleasure at the panorama spread out before her. After all these years it still gave her a buzz to look out from the house her ancestors had lived in for hundreds of years over the land they had tended and planted. And it was all due to Walter, her late husband. He had been dead over twenty-five years but she still missed him and resented the cruel fate that had parted them and allowed him so little time to enjoy the fruits of his labours.

Her family, the Greshams, had lived at Monkbeggars Hall since the time of Henry VIII but, by mismanagement and a series of ill-judged ventures in the last century, the ancestral home had been lost to the few remaining descendants. It had become, in turn, an orphanage, a prep school for boys, a hospital for shell-shocked victims in the Second World War and, after that, a private nursing home that had gone bust in the early 1950s. She and Walter had lived at Shendon in a rambling old rectory when they were first married but he had known of her hankering after the old house and had vowed to buy and restore it for her. And he had too. After the war, when he had retired with the rank of colonel, he had used his gratuity and a small legacy to set up his own business of car-exporting. It had flourished, the American trade sending the profits soaring. How those Americans had loved the prestige of owning a vintage Rolls-Royce, and how well they had been prepared to pay for the privilege. The Calder-Browns moved into Monkbeggars Hall while the children were still young and in those too few years before Walter's death they had battled to turn the old house once more into a family home.

Celia Calder-Brown looked round the beautifully proportioned room, with its linenfold panelling and a log fire burning in the open grate, and sighed. They had succeeded, but now the money was nearly all gone and neither her son nor her daughter had half the drive or presence of their father. The sound of a car approaching fast through the avenue of trees disturbed her reverie. She frowned at her watch and went to the entrance hall to greet her overdue visitor.

Ten miles away, her granddaughter, Lucy Hanson, huddled behind the wheel of her stationary Mini and also fretted at the passing time. She was parked in a lay-by near the entrance to the Felstone dock complex and although, ostensibly, she was checking an AA reference book, she was actually keeping a sharp eye on all incoming and departing traffic.

She was a slightly built girl of twenty with dark eyes, a dead white complexion and a tangled mop of hair that was a too uniformly dense black to be her natural colouring. She tugged at her black-mittened hand and squinted at her watch. He ought to have been here ages ago, what was keeping him? Something had gone wrong, he had been picked up by the police or the dock security men. What should she do now? She glared through the windscreen at the convoy of lorries rumbling by and pushed the AA book back into the glove pocket, giving a squawk of fright as somebody opened the passenger door and slid in beside her.

'Rick! You scared the life out of me.'

'I thought you were supposed to be on lookout?'

'I didn't expect you from that direction. How did it go − did you do it?'

'Yes.' The man was in his late twenties, as dark as the young woman but with a ruddy complexion and a beard.

'Did anyone see you?'

'A great many people, but I preserved my anonymity with this.' He shrugged out of the yellow fluorescent PVC

11

sleeveless jacket, folded it and laid in on the back seat. 'It gives me entrance to all sorts of prohibited areas.'

'There's a large police presence around this morning.'

'I know, and it's centred on the *Mercia* ferry.'

They met each other's eyes and Lucy shivered.

'We'll never bring it off and get away with it.'

'Having cold feet? I tell you it's foolproof, but I've discovered one snag: they've got guard dogs in.'

'Then we'll have to involve Netty. She really is marvellous with animals, has this natural affinity with them. You should see her do her Crocodile Dundee act.'

'Lucy, this is not a game, it's for real.'

'You're a real shit sometimes. Where would you be without me? Whose idea was it in the first place?'

'Come on, let's go.' He glanced through the rear window and knuckled her neck. 'We can discuss this later but let's get the hell out of here.'

The Mini roared into life, edged out of the lay-by and cut across the dock roundabout, narrowly missing the anonymous mortuary van that was on its way to Terminal 1.

George Brasnett, the pathologist, straightened up and looked over his glasses at Roland.

'Nasty business. Established any motive yet?'

'I'm hoping what you can tell us will point us on our way. How long has he been dead?'

'Now, James, you know better than to ask me that at this stage.'

'You won't commit yourself and you won't be quoted. I know, but you must have some idea off the cuff.'

The pathologist pursed his rubbery lips and fingered his chin with a pudgy, gloved hand. 'Not more than nine hours, not less than five; say between two and six o'clock.'

Roland sighed. 'And the murder weapon?'

'All I can tell you at this stage is that it was a two-edged blade.'

'So it was a dagger rather than a domestic knife?'

Brasnett shrugged. 'I'll tell you more when I've had him on the slab. You might as well take him away now, I can't do much more here.'

'Did he put up much defence?'

'For what it's worth – and this is just my opinion, mind – I reckon he was asleep when he was first attacked. The initial blow didn't kill him, he came to and tried to escape, which triggered off this frenzied bloodbath. He's got deep cuts across his right palm – look – where he tried to deflect the blade. That stain on the wall probably happened because the ship lurched just as the murderer was pulling the knife out of one of the wounds – probably that one at the base of the neck – and the blood splashed upwards. I can tell you something else: his attacker must have got covered in blood.'

Roland had already worked all this out. 'What about drugs?'

'I can see no outward sign of drug-taking. You say the dog found nothing?'

'Not a whisker. OK, I'll arrange for him to be taken to the mortuary. Have you finished?' This to the scene-of-crime team who had been bustling around.

'I've got this feeling that I've seen him before somewhere,' said Steve Copping, the photographer, screwing the lens cap back on his camera.

'Is that a positive fact or just a hunch?' asked Roland sharply.

'Probably just a fleeting resemblance to someone I've seen on the box or in a magazine.'

The inspector stared down at the corpse. Was there something familiar about the waxen, drained face or was Copping putting ideas into his head? 'It's difficult to imagine just what he did look like in real life. Right, if you've finished in here I want you all down on the car deck. There's a car unaccounted for that probably belonged to this joker. With any luck we may turn up something that will help with identification.'

The car deck was a vast, empty cavern reeking of stale exhaust and oil. At one side, near a large opening through which they could see the warehouses on the far shore of the estuary, was an oblong metal cylinder about the size of a railway goods wagon that throbbed and rumbled internally as if it were suffering from an attack of indigestion. The

13

Volkswagen looked very small and abandoned in the empty space.

'Let's hope that he's left some documents inside or there is something in the boot. Let's have that open first, but be careful of the dabs. The killer is hardly likely to have come in contact with the car, unless he was known to his victim and actually travelled with him, which is something we can't discount at this stage.'

'Suppose he was a crew member or company employee,' said Mansfield, shivering and turning up his collar as an icy blast struck the back of his neck.

'That's a possibility we can't ignore and it would explain the locked door. It was someone who either had a key or access to a key; or maybe the victim knew his killer and invited him in – don't forget the top bunk bears the impression of a body as if someone had lain on it recently. On the other hand, the victim could have forgotten or not bothered to lock the door when he turned in.'

'Which is quite likely if he was feeling ill and queasy. But why did his killer lock the door afterwards and remove the key? He knew the body was bound to be discovered as soon as the ship docked.'

'To make sure it didn't happen until he was ashore and well clear.'

'H'm. You'd think, especially in last night's weather, that the easiest way to carry out a murder would have been to give your victim a helping hand over the side. A quick shove on a dark, filthy night and no one would have been any the wiser. When someone was reported missing later it would pass as an accidental death.'

'There's just the little problem of getting your victim out there on the empty deck conveniently near to the side. By all accounts nobody was abroad last night and anyone seen taking the air under those gale-force conditions would have been conspicuous in the extreme.'

'Ah,' said Roland, turning back to the car. The boot had been opened and inside was a slim, black case, larger than a conventional briefcase but of similar design. The two locks were forced and he opened the lid revealing a collection of photographs and posters, a sheaf of letters paperclipped together and a small wad of business cards. Roland pounced on these.

'"John Hargreaves, Langdale Gallery, Bruton Place." It looks as if our stiff is an art dealer.'

The photographs were of paintings, some of which Roland felt sure he recognised, and much of the correspondence was on paper embossed with the Langdale Gallery address.

'This should get us somewhere.'

'Excuse me, Detective Inspector, but can I arrange coffee for your men — and some sandwiches?' It was Jack Paynter, the purser. He eyed the scene with open curiosity and Roland snapped shut the lid of the briefcase.

'You can indeed, some refreshment would be very welcome. By the way — ' as the purser reluctantly turned away — 'what is that?' Roland indicated the contraption that was still clanking away beside the far wall.

'That's the Muncher, our waste-disposal machine.'

'Oh? How does it operate?'

'You see that shaft leading into the end? All the rubbish comes down that and when it reaches the compactor it is pulverised and compressed.'

'And then what happens to it?'

'Every three or four days it is coupled up to a tug master and taken off.'

'You mean ashore, here in Felstone?'

'No, it's always dealt with over the other side in Zeebrugge, it's their pigeon.'

'I see. Where's the actual opening to the duct?'

'Up on B Deck.'

'Show me,' said Roland crisply, and he and his sergeant followed the purser back up the companionway. He led them through a door marked PRIVATE beside the boutique, only a short distance from the cabin area. They walked a few yards down a passage and turned a corner to find themselves confronted by a large, square aperture in the wall facing them. The purser jerked his head towards it and Roland looked inside at the gaping black shaft leading downwards out of sight.

'What goes into it?'

15

'Anything and everything. Galley refuse, packaging from the shops, litter ... you name it, it's all grist to the Muncher.'

'I take it this is out of bounds to the public?'

'You saw the notice on the door. Mind you, I'm not saying that someone couldn't have got in here undetected last night. You're wondering why the murderer didn't tip the body down here?' he asked with relish.

That possibility had not crossed Roland's mind, he was thinking along other lines. He kept his distaste at the purser's ghoulish curiosity out of his voice.

'Are you telling me that security is so lax aboard this ship that such an action could have gone unwitnessed?'

'Last night anything could have happened – and it did, didn't it?'

'Well, thank you for your help, Mr Paynter. We'll have that coffee now if you would be so kind as to send it to the cabin we're using.'

'Are you thinking the same as me?' Roland asked after the purser had departed.

'The murderer could have got rid of the murder weapon down this shaft?'

'And his bloodstained clothing. He could have bundled it up together with the knife and the victim's belongings, slipped through the door marked PRIVATE hoping to find somewhere to hide them until he could chuck them overboard, and come face to face with this ingenious monster – the answer to his prayer, or maybe he already knew it existed. Let's have a closer look.' He produced a torch and flashed it down the shaft, then bent forward and carefully ran a finger over a stain darkening the metal funnel.

'Want to take a bet that's not blood? It's still damp.'

'It's not necessarily human – could be kitchen offal.'

'We'll soon find out. Get the team back up here. I want samples taken for analysis and we'll check the floor and walls leading here, we may find further traces.'

'There'll be no way of retrieving anything that's gone inside its maw, will there?'

'I doubt it. It appears to be a very efficient machine,

which is more than can be said for the recording of passengers. You'd think after the 1987 disaster things would have improved in that respect.'

Traces of blood were found on the washbasin in the cabin, on the flooring and also on the inside of the door between the public and private sections of B Deck. These, together with the bloodstained smears inside the shaft, were proved to be of human origin and were later matched to the victim's own blood. There were no traces of fingerprints anywhere.

Roland had another lucky break that first morning of the investigation. A thorough search of the surrounding area took them into the boutique. This shop contained a very eclectic array of goods, ranging from leather handbags and silk scarves to cheap souvenirs. Mansfield was poking among the latter when he pursed his lips in a low whistle and called his superior over.

'How about this?'

Close to the entrance there was a stand of articles bearing a Union Jack crest; ashtrays, spoons, tankards, key rings. Mansfield pointed out a display card on which were slotted paperknives bearing a crest on their hilts. There was an empty space at the top where one had been removed.

'The murder weapon?'

'It's too obvious and these wouldn't be sharp or strong enough to have inflicted those injuries.' But Roland carefully slipped out a knife from further down the card, balanced it on his palm, and ran a tentative finger up and down the blade. He looked in disbelief at the beaded line of blood oozing in its path.

'Hell, it *is* sharp and this is well-tempered metal. These are lethal weapons, they shouldn't be on sale as harmless souvenirs.' He wound his handkerchief round his index finger. 'This goes straight to Doc Brasnett. If the murder weapon did come from this batch he'll be able to match it to the wounds; it's about the right length and size.'

'I suppose the killer saw these just sitting within reach of the doorway and pocketed one when no one was looking.'

'We'll have to check with the shop assistant on duty last night. He or she will know whether one was sold overnight or during a previous crossing. It's too much to hope that the murderer actually paid for it over the counter and could be fingered.'

'If it is the murder weapon.'

'I think, Patrick me boy, that it is and you see what this means? Our murder was unpremeditated, at least until the murderer boarded ship, otherwise he'd never have left such an important thing as the murder weapon to chance.'

'Unless, as we've already pointed out, he intended tipping his victim overboard and when that was ruled out by the weather he changed his plan and grabbed the first thing to hand.'

'This is all speculation so far. We've got the contents of the briefcase to follow up. And someone on board ship may have heard or seen something significant during the crossing, so we'll make a start first on interviewing the crew − before Captain Bell-Jones busts a gut.'

Chapter Two

A couple of hours later Roland and Mansfield were none the wiser as to the victim's last hours or the movements of his killer. The bad crossing had strained the resources of the ship's company and no one had noticed anything untoward. They only helpful piece of information had come from a crew member who had been on duty near the gangway after the ship berthed. He reported noticing a man going ashore who was not wearing outer clothing. He could give no description and could not even hazard a guess at the man's age. As he had said, 'I saw this bloke in sweater and slacks and I thought he must have been mad travelling without a coat or anything.'

'It could have been our killer. He'd got rid of his outer clothing as we'd conjectured because it was bloodstained, but I don't know that that's really of much help to us; it only means that he definitely left the ship and is now God knows where.' Mansfield pulled out his pipe and commenced the ritual of lighting up.

'If it was the killer it adds weight to our opinion that he was a fellow passenger and not a crew member. I can't see what connection a director of a well-known art gallery could have had with an employee of the Mercia Ferry Company.'

'Unless it is drugs.'

'Drugs, yes.' Roland sighed. 'And we've got the tie-up with Holland to consider.'

The contents of the briefcase had provided them with valuable information. A phone call to the Langdale Gallery had elicited that the dead man had been a director of the gallery and an expert on sixteenth- and seventeenth-century Dutch art. He was divorced from a Dutch woman who now lived in Amsterdam; Hargreaves had lived since the divorce in a flat in Brentwood. At the time of his death he had been involved in organising an exhibition of the work of lesser-known Dutch portrait painters and had been returning from a trip to Amsterdam and Bruges, where he had been arranging the loan of paintings for this exhibition. The letters in the briefcase had all been correspondence connected with this exhibition and one, in particular, had interested Roland.

It had been written locally by a Celia Calder-Brown of Monkbeggars Hall confirming an appointment with John Hargreaves for that very day. He was to have examined a portrait by Gerard Ter Borch which was in her possession, with a view to borrowing it for the London exhibition.

'That's Monkbeggars Hall out Barndon way. Do we know anything about this Celia Calder-Brown?'

'Isn't that the old Tudor house where they stage these historical re-creations and pageants? She must be the owner.'

'We'd better go and see her. I don't suppose for one moment that she can be tied in with the murder, but she may be able to shed some light on John Hargreaves. We'll also have to go up to town, investigate the Langdale Gallery and check out his colleagues and friends – which means searching his flat for leads. His Dutch wife too. According to the chappie I spoke to at the gallery, they have remained on good terms and he always stayed with her when he visited Holland, which he did frequently in the course of his business. We'll get Interpol to alert the appropriate forces in Amsterdam and Bruges to check him out that end and inform his ex-wife of his death.'

'So he was a regular visitor to the drugs centre of Europe,' Mansfield mused, tapping out his pipe. 'Could have been a courier.'

'If we find any connection with the drugs scene it will be the Drugs Squad's baby and out of our hands, but in the meantime I think we may have to embrace a little foreign travel – how's your Dutch and Flemish?'

'Will the Super ride it?'

'That remains to be seen. I want his blessing for a photograph of the dead man to be shown on TV and in the press with an appeal for his fellow passengers to come forward. Someone

20

may remember seeing him or quite unknowingly have some scrap of information tucked away in their subconscious that could help us. For now, I think we've finished here. We'd better tell Captain Bell-Jones that he's back in business.'

'What do you know of Dutch art, Patrick?'

Roland and Mansfield were on their way to Monkbeggars Hall, which lay inland about ten miles from Felstone. They had just taken part in a high-powered briefing with Superintendent Bob Lacey at Felstone HQ and telexes had flown backwards and forwards between the Met, Interpol, the Dutch criminal intelligence service CRI and the Belgian *Procureur des Konings*.

'Well, of course I know of Rembrandt and Vermeer and people like that, but I've never heard of this chappie Gerard Ter Borch. Your Ginny would know, wouldn't she?'

'Yes,' said Roland shortly.

'How's the courting going?' Mansfield stole a sideways look at his superior and wondered how fast and how hard he would be slapped down.

'I think it would be optimistic to call it that.'

'You do still see each other?'

'Yes, but that's as far as it goes.'

'You mean she's holding out on you?'

'I mean its none of your damn business!'

As Roland glared through the windscreen and put down his foot, Mansfield reflected on his companion's private life. James Roland's first wife had left him for another man, and it still rankled. Since those days he was reckoned in the force to have had more women than hot dinners but had taken care never to get involved with anyone; that is, until he met Ginny Dalton. She was the head of art at the local comprehensive, a young widow with a son of fourteen, and she and Roland had met when the latter was working on a murder case in Ginny's home village of nearby Croxton. At one point, Ginny had been one of the chief suspects, and it was through the evidence of her son Simon that the real murderer had eventually been apprehended. Since the trial Mansfield knew that Roland had been seeing Ginny regularly, but apparently all was not sweetness and light. It looked as if she were one of the few who had not succumbed to his fatal charm; perhaps the boy was being awkward. It was a difficult age and he was probably cutting up rough about the new man in his mother's life. Mansfield had it in him to be sorry for his superior. It would do James Roland no harm at all to realise that he had met his match in Ginny Dalton; yet, on the other hand, Mansfield thought that in many ways they were ideally suited. He changed the subject.

Monkbeggars Hall was situated on the outskirts of the sprawling village of Barndon. As Tudor mansions go it was on the small side, but it was a little gem of mellowed red brick, high chimneys and cream stonework built around three sides of a courtyard, the whole encircled by a moat. It was approached by a long, narrow drive that bisected the parkland surrounding the house and wound between fine stands of oak that were faintly outlined in a sulphur haze from tight, swelling buds.

Roland and Mansfield arrived at the gatehouse to find their way barred by tall wrought-iron gates hung between slender columns of tawny brick. The gatehouse was octagonal with mossy tiles clinging to the conical roof; it appeared to be derelict. Mansfield got out of the car and went over to the gates, which were decorated with two lozenges depicting a coat of arms. They were not locked and he slid the hasp and pushed them open. From here one could not see the house; the drive took a sharp-angled bend a little farther on and the house was hidden by a screen of trees. Roland drove the car through the gates and waited for Mansfield to close them again. What happened next took them both by surprise.

A car shot round the bend towards them. It appeared so suddenly that Roland was unable to take evasive action. He saw the car leap towards him on a collision course, then, at the last moment, it slewed sideways and careered off the driveway onto the grass verge, missing him by a centimetre and embedding itself in the soft bank.

'The bloody fool!' Mansfield ran back and the two men advanced on the car. Its driver was revving up violently in an attempt to shift his immobile vehicle. He glared at Roland and Mansfield as if the near collision had been their fault.

22

'I should stop doing that if I were you, you're making matters worse.' Roland leaned forward and spoke to him.

'Who the hell do you think you are, giving me orders?'

The man switched off after a final jab at the accelerator and got out of the car. He was a slim, fair-haired man of average height and Roland reckoned him to be in his early forties. At that moment he was seething with anger and he gave them a daggers look out of blue, narrowed eyes.

'I was going to ask you the same question. Can we have your name, please?'

'It's no business of yours — I didn't touch you!'

'We're police officers.' Roland produced his ID and flashed it under the man's nose. 'You were driving far too fast and in a most dangerous manner.'

'Just my luck. Look, this is a private road and there was no crash. You can't charge me with anything!'

'So far all I've asked is your name.'

'Hugh Calder-Brown.' The man hesitated and changed his tune. 'Look, officer, I know that I was going it a bit but I wasn't expecting to meet anyone. I apologise if I gave you a few nasty seconds, but no harm done, eh?'

Roland ignored this. 'Do you live at the Hall?'

'That'll be the day.'

'Are you related to Mrs Celia Calder-Brown, sir?'

'I happen to be her only son, not that you would think it from the way she treats me. We are, as they politely call it, estranged.'

'But you're on visiting terms?'

'I have just been to see her. I happened to be in the district and as I was passing by I thought I would call and see how she was, but ...' He shrugged and changed the subject. 'You haven't told me why you are here. Don't tell me that Mother has run foul of the law?' His eyes glinted, a wry grin crossed his face and he suddenly looked much younger and more personable. I bet he goes down well with the women, Mansfield thought. That sort of fair, rather delicate looks always wowed the ladies.

'Just a private matter.'

'Is anything wrong?' The man was itching to know the reason for their visit.

23

'Nothing for you to worry about, sir. Now, can we give you a push?'

A short while later the combined efforts of the three men had got Hugh Calder-Brown's car back on the driveway. By this time he was in a conciliatory mood.

'I'm sorry about that piece of bad driving, Inspector, and losing my temper. The truth of the matter is, I was as shaken up by the incident as you.'

'Just drive more carefully in future. It could have been a nasty accident.'

'Yes. Are you sure that I can't help you – with whatever it is you've come about?'

'No. We won't detain you any longer, you were in a hurry – remember?'

'Er, yes, well, thank you for the help, I'll leave you to it.'

He still hesitated, but as Roland and Mansfield waited with impassive faces he started up the engine and drove decorously away.

'In a proper old dander, wasn't he?' said Mansfield as they resumed their journey. 'I wonder what he and his mum have fallen out over.'

'I don't suppose we shall ever know. Mrs C-B is hardly likely to regale us with the family gossip, no matter how sypathetic our ear.'

'Look at those sheep over there.' Mansfield nodded towards the small herd grazing under a clump of tress. 'Have you ever seen anything like that before?'

The sheep in question were white with dark blotches on their coats and sported ferocious, curved horns.

'Can't say I have. Not your usual domestic animal at all.'

At that moment the Hall came into view. Roland slowed the car down.

'Very impressive, isn't it? How would you like to own a pile like that?'

'In this day and age a place like that would be a liability rather than an investment, I would say.'

'But a very decorative millstone round one's neck for all that. The lady must have money and we know that she owns at least one valuable painting. I wonder what the insurance

24

premiums are and the security arrangements. If the house is open to the public it must present problems.'

An elaborately carved portico enclosed the main front door of heavily fumed oak studded in traditional manner. It was opened by a middle-aged woman who admitted to being the housekeeper. Roland showed her his ID card and asked to see Mrs Calder-Brown. The woman looked at them suspiciously as if uncertain how to treat their visit. She was loath to let them into the house but in view of their status she couldn't just shut the door on them.

'You'd better wait here,' she said grudgingly. 'I'll tell Mrs Calder-Brown you wish to see her.'

'One expects to be viewed with suspicion by a vast percentage of our clientele but I had hoped for better treatment here.'

'Perhaps we should have used the back entrance.'

Roland stepped back and looked up at the front facade. A magnificent specimen of tree peony clothed the wall to the left of the door. From the rustling and cheeping issuing from its glossy depths it was host to a number of nesting birds. White and blue hyacinths and purple iris reticulata filled the large tubs flanking the porch and a clematis montana ran riot over the curved arch. This must take a lot of upkeep, he thought. I wonder how many gardeners she employs?

The housekeeper reappeared. 'Will you please come this way?'

She led them into a large panelled hall and Roland had a sense of stepping back into history. This was how the house must have looked in Tudor times; the long refectory table at one end laid with pewter plates and flagons; the heavy oak chairs fashioned for strength and durability rather than comfort; the fire irons and basket grate in the vast inglenook fireplace; the minstrel gallery overlooking the dining area and hung with tapestries. Surely nothing on display was later than the sixteenth century, and yet the portraits of lords and ladies in Elizabethan costume looked too bright and garish to be genuine.

They crossed this hall and the housekeeper took them through a doorway in the far wall that led into another, smaller but similarly furnished room, whose windows overlooked a stretch of lawn flanked by a massive cedar of Lebanon. A flash of blue and an unearthly shriek from high up in its branches resolved itself as a roosting peacock to Roland's startled eyes as he and Mansfield followed their guide through yet another door, this one marked PRIVATE. The room they now found themselves in was a small drawing-room furnished in a mish-mash of styles. It was light and airy, a room that was lived in rather than a museum piece. Chintz-covered chairs and a sprawling sofa colonised a faded Wilton carpet, and an elegant Queen Anne bureau stood near the window alcove. Seated at it was an elderly, diminutive woman with a halo of white hair and china-blue eyes. She was dressed in a mauve tweed suit with a toning blouse and there was something doll-like and fragile about her appearance. Her deep, cultured voice came as something of a shock.

'Detective Inspector Roland, Detective Sergeant Mansfield? What can I do for you?'

'Mrs Calder-Brown? It is very good of you to see us. We won't take up much of your time but I'm hoping you may be able to help us.'

'I'm intrigued, Inspector. I can't imagine how I can help you, but do enlighten me. Please sit down, and will you take coffee?'

'That's very good of you, ma'am, coffee would be most welcome.'

'Madge, coffee for three, please, and find me my cigarettes — I seem to have mislaid them since I came in from the greenhouses.'

'You've already smoked your quota for today,' was the surly reply.

'Nonsense, I couldn't possibly have, you've hidden them. Now hurry up with that coffee *and* my cigarettes. Poor Madge Hatfield,' Mrs Calder-Brown continued as the housekeeper exited with bad grace, 'she's been with me for over twenty-five years and she's more of a friend than a housekeeper but she bullies me; thinks I should cut down on my smoking. When you've reached my age, Inspector, it is really too late to worry about such things; we all have to die from something.'

'I'm not sure the medical profession would agree with you, ma'am, but at least you know the risks.'

'Quite so, and it should be my decision. Now, what do you want?'

'I believe you had an appointment this morning with a Mr John Hargreaves?'

'Why, yes, but he didn't turn up. May I ask how you knew about his visit?'

Roland ignored this. 'Could you tell me what happened?'

'Nothing. He arranged to see me at nine thirty but he didn't arrive and I've heard nothing from him since — no phone call to apologise, nothing.'

'How well did you know him, Mrs Calder-Brown?'

'I don't know him at all. We've never met and his appointment was made by letter. You say "did" — has something happened to him?'

'I'm afraid he's dead.'

'Dead! Good heavens, how awful! What happened — a car crash?'

'He was found dead on the *Mercia* ferry when it berthed at Felstone this morning.'

'The poor man! I suppose it was a heart attack? But I don't see why you are involved — you are CID officers, aren't you?'

At that moment the housekeeper returned with a tray of coffee, which she put down on the occasional table near the fireplace. Roland noted that there were no cigarettes on the tray; so did Celia Calder-Brown. She dismissed the housekeeper curtly and went over to the corner cupboard, from which she produced a new packet. As she rose to her feet Roland saw that she was scarcely more than five foot tall; a dainty Dresden figure impeccably dressed, except ... His eyes travelled downwards and he did a double take. She was wearing training shoes and with them fluorescent pink socks. With great difficulty he dragged his attention away from her feet, catching Mansfield's eye in the process.

Regally unaware of the momentary confusion her appearance had wrought in her two visitors, Celia Calder-Brown busied herself pouring out the coffee. When she had handed it round she sat down again at the bureau, broke open the packet and extracted a cigarette. Mansfield lumbered to his feet, his box of matches at the ready, but she waved him away and lit her cigarette from an onyx lighter which she took from a cubbyhole in the bureau.

'Well, Inspector, you haven't answered my question.' She inhaled deeply and blew a draught of smoke towards the ceiling.

'I'll try and put you in the picture. We are treating Mr Hargreaves' death as suspicious. He was murdered in a particularly brutal fashion.'

'Murdered!' She set her coffee cup down with a rattle, slopping liquid over the edge of the saucer. 'But why?'

'That is what I'm trying to find out. His personal effects were stolen, possibly to prevent identification, but we found his briefcase. It contained documents and letters which gave us his name and address and told us that he was professionally connected with the Langdale Gallery. There was a letter from you among the others, confirming an appointment with him for this morning, here at Monkbeggars Hall.'

'I see, so that's why you're here. Well, I don't think I'm going to be of much help to you, Inspector. As I already said, I've never met Mr Hargreaves; we have only corresponded and spoken over the telephone. He got in touch with me because the gallery wants to borrow a painting in my possession. It is a portrait of one of my ancestors by the Dutch artist Gerard Ter Borch. He visited England in the 1630s, when this was executed, and apparently it is one of only a few works still in existence from that period of his life; hence the gallery's interest.'

'It would be very valuable?'

'I know that for insurance purposes it's worth in the region of £200,000 but to me it has a value far beyond the financial one. It is the sole surviving heirloom of my family. I was a Gresham, Inspector.' She spoke as if he ought to be au fait with the pedigree of her ancestors. 'And the Greshams have lived here since the time of Henry VIII. However, my predecessors fell on hard times in the last century – a common enough tale, I fear – and everything was sold, including the Hall. There had been a Holbein and a Gainsborough and they went, but my great-grandfather refused to part with the Ter Borch. Apparently it was the spitting image of his twin

sister, who had been tragically killed in a hunting accident —
obviously some family likeness rearing its head three hundred
years after the original Gresham was immortalised in paint.
He hung on to it and eventually it came down to me.'

'You say the Hall was sold?'

'Yes. You're wondering how I come to be living here. It's
quite simple. My late husband bought it in the 1950s when it
was in a state of advanced dilapidation; it was practically in
ruins and hadn't been lived in for years. Together we restored
it and moved in a few years before he died.' She sighed and
tapped out her cigarette. 'But all this is not helping you, is
it? All I can tell you is that I was expecting Mr Hargreaves
this morning. He was coming to check out the painting, make
arrangements for its transportation to the gallery, sort out the
insurance and so on.'

'How long ago was this appointment made?'

'About two weeks. He rang me up, after the initial approach
by letter, told me that he would be in this area today and
asked if it would be convenient to call then. Surely his . . .
murder . . . can have no connection with this?'

'Extremely unlikely, but we have to check out all possibilities, no matter how tenuous. Well, thank you for your help,
Mrs Calder-Brown.' Roland got to his feet. 'May we see the
painting before we go?'

'Certainly, Inspector. It is not on public display for security
reasons.'

'I was wondering about that, with the Hall being open to
the public.'

'Only part of it. The painting is hung in a room to which
the public doesn't have access. Come with me.'

She led them back through the banqueting hall and
Roland tried to draw his eyes away from the lurid pink
socks illuminating the dark, polished floorboards ahead of
him. He looked instead at the walls, at the larger-than-life
Tudor portraits, and she intercepted his gaze.

'You're not taken in by those, are you, Inspector?'

'I wondered . . .'

'Painted a few years ago, purely as props for our historical
re-creations.'

'Ah, yes, the historical re-creations — tell me about them.'

29

'Running this place is a great drain on my resources. Although we were already open to the public, it was becoming increasingly difficult to make ends meet. Then my daughter and her husband, who run the adjoining home farm, hit on this idea of staging Tudor re-enactments. It's been done elsewhere and it has really taken off here. People come from all over the country to take part and also the local schools participate. We choose a year from the sixteenth century and try to re-create what would have been happening then; everyone wears the correct costume for that period, they talk in the language of the time and discuss relevant topics and they work at the various crafts and occupations that would have been going on here in Tudor days. My son-in-law was already raising rare breeds of farm animals so that helps to re-create the atmosphere. You must come and visit us then. We start next week and go on until the end of June.'

'It sounds most interesting.'

By this time they had ascended the main staircase and were walking along a narrow corridor which Roland reckoned must run along the length of the right wing of the building. She stopped when they reached the door at the end.

'The painting is in here, Inspector.'

'What sort of alarm system have you got in operation, Mrs Calder-Brown? An infrared sensor that is activated when the threshold is crossed?'

'No, there is a device attached to the actual painting.'

'Ah, a vibration sensor?'

'Yes, I believe that is what it is called. If the picture is touched or moved at all it triggers off an alarm which goes through to the police headquarters.'

She opened the door and switched on the light. It was a small room, heavily panelled in dark wood, containing a modern single divan, a small chest of drawers and a couple of chairs. The painting hung on the wall opposite the doorway in which they were standing; there was another door in the wall to the left of them, opposite the window.

'Well, you certainly keep it tucked away.'

'It would be very difficult to protect it adequately if it were hung downstairs in the main hall, and it is not a Tudor portrait so it would look out of place anyway. This is the

30

dressing-room to the master bedroom, which is through that door over there. My late husband liked to have it in here where he could keep an eye on it and appreciate it all by himself. He thought the sitter resembled me.'

'Where is the control box?'

'On the ground floor in the old butler's pantry. Do go in and look at the picture properly.'

The two detectives accepted her invitation, both having to duck as they entered to avoid a low beam.

The portrait was surprisingly small, about eighteen by twelve inches, and depicted a woman dressed in typical seventeenth-century costume. She wore her fair hair with a wispy fringe and the rest drawn back behind her ears in bunches of ringlets; a lapdog nestled against her voluminous skirts. The pert, smiling face did bear a slight resemblance to Celia Calder-Brown. Perhaps the family likeness was still perpetuating itself, he thought. The brushwork was fresh and glossy.

'It's in fine condition.'

'It was cleaned and restored about a year ago. A Miss Cordingley, a very competent picture restorer, carried out the work and did a first-class job. It was badly stained with nicotine – I have not been the only smoker in the family over the centuries – and my son persuaded her to take on the commission.'

'Would that be Mr Hugh Calder-Brown?'

'You know Hugh?' she asked sharply.

'We met a short while ago on your driveway and exchanged words. Does he also live here or is he married?'

'He is not married and he doesn't live here.' She sounded aggrieved on both points. 'We don't see eye to eye on many topics. I don't really know why he called today, he's certainly shown no concern for my health recently. He lives in Felstone, not very far away – he owns an antiquarian bookshop – but I haven't seen him for months, and when he does come he spends the short while he *is* here haranguing me about security arrangements and telling me that I would be a fool to lend out the painting.' She waved a hand in its direction. 'He thinks it would draw attention to its existence and would be an open invitation to any would-be art thief.'

'He could be right, but your security arrangements appear to be adequate. Well, thank you for your help, Mrs Calder-Brown. I don't think we need trouble you further.'

'You haven't told me yet what actually happened to Mr Hargreaves — how did he die?'

'He was stabbed to death, ma'am. His body was found after the *Mercia* docked.'

'What a terrible thing to happen! I suppose he got caught up in a fracas between two of these gangs of hooligans one reads about.'

Roland didn't enlighten her.

They retraced their steps. As they started to descend the staircase, a girl's voice could be heard echoing upwards from the direction of the main hall.

'It's all right, Hatty, I'll find her.'

A young woman dressed all in black burst through the doorway at the bottom of the stairs. She was wearing a leather jacket, a leather miniskirt and leggings, and her shock of black hair was teased out so that it stood on end. It reminded Roland of the pictures of Struwelpeter that he had seen in his grandmother's bookcase as a child.

'Lucy! How nice to see you, dear!' Celia Calder-Brown's voice was warm as she hurried down the remaining treads.

'Hello, Gran. Sorry, I didn't know you had visitors.'

'It's all right, dear, the inspector is just going.'

'Inspector?' The girl looked the two men up and down and visibly stiffened. 'You're surely not entertaining the fuzz?'

'Now, Lucy, don't be silly. I've just been helping the police with their inquiries — isn't that how it is put, Inspector?';

'That's what they say when they arrest someone without a warrant,' said the girl belligerently. 'Why are you pestering her?' she demanded of Roland.

He raised his eyebrows. 'May I ask who *you* are?'

'This is my granddaughter, Lucy Hanson,' said the elderly woman.

'You are popular with your family today, Mrs Calder-Brown. We'll leave you to your reunion. We can see ourselves out.'

But the housekeeper appeared as if on cue. As they followed

her to the door, they heard the next part of the conversation between grandmother and granddaughter.

'Are you on your own?'

'No. Rick's in the car.'

'You can bring him in dear.'

'No. That would – ' The door closed behind them, cutting off her reply in midsentence.

'I wouldn't have expected someone like Mrs Calder-Brown to number a Gothic among her kith and kin or to give her such a warm welcome.'

'Is that what they call them? You're a mine of information sometimes, Patrick.'

'You forget I've got a teenage daughter, though fortunately she's not into the raven touch yet. The old girl herself was quite a character too.'

'You mean the footwear?'

'I could see you couldn't take your eyes off it. What did you make of her?'

'She's either going gaga, or she's very eccentric, or ...' Roland paused and glanced back at the house. 'Or she's one of those confident people who are supremely indifferent to the image they're projecting; and for my money I think that's the correct explanation. Of course, she could have been jogging!'

They had left the car beyond the bridge that spanned the moat on a gravel square beside an ancient dovecote. There was another car parked nearby when they returned. It was an old Mini, purple in colour and looking the worse for wear. A bearded man was sitting in the passenger seat and he looked up curiously as they walked past.

'Well, well, did you see who that was?' asked Roland, unlocking his car door.

'Mr Richard Coates, unless I'm mistaken.'

'I don't think both our pairs of eyes are deceiving us. Now where does *he* fit into the picture? This is the last place that I should expect one of his ilk to frequent.'

'Looks as if he's hanging around the granddaughter, and she is something of a rebel if the get-up is anything to go by. He must be years older than her, though. What's he up to these days?'

'He continues to be a thorn in the flesh but he's careful to keep within the letter of the law. I bet the college authorities are ruing the day they appointed an anarchist as senior lecturer in economics and sociology. But he keeps his nose clean – just.'

Richard Coates taught at the local polytechnic. A product of the LSE, he was extremely left-wing in his views; a champion of all the minority groups and a prime mover behind most protest marches and demonstrations in the area.

'Perhaps she's one of his students.'

'Could be. Never mind, we've got more important things on our plate than the subversive activities of Richard Coates. Back to base and see if anything helpful has turned up.'

When they got back to Felstone police station, William Evans, the young Welsh detective constable who had been consigned to their team, had some news for them.

'The manageress of the boutique on the *Mercia* has stated that no paperknives were sold during the crossing and she is sure that the display card was full at the start of the journey.'

'So it looks as if it was the weapon, and the murder was unpremeditated. But why was he killed? We shall have to dig deep into his background and try and come up with an answer. I presume we've checked that he hasn't got form?'

'What about his business associates?'

'I'm hoping that our visit to the Langdale Gallery will take care of that angle and perhaps throw some light on his private life. We may find something to help us when we search his flat. He must have had friends and acquaintances, though, according to one of the telexes from Amsterdam, his ex-wife says that he had no other living relatives.'

'I wonder what his financial situation was,' said Mansfield tilting back his chair and playing with his pipe scraper. 'He must have earned a good screw and he doesn't appear to have had any family commitments, though I suppose he could have been paying out alimony. I don't know what happens in these cases where the ex-wife is a foreigner and doesn't reside in this country any longer.'

'Perhaps he's involved with another woman. It may turn out to be a crime of passion.'

'You're not saying his killer could have been a woman?'

'I know it's unlikely, seeing the nature of his injuries, but we can't rule it out. It has been known – a woman scorned and all that – and remember, he was probably asleep at the time of the attack, it wouldn't have taken superhuman strength to inflict those wounds.'

'Did you ever see that film, *Katefa's Revenge* I think it was called, where the heroine sacrificed her lover to appease the rain gods?' Evans asked with relish. 'She gave him a stab wound for each time they had slept together; he looked like a stuck pig at the end and – '

'Whatever sort of nasties did they show in the ghettos of Cardiff?' Roland interrupted him in full flow. 'I don't think that has any relevance to the case in hand, do you? As soon as we get a photo of the dead man I'll fax it through and I want you to arrange for it to be splashed over all the front pages.'

'You mean the local papers?'

'I mean the national ones, too. Don't forget, the passengers came from all over the country. And I want to know the minute the pathologist's report comes through or there's anything from Forensics. Come on, Patrick, there's work to do.'

'Where to first?'

'Up to the big city and the Langdale Gallery, I think, and we can call at Brentwood on the way back.'

'I must just let Jean know that I'm not going to be home this evening,' said Mansfield as they clattered down the stairs. 'You haven't got these domestic ties to think about.'

'Actually I'm supposed to be going to a concert with Ginny this evening; the local choral society are doing *Carmina Burana* and she managed to get tickets.'

'Jean mentioned that she wanted to go to that.'

'Well, there you are then, they can go together, they know each other well. Suggest it when you ring her.'

'Don't you think the suggestion would be better coming from you?' said Mansfield innocently. 'I presume you intend telling Ginny Dalton that you're standing her up tonight?'

Chapter Three

The Langdale Gallery was much larger than Roland had envisaged. From the outside the building was a good example of early Victorian architecture but the inside had been gutted and modernised and the overall effect was one of space and light with expanses of white wall and stainless-steel fittings. It was nearly six o'clock by the time they arrived and the gallery was closed for the day, but the exhibitions director and his secretary were waiting for them in the former's office.

'Jeremy Mickelsen, Inspector, and this is my assistant, Mrs Haynes. I can't believe that John has been murdered, it is just too shocking to be true!'

He was a tall, slightly stooping man in his late fifties with receding hair and rimless half-moon glasses.

'I'm afraid it is true, Mr Mickelsen.'

'But who could have done such a terrible thing?'

'That's what we're here to try and find out. Anything you can tell us about Mr Hargreaves – his work, friends and associates, habits, pastimes – no matter how insignificant you may think it, can help us to build up a picture of the dead man and assist us to establish a motive.'

'That's just it, Inspector. Ever since the news was broken to me I've been trying to think why he has been killed. It doesn't make sense; John Hargreaves is the last man you'd think of in connection with violence.'

'What do you mean?'

'I mean – ', he took off his glasses and swung them gently by an arm while he strove to express himself – 'he was such

36

a private man. Wrapped up in his work. He is – was – completely absorbed in his subject, and he was *the* expert on sixteenth- and seventeenth-century Dutch art. He lived quietly and modestly, no extravagances or self-indulgences as far as I know. He was not a man to make enemies or incite violence.'

'How did he get on with his colleagues and business associates?'

'Very well. He was greatly respected in the art world.'

'But was he liked?'

'Well, yes, but ... how can I put it?'

'He kept himself to himself,' Mrs Haynes interrupted. 'He was not a man you could get close to, but I'm certain nobody had any cause to dislike him.'

'He was something of an ascetic, engrossed in his work, as I said, and with not much time for socialising.'

'No women?'

'Oh no! That's completely out of the question. In an earlier age he would probably have been a monk.'

'And yet he had been married?'

'That's true, but it must have been the mismatch of the century. Anneke, his ex-wife, is the complete antithesis of him, a large woman in every sense of the word, full of life, gregarious, flamboyant and, incidentally, a very fine sculptress. That's how they met, through connections in the art world, but how they ever came to tie the knot remains a mystery. I think they both realised, before the ink was dry on the marriage certificate, that they had made a mistake. They parted amicably soon afterwards and remained good friends. He always stayed with her when he was in Holland and he went over there quite frequently in the course of business.'

'So he would have stayed with her on this last visit?'

'Yes, he was in Amsterdam before going on to Bruges.'

'And do you know exactly what he did on this trip, who he visited and where he went?'

'I've already made out a list of the people he intended seeing and the galleries he intended visiting; I thought you might need one,' said Mrs Haynes. 'I'll just get it for you.' She went into the next room, shutting the door behind her.

'An efficient woman,' said Roland. 'I wish all our witnesses were so cooperative. Now, could he have had any money troubles?'

'I really don't think so. He earned a very good salary and had few drains on his income.'

'Would he have been carrying much cash on his person?'

'You mean he was robbed?'

'His personal belongings were missing. I'm trying to establish whether he could have been killed for his money or for something he was carrying.'

'He wouldn't have had much actual cash on him. He would have paid for most things by credit card and his expenses would have been reimbursed later. What else could he have been carrying?'

'A valuable canvas? If he was borrowing paintings for the exhibition ...?'

'Oh dear me no! John just made the arrangements. The actual transportation is done through a firm of carriers who specialize in this sort of thing.' He mentioned a name and Mansfield noted it down. 'He never handled the exhibits, he certainly never carried any paintings on his person, only photos and specifications ...'

Roland cut into his protests. 'Drugs?'

'This is ridiculous! I've never heard of such an absurd idea!'

'Are you sure? You say he travelled regularly between here and the Continent. He was ideally placed to be recruited as a courier.'

'Inspector, this is preposterous! A valued friend and colleague has been brutally killed and all you can do is try to blacken his name! He was the victim, not the perpetrator of this terrible crime!'

'We have to consider all possibilities, Mr Mickelsen. There has to be a reason for his killing. If we can establish a motive we're more than halfway to discovering his murderer.'

'You're saying that John led a second, secret life of which I and my colleagues knew nothing?'

'I'm not saying. I'm asking.'

'You say he was a very private man.' Mansfield took up

the questioning. 'Not the sort of person to take anyone into his confidence; in fact, something of a dark horse?'

'Ye-es, I see what you mean.' Jeremy Mickelsen looked unhappy. 'I suppose it *is* possible. Who ever really knows his fellow man? We think we do but what we see is only the front he chooses to present to the world. But, having said that, I'm positive John was just as he appeared, a very solitary, law-abiding man, something of a recluse. Of course, much of his spare time was spent on the book he is researching.'

'Book?'

'He's been working on it for several years; the influence of Flemish artists on seventeenth-century Dutch landscape painting. It's a very complex subject and I don't think he had got down to the actual writing; he was still collating facts and making notes.'

'H'm. When he went on these business trips I presume he made his own arrangements, worked on his own initiative – he didn't have to have every move vetted and approved by you?'

'Of course not. He was a very senior member of staff, an executive director, and as such he was his own master.'

'So he could have fitted in all manner of extramural activities without the gallery being any the wiser?'

'Well, yes, I suppose so,' he admitted grudgingly.

At that moment Mrs Haynes reappeared.

'Here we are, officer, the itinerary that Mr Hargreaves followed. He went over from Harwich to the Hook of Holland on Saturday, visited the Mauritshuis in The Hague, went on to the Rijksmuseum, staying with his ex-wife while he was in Amsterdam, and then yesterday he travelled to Bruges, where he went to the Groeninge Museum and a private house before returning from Zeebrugge.'

'He was working over the Easter weekend?'

'It often happens that way in our business,' said Mickelsen. 'We don't keep office hours. John sets up his contacts and arranged times convenient to them and himself.'

'I can see that there's more similarity than I had thought between your profession and ours. Have you got a photo of John Hargreaves?'

'There were those ones taken to advertise the television show.' Mrs Haynes spoke to her boss.

'Yes, of course. May I ask why you need a photograph, Inspector?'

'To publicise it in the hope that someone will recognise the dead man and come up with some information to help our inquiry.'

'Oh, dear, you may get more results from this action than you anticipate. John took part several times in the *Connoisseurs' Art Show* on television; I'm sure a lot of people will remember him from that.'

So that was why Copping, the police photographer, had thought he recognised the corpse and why some vague memory had niggled away in the back of his own mind, Roland thought. Still, it had been a somewhat esoteric programme on Channel Four, not the sort of viewing the masses enjoyed.

'That can't be helped. It'll be a case of sorting out the sheep from the goats, and if he's achieved some fame on the box it will grab the public's interest. May we see his office and have access to his effects?'

'Certainly. Mrs Haynes will show you round and help you.'

'That won't be necessary. While we're busy perhaps Mrs Haynes can find us those photographs of Mr Hargreaves?' He mollified the middle-aged secretary with a smile and she departed to do his bidding.

John Hargreaves' office revealed no clues. He appeared to have been a very orderly man, completely bona fide. If he had led a secret life, no trace of it was to be found in his working environment. There were no paintings or prints hanging on his walls, which Roland thought rather strange, but his bookshelves were crammed with art books and exhibition catalogues. Ginny would be interested in these, he thought; she had probably visited some of these exhibitions. He glanced at his watch. They should now be together listening to the exciting melodies of Carl Orff. Instead, here he was, some eighty miles away, searching through material with which she would be far more familiar.

'Is there anything I can do to help?' Jeremy Mickelsen was

waiting for them with a folder of photographs when they had finished in John Hargreaves' office. Roland glanced through the photos.

'These will do fine. I'd like a list of names and addresses of all the employees of this gallery.'

'You surely don't think anyone here had anything to do with his murder?' Mickelsen was quite aghast.

'I'm trying to build up a picture of the dead man. According to you he led a life of seclusion, but he must have had some contact with the outside world apart from his work; no man is an island, as John Donne so rightly said. I'm hoping that some of his colleagues may be able to throw some light on his private life.'

'Yes, I see. Well, he certainly shunned parties and social gatherings. He had to attend a certain number of those in the course of his work, but he was a very reluctant participant. Very occasionally he would accept a dinner invitation from myself and my wife, and I believe he played bridge – but there again, I don't know with whom or whether it was a regular commitment.'

'Well, thank you for your help, Mr Mickelsen. Just one point – will the exhibition still go ahead?'

'Of course. This will be one of the most prestigious exhibitions we have ever mounted. It is a real feather in our cap. Fortunately John had already done most of the groundwork – oh, dear, that sound callous, doesn't it? But I'm sure he would have wanted it to go ahead. What about the funeral?'

'The coroner has been informed and the inquest will probably be set for early next week, but it is sure to be adjourned.'

'You will keep me informed?'

'Oh yes, Mr Mickelsen. We shall be in touch, you may be sure.'

'We've had our excitement and thrills, now for the soothing of the savage breast. Do you know the Elgar?'

Ginny Dalton and Jean Mansfield were sitting in the bar of the Jubilee Hall sipping their interval drinks. The latter consulted her programme.

'*The Music Makers*. I think I heard it performed a long while ago but I don't really recall it. I need something to bring me down to earth after *Carmina Burana*. It was exhilarating, wasn't it?'

She was a small, dark, vivacious woman in her early forties, a complete contrast to her companion, who was some ten years younger, at least six inches taller and the owner of an abundance of red-gold hair and a pair of odd-coloured eyes.

'I first heard it at a Prom many years ago and I was absolutely riveted. I think the local society gave it a very good rendering and they deserve the full house.'

The hall had been packed, every seat taken, and there was a crush in the bar.

'Thank you for the invitation. I had intended booking ages ago but somehow I hadn't got around to it.'

'It was James' idea. He thought it was a shame to waste the tickets and your husband had said that you wanted to go. They were both being altruistic.'

'Don't you believe it! It was just a sop to their consciences,' said Jean Mansfield sagely. 'How do you like being a police widow?'

'But I'm not, am I? I'm just a widow, full stop, and Alec has only been dead two and a half years. I don't want to be pressurised into another relationship yet.'

'And is James pressurising you? I'm sorry, I don't mean to pry, it's none of my business.'

'Don't worry, Jean, it is a relief to have someone to confide in. And I envy you; you and Patrick seem to have a very good marriage and yet you're a very independent person. How do you manage it?'

'I suppose by accepting the inevitable. If you're married to a policeman you have to understand this and not fight the system, which means, in my case, having interests and a life of my own outside the shared one. A lot of women can't come to terms with this, James' former wife for one.'

'The wayward Karen. Did you know her?'

'Not very well. She directly related James' devotion to duty to a lack of interest in her − stupid woman. I must say I don't think they were really suited, she wasn't good enough

42

for him. I still think that it was his pride that took the worst battering when she left him rather than his heartstrings – but don't ever tell him that I said so.'

'She certainly soured him for other women. I have this feeling – oh, it's difficult to explain – that although he wants me badly, underneath he resents me for the sexual attraction I exert over him.'

'I think you may be right to a certain extent. He's fallen for you against his will. But how about you?'

'You mean how do I feel about him? I'm very attracted to him sexually – I've got the hots for him – but although I lust after him I'm not sure if I actually like him. There's something rather cold and ruthless about him, which I suppose is why I've held out so far. If I slept with him I know that it would be marvellous physically but that might be all; just the assuaging of a physical appetite. I don't want that sort of relationship with James Roland or anybody else. Besides, there's Simon.' Ginny Dalton toyed with her glass and looked worried.

'He doesn't like James?'

'He's so prickly. I suppose it is partly his age.'

'But is it James he resents or would he be the same about any man who showed an interest in you?'

'I don't know. You would have thought, especially after that ghastly murder hunt and trial, that Simon could have been expected to hero-worship someone of James' calibre and charisma, but it hasn't worked that way. And James has been very good with him, handled him so tactfully and all to no avail. I feel positively guilty about my son's behaviour. He's downright rude at times and sometimes I feel that I could wring his neck!'

'I shouldn't worry about it too much. If you and James eventually make a go of it, I'm sure he'll come round to accepting it.'

'Thanks, Jean. It's done me good to talk about it, though I don't usually go around opening my heart to all and sundry.'

'I'm not all and sundry, I hope you look on me as your friend. There's just one thing that intrigues me mightily – how have you managed not to succumb to James Roland?'

'With great difficulty.' Ginny Dalton grinned at her companion.

'That must be quite a novel experience for him and one that will do him no harm.' Jean Mansfield smiled back. 'Now, to change the subject completely, isn't it good to see so many young people here? I can remember a time, not so many years ago, when a choral-society concert wouldn't have attracted anyone under the age of fifty.'

'That's true and it must be partly due to their moving with the times. The *Messiah* and the other oratorios are all very well in their place but there *have* been other composers after Handel and Bach. It's good to hear them tackle twentieth-century composers, and it pays off if it encourages the youngsters to develop an interest in classical choral music. I've noticed several of my sixth-formers here tonight and some even younger.'

'The young people are so much more attractive nowadays, especially the males. Goodness, I sound really ancient, don't I? But when I was young in the sixties it was the age of the flower people and hippies, and to me they were a race apart. Today they know their place in the world, they're so much more confident and interesting as people. I fantasise sometimes about what it would be like to have a toy boy.'

'Jean!'

'I've really shocked you, haven't I? I can assure you it's all in the mind. I'm happily married and I have no intention of rocking the boat, but one can't help wondering . . . Apparently it's the in thing at the moment.'

'Well, you won't get me climbing on that particular bandwagon. I teach too many of the little beasts! I prefer them a little maturer.'

'Speaking of maturer men, there's a rather well-preserved specimen sitting over there behind you who's been staring at the back of your head ever since we sat down.'

Ginny set down her wine glass and turned her head casually, at the same time edging her chair sideways so that it wouldn't look too obvious.

'Good heavens! It's Hugh Calder-Brown. I didn't know that he was into choral music.'

'He does know you?'

'You could say. You'll have a chance to meet him, he's

coming over.' She smiled and raised her hand at the man who had risen to his feet and was now pushing his way towards them.

'He looks as if he could do with a good night's sleep.'

'Those haggard good looks are part of his stock in trade. You're supposed to liken him to a consumptive poet.'

'I read somewhere that consumptives were highly sexed. Help — we can't seem to get off the subject this evening ...'

'Hugh! Fancy seeing you here.'

'I could say the same of you, my dear. Enjoying the concert?'

'Very much. Jean, meet Hugh Calder-Brown; Hugh — Jean Mansfield.' They acknowledged each other and Ginny Dalton continued, 'Jean stepped in at the last moment when I was stood up.'

'Stood up? I can't believe that,' he said gallantly.

'It's true all the same. Hugh is an antiquarian bookseller.' Ginny turned to her companion. 'He owns the second-hand bookshop in Goths Yard.'

'I've often looked in the window when I've been passing but I'm afraid that I've never been inside.'

'We must remedy that. I cater for all tastes and purses.'

'How is business?' Ginny asked.

'Fluctuating. I've been to a couple of book sales on the Continent recently and bought some nice first editions to add to my collection. The trouble is, I'm supposed to sell books, not add them to my shelves. Now you know why I'm not a rich man.'

'Well, you haven't a wife and family to support. Or has some designing female managed to get you to the altar at last?'

'That's unkind, Ginny. Since you weren't interested, I've abjured the company of women.'

'That I don't believe. A good woman would be the making of you.'

'You sound just like dear Mama; she doesn't approve of my life style.'

The two-minute bell went at that moment and there was a general movement towards the doors.

45

'We must get back to our seats. It's been lovely seeing you, Hugh.'

'The pleasure is mine entirely.' He shook hands with Jean and bestowed on her a charming, lopsided smile. 'I'll be in touch, Ginny. *Au revoir.*

'Well, well, another of your admirers,' said the older woman as they moved back towards the concert hall.

'I've been out with him a couple of times but one doesn't take a person like Hugh Calder-Brown seriously. He has a very mercurial temperament.'

'He looks like someone left over from the nineteen-twenties.'

'I know what you mean. One feels he would look more at home in a Noël Coward dressing-gown waving a cigarette holder around.'

'How did you meet?'

'At the annual Anglia Antiques and Craft Fair. I was helping out a friend who ran a pottery stall and he had the stand next to us.'

They took their seats in the auditorium and, as the orchestra tuned up, Jean whispered to Ginny, 'I wonder what Patrick and James would say if they knew that we'd spent most of the interval discussing our love lives and being chatted up by a rather gorgeous male.'

'Do you think they've given us a thought?'

'You're learning. I presume they're tied up with this body that was found on the *Mercia* ferry. Patrick didn't say but I heard about it on the local news. It sounded nasty. I'm not expecting to see much of him in the near future.'

A detective sergeant from the Brentwood station was waiting for Roland and Mansfield at John Hargreaves' flat. This was situated in a quiet cul-de-sac not far from Weald Park.

'We've had a quick look round but everything appears to be in order. No sign of a break-in or anything like that. What are you looking for?'

'Anything that might give us a clue to his murder. We're working in the dark at the moment. I presume he wasn't known to you?'

46

'No. According to the people downstairs, he was an exemplary character who commuted to the City most days and never harmed a fly.'

Roland could well believe this. The inhabitants of this sort of property were more likely to be sinned against than sinning. They were the victims of theft and homicide, not the instigators. The house was one of those substantial double-bay villas built in the early 1930s and from what he could see in the dark it appeared to have a sizeable, well-kept garden.

'He lived in the upstairs flat?'

'Yes, but I think it might be a good idea to talk to the Peters couple in the downstairs flat first. They've lived here for years and probably knew him as well as anyone. They're elderly, retired colonials and the wife is very cut up.'

While the wife was weepy and practically incoherent, the husband was made of sterner stuff.

'Lived in Kenya most of my life; we came back twenty years ago. Used to violence out there, it was always round the corner, but we didn't expect to find it here.' He had a quick, staccato way of speaking that went with his clipped military moustache and upright bearing. 'Things are not like they used to be, this country is going downhill fast.'

'I can't believe it officer, he was such a quiet, pleasant man — a real gentleman.' Mrs Peters peered up at Roland through faded, myopic eyes. 'Who could have done such a terrible thing?'

'That's what we're here to find out, ma'am. How well did you know him?'

'He kept himself to himself but he was a very kind man, would give a helping hand if needed.'

'He was a good landlord,' her husband interposed,'and what will become of us now? We're too old to move house and start somewhere new.'

'He owned the property?' Roland hadn't known this.

'Yes. He divided the house into two flats just before we moved in. Originally we lived in the top one and he had this one, but my wife suffers badly from arthritis and she was finding the stairs impossible so he suggested we change over.'

'Did he do much entertaining?'

'Not as far as we know. He was a very quiet man, spent most of the summer months in the garden. Very keen gardener he was, I used to give him a hand sometimes.'

'But living in the downstairs flat you would be aware of his visitors?' Roland persisted. 'The stairs to his flat lead off your hallway.'

'You're not suggesting that we spied on him, pried into his activities, are you?' A fresh wave of distress engulfed Mrs Peters.

'You want us to find his killer, don't you?' asked Roland gently. 'It's quite possible he knew his attacker and may have entertained him here. Living as you do in such close proximity you must have seen much of his coming and going. Are you aware of anyone who visited him regularly, male or female?'

'You think he had a lady visitor? You're barking up the wrong tree there, Inspector.' Her husband was quite derisive. 'John Hargreaves wasn't one for the ladies. I'm not saying he was queer, mind you, don't get me wrong, but the fairer sex were a closed book to him, he just wasn't interested. Spent his time at home reading and writing – he was working on a book, d'you know – and as I said, a very enthusiastic gardener.'

'He really wasn't here a great deal,' said his wife. 'He went into town most days – he had a very important job in an art gallery – and he was away quite often. But he did play bridge; you've forgotten that, Harold.'

'Did he play with a regular group?'

'I think it was always the same people, sometimes they came here to his flat. Two of them were a local solicitor and his wife and there was a lady, a very respectable lady who I believe is a retired schoolteacher.'

It didn't sound very promising, Roland thought, but they would have to be checked out. The man was becoming more of a mystery as they delved into his background; an estimable character with no faults. He was too good to be true, there must be skeletons in the cupboard somewhere; perhaps the flat would reveal something.

Some while later Mansfield replaced the last book in John Hargreaves' bookcase and rocked back on his heels.

'Well, we seem to have found his secret vice: sci-fi.' The bulging shelves in the bedroom were stuffed with science-fiction books, both hardback and paperback. Frank Herbert rubbed shoulders with J. G. Ballard and Isaac Asimov.

'At least he kept them separate from his others.' The study and living-room contained a comprehensive collection of art books, many of them in Dutch. 'I suppose being an expert in Dutch art and having been married to a Dutch woman he naturally learned the language. Any luck with his papers?'

'Nothing to help us.' Roland sighed and tapped his fingers on the desktop. 'He has a healthy bank balance, ditto building-society account. No sudden withdrawals of large sums or mystery windfalls and it looks as if he wasn't paying any alimony. All in all it adds up to him having been comfortably off with no financial worries. His diary is purely an engagements one; mostly business appointments, by the look of it, though there's a fortnightly date which was probably the bridge evening. We'll have to check up on it but I'm sure it's perfectly innocent.'

The flat was comfortably furnished and in a reasonably clean and tidy condition.

'The couple downstairs made no mention of him employing any domestic help, it looks as if he managed by himself.' There were enough well-used kitchen utensils to assume that John Hargreaves had also been capable in the cooking stakes. The fridge revealed a carton of long-life milk, a tub of margarine and a jar of mayonaise.

The wardrobe contained several good-quality, conservative suits and a dinner jacket, and the drawers of the dressing-table and chest of drawers contained the underwear, shirts and sweaters that one would expect an austere middle-aged man to own.

'Not even one tie in doubtful taste.' Mansfield turned his attention to the bathroom. The cabinet contained the normal medicaments to be found in any household, and on the windowsill were a new tube of toothpaste, a jar of medicated cream and a disposable razor. John Hargreaves obviously hadn't believed in adorning the male physiognomy. Mansfield thought of his student son's bedroom, of the talcs, aftershave lotions, deodorants and hair gel that were an essential part of his son's grooming routine, and the said son was existing on a grant which he and Jean were having to subsidise. He shut the bathroom door and went in search of his colleague.

'Do you want us to run a check on dabs?' asked the local sergeant.

'I don't think there's much point,' said Roland. 'The murderer did a good job in removing all traces of his and anybody else's on the ferry. Every surface had been wiped clean.'

'I can't see our victim as the mastermind or even a humble courier of a drug ring,' said Mansfield pensively, 'but do you think he could have been used? Suppose he was an innocent carrier — someone hid something in his baggage without his knowledge — and he found out and was killed to shut his mouth?'

'If there had been any drugs in that cabin I should have thought the dog would have found traces. I'm beginning to wonder if he was killed by mistake, if the killer got the wrong man. And if so, where does that leave us?'

'Holland in bulb time. This job is becoming a rest cure. I shall have applicants beating a path to my door, begging to be recruited, if this gets around.' Superintendent Bob Lacey glared at the two men facing him across his desk and then snorted. 'Don't look so belligerent, James. You've got the OK, but, by God, you'd better get some results!' He heaved his bulk out of his chair and padded over to the window. 'Shouldn't take long, should it? We're hard pressed at the moment; I can't afford to have two of my best officers gallivanting about on the Continent.'

'I think it's important to follow the same itinerary that John Hargreaves took,' said Roland firmly. 'Travel to the Hook on the morning ferry, stop by this museum in The Hague and then go on to Amsterdam. Visit the Rijksmuseum and interview the ex-wife — this will mean staying overnight in Amsterdam — and then move on to Bruges and the contacts there, and come back on the overnight boat, the *Mercia* ferry, from Zeebrugge.'

'Got it all worked out, haven't you? Well, mind you don't

step on the toes of our Dutch and Belgian counterparts. Cooperation is the name of the game, we don't want to upset our foreign friends.'

'We're liaising closely. They're running the story over there in the media in the hope that someone will recognise the dead man and produce some relevant information.'

'Ah, yes, the media interview. I'm told you're building up quite a fan club.'

'Sir?'

'Don't look so innocent. What's this I hear about females phoning through with information which they refuse to divulge unless they get a personal interview with Detective Inspector James Roland?'

'I think someone is kidding you, sir. Just a hiccup in communication.'

'H'm. Has it produced any results yet?'

'Too many. An awful lot of people think that they saw Hargreaves aboard the *Mercia* that night, but a good 90 per cent of them probably only recognise the photograph because it was familiar to them from his television appearances. However, we've got one lead. A woman, an elderly, retired civil servant, reported that she was sure she saw the murdered man drinking with a companion in the bar not long after they left port and that she saw them get up and leave together a little later. She can give no description of this drinking companion, only insists that it was a man, but he had his back to her all the time and she has no idea of his age, appearance, or even if he was white. She did say that she thought that he could have been a sailor but when pressed admitted that this was because he was wearing one of those peaked denim caps. I think they're called Guernsey caps, that all and sundry wear nowadays. So far nobody has corroborated her story.'

'No help from the autopsy?'

'It's almost certain that the weapon used was the missing paperknife from the boutique or an identical knife; the stab wounds match up. It was wielded by a right-handed person who used excessive force – the sternum was cracked.'

'Not a great deal of help.' Lacey pulled gently at his ear lobe. 'Well, off you go then and do what you have to do over the other side.'

51

The superintendent waited until they were at the door and added maliciously, 'And that's not licence to sample the red-light district!'

The crossing from Harwich had been uneventful, the sea as calm as the proverbial millpond. The train journey from the Hook of Holland had taken them through scenery that had come straight out of a travel brochure; low-lying rectangular fields ablaze with colour, the gold and white of daffodils and narcissi now giving way to the crimson, blue and pink of tulip and hyacinth. At the Mauritshuis Museum, a beautiful old building beside the Vijver Lake in The Hague, the director had received them courteously but what he had to tell them added little to what they already knew, Mijnheer Hargreaves, an old and revered friend, had arrived as expected and they had discussed the arrangements for the loan of two paintings, by Jan Steen and Bartholomeus van der Helst respectively, to the Langdale Gallery. They had then shared a meal and the Englishman had continued on his journey to Amsterdam.

In Amsterdam Roland and Mansfield met up with *Adjudant-rechercheur* Pieter Hendriks of the CRI, who had been conducting inquiries on their behalf in Holland. He was a burly man in his early forties with fair hair and eyebrows so blond that they appeared almost nonexistent and gave his face a look of perpetual surprise. He spoke good English.

'Your Mr Hargreaves was not known to us. He had, as you say, no form, and none of our contacts in the drugs world have any knowledge of him. He came to the Nederland many times — all very innocent. He visits his wife.'

'Ah, yes, his wife. Anneke Kellermans. Has she remarried?'

'No, that is her professional name. I will take you to her after you have registered at your hotel. You have been booked in at the Hotel Amsterdam on Hoofstraat, which is not far from Vondelstraat, where she lives, and also the Rijksmuseum is nearby.'

It was Mansfield's first visit to the Dutch city and he was impressed by the sheer volume of traffic, so chaotic and yet so ordered at the same time; the cars and vans and lorries

52

speeding in all directions, the hordes of cyclists and the yellow, clanking trams whose tracks seemingly cut across the roads and pavements indiscriminately and posed great peril to pedestrians and drivers alike.

They left their overnight bags at the hotel. Pieter Hendriks took them by a short cut across the nearby Vondelpark to the house of Anneke Kellermans. The cherry trees were in full bloom, pink and white cones of candyfloss anchored to gnarled black trunks, dripping onto the grass through which magpies bounced and chattered. There were children romping along the tarmac paths, courting couples enjoying the spring sunshine, and through the trees the lake glittered like a silver spoon. The noise and bustle of the city seemed a world apart.

The ex-wife of John Hargreaves lived in a tall house on Vondelstraat. Her studio was on the ground floor and her living quarters on the floors above. Pieter Hendriks rang the bell and spoke gruffly into the intercom. While they waited Roland quizzed him about the lady in question.

'Is there anything we should know about Mevrouw Kellermans?'

'She is very *geducht* – formidable – but she likes the English.' A smile fleetingly crossed the Dutchman's rather solemn features. 'Treat her with respect.'

The door opened to reveal a very large woman with a florid complexion and greying hair skewered on top of her head in an untidy bun. Roland wasn't quite sure whether she really was as fat as she looked or whether her voluminous smock was disguising her true figure. His first thought was: my God! She's certainly got the physique to have carved up her ex!

Hendriks introduced them. Anneke Kellermans clasped the startled Roland's hand with her own dusty ones and burst out, 'Ah, officer, my poor Jan! This is a terrible thing that has happened! You must find the villain who did this terrible thing.'

'That is why we are here, Mevrouw Kellermans. Shall we go inside?'

She surged ahead of them up the stairs, panting and gasping, and the three policemen followed in her wake.

The room into which she led them ran the length of the house and there were large dormer windows at either end that overlooked the rooftops of Amsterdam. There were several vividly coloured modernistic paintings on the walls and some large pieces of avant-garde sculpture on the polished floorboards. She obviously hadn't shared her ex-husband's enthusiasm for the old masters. Roland wondered what point of contact they could ever have had and whether the sculptures were her own work.

'How can I help you?' By this time she had divested herself of her working smock but underneath she wore another tentlike caftan.

'By telling us all you know of John Hargreaves' background. You were divorced a long while ago, yet you appeared to be on good terms. Was there no animosity?'

'Never.' The tears brimmed in her eyes as she clasped her hands and leaned towards Roland. 'He was a dear friend. I have suffered the death of a dear friend ...'

Chapter Four

'Do you know if he had any enemies?'

'Jan did not make enemies, he was very *Aangenaam* – an agreeable man.'

'What about his work, Mevrouw Kellermans? Could anyone have been jealous of his success? Had he rivals?'

She considered this. 'In the art world there are always little rivalries, little upsets, storm in a bowl, but nothing to kill for. It is crazy!'

Roland was inclined to agree with her. Nothing they had learned so far could account for a character like John Hargreaves meeting such a nasty end.

'Did he have appointments with anyone else while he was here?'

'Not that I know, I think not.'

'How often was he over here?'

She shrugged. 'Several times a year. There were no regular visits. He came on business and sometimes to research for his book. Who will finish it now?'

'Perhaps you?'

'*Neen, dank U zeer*. It is not my period. I have not the knowledge or the interest.'

'Did your ex-husband suffer from seasickness?'

'Very much so. He was a bad traveller always, even when calm was the sea.'

'Why didn't he fly?'

'Because he was afraid of the flying. Never would he go in an aeroplane. If only he had, officer – ' the tears welled up again in her eyes – 'he would be alive today. People don't

55

get stabbed to the death in aeroplanes.'

Roland left Vondelstraat convinced that Anneke Kellermans was genuinely grieving for her ex-husband and bewildered by his murder. Perhaps they would get more help at the Rijksmuseum or in Bruges. There was nothing more they could do that day and Pieter Hendriks suggested that while they were in Amsterdam they should sample some international cuisine. He regretted that he could not join them, a prior engagement, but he escorted them to an Indonesian restaurant near the Singel flower market and recommended the Rijsttafel.

'I don't eat this sort of food,' Mansfield complained, his eyes watering, as he bit into a particularly highly spiced morsel he had speared out of his rice platter.

'You're never too old to start. Think of it as broadening your education.'

'Talking about age, have you noticed anything about this city?'

'Such as what?'

'The age of the inhabitants. They're all young, teenagers and students. I've seen hardly anyone over forty, except Mrs K. I feel positively geriatric.'

'It does seem to have a youthful population. Perhaps they discreetly put the older generation out to grass when they reach a certain age.'

'You can see why they have a drugs problem. The good *Adjudant-rechercheur* wasn't very forthcoming about it, was he?'

'I should have liked to have discussed it with him more thoroughly but he was obviously unwilling,' said Roland, referring to an earlier conversation they had had with Pieter Hendriks, 'and as it appears to have no direct bearing on our inquiry I didn't like to press it.'

'Sombre chappie, isn't he? Very unbending and proper.'

'I think that's a characteristic of the Dutch. They're a very moral people.'

'And yet Amsterdam is notorious for its vice and drugs.'

'It's a strange anomaly, but apparently the scene is not as black as it is painted. I was reading a report the other day; since the Dutch decriminalised soft drugs the proportion of

56

young people using cannabis has dropped dramatically while it has gone up in Germany and Switzerland.'

'You mean they don't prosecute for the possession of pot?'

'Soft drugs have not been legalised but although, in theory, you can still be prosecuted for being in possession of even a small amount, in reality it doesn't happen. The Dutch seem to have managed to separate soft drugs from the hard stuff and they claim that they have proved that one doesn't lead on to the other.'

'Who are they trying to kid? We've only been here a few hours and we've seen junkies lying in the gutter. I wouldn't be happy if either of my kids came to live here in Amsterdam — there's too much temptation.'

'Perhaps we're exaggerating the problem because it's more in the open here and not swept under the carpet. Are you having any more to eat?'

'Not for me. But I need another beer, my mouth and throat are on fire!'

Later they strolled back to their hotel, crossing the Leideseplein with its throng of young, cosmopolitan people crowding the square beneath the strings of fairy lights. Mansfield wondered if John Hargreaves had felt as alien in this city as he did.

The next morning found them at the Rijksmuseum, which to Mansfield looked identical from the outside to the Central Station at which they had arrived. Their visit there followed the same pattern as the one to the Mauritshuis. John Hargreaves had discussed the loan of certain paintings with the director of that department and afterwards had remained on the first floor to carry out some private research for the book he was writing.

'Now we're here we'd better have a quick look round,' said Roland after they had taken their leave of the curator. 'I think that's allowed under our terms of reference.'

'I bet the Super wouldn't buy it, but I consider it vital to our understanding of John Hargreaves.'

They joined the throng of visitors and moved round the galleries. Mansfield looked admiringly at 'The Night Watch', which faced them from the other end of the room. 'Now that really is something. But you'd never see that happening in England.' He nodded towards the group of very young schoolchildren who were seated quietly on the floor near the painting, raptly absorbing the lecture their teacher was giving them on Rembrandt.

'Perhaps here they are taught to appreciate their national treasures at a young age.'

They moved on and Roland consulted his guidebook. 'Here we are, some paintings by Gerard Ter Borch.'

'He believed in working on a much smaller scale, didn't he?' Mansfield looked at a portrait of a wizened-looking little girl who had an old head on young shoulders. 'Bet this one kicked the bucket young, she looks like a dwarf rather than a child. But no ...' He peered closer. 'I take that back: "Helena van der Schalke, painted as a child." She must have been painted again as an adult, so she did reach maturity. Poor little kid, she can't have had much fun rigged out in that costume.'

'People dressed their children as miniature adults in those days. They certainly didn't have the freedom they have nowadays.'

'It's gone too much the other way,' Mansfield growled. 'What time is the train to Bruges?'

In Bruges they were greeted by the carillon in the main square playing what Mansfield swore was 'Twinkle, Twinkle, Little Star' although Roland assured him it was part of a suite by Beethoven. They left the city to the strains of a Mozart symphony, no further forward in their inquiries. John Hargreaves had carried out his itinerary as planned, efficiently arranging the loan of the pictures required and leaving behind no clues to explain his violent death a few hours later. As the train carried them the ten miles from Bruges to Zeebrugge, past toy-town farms and hamlets, Roland admitted to feeling thoroughly frustrated.

'I'm coming round more and more to the idea that he was killed in mistake for someone else. It's the only explanation.'

'Which means we may never find the murderer.'

'Unless he kills again. I'm afraid this has been a wasted trip. Bob Lacey is not going to be very happy.'

'I've got something out of it. I've made a momentous decision.'

Roland cocked an eyebrow.

'I'm going to take Jean on one of those weekend breaks to Bruges. There's no reason why we shouldn't do something like that now and again, the children are practically off our hands.'

'Good for you. You really fell for Bruges, didn't you?'

'It's a beautiful city. All those lovely old buildings and the canals. It was like stepping back into the Middle Ages – so peaceful and yet full of life. People go there for their honeymoons,' he added, looking slyly at his companion.

'So I believe,' Roland replied blandly.

A cabin had been booked for the two men on the *Mercia* ferry; not number 32, which was still out of commission, but an identical one farther along the passage. They did not go to it straight away. As Roland said, they had a few little experiments to conduct first. They sampled the self-service cafeteria and then sat in the nearby bar area surveying their fellow passengers. There were many of them. If not carrying her full quota, the ferry must have been pretty close to it. There was plenty of coming and going, people drifting in and out of the duty-free shop and boutique, and eating and drinking. As the night wore on, those who had not been fortunate enough to secure a cabin or a reclining seat stretched out on the lounge seating or lay on the floor, their heads cushioned by rucksacks and bags.

'Go into the boutique and see how easy it would be to whip one of those paperknives,' Roland ordered.

Mansfield returned a short while later. 'They've been removed from the display, but there's a card of souvenir spoons in their place. I could have palmed the lot, it's a shoplifter's paradise.'

'I thought as much. Well, I think that this is where we retire for the night – but not, I'm afraid, my friend, to sleep.'

'You're lying on the bottom bunk asleep ...'

Roland and Mansfield were threshing out what could have happened on the night of the murder.

'The murderer creeps in through the door. He dare not risk switching on the light and waking you up, so he lunges at you in the dark. He can't really see what he's doing – which accounts for the apparent butchery.'

'And it could mean, if it was done in the dark, that he thought John Hargreaves was someone else and didn't realise his mistake until afterwards. He must have had a key or the door was unlocked.'

'Or how about this: the murderer – we'll call him M for convenience – sees his victim, V, in the bar and contrives to fall into conversation with him. V tells him that he's a very bad traveller and M says that he has some marvellous seasickness pills. He offers to give one to V but says he daren't take one himself because they knock you out and he hasn't been fortunate enough to secure a cabin. V accepts the offer, takes pity on M and tells him that he may use the spare berth in his cabin. They both retire to the cabin and M gives V a powerful sleeping pill and pretends to take one himself. He lies on the top bunk, waits until V falls asleep and then attacks him.'

'But that would mean that John Hargreaves didn't know his killer, and if so, why was he killed?'

'Because he had something in his possession the murderer wanted? Or perhaps he had witnessed something incriminating of which he was unaware and he was killed to shut his mouth.'

'This is all supposition.'

'I know, we're groping in the dark. Let's carry out another experiment. Roll up your coat into a bundle and see if you can get from here to the waste-disposal unit with it without anyone seeing you.'

Mansfield disappeared and within a short time was back again.

'Well?'

'I managed it. There's no one about at all.' He looked at his watch. 'It's two a.m. The passengers are all asleep or resting and the crew are otherwise occupied.'

Roland waited a short while and then carried out the same experiment himself. The *Mercia* was a ghost ship. It was only a short distance from the cabins to the door beside the boutique, and this area was out of view of the passengers in the lounge and cafeteria beyond. Roland pushed open the door and slipped through. The passageway was dimly lit and he felt rather than heard the throb of the engines. The voice behind him made him jump.

'Excuse me, sir, but this is private. Where do you think you're going?'

Roland and Jack Paynter, the purser, recognised each other simultaneously.

'Why, it's the inspector! I didn't know you were on board. Does the Master — '

'I'm not here officially.'

'Travelling incognito, eh?' He gave a barking laugh. 'And still interested in my Muncher?'

'I'm checking out certain possibilities.'

'You see how difficult it is for an unauthorised person to enter this part of the ship.'

'My sergeant has already moved around here quite freely and undetected,' said Roland crisply.

'Well, we do our best. I must say you've had good publicity. Are you any nearer to finding out who did it?'

Roland ignored the question. 'Tell me, how easy would it be for someone to get hold of a cabin key?'

'Strictly speaking, it's not on, but off the record, many of the keys are interchangeable.'

'You didn't tell me this before.'

The steward shrugged. 'It doesn't really matter, does it? It was just that poor sod in number 32's bad luck that he was the one to get scrubbed out. I mean, if it hadn't been him it would have been someone else.'

'What *do* you mean?' Roland was intrigued in spite of himself.

'Well, it stands to reason it was a psychopath that did it and we reckon if there's a psychopath at large anyone could have been killed.'

'We?'

'Myself and some of the ship's crew. Now don't tell me you're not working on the same theory, Inspector? Serial murder, they call it, don't they? When is he going to strike again?'

*

Beattie Jones unlocked the back door of the Oxfam shop and dumped her handbag and shopping basket on the floor inside before turning back to manhandle the black plastic sack that was propped up on the step.

'Another donation,' she called back to her companion, who was still locking up her car. 'Have we got time to sort it out before we open?'

'It's only a quarter to ten. Plenty of time to do that and have a cup of tea. Put the kettle on, there's a dear, and I'll get the book.'

The two women went into the room at the back of the shop which served as restroom, office and general workshop. It was a dark, overcast day. Mary Fenton switched on the light and took off her overcoat while her friend filled the kettle, set out two mugs on the draining board and extracted tea bags from the jar on the shelf above the sink.

'Did you have a good weekend? How did the christening go?'

'Very well. She behaved beautifully, didn't even whimper, and she looked lovely in that broderie anglaise gown Chrissie made for her. Thank goodness it was better weather than today.'

Beattie Jones looked through the open doorway into the dimly lit shop beyond. The racks of clothing cast black shadows across the floor and between the two mannequins silhouetted at either side of the window she could see scurrying pedestrians pounding the pavement on the other side of the glass. The grass mats, canework and third world jewellery, products of a warmer clime, looked out of place hanging on the wall amid displays of cards depicting the English countryside. Not that there was much call for these goods at the moment. Christmas was when the sale of ethnic goods soared, at this time of year people were more interested in spring clothes, though with this sort of weather she doubted whether they would do much trade that day.

'I can't believe Chrissie is a mother. It seems only yesterday that she was a child herself. I don't know where time goes. What did you wear?'

'My navy suit. It was the one I wore for the wedding but I had a new blouse – a pink and cerise one – so it looked

62

different and of course I didn't wear a hat. My goodness, this sack's been knotted up tight, I'm having a job undoing it.'

She dragged the sack into the centre of the floor beneath the light. Her friend reached for her glasses and the box of price tags.

'Ugh, whatever it is it smells horrible.' Beattie Jones had managed to undo the neck of the sack.

'It's disgusting the way people dump their rubbish on us,' said Mary Fenton irritably. 'I know its charity and we're grateful for all donations but you'd think they'd at least make sure that clothes are clean and washed before they pass them on. Some of the stuff we take in would disgrace a jumble sale. What's the matter?'

'They're *wet*!' Her friend's voice rose in indignation. 'This really is the limit, and what a stink!' She plunged both hands inside the black plastic and tugged at the clothing inside.

'What have you got?'

'Looks like a boiler suit or dungarees of some sort. What are you staring at?'

'Beattie! Your hands, your skirt – they're *red*!'

There was dawning apprehension on the other woman's face. Beattie Jones dropped her bundle and stared at her outstretched hands in horror.

'It's blood! My God – it's blood!'

She clapped her hands over her mouth and then realised what she had done and went into hysterics.

'Right ma'am, we'll get someone along straight away. Yes, I know the place, the Oxfam shop on the corner of Datchet Street and Peel Road. Don't worry, we'll be right with you.' The young constable swung round from the switchboard and called across to the duty sergeant. 'Some old bird in hysterics ringing from the Oxfam shop. They've had a bag of bloodstained clothing dumped on the doorstep, thought it was a hand-out.'

'Bloodstained clothing? Sounds as if it could tie in with the *Mercia* ferry case. The boys upstairs will want to handle this one. Put out a call for DI Roland.'

James Roland was in court, but Patrick Mansfield knew

that DC Evans was spending that morning checking signatures in connection with a fraud case in the building society at the other end of Datchet Street. Mansfield and the young Welshman converged on the Oxfam shop and its shocked helpers.

'Now just take it calmly and tell us exactly what happened. Where was the sack?'

'On the back doorstep. It was there when we arrived.'

'We just thought it was charity goods someone was donating to Oxfam. We often get bundles deposited outside the door if the shop isn't open.'

'There's an identical black sack outside your front door now.' A look of momentary horror was replaced by one of understanding.

'That's the rubbish. It's always collected on a Monday morning. All the shops leave their dustbin bags out in the front where they are picked up by the dustcart.'

'So you found this bag on the doorstep. What happened next?'

'Well, we opened up and took it inside.'

'We decided we'd got time to sort out the . . . the contents before we opened the shop at ten. Beattie undid it while I put on the kettle and got out the record book.'

'It was horrible!' The woman called Beattie was still doing a good imitation of Lady Macbeth, wringing her hands and scrubbing at them with a pink-stained towel. 'I pulled that . . . that garment out of the bag and it felt wet . . .'

'The material was too dark to show what the damp was, but it brushed against her clothes and left a red stain,' said the second woman, who had recovered from her initial shock and was now starting to enjoy the drama. 'And then I saw her hands!'

'Don't!' her friend moaned. 'Officer, it *is* human blood, isn't it?'

'We can't tell at this stage, but it's more likely to be animal blood,' Mansfield lied soothingly. 'Probably somebody playing a practical joke.'

'A joke? What a macabre sense of humour! And where would they get the blood?'

'It's probably chicken blood,' said William Evans knowingly. 'There's a poultry butcher in the next street.'

Mansfield turned back to the two women. 'We'll take this little lot away and run some tests on it, but I'm sure it'll turn out to be a hoax, someone with a morbid sense of fun.'

'So we've found the murderer's clothing,' said Evans enthusiastically as they drove back to the station.

'Have you lost all your marbles?' Mansfield growled. 'Any bloodstained clothing belonging to our case would be dried and stiff by now.'

'But if it was sealed up in this plastic sack it would have kept moist.'

'It would be putrid by now.'

'It smells putrid,' Evans grumbled. 'How do you read it?'

'I don't like it at all. Let's hope it is animal blood and a joke, otherwise, William boyo, I fear we may be looking for another corpse.'

Roland was back in his office and together they examined the bloodstained clothing. The front of the garment was soaked in blood and there were heavy stains round the cuffs and splashed down the legs.

'You say it was left on the back step of the shop. If it's not a hoax I wonder why.'

'I have a nasty theory about that. Today is the day the dustcart collects from those streets. Every shop and household had identical black plastic bags standing out in the front. The Oxfam shop is on a corner; someone wanting to get rid of a sack of bloodstained clothes could have mistakenly dumped it at the Peel Road door instead of the front entrance in Datchet Street, expecting it to be carted away and disposed of.'

'Get this straight to the lab. We must know whether it's animal or human blood and I hope to God it isn't human. Someone didn't lose this amount through cutting a finger.'

You've been to the Rijksmuseum, I presume?' James Roland tightened his hold on Ginny Dalton and nuzzled her neck. They were sitting on the sofa in her cottage.

'Yes, and the Mauritshuis. I spent a couple of months in Amsterdam when I was a student. It's a fascinating place.'

'And you shall go back. How about a holiday there when I can get a weekend off?'

'And when is that likely to be, Inspector Roland?' Treat it lightly, she told herself, carefully extricating herself from his embrace and moving farther along the sofa.

'God knows. I'm working all hours of the day and night and getting nowhere fast.'

'I know you don't usually discuss your work, but you're working on this murder on the *Mercia* ferry, aren't you?'

'There's no reason why you shouldn't know. The press are having a field day. The April Fool Murder, they're calling it − "When will the April Fool joker strike again?" The dreadful thing is, I think he has.'

'Oh, James, no!'

'Sorry, forget I said that.' James Roland shook his head and ran his fingers through his black hair. 'What were we discussing?'

'I'm going to make some more coffee.' She got to her feet and padded to the kitchen, and he leaned back and sighed. Across the room Faience the cat looked at him with inscrutable eyes, then she blinked, lay her head down on her paws and went back to sleep. That damn cat probably slept on her bed, he thought. She got nearer to her mistress than ever he did.

'Here we are.' Ginny handed him a pottery mug. She sat down decorously beside him and sipped at hers. 'Have you got no leads at all?'

'Nothing significant. It's one of the most frustrating cases I have ever worked on. All I seem to have done is go on a lot of wild-goose chases; Monkbeggars Hall, the trip to Holland and Belgium ...'

'Monkbeggars Hall? How does that come into it?'

'It was completely irrelevant − a real time waster. Have you visited the place?'

'Yes, and I'm going back again soon with the first form. We're taking part in one of the historical re-creations next month.'

'You are? What a coincidence! The old girl who owns the place told me something about them. It seems a complex undertaking.'

'Oh, it is. We're well rehearsed and the kids really enter into the spirit of the thing.'

'So you dress up in costume and speak with all that thee-ing and thou-ing?'

'Don't mock, it's very educational. I'm in the middle of making my costume at the moment, it's green velvet.'

'I'm sure you'll look adorable with all this hair flowing down your back.' He threaded his fingers through the loose knot at the base of her neck and tried to undo it.

'It will all be bundled inside my cap.'

'What a waste! Still, you'll look just like Anne Boleyn. She had red hair, hadn't she?'

'I believe you're thinking of Henry VIII. She had a sixth finger on her left hand, did you know? A witch mark. They claimed that she bewitched him.'

'Then I've certainly got the right character, because you've bewitched me. Come here, you sorceress, and practise your spells on me.'

He took the empty coffee mug from her and set it carefully on the floor, then pulled her into his arms and pressed his body against hers as he sought for her lips.

The shrilling of the phone shattered their embrace. They sprang apart, she looking guilty, he trying to curb his annoyance.

'It may be for me. I had to leave your number.'

She walked across the room and picked up the receiver. They stared at each other across the room as she answered and then she held it out to him.

'It is. How did you know?'

Mansfield's voice came urgently down the line. As Roland listened, he stiffened and his face became a tight mask.

'Where? When? OK, I'll be right with you. Yes, I've got my car, I'll come under my own steam. Yes, about half an hour.' He put the phone down and she asked quickly:

'Something wrong?'

'You could say. I've got to go, something has come up.'

She wanted to ask him what it was but she bit back the question. This was what she would have to learn to live with if they ever made a commitment to each other. Already he was distanced from her, a professional policeman taking over. Could one, should one, be able to change so quickly from importunate lover to upholder of law and order? To slip from one role to another with such ease?

'I'll be in touch. Thanks for the evening.' And he was gone.

As she collected up the dirty mugs and took them into the kitchen, she reflected that it was a good thing that it had been a phone call that had broken up their embrace and not Simon bursting in on them.

'It has to be the work of the same person, it has all the signs. Someone who enjoys killing.'

'Or who gets in a frenzy at the sight of blood.'

'But what possible connection can there be between a body found on the *Mercia* and another one turning up two weeks later in the wilds of Suffolk?'

Roland and Mansfield, with a subdued Evans, paced the floor of the cottage while around them the team went into action. It was a woman this time. A small, slight figure with greying mid-brown hair, clad in a blue velour dressing-gown. She had been stabbed repeatedly in the back and her body lay slumped, face downwards, across the kitchen table in a pool of congealed blood.

Roland was awaiting the arrival of Doc Brasnett before the body was touched.

'The lab has already confirmed that the blood on that boilersuit was human. It looks as if we've found its source. Do we know who she is?'

'Yes, sir, a Lydia Cordingley.' PC Stephen Morton, the local bobby from the nearby village of Helsby, spoke up. 'She was unmarried, in her early forties and she lived here on her own.'

'Really out in the sticks — it must be all of two miles to Helsby, isn't it? How was she found?'

'It was because of the dog, sir. She had a Jack Russell terrier and it crawled into Manor Farm — that's on the outskirts of the village — more dead than alive. The people at the farm raised the alarm. It looks as if whoever did it struck the dog first and put him out of action before attacking his mistress, but they didn't quite kill him. He must have come round and

68

dragged himself over to the nearest neighbour. He'll have to be put down, he's in a bad way.'

'Not as bad as his owner. Is everything just as you found it?'

'It looks as if it's been ransacked but it could be a cover-up.'

'I suppose there'll be no way of knowing what, if anything, has been taken. Had she any relatives living nearby or close friends?'

'I think she was alone in the world. She didn't mix much locally, I expect because of her disablement, but she had business acquaintances.'

'Disablement?'

'She was partially crippled — polio as a child, I believe. She limped and walked with the aid of a stick.'

Roland had noticed the cane lying under the table. 'I didn't think people still got polio; still, I suppose it was a long while ago. Was she a wealthy woman? I mean, was she one of those eccentrics who don't trust banks and keep their money stashed away under the matress?'

'From what I knew of her I wouldn't have said that she was eccentric, just quiet and retiring. I don't think she was rolling in the readies but she seemed to be comfortably off.'

Roland pointed to a door with a double Chubb lock. 'What's in there?'

'That's her studio, sir. It was built onto the cottage when she moved here.'

'Have you found the keys?'

PC Morton pointed to the handbag that had been upturned on the dresser. There was no purse or wallet but among the scattered contents was a bunch of keys.

'Those?'

'Have you checked here for dabs?' Roland asked his colleague who was dusting for fingerprints.

'Yes, everything appears to have been wiped. I think the only ones we're going to find are those belonging to the dead woman.'

Roland unlocked the studio door and they went inside.

'This is like a strong-room' he said, looking round and

noting the windows with their bars and security locks. 'What did she do in here — forge banknotes?'

There were canvases and empty picture frames propped up against the walls and the worktops were littered with paints and pots of brushes. In a wall cupboard was a camera, an excellent little Nikon, and a folder of photographs which were all of paintings. A large rectangular metal table to which blocks and clamps were fixed stood in the centre of the room.

'Whatever is that? It looks like a rack.'

'It's her hot-table, sir. She was a picture restorer, not an artist. I think it was used for relining canvases or something of that sort.'

Picture restorer. Something clicked in Roland's memory. Lydia Cordingley: surely that was the name that Celia Calder-Brown had mentioned in connection with her painting being cleaned? Was there a link between the two murders that somehow involved the art world? He stowed it away in the back of his mind for further contemplation later and returned to the task in hand.

'You seem to be very knowledgeable, constable.'

'She cleaned and restored some panels for the local church a few years ago and I got involved in arranging their removal and transportation.'

'Did you now?' Roland regarded the constable thoughtfully. 'She couldn't have been all that much of a recluse if she was a professional picture restorer. She must have travelled around and had plenty of people here on a business footing.'

'I didn't say she was a recluse, sir, it was just that she lived all on her own and didn't encourage social visitors.'

By this time Doc Brasnett had arrived. He stared down at the corpse as he stripped off his coat and pulled on surgical gloves.

'How many more of these are you going to turn up, James? Is it the work of the same person?'

'I'm hoping that's what you're going to tell me.'

'Has the photographer finished?'

'Yes, you can move her now.'

George Brasnett grunted and started his examination.

'Blood congealed ... h'mm. Rigor mortis developed in the face and arms but not fully developed in the legs. I suppose you want an approximate time of death.' He busied himself with a rectal thermometer and Mansfield, who was more squeamish about this sort of thing than he liked to admit, looked away and tried not to think of the indignities being inflicted on the dead woman's body.

Brasnett straightened up. 'Twenty-seven degrees Celsius,' he said, squinting at the thermometer. 'Well, bearing in mind the ambivalent temperature − I presume the radiator's been on that low setting all day − I should say she's been dead about ten to twelve hours, possible a little more. That's only a very rough approximation, mind. I can tell you something else, though, it was a different weapon this time − a single-edged blade.'

'A kitchen knife?'

'Could well be. I'll be able to give you more details about the length of the blade when I do the autopsy. Her killer certainly went to town; a frail little body, taken unawares from the back − he didn't have to inflict all that damage.'

'What are you trying to say?'

'I don't like it, James, and I'm sure you're thinking along the same lines.' Brasnett looked at Roland over the top of his glasses.

'A homicidal maniac on the loose?'

'Your psychopath, so beloved of crime novelists.'

'But serial murders usually have some common denominator.'

'They were both killed on a Monday,' Mansfield put in.

'God help us if that's all we've got to go on. Perhaps when we go through her papers we'll be able to get a list of her business contacts. They'll have to be checked out and it will also mean a house-to-house in the neighbourhood, though maybe I should say a field-to-field.' He stared out of the window at the countryside that lurked blackly beyond the squares of light from the windows falling across the lawn outside. 'It will be too much to hope that someone actually saw her murderer arrive or leave, but hopefully somebody may know something about her habits and whether she had any regular visitors.'

PC Morton spoke up. 'If it hadn't have been for the dog,

her body wouldn't have been found so soon. It could have lain here for several days before anyone realised anything was wrong.'

'Perhaps her killer was counting on that, in which case he slipped up by not making sure that he had put the dog permanently out of action.'

A search of the downstairs rooms revealed little to help them, but Mansfield struck lucky in the dead woman's bedroom.

'Look what I've found in the bedside cabinet drawer.' He held out a round tin containing a dutch cap to Roland.

'So she wasn't as stand-offish as all that. It looks as if she had a lover. I wonder who he is and whether he can throw any light on her murder.'

'Someone local?'

'If it's someone in the village it will be known. You can't keep a thing like that quiet in a village community.'

'Perhaps it was a lovers' quarrel.'

'If only it were, but I fear it's not as simple as that. We'll have to try and find out if she had a regular man-friend, but what's the betting it'll turn out to have nothing to do with this case?'

It was the small hours before Roland and Mansfield got back to Felstone. The scene-of-crime team had departed earlier, the fingerprint expert having established that the murderer had worn gloves and had wiped clean all the surfaces with which he had come into contact. An incident room had been set up and the body removed to the mortuary to await the further attentions of Doc Brasnett. DC Evans had been sent off to the forensics laboratory at Aldermaston with the dead woman's clothing and an urgent request for tests to be done to ascertain if the blood matched up with that found on the boiler suit.

Having done all that could be done for the time being, the two detectives returned to their respective homes to snatch a few hours' sleep.

The house on the outskirts of Felstone was a respectable Edwardian semidetached residence. The owners of the neighbouring houses were not so sure that the occupants were respectable. Living as they did in close proximity to Felstone Polytechnic, they were used to the annual influx of students renting property or lodging in the immediate area, but the ménage at number 46 was something else again. No one was quite sure exactly how many were in residence and with an absent landlord it was difficult to establish how many people it was supposed to house and whether any laws were being contravened, but the comings and goings at all hours of the day and night and the bizarre appearance of some of the tenants caused raised eyebrows, to say the least.

For a start, they weren't all young. Many were middle-aged or older and men seemed to predominate. It was the consensus of opinion among the owner-occupiers in the district that possibly the house was being used as a brothel.

If he had known this, Rick Coates would have been amused; there was more than one way of cocking a snook at the Establishment. As it was, he cohabited with Lucy Hanson on the top floor while her fellow students, four in all, occupied the rest of the house. Much of the activity noted by the neighbours was connected with the conspiracy he was hatching. To be honest, the initial idea had been Lucy's and it was through her contrivance that the project was being financed. He pondered on this now as he sat at the head of the table and watched her hand out leaflets.

Who would have thought that a background such as hers would have spawned such a rebel? That snob of a mother with her rigid class conformity and the father, not much better, with his braying accent and huntin', shootin' and fishin' mentality. The best of the bunch was the grandmother; she was a bit of a rebel herself and there was a sneaking regard between them. Lucy took after her grandmother, there was nothing of her parents in her. He wondered if the old lady would be good for a touch. Finances were becoming strained. It was all very well people giving their moral support to the scheme, but they needed to put their wallets where their mouths were.

He called the meeting to order and addressed his fellow conspirators. The authorities would have been very surprised to have seen who were rubbing shoulders in that room.

'Everything is going to plan. There're just a few last-minute

73

details to finalise.' He hoped he sounded more confident than he felt.

'The date still stands?'

'Yes. It has to be a weekend when the tide is right and there is no moon, and fortunately that coincides with the barge races.'

'I still think it is risky to do it then with all that extra activity in the area.' The speaker was a man in his sixties with shrewd eyes and a somewhat pugnacious manner.

'It is the perfect cover-up. You're happy with the arrangements, aren't you, Lars?'

'Yes. I'll sail her in the day before and hove to upriver from the docks. That night I'll bring her in and when she's loaded I'll slip out with the tide under cover of darkness. We'll be over the North Sea before anyone realises that one of the competitors has gone missing.'

'Is she big enough for the job?'

The man Lars chuckled. 'You've obviously never been below hatches on a Thames barge, Lucy. She'll hold a king's ransom.'

'Is everything fixed up over on the other side?'

'Yes. We unload near Blankenberge and the lorries will be waiting there.'

'It's a hell of a journey.'

'We have to go overland through Europe, there's no way we could arrange to fly the stuff. The paperwork is all in order, isn't it, Bernard?'

'It will be by the time you want it,' came the laconic reply. 'How many are standing by over there? The Belgian authorities can be very sticky.'

'I think I sorted that out on my trip over there.'

'That business on the *Mercia* ferry ...' The middle-aged speaker dressed in black looked unhappy.

'It was most unfortunate,' said Rick Coates shortly and changed the subject. 'The thing I'm most worried about is the sleds. They've got to be silent. Even at this stage I think we may have to go back to the drawing-board.'

'I guarantee there won't be a squeak. I'm in charge of that part of the operation, leave it to me.' The speaker got to his feet. He was a thickset man in his early thirties wearing jeans and a donkey jacket. 'I must be off, got to see a man about a dog. Lucy, me darling, don't forget your contribution.'

'They'll be there and we won't have to pay a penny for them.'

The meeting broke up shortly after that and the conspirators went their various ways. Unbeknown to them, a certain ambitious young officer, who worked for Customs and Excise and lived nearby, was keeping an eye on their activities. He added to his report and decided to pursue the friendship he had struck up with one of the group, a young woman called Annette who had fabulous long legs and was crazy about animals.

Chapter Five

'Dad, haven't you finished with the paper yet?' Charlotte Hanson edged her chair further alongside the table and tried to read over her father's shoulder. She was a complete contrast to her elder sister, Lucy, being plump with fair hair and blue eyes.

'Your mother's finished with *The Times*.'

'I don't want *The Times*. I want to read about the murders. Katy reckons it's all to do with black magic and sacrificial rites.'

'Who's Katy?'

'Katy Gorham. Dad, don't say you've forgotten her, she came here to my last birthday party.'

'I thought I told you not to get involved with the Gorhams?' Marian Hanson came back into the breakfast room in time to catch the last part of the conversation between her husband and younger daughter. She was a large woman with greying hair and a rather horsy face. What was puppy fat on her daughter was in her solid middle-aged spread. 'They are not at all the sort of people I like you mixing with. I don't know what your headmistress was thinking of, taking a person like that into the school. And another thing, you're too young to read the local gutter press. I don't know why your father insists on taking it.'

'I'm fifteen!'

'Quite. The stories they print in there are not for a young girl's eyes.'

'You let Lucy do far more at my age!'

'If we had been stricter with her then perhaps she wouldn't

have turned out the way she has. I'm not having you throw yourself away like her. She has a first-class brain, she was Oxbridge material and instead she's wasting her talents at the local polytechnic.'

'She can still get a good degree from there,' her husband protested, trying to diffuse the situation. 'Though I must say I don't like the group of people she's got herself involved with, all living together in one house.'

'If she won't live at home at least I feel happier about her sharing with other young people, and her tutor also lives there. I expect he keeps an eye on them all, though I must say I feel he has had a bad influence on her, encouraging her left-wing fantasies.'

Charlotte Hanson eyed both parents slyly. 'She sleeps with him.'

The response was gratifying, living up to her wildest expectations.

'Charlotte!'

'Don't tell such wicked lies!'

'It's not a lie, it's the truth. She's been having it off with him for two years − ever since she went to college. Why don't you ask her?'

'Just you tell me where you got such a ridiculous idea from.'

'Oh, Dad, you're still living in the middle ages. Everyone does it now.'

'Don't talk to your father like that! Where are you going?'

The girl pushed back her chair with a crash and rushed towards the door.

'To the stables. You never believe anything I say! At least Turk will be pleased to see me!'

'If you don't exercise her more she'll soon be as fat as you. But you'll just answer a few questions first, my girl.'

'Oh, let her go, Nigel, I will not have these upsets at the breakfast table. We'll talk later, Charlotte,' she warned. 'And be back in good time. I want you cleaned up and looking presentable at lunchtime.'

'I can't believe she really meant what she said.' Nigel Hanson took off his glasses and made a play of replacing them in their case and stowing it in his pocket. 'She was just trying to shock us. If I thought that bearded scoundrel was really taking advantage of my daughter I'd ... I'd ...'

'What would you do? You don't seem to realise, Nigel, that Lucy is twenty. She is of age and we no longer have any control over her, so it is no good coming the Victorian father. Though I can't think why she's turned out like this. We were always so careful over her upbringing. She went to a good school and only mixed with the right people — why has she turned into such an unmanageable young woman.'

'Perhaps you've rammed it down her throat too much.'

'What *do* you mean?' Marian Hanson's voice rose.

'Well, you do come it a bit strong, old girl. All young people rebel a little. It's probably a case of forbidden fruit. This is the first time in her life that she has met a different class of person with differing ideals and outlook to ourselves and it's gone to her head; she's fascinated by them.'

'Why are girls so difficult? We've never had any trouble with Michael.'

'We don't know what he gets up to, away at boarding school. We just don't get to hear of it.'

'His reports are good. His teachers think he'll get good A-level results.'

'Have you seen anything of Lucy lately?' There was wistfulness in his voice.

'No, but Mother has. She turned up at the Hall out of the blue.'

'Your mother encourages her, you know. I blame her for a lot of Lucy's behaviour. She never had the chance to kick over the traces herself and she took great care that you and Hugh conformed, but she seems to take a delight in encouraging Lucy's waywardness. It's as if she is trying to spur Lucy on to do the things she never dared do herself.'

'You're exaggerating. It's just that Mother seems to be the only one of us who exacts any influence on her these days.'

'What did she want?'

'Apparently she wants to take part in the re-creations again.'

'At the high table?'

78

'Don't be ridiculous, Nigel. She'll be in rags and bare feet, boosting the ranks of the lower orders.'

'That alarms me rather. I can just see her leading a peasants' revolt, and that is not something I want re-enacted at Monkbeggars Hall.'

'Hugh is also going to honour us with his presence.'

'I thought he and your mother weren't on speaking terms?'

'Apparently they've agreed to bury the hatchet, at least for the time being. He'd hate to pass up the opportunity of exposing himself in doublet and hose. He ought to have been an actor instead of a bookseller.'

'There's nothing wrong with Hugh that a good woman wouldn't put right. It's time he settled down. He's over forty now, isn't he?'

'I don't know why you're so keen to get him married off. If he produced a family it would put paid to any hopes of Michael inheriting the Hall. I would pity any woman who got herself permanently involved with Hugh, he is a very unstable person.'

'You've never liked him, have you?' As one from a large, happy family, Nigel Hanson had never been able to understand the gulf between his wife and brother-in-law.

'Don't be absurd, Nigel. It's just that we've never had much in common, there's too big a gap in our ages.'

'Why did he fall out with your mother?'

'I don't know.' Her mouth tightened. 'It must have been something really serious, he always was her favourite.'

'Well, I must be off. Promised Jeff Prescott I wouldn't be late.'

'Where are you going?' His wife's voice was ominously quiet.

'To the golf club.'

'And what time do you propose getting back?'

'We'll get in a round before lunch. I'll get a bite in the club-house, should be back some time late in the afternoon.'

'You've forgotten!'

'Forgotten what?'

'It really is too bad of you, Nigel. I reminded you only a couple of days ago. The Hendon-Bretts are coming for lunchtime drinks. I arranged it ages ago. The colonel is very keen to learn about your breeding programme with the Jacob sheep.'

'Oh, hell! I *had* forgotten. Can't you put them off?'

'I most certainly cannot. You'll have to cancel your golf.'

Her husband looked mutinous. 'If I promise to be back by lunchtime?'

'No, Nigel, I know how you get carried away once you're on the links, you lose all sense of time. You'll have to cancel.'

'He's a bore, that man. All he can talk about is his experiences in the brigade; I wouldn't mind betting he was never a commissioned officer. And as for that wife of his – that bleating voice and all that name-dropping ...'

'They're very influential people. Promise you'll behave?'

'I don't have much choice, do I? I'll go and ring Prescott.'

'Why don't you do it from here?'

'No, I'll use the office phone, I want to have a smoke.'

Back in the farm office, Nigel Hanson threw himself back in his club chair and sulked. Damn Marian and her social calendar. He'd been looking forward to today, his first off the leash for nearly a fortnight – or so he had thought. And to make matters worse it was a glorious day; blue skies with just a hint of cotton-wool cloud, sunshine that was gaining strength and warmth hourly, and the whole countryside bursting into leaf and blossom. Was it old Will Shakespeare who had written of springtime being the time when young men's fancies turned towards thoughts of love? Middle-aged men's too. He pulled the phone towards him and dialled a number.

'Olive? I can't make it, something's come up ... No, I know, I desperately sorry. Marian's fixed up this social engagement, there's no way I can get out of it ... Yes, me too ... Can't wait, I'm feeling really lechy .. Don't you dare ... Yes, keep yourself on ice. I'll be in touch as soon as possible. And Olive – not a word to anyone about that weekend, especially under the circumstances.'

He put down the phone and stared out of the window. Marian chose that moment to come into view, walking across the corner of the yard towards the stables. She looked supremely confident, striding out in her brogues and well-cut tweeds; the typical English County lady in control of her life and destiny. What would she say if she knew what a mess he'd got himself into? It was hell being married to one woman and lusting after another. The French managed these things so much better.

Lydia Cordingley had been a competent and business like woman, as Roland and Mansfield discovered when they went through her personal papers. As Mansfield said, it was as if she had known that she was going to fall off the perch and had put her affairs in order. Her solicitor was a certain David Poultney, partner in a well-known firm in Woodford. He had drawn up her will, was her sole executor and the document had been lodged with him. It was perfectly straightforward: the estate was to be divided between several well-known charities with a special bequest going to the local RSPCA branch.

'How much simpler it is when people leave a will, especially if they have no family,' said Roland after he had been in contact with the solicitor. 'It's amazing the number of would-be relatives who would have come crawling out of the woodwork if she had died intestate.'

'Well, she wasn't killed for her inheritance, nor John Hargreaves either, so that rules out one of the most usual motives for murder. They both left the bulk of their estate to charity, apart from his small legacy to his ex-wife and I can't see the Mevrouw knocking him off for that.' Mansfield sucked at his pipe and produced a satisfying sizzle. 'Why were they killed? They were both apparently harmless, solitary people who had nothing in common to connect them.'

'At least we now know that the blood on the boiler suit was that of the dead woman. Forensics came up trumps. I stressed that it was of the utmost priority but they're so short-staffed and overworked that I thought we'd probably have to wait longer for the results. By the way, Lydia Cordingley was the person who cleaned Mrs Calder-Brown's picture. I've been in touch with her. The dead woman worked on it thirteen months go and was recommended to her by her son, as I'd remembered her saying. Apparently he organised it; arranged for the painting to be transported to her studio and installed back at Monkbeggars Hall after the operation. I think a visit to Mr Hugh Calder-Brown might pay off. He must have known her, if only on a very cursory footing.'

The house-to-house inquiry in Helsby had produced no tangible results. The dead woman had been respected by the community but had kept herself apart from village life. There had been no mention of any regular visitors who might or might not have been her lover. The idea of her having an enemy or enemies had been ridiculed by all those interviewed.

'I can believe that it is possible that John Hargreaves was killed by mistake or because he unwittingly got mixed up in something nasty, but that doesn't apply to Lydia Cordingley. She wasn't a drugs courier and living out in the wildest Suffolk she's hardly likely to have been an unknowing witness to some piece of skulduggery.'

'Perhaps the two murders haven't any connection and it was a tramp after all. There was no money in the cottage – her loose change had been taken and it looked as if her jewel box had been raided.'

'No, I won't buy it. We were meant to think that but I can't believe the two deaths are unrelated. We shall have to delve deeper into her background. I wonder what the bank was holding in safekeeping for her.'

David Poultney had learned from her bank in Woodford that a large, sealed envelope had been deposited in their vaults by Ms Cordingley and since he was her executor it would be opened in his presence by the bank authorities when he cared to call in.

'He's promised that if it is likely to be of any significance to our inquiries he'll come across with the goods.'

'Perhaps she was a blackmailer.'

'Well, that's certainly a high-risk occupation.'

The inquest on Lydia Cordingley was held and adjourned pending police inquiries. Roland was convinced that the two murders had been carried out by the same person but how to connect them was another matter. If he had been unsuccessful at finding a motive for John Hargreaves' killing, the death of the woman posed even greater problems.

'The murder weapon was a singled-edged blade about six inches long. Brasnett reckons it was a kitchen knife of the sort used for preparing vegetables. On the other hand, she must have had a sharp knife for cutting canvas, it could have been that.'

'There was a Stanley knife and some loose blades lying on the work top in the studio,' said Mansfield. The two men were going over the post mortem report in Roland's office.

'Maybe she used that in preference to a knife, but whether the weapon was a knife from her studio or her kichen it makes no difference to the result and is not going to help us in nailing her killer, unless we can find it complete with a nice set of fingerprints.' He read aloud: '"Stab wounds puncturing the lung; blood and air in the chest cavity ... collapse of the punctured lung ... A wound in the left mid-back directed towards the spine ... lacerated the aorta and caused massive haemorrhage internally ... Soggy bread in the stomach suggests a breakfast of toast just prior to her death ..."' Roland threw down the report. 'There you are, it all adds up to a vicious attack like the one that killed Hargreaves, but where that leaves us – '

'Maybe her killer was her mysterious lover and he deliberately made it look like the other killing to throw us off the scent? There's been enough publicity about the first murder.'

'True. We're still getting people phoning in to say that they think they recognise the dead man from his photograph. It's a wild-goose chase but we've got to follow them all up. There's just a chance something may come up that will link him with Lydia Cordingley.'

'*He* couldn't have been her lover?'

'If he was, how do you account for them both being killed? I don't think she, in her frail physical state, could have possibly killed him, and even if she had, who finished her off and why?'

'Yes, it's crazy, isn't it?'

'Let's sift through these reports again and see if we've missed anything that could give us a lead.'

Later that day came the first hint of a breakthrough with a phone call from the solicitor David Poultney.

'The package Lydia Cordingley deposited with the bank has been opened in my presence.'

'And . . .? Did it contain anything of importance?'

'I'm not sure.' There was a pause over the line and Roland heard the solicitor clear his throat. 'There were some share certificates and several papers of a similar nature, which was what I expected, but there were also some photographs.'

'Photographs? Of what?' Roland felt his pulse quicken and the word 'blackmail' flashed across his brain; perhaps Mansfield had been right.

'They appear to be of paintings, or rather, of one painting photographed from different angles.'

Paintings: it had to be significant. John Hargreaves had been involved with the buying, selling and exhibiting of paintings; Lydia Cordingley had repaired and cleaned them. There had to be a connection.

'May I see them? Have you got them at your office?'

'Oh no, Inspector. The bank won't release them until probate of the estate has been granted.'

Inwardly Roland cursed. Of course they wouldn't, as he knew only too well. 'But they will let you examine them' the solicitor continued, 'in the bank vault in the presence of myself and the bank manager.'

'When can that be? Immediately?'

'I'm afraid not. I'm tied up with an important client for the rest of this afternoon and the bank has already closed for the day.'

'This *is* a murder inquiry!'

'I'll arrange it for first thing tomorrow morning.' And with this Roland had to be content.

As he and Mansfield drove over to Woodford the next morning the sergeant pondered out loud.

'The fact that the bloodstained clothing was left in Felstone surely indicates that the murderer is a local person.'

'Not necessarily. He could have been driving through Felstone purely by chance with the bag in his car and when he saw all the identical bags out in the street awaiting collection it struck him as an ideal way to get rid of the highly incriminating evidence. The fact that he left it in the wrong street suggests that he wasn't *au fait* with the street-collection rota. He could even have been on his way to the ferry terminal.'

'You mean he may have left the country?'

'We don't know that he's British, do we? Let's hope these photos give us some help.'

The bank manager was waiting for them with his chief clerk and together with the solicitor they filed through the security checks and entered the strongroom. The photographs were similar to the ones that Roland and Mansfield had found in the woman's studio, records of her restoration work, but it was the subject matter that excited the two men. They were all of the Gerard Ter Broch painting that they had seen at Monkbeggars Hall. There were two photographs of the complete painting and several close-ups of parts of the work; the sitter's hands, the elaborate folds of her dress, the stylised ringlets. What interested Roland most was the fact that one of the photos of the whole picture showed the frame, whereas the other one appeared to be unframed. On the back of the latter was a scribbled date prefixed by a single word: 'copied'.

'Do you recognise them, Inspector? Have they any significance for you?' The bank manager was curious and hiding it under the cover of polite enquiry.

'I think I've seen the original. We'll take charge of them.'

'I'm afraid that's impossible, Inspector. Until probate is granted to the executor of Miss Cordingley – in this case Mr Poultney – this package must remain here.'

'And how long will that take?'

'Several weeks at the very least,' said the solicitor.

'This is vital evidence in a murder inquiry.'

'I'm sorry, but you know the rules, Inspector. I'm not allowed to divulge any information about my customers without their written instructions. Officially I can't even give you an address even though it be in the telephone directory. I am powerless to release anything until I have the probate document as proof. But – ' he paused condescendingly – 'it would be in order for you to photograph them.'

'Get Copping here at once,' Roland snapped to his assistant. 'I want copies as good as the originals, if not better.'

'They're alike and yet they're different. For my money, one is the original and the other a copy.'

Roland and Mansfield were studying the blown-up copies of the photographs back at the station.

'Well that one did have "copied" written on the back, didn't it?' said Mansfield cautiously. 'It looks as if while she was cleaning the picture she made a copy of it.'

'But why?'

'For insurance purposes? Perhaps Mrs Calder-Brown has hung the copy and stashed the other one away for safety.'

'She never mentioned it when we looked at it, and if it is only a copy, why the elaborate security arrangements? And I'm sure John Hargreaves was going there that day to see the picture she showed us.'

'Perhaps she doesn't know herself that the picture is only a copy.'

'What are you getting at?' Roland regarded his sergeant with narrowed eyes.

'Supposing that when the picture was sent for cleaning it was spirited away and a copy substituted on return.'

'You mean Lydia Cordingley stole it and passed off her copy as the original?'

'She could never have sold it on the open market but with her connections in the art world she could have disposed of it to one of those unscrupulous art collectors in the States or South America who aren't bothered with the ethics of the business.'

'Or she could have been used.' Roland was now on the same wavelength and racing ahead. 'Maybe she was asked to do a copy — told it *was* for insurance purposes — when she restored the original. This would probably have seemed perfectly reasonable to her but she took photographs and wrote on the back of the copy as an insurance to cover herself in case at some later date it got into the wrong hands.'

'But surely, no matter how good an artist she was, one could tell a copy from the original? Even if it looked very similar one would see that it wasn't old.'

'Well, it does look identical, doesn't it? Could you really tell them apart?' Roland looked closely at the two photographs. 'And I believe there are ways these days of faking age, using old canvases and discolouring the varnish. I believe I even read somewhere recently of a painting being baked so that the surface looked old and cracked.'

'But it wouldn't fool an expert.'

'It didn't have to, did it? It was hung where no one could get close to it and if it did look somewhat bright and pristine – as I remarked when we saw it – well, it had recently been cleaned, hadn't it?'

'But John Hargreaves would have known as soon as he saw it.' Mansfield dismissed his chief's reasoning, pulled his pipe out of his pocket and proceeded to stuff the bowl with tobacco. Aware of a strange tension emanating from the still figure looming over him, he looked up and caught Roland's eye. 'Well, what's the matter?'

'Do you realise what you've just said?' Roland demanded. 'You've just come up with a motive for his murder!'

'What?'

'If that picture is a fake it would have been discovered the minute he set eyes on it, so he had to be prevented from doing so.'

'Surely it would have been easier to remove the picture than to scrub out Hargreaves?'

'Would it? Remember the security arrangements? It would take time and expertise to set up a snatch, neither of which perhaps our murderer had.'

'But why kill Lydia Cordingley too?'

'Think, man. She knew that there was a copy at large – she painted it. If ever a connection was made between John Hargreaves' murder, Monkbeggars Hall and the painting, she would have become suspicious. She was killed to shut her mouth!'

'So who is the murderer? You're surely not suggesting that Mrs C-B set it up herself? She hasn't got the physique to swat the proverbial fly.'

'I'm sure she wouldn't have done the actual killing but she could have had an accomplice. She as much as admitted that running the Hall was sucking her dry. The proceeds from the sale of that painting would have provided a nice little windfall to tide her over for a good few years ... But no, I don't think she's the culprit.'

'What about her son?'

'Hugh Calder-Brown? Yes, indeed, what about him? He made the arrangements for the picture to be cleaned. It'll be interesting to hear what he has to say. I think we must definitely have a little probe into his background and suss out his financial position. For what could he have needed a large sum of money? The same applies to her other relations.'

'You think it would be one of the family.'

'It doesn't have to be, does it?' Roland sighed. 'It could just as well be someone who knew Lydia Cordingley − her mysterious lover, perhaps − who knew about the copy and persuaded her to connive at the substitution. It doesn't have to be someone with a connection to Monkbeggars Hall at all.'

'So how do we find out?'

'Firstly, we establish whether the painting hanging in Monkbeggars Hall is the original or a copy. After all, this has all been supposition so far. We could be talking off the top of our heads.'

'You're saying we've got to call in the Art and Antiques Squad?'

'Don't spoil my day, Patrick. This is a murder inquiry, we're not investigating a full-scale art fraud, it's a one-off thing. No, we've got to find out whether our theory is correct.'

'So we get an expert to examine the picture?'

'Not straight away. I want to be certain first that we're on the right track before I stick my neck out. I don't want anyone thinking I've fallen off my trolley and I don't want to alert the villain. No, first of all, you'll take copies of these photos to Mr Mickelsen at the Langdale Gallery; see what he makes of them. He should either be able to tell if there are grounds for our suspicions or dismiss it out of hand. Do this first thing in the morning. In the meantime − ' Roland gathered together the photos – 'there is someone to whom I'd like to show these.'

The phone rang as Ginny Dalton was stuffing rolls of paper and packets of crayons into her work bag. She called out to her son, who was in the next room.

'Answer it, please, Simon. I'm late already.'

She struggled to shut the bag and, after adjusting the contents, managed to zip it up. She sank back on her heels and pushed the hair out of her eyes. Simon stuck his head through the doorway.

'It's your 'tec.'

'Simon!' She looked at him in exasperation.

'Well, he is, isn't he? Shall I tell him you're busy?'

'No, I'll take it. If you still want a lift into Felstone you'd better hurry up and get ready.' The boy shrugged and reluctantly went towards the stairs. When she reckoned he was out of earshot, she picked up the receiver.

'Ginny? It's James. Are you busy this evening?'

'Yes, it's one of my evening-class nights. I take a still-life class at school.'

'Oh, damn, I'd forgotten. There's something I want to show you, something on which I want your opinion.'

For a few seconds her imagination ran riot, encompassing such ideas as engagement rings and desirable residences, then reality took over.

'Is it important? Something to do with me personally?'

'No, nothing for you to worry about. I just want some help with something that's come up to do with the case I'm working on.'

'I might have known. At least you don't bother to pretend that it's me you want to see.'

'Ginny, don't be like that! I tell you what. I'll meet you out of school, we'll go for a drink and then I'll spend the rest of the night with you.'

'Nothing doing. You don't pass up an opportunity, do you?'

'At least you can't say I don't try. But seriously, can I meet you afterwards? What time do you finish?'

'Nine thirty. I'll have my car so I'll meet you in town. Where were you thinking of going?'

'The Albany? I'll be waiting for you there, just after nine thirty.'

'I can't stay long, I have to pick up Simon.'

'Tell him you're going to be late. What are you fixing up for your students tonight?'

'I thought something along the lines of a jar of sticky buds with a gardening trug and tools in the foreground.'

'It sound fascinating. I wish I had the time to join your classes.'

'You know you'd be bored to tears. I must go, goodbye for now.'

She put down the receiver and gathered up her paraphernalia. Simon came thundering down the stairs, dragging his coat behind him.

The Albany was a popular hotel in the centre of Felstone. James Roland arrived early and managed to secure a table in the corner away from the hubbub near the bar. He bought a lager for himself and a vodka for Ginny and settled down to wait. It was nearly ten o'clock before she arrived. He watched, with a mixture of pride and annoyance, the admiring glances she received as she walked across the room and joined him.

'Hello, James. Sorry I'm late but I had some clearing up to do after the class finished.'

He held out the chair for her. 'I've got you a vodka and lime, is that all right?'

'Fine, just what I need.' She sunk onto the chair and raised her glass. 'Cheers.'

'How did it go?'

'Much the same as usual. Out of a class of twenty there are only two with any real artistic talent, but I suppose that makes it worthwhile. And they all enjoy themselves, or so I like to believe; but between you and me, I don't want to set eyes on another sticky bud for a very long time.'

He laughed. 'What about when you have a nude model?'

'Trust you to think of something like that. These are still-life classes. Life classes are very much a closed shop,

90

run by the art school for genuine art students only. What did you want to show me?'

'The light's not very good in here.' Roland squinted up at the nearby wall-light which was an elaborate candlelabra with bulbs shaped like candles and ornate fringed shades. 'But have a look at these and tell me what you think.'

He took out the photos of the Ter Borch painting and spread them on the tabletop. Ginny bent over them.

'What do you want to know?'

'Just tell me what they say to you.'

She gave him a quizzical look, then turned back to the photos.

'They are photos of a painting. It looks old. I would hazard a guess that it is seventeenth-century and probably Dutch.'

He looked at her admiringly. 'Go on.'

'What is this all about, James? Is it a painting that's been stolen or one you've had handed in?'

'Concentrate on these two, the full-length ones. Would you say they were identical?'

'The obvious difference is the fact that one is framed and the other isn't, but apart from that they certainly look identical at first glance.' She studied them closely and frowned. 'Having said that, I'm not so sure − I think the unframed one could be a copy of the other one. Who is it by?'

'Gerard Ter Borch. Does that mean anything to you?'

'Oh yes, it figures. This is his style and the period is about right. If it's genuine it would be very valuable.'

'Valuable enough to have caused two deaths, possibly.'

'James!'

'So you really think one could be a copy of the other?'

'Please don't quote me. I'm only saying that it could be, but it would be impossible even for an expert to tell just from a photograph.'

'I realise that, but before I stick my neck out I just want your off-the-cuff opinion as an informed outsider.'

'Well, for what it's worth, I think that one could be a copy.' She pointed to the photo of the unframed painting. 'But it could still be old − a contemporary copy.'

'What do you mean?'

'Artists of the calibre of Ter Borch always had students

working for them who copied their master's work and often even helped with the painting of the original canvases; they were given unimportant bits to paint while the master concentrated on the main subject. That second photo could be of a copy by one of his pupils; it would still be pretty valuable catalogued as attributable to his studio.'

'That's a complication I could do without. You really know your stuff, don't you? Before we leave the subject, can you tell me anything about picture restorers?'

'What do you want to know?'

'Professional picture cleaners and restorers — are they competent painters themselves, or doesn't it follow?'

Ginny set down her glass and looked at her companion shrewdly. 'James, has all this got anything to do with that woman who was killed at Helsby?'

'Lydia Cordingley? Yes, but I can't tell you any more. You didn't by any chance know her, did you?'

'Not personally, but I knew of her. As well as being a skilful picture restorer, she was also a gifted painter — she used to exhibit regularly. Does that answer your question?'

'Yes, bless you.' He picked up the photos and replaced them in the envelope. 'Can I get you another drink?'

'Not for me, thanks. I shall have to be going soon.'

'Now don't start your Cinderella act. Did I tell you that — '

She never found out what he was about to tell her, because they were interrupted at that moment.

'Hello, James!'

'Karen!' He looked up, startled to see his ex-wife standing beside their table. 'What are you doing here?'

'It's still a free country, darling, I've as much right to be in here as you; aren't you going to introduce us?'

He pulled himself together. 'This is Ginny Dalton. Ginny, this is Karen, my ex-wife.'

The two women acknowledged each other and took in each other's appearance. Ginny Dalton saw a dark-haired woman of about her own age who was attractive in a rather flamboyant way. Roland's ex-wife took in the unusual colouring of the woman seated at the table and recognised in her a quality that she couldn't put her finger on but it made a curl of jealousy snake through her.

92

'You're looking well, Karen, how's life treating you?' James Roland tried to sound unperturbed.

'I can't grumble, and what about you? You've been getting a lot of publicity just lately.'

'One of the penalties of my job, as you should know.'

'And has the big police machine actually managed to spare you for an hour?'

'Still the old Karen!'

'Still pulling them in, James?'

Ginny got to her feet. 'I'm sure you two have plenty to talk about. I must go and powder my nose.'

'An independent woman,' said Karen, watching her walk across the room. 'I heard that the bit you were currently sniffing after had more than open legs beneath her skirts.'

'You didn't used to be as vulgar as that,' said Roland, making an effort to curb his anger.

'I've changed. Or maybe you could say that I've learned to view life more realistically.'

'How is Don?'

'Don? Oh, that's all over. I guess you could say that we outgrew each other.'

Roland listened in dismay, startled by how the news unnerved him.

'We had some good times, didn't we, James?' she went on. 'Perhaps we should have tried harder to make it work.'

'You were the one who walked out on me. You couldn't stand my commitment to work and you committed adultery, not me. You're the one who didn't try to make it work.'

'You're still bitter, aren't you? Perhaps that should give me hope.'

Before he could ask what she meant, she touched him lightly on the arm and turned away.

'Go and find your friend and try not to blacken my character too much.'

Ginny Dalton stared at her reflection in the cloakroom mirror and tweaked a strand of hair back into place. So that was James' ex-wife? Karen worked as a library assistant, not in Felstone but over at the Woodford branch, and their social paths had never crossed. She didn't look like a librarian, Ginny thought and then took herself to task;

how ridiculous, trotting out that old cliché. Why did she still connect the word 'librarian' with an elderly, bespectacled spinster? Nowadays they were more likely to be young and trendy and well entrenched in the world of computers and high tec. Karen — Ginny realised that she didn't know her surname; had she remarried, had she reverted to her maiden name or did she still call herself Roland? James hadn't made it clear when he introduced them. Anyway, Karen was certainly a modern, sophisticated woman, but there was something faintly predatory about her. How did James really feel about his ex-wife? He was supposed to be somewhat bitter but was there still a residue of attraction lingering between them? And where did that leave her, Ginny?

She gathered up her handbag and made her way back to the lounge bar of the Albany. James was sitting staring into his empty glass and there was no sign of his ex-wife. Unbeknown to them both, Karen had gone back to her escort, who was sitting at a table behind a bank of plants that effectively hid him from view. He, however, between the fronds of an outsize fern, had been a witness to everything that had taken place on the other side of the room.

Hugh Calder-Brown was both diverted and piqued. Who would have thought that Karen's ex-husband was none other than that damn detective who had caught him on the raw the other week over at the Hall? And now he seemed to be interested in Ginny Dalton. She was an extremely attractive woman, as he knew to his cost. He had tried to make it with her on a couple of occasions but it had been too soon after her husband's death and nothing had come of it. It looked as if she was now back in circulation. He had been meaning to get in touch with her again ever since that chance meeting at the Choral Society concert; well, perhaps now he would. He had an urge to get even with that dark, undeniably handsome policeman who had made him look such a fool, and what better way than to carry on with both his ex-wife and his current girlfriend? Hugh Calder-Brown smiled to himself and refused to tell the woman sitting opposite him what he found so amusing.

*

Jeremy Mickelsen looked over the top of his glasses at Patrick Mansfield.

'Yes, this is the painting we were hoping to borrow for the exhibition. A fine example of his early work, far more sophisticated than most of the work he produced at that age. He was only a very young man when he visited this country. What's the problem?'

'What about this one?' Mansfield produced the photo of the unframed painting and laid it on the desk beside the other one.

Mickelsen examined it, looked up at Mansfield with a puzzled expression on his face and then perused the photo more closely.

'Was there ever a copy painted for insurance purposes?'

'You think this one is a fake?'

'A fake is a painting that is deliberately passed off as someone else's work. I'm saying that this one looks like a good copy but I should have to examine the actual painting to be sure.'

'We think it may be hanging on the wall at Monkbeggars Hall.'

'Really?' Jeremy Mickelsen looked dubious. Then, as the full impact of what he had just heard penetrated his understanding, he said sharply, 'Is this connected with John's death? You're not trying to imply that he was mixed up in an art fraud, are you?'

'I think there may have been some hanky-panky going on but I'm pretty certain Hargreaves was completely innocent of it. He was just unfortunate enough to get involved.'

'I'm not sure that I understand.' The gallery director looked bemused. 'But how can I help?'

'We think he may have been killed to prevent him identifying the painting at Monkbeggars Hall as a fake. Now this is strictly confidential. I would be roasted if my superiors knew that I'd told you this, but I need your cooperation. Is there an easy way of proving whether the picture there is genuine or a copy? What about signatures?'

'Ah, that's a very grey area. If only our old masters had always signed their work, how much easier it would make things for myself and all my colleagues in the art world, though, of course, signatures can be forged. Gerard Ter Borch was somewhat lax in this respect; sometimes he signed his work, sometimes not, and some paintings contain his monogram. And of course the situation is complicated by the fact that he often did more than one version of a painting. A good example is "The Parental Admonition", one of his best-known works; there are several versions of that in existence, one of them in the Rijksmuseum, which you may have seen.'

'Yes,' said Mansfield, attempting to look knowledgeable while at the same time frantically trying to call the picture to mind.

'We know, of course, that this painting wasn't signed,' Mickelsen continued, indicating the photograph, 'but we have all the provenance we need.'

'How do you mean?'

'The painting has been privately owned by the same family since it was executed in the seventeenth century at their commission. There are family papers and records referring to it. Let me just examine the one we think may be a copy more closely.'

He took a magnifying glass out of the desk drawer and pored over the second photograph, turning it this way and that.

'Well, this is most interesting — there *is* a signature on this one.'

Mansfield craned forward to look. 'Where?'

'It's very easily overlooked. See the way the dog is crouched against her skirt? In the curl of its tail there is a little circle containing two initials. It certainly isn't Ter Borch's signature, it looks like an L and a C.' He handed the magnifying glass to Mansfield, who pounced on it eagerly. 'Does it mean anything to you?'

'Yes, this is most significant. Fancy us not noticing it.' Mansfield straightened up.

'I know what I'm looking for.'

'Well, you've been most helpful, Mr Mickelsen. I take it that if we find that the picture at Monkbeggars Hall contains this signature, we'll know that it is not the original. But are you prepared to prove or disprove authenticity in a court of law if necessary?'

'Anything that'll help to bring John's murderer to justice.'

Mansfield drove back along the A12, pleased with the results of his second visit to the Langdale Gallery. This one had not been a waste of time; it had produced some evidence that could be crucial to their inquiry. Lydia Cordingley had certainly been an astute woman and covered her back. When she copied the painting, whether knowingly or unknowingly for fraudulent purposes, she had taken care that she could never be accused of faking an old master.

It would be interesting to see which painting was hanging on the wall at Monkbeggars Hall, the original or the copy. Had they built up a good case for the motives behind the two murders or was it just a house of cards that could crumple at a touch?

Chapter Six

The hawthorn was out early that year. The hedgerow was thick with creamy-white bracts that intoxicated bees and flies alike and the sheep's parsley frothed alongside the verges like coarse lace. 'Never cast a clout 'til May is out,' Mansfield quoted to himself as he relaxed in the passenger seat while Roland manoeuvred the car down narrow country lanes towards Barndon. It had never been satisfactorily explained whether the old saw referred to the month or the blossom. Well, it was still April, the blossom was out and it was hot enough for June. He had removed his jacket at the start of the journey and now sat in his shirtsleeves feeling the warmth of the sun pleasantly burnishing his forearms.

As they reached the outskirts of Barndon the volume of traffic converging on the village increased dramatically. A very large poster fluttering between two oak trees on the green caught Roland's attention.

'Hell and damnation! You know what we've done, don't you? We've arrived in the middle of one of the historical re-creations! He pulled the car over into a lay-by and switched off the engine. 'We should have checked. Damn! I hadn't realised that they were starting so soon. What to do now, Patrick my friend?'

'Is it such a disaster? It would be a good chance to have a snoop around undetected, mingle with the crowds.'

Roland looked speculatively at his sergeant. 'You come up with some good ideas sometimes, don't you? The only trouble is, the public aren't allowed near the part of the house where the picture is displayed.'

'We can hang around until the crowds have dispersed and then make our presence known.'

'Yes, you have a point. And it'll give us an opportunity to check out the other members of the family, presuming they take part in the revels and we can sort out who is who if they're all dressed up in Tudor costume. Right, we proceed as ordinary tourists, which will mean putting our hands into our pockets Pat; no good flashing our ID cards if we wish to remain anonymous.'

As Roland swung the car back onto the road he thought of something else. Ginny: would she be here today with her schoolkids? But no, she had said they were taking part next month, meaning some time during May. He wouldn't have to deal with that added complication.

The gates to Monkbeggars Hall were wide open and he joined the stream of cars turning into the grounds. A youth, very much of the twentieth century in looks and gear, waved them on. When Roland rounded the bend in the driveway he saw that visitors' cars were being parked on either side of the drive beneath the trees, forming a neat herringbone pattern. He slotted his car in between a cloven-trunked oak and a Land-Rover and the two policemen got out. On foot the drive seemed much longer than it had when they had travelled it by car. Ahead, in the distance, a high barricade had been erected, effectively concealing the Hall from view.

As they drew nearer, Roland and Mansfield saw that this barricade was meant to represent castle battlements; in the centre was a gateway at which visitors paid their entrance fee and entered a tunnel. A well-built, red-complexioned, middle-aged man dressed in a Barbour jacket and corduroy breeches was overseeing this operation. Roland indicated that they should hold back so that they were the last of the present influx to gain admission. The man had a loud, affected voice of the kind that Mansfield thought of as haw-haw and he would have looked far more at home at a point-to-point, his well-upholstered rear underpinned by a shooting-stick, than ushering his visitors through the archway.

'A lovely day you've got for it,' said Roland blandly, handing over his entrance fee. Beside him, Mansfield winced as he also parted with a five-pound note.

'Yes, we're usually lucky with the weather. Have you been before?'

'No, this is our first visit. We saw the posters and decided to have a look but we're not sure what to expect.'

The man gave a barking laugh. 'I'll tell you what to expect; when you walk through that tunnel you'll think you've entered a time warp and been transported back to Tudor England.'

'It must take a lot of organising.'

'It certainly does. We started planning and rehearsing several months ago.'

'Where do the participants come from?'

'All over the country. We advertise in the national press around Christmastime and stop the recruiting when we've received several hundred replies.'

'As many as that?'

'Oh yes. We've been doing this for several years now and have a reputation as being among the foremost promoters of this sort of entertainment in the whole of the country. People fall over themselves to take part.'

'What type of people are interested?'

'People from all walks of life, from retired professionals to mothers with babes in arms. I suppose the only thing they have in common is a yearning after Thespis; many of them are out-of-work actors and I think they all welcome the chance to tread the boards, so to speak, and live in a fantasy world for a day. The only stricture we impose is that they dress in authentic costume and keep in character, which means taking on the mantle of a Tudor character, be it gentry or peasant, and speaking in the language of the time.'

'I presume you are the owner of the Hall?' asked Roland innocently.

'No, that's my mother-in-law. I farm the land around here and breed the endangered species of domestic animal you'll see in the course of your visit.'

'You don't actually take part yourself?' Roland indicated his modern dress.

'Not me,' he boomed. 'Somebody has to organise things. We can't all live with our heads in the clouds. But you'll find my wife and the rest of the family gallivanting around. What's the time?' He checked his watch. 'Just after midday – you'll be in time to see the dinner ceremony. If you go first to the kitchens you'll be able to watch the meal being prepared and carried through to the lords and ladies in the Great Hall; that's a good starting point. I hope you enjoy it.'

He waved them on and turned to the new group of people approaching the barrier.

Roland and Mansfield walked through the hardboard tunnel and emerged into brilliant sunshine. Facing them was Monkbeggars Hall transformed into a scene of frenzied activity. Tudor gallants swaggered across the courtyard with their ladies and minions in attendance; a group armed with bows practised at the nearby butts; and to the left of them was what looked like a gipsy encampment with men and women dressed in colourful rags juggling and playing primitive pipes while nearby a naked toddler crawled in the dust and an old crone poked at something cooking in a pot slung over a smoking fire.

'Extraordinary! Let's have a look round.'

The two men strolled towards the house, taking in the spectacle. Near the dovecote a man pinned in the stocks was being pelted with rubbish by a group of urchins. Close by, a woman in voluminous skirts squatted on the grass selling bunches of herbs from her hand-woven basket. An elderly cleric, majestic in black bombazine and tight-fitting cap, lectured to a group of Elizabethan schoolboys trailing in his wake. And everywhere, visitors and participants mingled and the discordant shrieks of peacocks rose above the general hubbub.

They located the kitchen and stepped across the threshold. The heat met them like a solid wall. An enormous fire burned in the open fireplace, which was hung with spits and cooking pots and attended by several wenches in rough, home-spun gowns. Gathered round the long, rough-hewn table that took pride of place in the centre of the room were several more women chopping, slicing and pounding a bizarre mixture of ingredients. Presiding over them was an elderly dame, nearly as broad as she was long, with apple cheeks and wispy grey hair escaping from her coif. She made Roland think of Mistress Quickly. As they watched, fascinated, she screeched at a hovering pageboy to tell the steward that the repast was

101

ready and cuffed him about the ears when he tripped on the uneven flagstones while scurrying to do her bidding.

A collection of platters containing prepared food was set out on the wide shelf that ran the length of the right wall. Mansfield looked at it suspiciously and peered at the menu that was propped up against one of the dishes.

'''Pottage of Cabige, Alos of Mutton, Chicken Cullis, Tarte of Apple and Oranges, Almond Pudding, Manchet of Bread'',' he read out loud. 'Are they really going to eat this?' he whispered to Roland, viewing the congealing food with horror. Most of the food was decorated with fresh flowers; marigold heads, rose petals and sweet william. Mansfield poked an experimental finger into the dish nearest to him.

'Master, remove thy finger from the victuals!' squawked the dame, brandishing a wicked-looking knife at him. Mansfield retreated with alacrity.

The knife caught Roland's attention; there was a murderous assortment lying around among the kitchen utensils. Many of them looked genuinely old, the dull metal blades honed to thinness, some of them two-edged like daggers. Had Lydia Cordingley been killed by a knife from the kichens of Monkbeggars Hall? Would he be justified in pulling them all in for forensic testing? It might still be possible for the experts to find traces of blood belonging to the victim even if it had been cleaned and reused since.

His musings were interrupted by a fresh surge of activity. A band of young pageboys descended on the kitchen and, under the supervision of an important-looking man in black and mulberry, whom Roland took to be the steward, were loaded up and marched off, each boy bearing a single platter held aloft to cries of 'Make passage!' Mansfield and Roland, with the other spectators, followed in their rear.

A fanfare rang out as the cortege crossed the threshold into the Great Hall. At the far end, seated round the table and resplendent in jewel-like velvets and satins, sat the Personnes of Qualitie, as they were quaintly called in the information brochure. The dishes were paraded before these people, who indicated which ones they wished to sample. The two men edged forward through the crowd and positioned themselves so that they could see but, they hoped, not be noticed by the participants in the meal. From the gallery above came the strains of music as a group of musicians played lute, recorder and shawm.

Celia Calder-Brown was seated at the head of the table. She wore a rich, tawny-brown brocade gown with a starched ruff at her neck, and her white curls were hidden beneath a matching cap and veil. Roland wondered idly what sort of footgear she was sporting beneath her hooped skirts. She certainly looked the part, which was more than could be said for the woman seated at her side. This second woman looked flushed and uncomfortable in her florid pink dress, fidgeting with the neckline and dabbing at her headdress as if embarrassed by the masquerade. The man seated on the other side of Celia Calder-Brown looked thoroughly at home in his black velvet doublet and a cap tilted at a rakish angle. As he looked up from his dish and spoke across the table to the companion sitting opposite him, Roland saw that it was Hugh Calder-Brown, looking for all the world like an Elizabethan buccanner.

He must have healed the rift with his mother, Roland thought, and how fortunate that he should be here too. He was top of Roland's list of people to be interviewed in connection with his new theory; he would be able to kill two birds with one stone later in the day.

'They haven't got forks,' Mansfield rumbled in his ear, watching as the diners speared their meat with daggers or scooped up the food with odd-shaped spoons.

'They weren't in general use in those days.'

'This reminds me of watching the chimpanzees' tea party at the zoo. Let's get out of here and see what else is going on.'

As they walked along the corridor to the servants' quarters they saw the notice pinned on the door leading to the private part of the house: PASS NOT WITHIN.

'I wonder what would happen if we did?'

'We'd probably be clapped in the stocks.'

They walked through the house to the dairy, where women were making butter and cheese, and climbed the rickety stairs to the still room above. Pots of plants and baskets of fruit and vegetables littered the floor and tables at which women, assisted by children of varying ages, mixed potions and pounded herbs and berries. Bunches of green leaves hung from the whitewashed walls and Mansfield pointed to these.

'What are they?' he asked of no one in particular.

'Why, master,' one of the women exclaimed, looking up from her task, 'they be elder leaves to keep off the flies. Hast thee no elder tree at they gate to ward off the flies and evil spirits?'

'What's wrong with a good old can of aerosol fly spray?' Mansfield mumbled in embarrassment.

'Patrick, you're not entering into the spirit of the thing,' Roland scolded. 'Tell me, mistress, what do you?'

'These be worm pills,' said the woman, indicating the pea-sized balls in the dish at her side, 'and I be making an ointment for the itch here with sorrel and goose grease.' She pounded with a pestle the concoction in the mortar in front of her. 'Do thee have the itch, Master?'

'I'll say he does,' said Mansfield sotto voce.

Roland extricated them from the still room. Outside they explored the outbuildings, where numerous activities were taking place.

In the forge, where the fire was boosted by a gigantic pair of bellows, they watched a horse being shod, and in a cart lodge nearby saw candles being made by a group of youngsters under the tutelage of another worthy dame, who managed her pupils, the tubs of molten wax and the rows of dripping tapers with the practised hand of one born to the task. Nearby, a barn was being erected by a team of labourers, who, stripped to their breeches, manhandled the rougly hewn beams of wood into position amid much swearing and bantering in what they supposed was Elizabethan colloquial English.

A young, poorly dressed girl stood in the doorway of a hovel wringing her hands and sobbing. As they approached, she cried out to them:

'Enter not, masters! My sister hath returned but a sennight past from London city and is stricken with the fever. We fear she hath the contagion!'

As Mansfield said afterwards, so strong was the power of suggestion that nothing would have made him cross that

threshold. Her sentences had spelled one word to him —
plague — and some tribal memory had stirred within him,
sending a trickle of fear up his spine and an overpowering
impulse to flee the scene.

A flock of chestnut-coloured pigs rounded the corner. The
girl flapped her apron and shooed them away as they tried to
push past her into the cottage. Rebuffed, they shot sideways
and thundered past the two men, who stepped hastily aside.

'Whatever sort of pigs are they?' Mansfield asked, looking
after them.

'God knows, but they're rather attractive, aren't they, the
exact colour of ripe conkers. What else is there to see?'

A curl of smoke rising above a screen of trees that barred
their way caught their attention. They followed a narrow path
that wound between mature trunks and scrubby saplings and
found themselves in a clearing, in the centre of which an
open fire burned in a shallow pit. Beside this a young woman
crouched on the ground, making coil pots out of sausages
of clay. Nearby was a kiln, shaped like an old-fashioned pie
funnel and built of clay blocks. A man with his back to them
was chopping wood to furnish the fires, a little way distant.

Roland leaned over and picked up one of the pots to
examine it closer, and the girl looked up. With a sense of
shock he recognised Lucy Hanson, the rebel granddaughter
of Celia Calder-Brown. She was dressed in a ragged gown with
a sacking apron tied round her middle and her black spiky
hair was drawn back in a dirty knotted kerchief. The biggest
surprise in her appearance was her face. Devoid of make-up,
her former dead-white countenance was now flushed and
rosy. A little voice at the back of Roland's mind said that
this was all wrong; surely it was the Elizabethan ladies, under
the examples of Good Queen Bess, who had used to whiten
their complexions with lead and poison themselves into the
bargain. She recognised them at the same instant.

'What are *you* doing here?' she snapped.

'Why, if it isn't Miss Lucy Hanson,' said Roland suavely.
'I would have expected to find you in the Great Hall, not
slumming it out here with the hoi polloi.'

'I'm experiencing at first hand the exploitation of the
masses. It was happening four hundred years ago and it's

still going on today. The privileged few grinding the face of the poor underfoot.'

'You appear to be an intelligent young woman, why are you repeating clichés lifted from some second-rate left-wing pamphlet?'

She flushed a deeper red. 'I thought that was the language you lot understood. Don't you police think and act in stereotype with your token gay and token black to appease the commonalty?'

'Sergeant, do we have a token gay on the force?'

'I wouldn't like to say,' said Mansfield ponderously. 'Even in these days of enlightenment not everyone has come out of the closet. But we certainly don't have a nigger.'

'Very remiss of us. We can do you a red-haired Celt, but not a black.'

'You may make fun of me, but you'll laugh on the other side of your face when − '

'I know,' said Roland wearily. 'When the revolution comes we'll be the first to the wall.'

'I was going to say that when those in power are corrupt someone has to take the initiative to correct injustice.'

'Now you're really frightening me. Anyone who takes the law into their own hands is either a fool or a knave and I don't think that you're either, Miss Hanson. You appear to be a privileged young woman who is rebelling against her background. That is a common enough occurrence and could almost be applauded; it is good to try and help those less fortunate, but don't delude yourself. You come from an affluent, middle-class family; you can never appreciate what it is like to really be an underdog, one of life's less fortunates.'

'Don't preach to me! You still haven't told me why you're here. Have you come to pester my grandmother again?'

'Now why ever should you think that? Your grandmother whetted our curiosity with her description of these historical re-creations, so we've come to see for ourselves.'

'And has it given you − '

'Wench!' A voice broke in on their conversation. 'What strange phrases drop from thy lips! In what foreign tongue speak thee?'

It was the woodcutter, who had laid aside his axe and come

106

over to see what was going on. He was a swarthily bearded man dressed in a sleeveless jerkin and ragged breeches that revealed tanned, sinewy muscles and bare feet. So much did he look the part that at first Roland didn't know him, then recognition flooded in. It was Richard Coates. Well, it figured; from what he had seen so far, wherever Lucy Hanson was to be found, the lecturer was not far behind. It was he, of course, who fed the girl with radical ideas, but Roland would have expected a more subtle approach from one of Coates' obvious intellectual standing. Perhaps Lucy was not such a good pupil ...

'Master, these men are from ... are from the Watch! They come to spy upon the Great House!'

The man shot them a shrewd look out of narrowed eyes. Roland was sure that he was recognised and filed away for future reference, but Richard Coates chose to disregard her information.

'Guard your tongue! They are but visitors to our poor domain. Show them thy wares.'

The girl hesitated, then plunged to her knees and embraced her crude pottery with outstretched arms. 'Masters, please buy my humble wares! Take pity on a poor girl!'

It was a parody of grovelling. Her voice whined but her eyes flashed defiance.

'Mistress, I have no groats. Good-day to thee.'

As they walked away, the two men heard Lucy Hanson's voice raised in protest and the deeper tones of Richard Coates overlaying her arguments, and then the sound of chopping as he swung his axe among the timber.

'What do you actually do, Alan?'

Annette Shaw, Netty to her friends, leaned on the table with both elbows and cradled her coffee cup in her hands.

'I'm a Civil Service employee,' prevaricated Alan Scopes, executive officer of HM Customs and Excise.

'That sounds very dull and conventional. Don't you get bored?'

They were seated in the Merlin, a restaurant in the centre of Felstone that specialised in vegetarian food and a wide selection of teas and coffees. It was frequented by the

107

young professional classes and was not a place Netty was in the habit of patronising. Her friend Lucy would be very scathing if she could see her here, making remarks about the bourgeoisie and the propping-up of an outdated class system. Lucy was rather a fraud really; she came from just such an environment herself. She would probably disapprove, too, of the young man sitting opposite her, and of his method of cultivating Netty's friendship. She had been picked up. There were no two ways about it; she who supported the women's movement and should have scorned his approach had instead actively encouraged it. He lived near the house where she lodged and she had noticed him several times in the street where his appraising glance had left no doubt of his interest in her. She had been flattered, had even at one point thought he was following her, and when he dashed out of a shop one evening, colliding with her and knocking her books out of her arms, she had been sure that it was deliberate. But she had allowed him to strike up an acquaintance and this was their third date. He attracted her and, for all he might be a prosaic civil servant, there was something bright-eyed and bushy-tailed about him.

'There are various departments, we get moved around,' he said vaguely.

'You're not a local person, are you, Alan? Where is your home town?'

'I was born and brought up in London, in Finchley, and I worked in the City for a couple of years before moving up here.'

'I can't imagine anyone wanting to live and work here if they had the chance to stay in London.'

'I thought you missed your animals and were keen to move to a place where you can keep a dog? It would be even more difficult in London.'

'Yes, I suppose that's true. I'm not being consistent, am I? It's just that Felstone is such a parochial place; it may have grown enormously in recent years with the docks expansion and new industries springing up like mushrooms, but at heart it's still a sleepy little town that only pays lip service to the idea of being a holiday resort.'

'It's not such a bad place, and the Poly has a very good

reputation; you're enjoying the course, aren't you?'

'Yes, it is interesting. I should have gone to university, you know, but I fluffed my grades and I was lucky to get taken on here. Still, there are other things in life besides my degree course.'

'Such as? You're a very intriguing woman, you know, Netty. You hint at all sorts of mysterious excitements but you don't let on. Are you living a second, secret life of which I know nothing? Do stop tantalising me.'

She flashed him a glance from beneath the lowered fringes of her long eyelashes and he felt his pulse quicken. She was a very attractive young woman; was she also involved in some criminal activity? He wanted to get to know her better, to get involved in her life, but it was his heart speaking, not his head. What had started out as a cold-blooded surveillance was now developing into an *affaire de coeur*, which was strictly against his professional ethics. Watch your step, Alan, he told himself, but hang in there.

For her part, Netty Shaw wondered just how far she dare go. She had already, during their short acquaintance, been too indiscreet. She was sworn to secrecy but thought they could do with people of Alan's obvious calibre. She decided to drop a few more hints and try to gauge how he would be likely to react if he knew about the plot. If she thought that he agreed with it in principle perhaps he could be recruited to the team. As her protégé he would boost her standing with Lucy, who was inclined to lord it over her because of this thing she had going with Rick Coates. Rick was attractive, resourceful and a brilliant leader but she herself wouldn't want to be involved with him sexually. There was something selfish and unsympathetic about him; she sometimes felt he was into power politics for the kicks rather than for any spirit of altruism.

'Tell me Alan, what do you think about the unfairness of the distribution of wealth; the dreadful gulf between rich and poor?'

'Come again?' He stared at her in surprise. Whatever he had expected to hear, it certainly hadn't been this.

'Don't you agree that a vast majority of the world's wealth and resources is invested in just a very small proportion of

109

the population? On a different scale, wouldn't you say that the wealthy countries have grown rich and powerful at the expense of the Third World?'

'Well, I think that's an exaggeration and an over-simplification, but I know what you mean. Still, it's a situation that had existed since time began; there will always be sections of the community that are more prosperous than others – everyone is equal but some are more equal than others, and all that. The ideal world where everyone has their fair share of what's up for grabs is very commendable but equality in that sense is an unworkable hypothesis.'

'It doesn't have to be.' She leaned towards him and her face was lit with enthusiasm. 'Robin Hood had the right idea.'

He listened in growing excitement and dismay. Was she really hinting at some large-scale racket to embezzle under the guise of philanthropy, and was this what the suspicious gatherings at the house where she lived were all about? Or was he completely mis-reading her?

'Netty, you're talking in riddles.'

'Supposing that I tell you that some people intend doing something about it? We're not going to sit back and wait for the politicians to come to their senses, we're taking things into our own hands.'

'What are you going to do – rob a bank and distribute the money among the needy of the district?' He deliberately kept his tone light and bantering.

'Not a bank, no. Currency is not the only valuable com-modity and you've got to think on a wider scale than local issues.'

'Netty, I think someone's having you on. It's a nice idea and you're a nice girl to have such altruistic sentiments – '

'Don't humour me, Alan!' she snapped. 'I'm not off my trolley. I had hoped that you would be more sympathetic and might be interested in joining us, but you're not taking me seriously, so ...'

'I'm not sure what you're talking about. These hints and innuendos don't add up to much. If you want my support in whatever you're involved in, you'll have to be a little more explicit.'

She regarded him speculatively. No, she had made a

mistake, he was far too conventional and middle-class to be considered as a recruit. It was a pity, he was really quite dishy and she had been almost criminally indiscreet; but she couldn't resist a little teasing.

'Forget it. You're not the right material. I should have realised you weren't suitable.'

'Suitable for what? You mean you're holding out on me now?'

'Don't worry, you'll know all about it before long – just watch the press.'

'And what am I to look out for?'

'That would be telling, but on a certain night, very soon now, something is going to happen that will make the man in the street sit up and take notice.'

'You're winding me up, aren't you? Is this some rag-week hoax? Are you planning, on the night of the full moon, to kidnap all the local dignitaries and hold them to ransom?'

'This has nothing to do with the college and it's no joke; it's deadly serious. But I can tell you one thing, it most certainly won't be when the moon is full.'

'No?'

'Remember the Runners and "Watch the Wall, my darling, while the Gentlemen go by!"'

'Runners?' He hoped he hadn't spoken too sharply but he recognised her quote as coming from Kipling's Smuggler's Song.

'Isn't that what the duty men, the Customs and Excise, used to be called in the olden days? They knew that the action always took place on a night when there was no moon and the tide was high. The same formula holds good today. Remember that, Alan.'

'I will, I most certainly will.'

Roland and Mansfield walked back towards the house. The lords and ladies from the Great Hall were now relaxing on the lawn under the canopy of the cedar tree. Some were dancing sedately to the accompaniment of the music consort; a few of the men sprawled on the grass playing chess while their ladies stitched at their tambour frames; and the more elderly, Celia Calder-Brown among them, sat on high-backed chairs and watched the activities around them.

'Do you think that woman in the pink dress is the daughter, Lucy's mother?' Mansfield indicated the woman seated beside their hostess.

'Could be. She looks as if she's doing it under duress and not for fun like the rest of them. I can't see the son anywhere.'

'Perhaps he's tumbling the wenches in the haystacks.'

Celia Calder-Brown fanned herself and hid a yawn behind her dainty, feathered fan as her gaze ran idly over her audience. She recognised the policemen and her eyebrows shot up in surprise, then she acknowledged them with a regal nod. Roland, across the stretch of manicured lawn, bowed in return.

'You're really into all this, aren't you?' Mansfield grumbled. 'Personally I can't see much point in it.'

'The trouble with you, Patrick, is, you've got no soul and no imagination. I'm sure Jean would enjoy herself here. Did I tell you that Ginny is going to take part with some of her pupils at a later date?'

'Is she now? Perhaps that accounts for the way you're lapping it up. I think you fancy yourself dolled up in doublet and hose and tripping a measure with Mistress Dalton.'

'I can think of worse ways of passing a day, but opportunity would be a fine thing. May I remind you we're here on duty, not for pleasure.'

At that moment there were sounds of a commotion coming from round the side of the house; raised voices and thudding feet. A man burst round the corner waving his arms.

'Fire! There's a fire in the servants' quarters!'

In that instant they heard and smelled it; the crackle of flames and the acrid stench of smoke. There was a murmur and movements of panic among the visitors thronging the area, and the costumed group on the lawn seemed to freeze into a tableau. Celia Calder-Brown stared white-faced at the house. Roland ran across to her.

'Where's the nearest phone?'

'In the entrance hall beside the press.'

112

He turned to the pink-robed woman beside her. 'Call the fire brigade and tell them it's urgent!'

'They won't be able to get through the barricade.'

'It must be dismantled at once.'

'My husband is down there on the gate – I'll see that it is organised.'

'Mansfield, control the crowd here and stop them coming near the scene. Where actually is the fire?' He turned to the man who had raised the alarm. 'Tell me as we go.'

'I think it started in the little room behind the bakery.' The man was panting as he tried to keep up with Roland. 'There was a whole group in there earlier making baskets and plaiting rushes. The whole lot has gone up and the fire has spread to the panelling in the corridor near the back entrance.'

'Is everyone out of that part of the building?'

'As far as we know. Most people were having their lunch break.'

They pushed their way through the people gathered round the archway leading to the domestic quarters.

'Here! Who do you think you are?'

'A police officer,' Roland snarled, shouldering the man aside. 'If you want to make yourself useful, get all the able-bodied men and women together and collect all the pots and pans you can lay your hands on from the kitchen. We'll make a chain from the moat – it may help to contain the fire until the brigade arrive.'

It was not as bad as he had feared. The room beside the bakery was gutted and there was a stench of burning toast that told its own tale of the baker's wares being devoured by the flames, but the fire had not progressed towards the main building. Instead, it had raged the other way, fanned by the draughts, down the corridor to the stone gatehouse that spanned the moat. With nothing to feed on the fire was already dying down and Roland was sure that the worst was over, but the next quarter of an hour was hectic as he joined the human chain dipping and dousing with its makeshift buckets.

The fire brigade and Celia Calder-Brown arrived on the scene together. By then the fire was well under control and Roland thankfully relinquished his task and went over to her.

'I don't know what you're doing here today, officer, but thank goodness for your presence. How did it start?'

'I should imagine a careless match or cigarette stub among the rushes and canes. It would have gone up like a tinder box.' He guided her to one side to avoid the hose pipes and she clutched his arm.

'That panelling that's smouldering — it backs on to the old butler's pantry where the security control box is housed. I fear the alarm may have been activated.'

'Well, if it has, you'll have a visit from a few more coppers.'

'Can't you ring the police station and explain what has happened?'

'I'm sorry ma'am, but if that alarm has gone off there's nothing I can do to prevent a security check. Wheel's will have been set in motion and must run their course.'

'Mother! What on earth is happening?' Hugh Calder-Brown pushed his way through the firemen. He looked alarmed and out of breath. The black velvet cap was missing and his fair hair stood on end as if he had been running.

'There's been a fire behind the old bakery. The firemen have got it under control now and I don't think there's been too much damage.'

'I was organising the archery contest down in the park when this damn great fire engine came roaring up the drive; then I noticed that Nigel and a team of men were dismantling the barricade to let it through. Marian was running round in circles screeching like a stuck pig and I had a job getting any sense out of her — she said something about a fire so I rushed back ...'

'Are people panicking?'

'No. I don't think many of the crowd realised anything was wrong till the fire engine arrived, and there's some chappie out there keeping control — must be a policeman.'

'Go and help him, dear. Look, they've put out the fire but we must keep this part of the house out of bounds for the rest of the day. Can you make some announcement to that effect?'

'Leave it to me. I'll make sure this area is sealed off from the public. How long ago did it start?'

'We're not sure, but thanks to the quick thinking of this gentleman here who organised a chain of buckets from the moat, it was prevented from spreading.'

She looked round to thank Roland, but he had quietly effaced himself. She shrugged and turned back to her son, who seemed to notice for the first time the team of dishevelled, smoke-blackened men and women who were flopped down on the banks of the moat, recovering from their recent exertions.

'Well done, everyone!' he said in a hearty voice. 'I suggest you go back to your quarters and clean up, and I'll lay on some refreshment for you. I expect you're all thirsty.'

Roland glanced ruefully down at his damp, soot-stained shirt and trousers as he slipped back to join his sergeant. Hugh Calder-Brown would organise things back there with his mother and the firemen. Roland had his reasons for avoiding an encounter with him for the moment.

A police car was parked in the courtyard, its blue light flashing. As he approached, another one sped up the drive and crossed the moat bridge, followed by a Range-Rover. He hurried towards them and reached the group of policemen tumbling out of the cars at the same time as Mansfield.

'The security alarm's been activated by a fire. It's a false alarm.'

'Who are you?'

The two detectives hurridly produced their ID cards.

'DI Roland and DS Mansfield of Felstone CID.'

'What are you doing here? What the hell is going on?' The speaker, a burly, uniformed sergeant, eyed them suspiciously.

'We're here on unofficial business. A fire was accidentally started in the servants' quarters; it burned through the panelling near the control box and must have set off the alarm. You took your time getting here!'

'Couldn't get through, could we!' The man glared back at the figure hurrying towards them from the Range-Rover. It was Nigel Hanson.

115

'What's the matter? What are the police doing here? The fire ...?'

'I was just explaining that the fire accidentally triggered off the security alarm,' said Roland soothingly, flashing his ID card at Hanson, who looked even more alarmed as he recognised him from earlier. 'The fire has been put out now and no damage has been done to the main part of the building, but these officers must check that the picture is still in position and unharmed.'

'Are you in charge around here?' the uniformed sergeant demanded of Nigel Hanson.

'You could say — I'm the owner's son-in-law. You'd better come in. I really don't know what to think. This little episode is going to spoil our image. Nothing like this has ever happened before.'

He led the way through the main hall towards the private quarters of the house. Roland and Mansfield discreetly tagged on behind.

'There you are — all present and correct!' Nigel Hanson flung open the door and stood back to let the policemen into the room.

The picture still hung on the wall opposite, as it had when Roland and Mansfield had seen it before. The former was thinking how opportune this new development was; they now had a valid reason for examining the painting without arousing the family's suspicions.

'Nigel — are you there?'

'My wife,' said Hanson in explanation. 'I expect she's worried about your presence.'

'You go and tell her what's happened and we'll just check in here,' said the sergeant, and Hanson needed no second bidding. He hurried down the stairs and missed the ensuing conversation between the sergeants and the two detectives.

'I still don't know what you're doing here, sir. This is out of order.'

'We have reason to be interested in this picture. Do you mind opening that casement so that we can see it better?'

The sergeant shrugged and carried out the instruction, and the two detectives approached the painting. With a sense of excitement and relief that his hunch was correct, Roland leaned forward and made out the circled initial hidden within the painted dog's tail.

'Very cleverly done,' he said to his companion. 'Nobody would notice it unless they knew what they were looking for, yet it's unmistakably signed with her initials.'

He called the uniformed men over to the painting.

'Sergeant, will you and your men please witness this?' He pointed out the signature to the mystified men.

'What is this? Are you saying there's something wrong with the damn picture?'

'Nothing that need concern you. You've verified that it was a false alarm and the picture is still safe. It should reassure Mrs Calder-Brown to know that the security arrangements work. I'll tell her the check has been carried out and we'll leave you to deal with Mr Hanson, the son-in-law.'

'What do we do now?' Mansfield asked as they clattered down the stairs.

'Sit tight until the revels are over. When the visitors have all gone, I presume the family will hold an inquest into today's proceedings. We'll spring it on them then. It'll be interesting to watch their reactions.'

'You really think one of them stole the original painting and murdered our two victims?'

'They seem to be the most likely suspects at this stage; maybe they're all in cahoots. On the other hand, the murderer could be someone known to Lydia Cordingley and have nothing to do with Monkbeggars Hall. Let's go and find something to eat.'

'I'm not sure I fancy what they're likely to serve up here.'

'I'm sure we'll find a genuine hot-dog stall tucked away somewhere for the likes of the more faint-hearted such as you. I need a drink.'

The last visitors straggled through the gates and the participants dropped their Tudor roles and set about the clearing-up operation. Roland had discovered that two barns belonging to the home farm had been converted into dormitories for their use and the more intrepid were camping out in the adjoining field.

117

He and Mansfield had spent the rest of the afternoon until closing time exploring the grounds and keeping out of the way of the family. The gateway leading to the back of the Hall had beeen locked and those activities that had been carried on in that quarter were moved to a different venue. The fire engine had departed and before very long the drama of earlier had been almost forgotten or relegated to the background. The two detectives waited until the last costumed performer had left the scene and then strolled back to the house.

As anticipated, they found Celia Calder-Brown together with her son, daughter, son-in-law and a young girl whom they hadn't noticed before, in the owner's private sitting-room. The two men were checking over the day's takings with the help of Marian Hanson. The older woman, her headdress removed to reveal her mop of crisp, white curls, was pouring out tea from a large, ugly, brown teapot that looked as if it belonged below stairs.

'Inspector, I didn't realise you were still here.' Celia Calder-Brown put down the teapot and looked at them in surprise. 'Is something wrong? I haven't thanked you properly for your quick thinking when the fire broke out.'

'All part of the day's work, ma'am. I take it everything is under control back there?'

'It looked much worse than it was. There's very little real damage – we were lucky. You haven't told me yet why you are here today.'

'Yes, I don't understand what you're doing here. Were you expecting trouble?' Nigel Hanson had laid aside the piles of coins he had been counting and was looking at them suspiciously. Roland ignored the question.

'You must be Mr Hanson? We weren't introduced earlier.'

'Yes, this is Nigel and my daughter Marian and this is Charlotte, my granddaughter.' Celia Calder-Brown indicated the plump young girl dressed in yellow satin, who was eyeing them with open curiosity.

'You would be Miss Lucy Hanson's sister?' Roland addressed the girl, but it was her father who answered.

'You know my other daughter, inspector? I hope not professionally!'

'Don't be silly, Nigel. This is my younger daughter, inspector. She's still at school.'

'It's a bore, but *I* still have to do what I'm told!' The girl gave him a gap-toothed smile, to which he found himself responding.

It was difficult to imagine a greater contrast between the physical appearance of the two sisters; but then, there had been no telling what was Lucy's true colouring beneath the macquillage. Neither she nor Richard Coates was in evidence – was this their choice or were they persona non grata with the family?

'Didn't we all, at your age? And it gets no better, I can assure you. I still have to do what my chief tells me.'

'And what would that be?' Hugh Calder-Brown got to his feet and sauntered over to them. He was still in costume, as were the others with the exception of his brother-in-law; but, while they looked as if they were masquerading in borrowed plumes, he looked like someone who had stepped from a Nicholas Hilliard miniature. He had put on the role with the costume and had not yet relinquished it.

'Ah, Mr Calder-Brown. We've met before, though in somewhat different circumstances.'

'You caught me on a bad day, Inspector.' He gave a boyish grin. 'But you haven't answered my mother's question as to why you and your colleague – ' he nodded to Mansfield – 'are here.'

'Mrs Calder-Brown gave us such an interesting account of the historical re-creations that we felt that we had to come and see for ourselves.'

'I don't think I believe you, Inspector. I think there is an ulterior motive for your presence here.'

'You're quite right, sir. We have reason to believe ...' Roland paused to make sure he had everyone's attention and to increase the drama of his coming announcements.'... that the Gerard Ter Borch painting that you have hanging on your wall is not the original but a clever copy.'

You could have heard the proverbial pin drop, thought Mansfield, watching their reactions closely. On all their faces was an expression of stupefied surprise. Then Charlotte giggled and broke the shocked silence.

119

'Lucy always said it should be sold and the money given to charity — what a pity it wasn't done!'

'Shut up, Charlotte! You can't be serious, Inspector?'

'This is preposterous!' said Nigel Hanson, outrage taking over from astonishment. 'What possible grounds could you have for thinking this?'

'Yes, you must have your reasons?' Hugh Calder-Brown chipped in, narrowing his eyes. 'I think you owe us an explanation.'

'Oh, we have our reasons; in fact, we have proof. Perhaps we can all go and look at the picture and I shall explain what I mean.'

For the second time that afternoon, Nigel Hanson led the way through the house towards the room where the picture hung.

'This is a very serious accusation you've made,' he protested to Roland as they climbed the stairs.

'I wasn't aware that I had made an accusation. I've only said that you're all labouring under a misapprehension if you think the painting is a genuine old master.'

'Here, Mother-in-law, you know the picture better than any of us,' he said, groping for the door-handle. 'Just tell him that he's talking off the top of his head!'

He pushed open the door and snapped on the light. Opposite them hung the gilt frame. It was empty. The painting had been neatly cut out and removed.

Chapter Seven

'I don't believe it! I just don't believe it! You were there investigating the bloody picture and you let it be snatched from under your bloody noses!'

Superintendent Lacey stomped up and down the office, thumping any furniture that impeded his passage. Mansfield was sure he could feel the floor reverberating under his heavy tread; it was like watching some prehistoric animal cornered in a small cave, and the superintendent was as dangerous as a caged animal. His bulk and gait might call to mind a dinosaur but his mind was probing, sifting and drilling to the heart of the matter. This was going to do James' hopes of promotion no good at all.

'Tell me it's not true, James,' he pleaded theatrically. 'Tell me it's just a bad dream from which I'm going to awaken. Because if it isn't, what, in the name of sweet Jesus, am I going to tell the CC?'

Roland had decided at the start of the interview that it was best to put up no defence at first but to let the full force of the tirade wash over him and salvage what he could at the end. He thought that it was now time to intervene.

'It was not the real painting that was taken, only a passable copy,' he said calmly. 'And at least it's proved that my theory was right.'

'How?' Lacey barked. 'There's a fire at Monkbeggars hall and in the kerfuffle that follows, one of the two or three hundred visitors, who may have had his eye on it for a long time, sees his chance and snaffles it. What has that to do with your theory? You make a complete balls-up of the

121

whole thing and then have the effrontery to claim that it's helping your inquiries!' His eyes bulged and Mansfield was afraid he was going to have an apoplectic fit. Rather James than me, he thought, and sat back to weather the storm.

'I'm convinced it was set-up,' said Roland. 'The fire was started deliberately for the purpose of causing a diversion and setting off the alarm. The call went through to the station and the nearest patrol car was sent to investigate. As expected, the picture was examined and pronounced in order, the police presence departed, and later our ingenious thief removed the picture from the frame ... because no one had remembered to reconnect the alarm after the alert.'

'Someone's head is going to roll for that!'

'You can hardly blame me for that, sir. It wasn't my responsibility.'

'And now you're trying to tell me it was not the real picture that was stolen? So someone is going to have a horrible shock when they try to flog it.'

'No, sir, I've already explained — it was stolen because it was *not* the original. Someone was trying to cover up the fact that the picture hanging in Monkbeggars Hall was not the real McCoy. Whoever it was hadn't realised that we already knew that it was a copy.'

'There's only your word for it.'

'No, I made sure that Sergeant Moyes and his colleagues witnessed Lydia Cordingley's signature on the copy.'

'You did? Quick thinking! But where does this lead us? Are you implying it was one of the family?'

'It was obviously someone with inside information but not necessarily one of the family. It could be someone who had been involved in a racket with Lydia Cordingley; after all, she would probably have known about the security arrangements at the Hall when she cleaned it and he or she could have contrived the whole thing for the purpose of destroying the evidence that the real picture had already disappeared.'

'You really think our two stiffs were rubbed out to stop them exposing the fake painting? Sound far-fetched to me. One of your wilder flights of fancy, James.'

'The original painting was insured for £200,000, which means it would sell for about £100,000 on the open market.

122

You and I know that people have been murdered for a few paltry pounds.

'True. So what is your next move?'

'Investigate the members of the family thoroughly, check their alibis for the times of the two murders and try and sort out just who was where during the fire and when the false painting went missing. We must also dig deeper into Lydia Cordingley's background and see if we can come up with anything else.'

'It might be a good idea to check out all the other pictures she's cleaned and restored in the last few years. We could find that half the stately homes in England are now displaying copies instead of originals on their walls!'

'Heaven forbid!'

'I know one thing, I shouldn't like to be the one who has to sort out the insurance claim over this one.' Bob Lacey eased his bulk onto his chair, which creaked audibly under the strain. 'Off you go then, and I want results. I'll buy your theory if you can back it up with facts. There are questions you need to ask, and you know which is the most important?'

'Sir?'

'Who, in the last year, has needed to find a hundred grand?'

Roland had sent Mansfield and Evans home. There was little more that could be done that day, and tomorrow they would make an early start on the planned interviews. But still he lingered on in his office late into the evening, mulling over facts and theories and trying to make sense out of them.

Below him, the station was almost as busy as during the day, but up here on the second floor, behind closed doors, he could believe himself alone in the building. From his window he could see across the dark rooftops of Felstone to the distant dock complex, which was enveloped in a white glow. By straining his eyes he imagined he could pick out the broad funnel of the *Bernicia* ferry between the black skeletal cranes and warehouses. There, on her sister ship, the *Mercia*, it had all begun; where was it going to end?

Most of the cases on which he worked had their roots in the underworld. His adversaries were mostly from the criminal fraternity; thieves, embezzlers, drug-traffickers, protection racketeers, GBH offenders; what Bob Lacey, spewing worn-out clichés, called the dregs of society, plus the occasional domestic homicide. Now he was investigating among the county set, verging on the realms of the lady novelists – Agatha Christie, Margery Allingham, the body-in-the-library syndrome. But no, the memory of those two horribly slaughtered bodies – John Hargreaves butchered in his bunk as he lay sleeping and the woman struck down in the fastness of her cottage – shattered any such thoughts. Was the murderer unknown to him, a total and, so far, unidentified stranger? Or was the culprit a member of Celia Calder-Brown's family?

His mind went into action replay over the events that had followed his announcement that the picture hanging on the wall was a copy. There had been genuine surprise on all their faces – but was one not the surprise of being told something unbelievable, but shock that his or her game had been rumbled? Equally they had all appeared stunned when they had found the empty picture frame. The shocked silence had been broken by Celia Calder-Brown.

'But Inspector, it was a false alarm!' she cried in distress. 'You checked and said the picture was here, safe.'

'It was here,' said Nigel Hanson. 'I saw it myself, as did you,' he shot at Roland.

Then had followed an exchange of recriminations among the members of the family about the fact that the alarm had not been reset. Nigel Hanson, feeling the blame was attaching to him, had tried to change the subject.

'How can we believe what you say about it being a copy?' he demanded of Roland. 'We have only your word for it. You can't prove it and it's a serious matter to make allegations like that that could mislead the insurance brokers.'

'Lydia Cordingley, the picture restorer, made a copy of the original painting when she cleaned it.'

'You mean she stole the real one and substituted a copy in its place?' screeched his wife.

'Is this true?' Celia Calder-Brown rounded on her son. 'Hugh, she was a friend of yours, how could – '

'Not a friend, Mother,' he interrupted her, 'just someone who was recommended to me as a very professional and competent worker. I didn't know her, and she's dead – remember?'

'Dead? Oh, my goodness she was that poor woman who was murdered. Inspector, you're not saying that her death had something to do with our picture?'

'I believe it has a direct bearing on it.'

'But I don't understand – are you saying she was a criminal?'

'What gives you that idea, Mrs Calder-Brown? Lydia Cordingley was innocent of any crime, that was why she was murdered; but she was unknowingly used to perpetrate a fraud.'

'But how do you know this? The woman is dead – what proof have you got?' Hugh Calder-Brown demanded.

'Miss Cordingley painted the copy at someone's instigation, probably thinking it was for insurance or security. Being a scrupulous person and worried, perhaps, that at some future date it could be used for fraudulent purposes, she signed it with her initials and left photos and papers in the safekeeping of her bank.' Roland looked closely at his audience as he revealed this piece of information; nobody looked horrified or guilty.

'You mean she left evidence behind of what she had done? You know who was behind it?' Nigel Hanson's brown, somewhat blood-shot eyes bulged in a way that called to mind the Super.

'No, unfortunately she didn't get to naming names.'

'Did you say she signed the painting?' Hugh Calder-Brown was looking at Roland quizzically.

'Yes. We knew from the photo records what to look for and Mr Mansfield and I both witnessed her signature on your painting, as did my colleagues who answered the alarm call. I can assure you there's no doubt about this.'

'But Inspector ...' His mother was rallying round to her original point. 'Surely it's obvious that this ... this peculation had nothing to do with us. The unfortunate woman has cheated us out of a fortune and you're trying to implicate the family –'

'Mrs Calder-Brown, I am investigating two particularly nasty murders which appear to have some connection with

Monkbeggars Hall. I am making no accusations, just examining all possibilities, no matter how tenuous. If you are innocent you have nothing to worry about and I'm sure you will welcome the opportunity to be eliminated from inquiries.'

'That's all very well,' Nigel Hanson blustered, 'but you've no right to come here and make these insinuations! There is such a thing as libel, you know – I think our solicitors should be present!'

'That is your prerogative, sir, if you think you need legal assistance . . .' Roland let it hang in the air and then changed the subject.

'Where is your elder daughter, Miss Hanson? I noticed her earlier taking part in the revels with her . . . friend.'

'Lucy doesn't live at home any longer,' said her mother shortly. 'She probably left as soon as the re-enactment was officially over.'

'You didn't see her at all today?'

'Lucy chose to join the ranks of the rustics, as I'm sure you must know if you saw her; the lower orders are not admitted to the house, in accordance with how things were run in Tudor times. There was no opportunity for us to meet.'

'Would she have known about the fire and its aftermath?'

'I should have thought every single member of the public knew, what with fire engines and police cars roaring up to the house,' said her father angrily. 'But she didn't see fit to enquire what had happened.'

Possibly because she knew already? Roland thought. There was no way Lucy and Richard Coates could be ruled out of his inquiries; they were just as suspect as the other people in the room.

He had taken his leave soon after that, satisfied that he had set the cat among the pigeons. He didn't normally reveal his hand so early in an investigation but he had hoped, by so doing, to stampede someone into action. Someone might now be scared shitless and would, as a result, make a slip.

He reflected on this now as he wandered over to the window and stood, hands in pockets, staring out at the night outside.

126

He had left them quibbling among themselves but they had been unanimous in one thing; they hadn't wanted the theft of the copy to be made public. Was this a significant fact, he pondered, or was it just a case of the family closing ranks? Outside, a clock chimed eleven and the luminous dial of St Benedict's, which had long ago lost both hands, glowed like a moon pinioned in the black, angular tower.

It was time to go home, he was getting nowhere fast. Perhaps a few hours' sleep would clear his head and make sense of the thoughts and images spinning round in his mind like a miniature whirlwind. He locked his office door and tramped down the stone staircase, hunching into his jacket. The duty sergeant called out good night and he replied. From below came the raucous bellowing of a drunk being locked up for the night. Sometimes he wondered why he strove so hard to rise in the ranks; how much simpler it would be, he thought as he got into his car, to carry out the more menial tasks and leave the brainwork to others.

The *Betsy May* shipped anchor and headed further downstream. Her engine was throttled down to half power, her tawny sails tightly furled along her weathered spars. It was very dark and still. Too still, thought Lars Svenson as he swung the wheel a degree; the river was like a sounding board, a flat sheet off which every little noise rebounded and echoed from shore to shore. He could hear the activity surrounding the port of Felstone as clearly as if he were lying alongside one of the terminals although it was several miles nearer the mouth of the estuary, its position heralded by a white glow in the sky. He hissed gently through his teeth, imitating the water creaming past his bows, and squinted at the other barges slipping astern, their black outlines quickly swallowed up by the pitch night.

Below deck Jan, his mate, slept off the effects of an over indulgent evening. The riverside pub, mecca of sailors and landlubbers alike, had echoed to the sounds of conviviality as the crews of the tall, stately barges had gathered to exchange news and banter before the serious business of racing. Even Jan's condition added colour to their subterfuge, Lars thought; the natural result of someone drinking

127

to drown his sorrows. They had dropped many a hint among their fellow seamen that they might have to withdraw from the races because of trouble with their mizzen mast. Tomorrow, they had insinuated, would be spent trying to correct the fault and to this end they would probably stand off farther downriver, away from the main shipping channel.

If they were missed the next day in the mêlée that surrounded the pre-race jockeying for position, someone would remember that the *Betsy May* had threatened to scratch. They would be pitied, Lars thought, but no one would query their absence. He sniffed the night air; unless they got a wind no one would be doing much sailing, they'd not even get under way. The forecast for the next couple of days had predicted a strengthening breeze but he could detect no sign of it.

He altered course slightly to avoid a channel marker buoy and stared out over the black water ahead. Jan should really be up forward helping to navigate. A collision with another vessel would be all they needed, but he wasn't really worried. Only the large freighters sailed at night and they were lit up like Christmas trees; any moored craft would be carrying riding lights. He shifted position and listened to the comforting sounds of the rigging creaking overhead and the water gurgling beneath the keel. The *Betsy May* had a far more important assignment than the East Coast Barge Races.

A train clattered out of a cutting on the port shore. For a few seconds it ran parallel to the river, a bright caterpillar of oscillating light, before plunging behind a wooded escarpment. Nearby a dog barked, startlingly clear across the expanse of water, and was answered by another farther off.

The next morning saw Roland and Mansfield back at the village of Barndon. Their venue this time was not Monkbeggars Hall but the home farm where Nigel and Marian Hanson resided. It was a beautiful old Suffolk farmhouse with tall gables and mossy tiles and the walls were covered with ivy. Marian Hanson opened the door to them. She was dressed in a tweed kilt and cashmere sweater and looked far more at ease than she had done the previous day masquerading as

128

an Elizabethan lady. She was surprised but not alarmed to see them.

'Inspector! You have some news of the painting?'

'Mrs Hanson, I'm conducting a murder inquiry. This takes priority, as I told you yesterday.'

'I really don't understand the connection ... You'd better come in.'

She led the way into a sitting-room complete with beamed ceiling and inglenook fireplace. A gas fire with imitation logs burned there and the glow burnished the copper pan filled with narcissi and forsythia that stood on a nearby coffee table. At first glance the room exuded an air of comfortable, unostentatious wealth, but Roland's trained eye quickly took in the threadbare patches in the carpet, not quite hidden by the strategically placed rugs, and the somewhat faded chintz covering the sofa and easy chairs. Marian Hanson had good taste and an eye for interior design but the ornaments in the room were modern, mass-produced articles, not the antiques one would have expected, and the hunting prints on the wall were cheap imitations of the nineteenth-century originals. Perhaps all the best artefacts were displayed in Monkbeggars Hall; it would be interesting to know how closely related were the financial affairs of the two establishments.

'Mother says that the death of that man – John Hargreaves, wasn't it? – has something to do with that murdered woman and our painting. I fail to see – '

'Mrs Hanson, we know that John Hargreaves and Lydia Cordingley were killed by the same person, and the connecting thread between them is the Ter Borch painting. You must appreciate that it is my duty to investigate everyone associated with this field of inquiry, if only to eliminate them and allow me to concentrate on the more significant factors. I'm sure, under the circumstances, you'll be only too willing to cooperate.'

'Well ... yes, what do you want to know?'

'Where were you and your husband on the night of the 1st April and on the 15th?'

'You mean we have to produce an alibi? This is preposterous!'

Her already high-coloured complexion flushed a deeper,

129

angrier red and her voice climbed half an octave. Hoity-toity, Mansfied thought, discreetly taking notes from the depths of a low-slung chair in a corner. But was she covering up for a guilty conscience?

'Mrs Hanson, please.'

'We were here, of course.'

'Both of you?'

'Er, yes, let me see ...'

'The first occasion was Easter weekend,' Roland prompted.

'Easter? Oh, of course, I had forgotten. Well, in that case my husband was away. He spent the weekend in Newmarket.'

'Newmarket?'

'The racing fraternity, Inspector.' She spoke as if explaining something to a child. 'Nigel has shares in a racehorse. It has yet to get within a mile of the winning post, but it is his great enthusiasm, his hobby, I suppose you could say.' She spoke wearily and Roland guessed that this had long been a bone of contention between them, but he felt his interest quickening; racehorses cost money.

'So your husband was staying in Newmarket and you were here — alone?'

'My son and younger daughter were here with me.'

'I didn't realise you had a son, Mrs Hanson.'

'Michael is at boarding school, in his last year, but he was home for the holidays.'

'And on the 15th April? Another Monday, incidentally.'

'I had better check my diary, Inspector. You seem intent on tripping me up.'

She made a great play of rifling through the voluminous leather handbag that had been lying on a nearby chair and taking out and putting on her glasses before she examined the diary she had extracted from its depths. She looked at him over the top of the glasses.

'Actually I wasn't here that day. Michael's school was putting on a play in which he was taking part and I spent the day up there. He is at Rapley Hall in Norfolk and I have an old schoolfriend who lives nearby so I took the opportunity of visiting her and killing two birds with one stone.'

'So on both occasions you and Mr Hanson went your

130

separate ways. Do you not participate in events together?'

'Inspector, this is a very busy farm. We carry a lot of stock, which means we are far more labour-intensive than most modern farms. Someone has to be here to see to things.'

Roland's mind boggled at the thought of Marian Hanson buckling down to the job of mucking out or whatever. He couldn't quite see Nigel Hanson in that role, either; riding his acres in a Range-Rover, yes, but ploughing a furrow?

'Quite. Well, perhaps I could have a word with your husband?'

'But I've told you what you wanted to know.'

'You've answered the questions I put to you.'

'Nigel should be in the farm office now,' she said stiffly, glaring at Roland. 'I'll take you to him. It's across the stable yard.'

'There's no need for you to bother, Mrs Hanson. I'm sure we'll find our way. One last thing − could we have the address of your daughter Lucy?'

'You surely can't be suspecting her of having anything to do with this ... this contretemps!'

'You do have her address?'

'Of course,' she snapped and, tearing a page out of her diary, she scribbled on it and handed it to Roland. 'But you won't find her there. She attends Felstone Polytechnic, she'll be at a lecture.'

'I believe Mr Richard Coates is one of her tutors?'

'I really have no idea.'

'I believe your brother, Mr Hugh Calder-Brown, also lives in Felstone?'

'He owns the bookshop in Goths Yard and lives above it; is that what you want to know?' she asked coldly.

'With his wife and family, I presume.'

'Hugh is not married and has no children, or certainly no legitimate ones. He's a bachelor gay − and I use that expression in the old-fashioned sense, Inspector.'

'Well, thank you for your help, Mrs Hanson, we won't take up any more of your time. Across the yard, you said?'

'There seems to be little love lost between her and her brother,' said Roland as they walked towards the farm office.

131

'She's one of those women, typical of her class, with masses of energy and no outlet for it.'

'I wouldn't say that. She seems to play an active part in the running of the farm and the shenanigans up at the Hall, and I wouldn't mind betting she's the mainstay of the local Conservative Club, the WI and all that jazz. Rather like your Jean in a way.' Roland cocked an eye at his sergeant.

'I can't see any similarity at all. Jean is not bossy and over-bearing like that; she occupies herself with various activities and does a lot of charity work.'

'I know; she's an excellent woman.' Roland smiled to himself. Jean Mansfield managed her husband beautifully, but so skilful was she that most of the time he had no idea that he was being manipulated.

Nigel Hanson had heard their footsteps and appeared in the doorway to the farm office.

'What is it now?' he asked ungraciously.

'Your wife sent us across. Just a few questions, sir.'

He shrugged and went back into the building. The two detectives took this as an invitation and followed him inside. It was a good-sized, comfortable room. A large desk, covered by a mountain of paperwork, stood near the window and there were two filing cabinets along-side one wall, floor-to-ceiling bookshelves along another wall and a gun cupboard in the corner. There were rugs on the floor and several leather easy chairs besides the chair behind his desk. This was Hanson's den as well as his office. Trophies and cups were displayed on every available surface along with rosettes and framed photo-graphs.

Roland walked across and examined these photographs. Most of them showed either Charlotte or Lucy at varying ages and on a variety of different ponies and horses; there were also a couple of photographs of youthful cricket teams, which probably included the son Michael.

'Your daughters are accomplished horsewomen?'

'Yes, although Lucy has outgrown it now. But you didn't come here to talk about my daughters' equine successes.'

'Indeed no. What were you doing over the Easter weekend?'

'Easter weekend, eh?' He appeared to search his memory. 'I spent a few days up at Newmarket – didn't my wife tell you?'

'Rather early in the year, wasn't it, sir? I understand the flat-racing season doesn't get under way until the middle of April in these parts?'

'I part-own a racehorse; a beautiful little goer but he hasn't quite come into form yet. I have great hopes for him this season.' He was suddenly fired with enthusiasm. 'Are you a racing man, Inspector?'

'Unfortunately my job leaves me very little time to sample the joys of the turf. It must be an expensive business, owning a racehorse?'

'You could say that. Of course, I only have a third share. There are three of us in it together.'

'Did you stay with one of these racing colleagues over the Easter weekend?'

'I really object to all this poking around in my private affairs. I can't see what it has to do with you. Why don't you concentrate on solving some of the real crime in the district? What about my sacks?'

'Your *sacks*, sir?'

'Yes. A couple of hundred of my sacks have gone missing from the shed beside the silo – and the stapling machine, too!'

'Have you reported it?'

'Yes, and a fat lot of response there's been. Nothing has been done – '

'I'm sure the local police are working on it. Now, would you mind answering my question?'

'I stay in a little pub on the outskirts of Newmarket when I go up there, the Laurel Bush.'

Mansfield took up the questioning. 'Alone?'

'What do you mean?' he snapped, his ruddy complexion taking on a purple hue.

'Does your wife go with you?'

'Good God no! I mean ... no, she usually stays here.'

'So, since you a regular visitor to this establishment, they'll remember you?'

'Yes, but ...'

133

'But what, sir?' Roland leaned forward and joined in with his colleague.

'Look, are you really going to check up on me?'

'I've already explained the situation. If you're innocent you have nothing to fear.'

'You don't understand ... I haven't been quite open with you.'

'You wish to change your statement?'

'The truth is, Inspector, I wasn't on my own. I have a friend ...'

'A lady friend?'

'Well ... yes. You see, it's like this: Marian doesn't share my interests and I get lonely ... and then I met Olive ...'

'Olive is the name of the lady concerned? And is she connected with the racing fraternity?'

'Oh no. Olive ... Olive helps out at the Laurel Bush.'

'You mean she's a barmaid?'

'She's a niece of the owner and she helps out when they're short-staffed,' he replied stiffly.

'So she lives there. Could we have her full name, please?'

'Olive Durrant. She's divorced but she still uses her married name. Inspector, my wife – she doesn't have to know, does she?'

'Your private life is only of interest to me in so far as it touches on my investigation. If it has no bearing on my case there is no reason for your wife to learn of your extramarital activities from me.'

'I can assure you that Olive and myself had nothing to do with those dreadful murders or the business of the painting. You must believe me.'

'If only we could believe all we're told, Mr Hanson, our task would be much simpler. Now, Sergeant Mansfield, have we covered everything?'

'There's just the matter of the second date, sir,' said Mansfield, going smoothly into their double act.

'Ah yes, the 15th April. What were you doing on the 15th April?'

'The 15th April?' Nigel Hanson looked blank.

'Your wife has said that she was in Norfolk visiting your son at school and spending part of the day with a friend.'

'Yes, that's right. Well, I was here, of course.'

'Alone?'

'You surely don't think I have Olive over here!'

'I mean, was your daughter here – the younger one?'

'Charlotte is at school during the day, but certainly she was here after four o'clock.'

'I presume you don't run this farm single-handed; there would be farmworkers around to vouch for your presence that day?'

'I'm sure that I can produce witnesses if I put my mind to it. Was that the day that woman was killed?'

'It was, sir. A very nasty business. Tell me, did you know her?'

'No, of course not! Why should you think that?'

'She was recommended to Mrs Calder-Brown when she was looking for someone to clean the painting. I wondered if it was you who suggested her.'

'Not me, I know nothing about that sort of thing.'

'Well, that will be all for now. If you think of anything that might be of help to our inquiries, please let us know.'

'Oh, I will; yes, I will. And Inspector ... you will be discreet, won't you?'

'I can't promise anything, sir.'

They left a very worried man behind them as they went back to the car.

'So he's got a bit on the side? Can't say I blame him,' said Mansfield, zipping up his jacket. 'What do you make of him?'

'On the face of it he doesn't appear very bright; not overendowed with the little grey cells, as Poirot would say. But appearances can be deceptive. I think he's more shrewd than he lets on, and remember, it didn't take much ingenuity to plan those two murders – more a case of using brute force with very little attempt to cover up.'

'So he's still one of our chief suspects?'

'Most definitely. We'll have to check out his alibi for the Easter weekend, but I don't know that it'll be of much help.'

'You mean he's probably in there now, ringing up his lady love to make sure her story agrees with his?'

135

'Most likely, but I think we'll let him stew for a little longer. I'm afraid he probably was just having a dirty weekend, but if we get any more evidence that points to him we'll have to follow it up. Let's get on and visit one of our other chief suspects — his brother-in-law.'

Goths Yard was situated in the old part of Felstone. It had once been the coachyard of a thriving hostelry but the inn had long since disappeared and the remaining buildings, mostly stables and coach houses, had been renovated and converted into individual shops, some little boutiques and other, larger units. A stone fountain plashed gently into a shallow bowl in the centre of the cobbled yard. This fountain had been a source of controversy since its inception a few years earlier. The traditionalists had deplored its mock-Gothic design, claiming that a modern monstrosity had been put in a genuine antique setting. There had also been claims that young children could drown in the unfenced pool at its base. But the fountain still played and no child had come to grief, though students from the Poly frequently colonised the stone coping and in hot weather dabbled their feet in the water, and on one New Year's Eve a drunken reveller had stripped naked and bathed in the icy bowl to the accompaniment of much raucous encouragement from his inebriated friends before being arrested and marched off to the police station.

The rents and rates in this part of the town were high and this was reflected in the type of shop established in Goths yard. There was an upmarket shoe shop that specialised in Italian shoes, a superior china shop, a shop that sold homemade Belgian chocolates, a very classy dress shop that appeared to carry very little stock, and an excellent restaurant that in the summer months set out elegant wrought-iron tables and chairs beneath a wisteria-hung trellis.

These tables and chairs were in place now, a response to the warm spring weather, as Roland and Mansfield crossed the yard. Hugh Calder-Brown's shop was tucked away in a corner, but the shopfront was deceiving; inside, the premises were far more spacious than they looked from the outside. He himself was sitting at a table towards the back of the shop, reading a newspaper. He was wearing a dark-green velvet jacket and matching trousers. Little Lord Fauntleroy grown up, Mansfield thought disgustedly, but he didn't look foppish, just suave and elegant. He got to his feet when he saw them and came to greet them.

'Inspector! Sergeant! You've come to patronise my poor establishment. What volumes can I produce for your erudition?'

'We have come, sir − ' Roland spoke ironically − 'to ask some questions in connection with two suspicious deaths and a painting that has gone missing − lost, stolen or strayed.'

'The painting ... yes. It's quite incredible but I suppose you know what you're talking about − you've got your facts right?'

'Oh yes, sir. Perhaps you could tell us how well you knew Lydia Cordingley?'

'But I didn't know her. Whatever put that idea into your head?'

'Your mother, Mrs Calder-Brown, said that you made the arrangements for Miss Cordingley to clean and restore the Ter Borch painting, so naturally we assumed you knew her.'

'Knew *of* her, Inspector. I didn't know her personally.'

'Perhaps you could explain just what you mean?'

'I'm an antiquarian bookseller, I attend auctions and fairs all over the district, and naturally I come into contact with people in the arts world, which impinges on my own profession. I had heard her spoken of with respect by various of these colleagues and when Mother started talking about having the picture cleaned, I remembered her and suggested her for the job. Actually, Inspector, I may be misleading you because I believe I did meet her a couple of times at functions. Am I right in thinking she was something of a cripple?'

He sounded very plausible, but Roland noted that he was not as relaxed as he would have them believe. There was a nervous blink to his eyes and he couldn't keep his hands still.

'I understood that you transported the picture from Monkbeggars Hall to Miss Cordingley's cottage and back again.'

'Good grief, no! That was done through a firm of specialised carriers who deal exclusively with works of art. That

137

picture was worth a great deal of money, it had to be properly protected in transit to meet the insurance precepts.' He gave them the name and address of the firm and Mansfield added it to his notes.

'Do you really think she switched paintings, Inspector — sent back a copy in place of the original?'

'Do *you* think so, sir?'

'Well, there's no way the picture could have been tampered with after it was re-hung at the Hall. You know how the alarm system works. So it must have been done at that end. I presume you're checking up on her contacts?'

'Among others. Would you mind telling me what you were doing on the night of the 1st to 2nd April?'

'Like that, is it? You're so short of leads that you're grilling everyone who swims into your orbit?'

'Just so. I fling my net wide and every fish, be it large or small, is examined before I throw it back.'

'Quite poetic, Inspector.' He couldn't keep the sneer out of his voice. 'And am I a big fish or a little one?'

'That remains to be seen. Do you want me to repeat my question?'

'You're referring to the Easter weekend, aren't you? I was recovering from a bad cold. I'd been to a sale earlier in the week and I must have picked up a bug; I was feeling very poorly.'

'You were here? I believe you have a flat over the premises?'

'Yes, I have a flat upstairs and I spent most of the weekend incarcerated here, feeling sorry for myself.'

'You're not married, Mr Calder-Brown?'

'No, so far I've managed to escape the net. What fishy analogies we seem to be using. How about you, Inspector?'

Roland ignored this. 'But you were fully recovered by the Tuesday?'

'Tuesday?'

'You were visiting your mother at Monkbeggars Hall the day after Easter Monday.'

'Ah yes, of course, where we had our little mishap. Yes, having spent the weekend indoors I felt the need for a change of scene. I drove over to Tilstead to visit a friend

138

but she was out so I called in to see Mother on the way back.'

'This shop is closed on a Tuesday?' Mansfield took up the questioning.

'Monday is my normal closing day but as Monday was a bank holiday that week, I decided to take the Tuesday off as well.'

'And what were you doing on Monday 15th April?'

'I was here doing a little stocktaking. I'm afraid I'm not being of much help to you, am I? I can't provide an alibi for either date.'

'It's yourself you would be helping, Mr Calder-Brown, rather than us. I suggest you try and remember if any of your neighbours or the tradespeople saw you. It might be to your advantage to provide an alibi − if only to stop us bothering you again.'

On this note they left him, Roland content that he had pierced his self-confidence.

'It's a pity we didn't get to see over his living quarters. That might have given us more of an idea about his life style. Get Evans to snoop around and find out what sort of car he drives and where he keeps it. He was expecting us to check his movements on those dates and he comes up with those deliberately inconclusive alibis. I don't believe he would have spent the entire bank holiday on his own. You know what his sister hinted at − he's a womaniser. It's my bet he would have had some dame around, soothing his fevered brow.'

'You think he was lying?'

'I think he may have been deliberately misleading us, probably because he doesn't want an irate husband on his trail.'

'Where to now?'

'The college and Mr Richard Coates.' Roland looked at his watch. 'We should catch him in his lunch hour.'

The polytechnic was on the other side of Felstone. It had been built in the 1950s on land reclaimed from the marshes to the south of the town, and only the dock railway spur and a new housing estate separated its grounds from the boundary of the dock complex.

It consisted of a vast square block of glass and concrete and numerous smaller cubelike buildings which had been added later as the college expanded.

Roland and Mansfield parked in the visitors' car park and walked towards the main entrance hall. A tall young woman with red-gold hair piled high on her head tripped down the steps towards them and for a few seconds Roland thought it was Ginny. His heart did a lurch and then he saw that it was a much younger girl, a student with blue eyes and a multitude of freckles across her snub nose. What was Ginny doing now? he wondered. Was she taking a lunchbreak in the staff room of Felstone High School, which was only a stone's throw away down the road, or had she gone into town to do some shopping or meet friends? It seemed an age since he had seen her and unless he cracked this case soon there would be no free time to spend in her company.

At the reception desk he asked for Richard Coates and gave their names.

'He has finished his morning lecture but he may still be in his office. I'll try and raise him for you.' She punched out some numbers with elegant, red-tipped fingers and spoke into the receiver.

'He is still in his office. Do you want me to get someone to show you the way?'

'We'll find it ourselves if you just give us directions.'

'Take the lift to the third floor.' She nodded towards the vestibule where the grey metal doors and rows of buttons proclaimed their function. 'When you get out, turn right and it's the third door along — his name is on it.'

Roland thanked her and the two men went towards the lifts. Students thronged the corridor. Most of them were in their late teens or early twenties, Roland supposed, but from their appearance they could be beings from another planet. It was difficult to tell male from female although the male of the species didn't wear his hair as long nowadays as he himself had as a teenager in the seventies.

'God! They make me feel old,' he remarked as they waited for the lift to descend. 'But you should be used to them, having two of your own.'

'I thought mine were bad enough but have you ever

seen anything as bizarre as that?' Mansfield indicated a girl walking along the corridor towards them. She had spiky magenta-coloured hair and was clad in a wonderful assortment of purple garments.

'I should think that Lucy Hanson is perfectly at home in this milieu.'

They rode the lift and found themselves in another corridor, whose windows gave a fine view of the port of Felstone and the river curling inland past the rows of warehouses and container stockades. A cluster of red-brown sails upriver in the distance caught Roland's eye. Of course, it was the East Coast Barge Races, they were taking place much earlier this year. Damn! He'd try to wangle a few hours off; he and Ginny could go and take a look. They could watch from one of the viewing places along the river wall and afterwards have a meal in one of the riverside pubs ...

'Here we are.' Mansfield's voice plucked him back to the present. 'Mr Richard Coates, Senior Lecturer in Economics,' he read from the lettering on the door. 'I wonder what sort of reception we'll get?'

Although he had known that they were on their way, Richard Coates took a long while answering their knock. When he did he pretended surprise.

'The inspector and his sidekick! To what do I owe the honour of this visit?'

Beneath the seeming affability the man was coldly, tightly angry. He too was dressed in a dark-green velvet jacket but he looked very different from Hugh Calder-Brown. He looked dangerous and insolent. You could understand an impressionable young woman of Lucy Hanson's age falling for him, Mansfield thought. It probably boosted her image among her peers to claim him as her boyfriend.

'You were present at a historical re-creation at Monk-beggars Hall yesterday, in the course of which a fire broke out and a valuable picture was found to be missing.'

'I was one of many hundreds of others present – are you interviewing each one personally? You're going to have your work cut out following up everyone who was there. Is there a shortage of crime at the moment that they can spare such important officers as yourselves for the task?'

'Let's cut the crap, shall we? I believe you're a friend of Lucy Hanson, the granddaughter of the owner of Monk-beggars Hall.'

'Sorry, Inspector, I'm forgetting my manners. Do come into my humble office, and you too, Sergeant.' He stepped back abruptly and it was only Mansfield's quick reaction that caught the door and prevented it slamming in their faces. Once inside, Coates made no attempt to offer them a seat but leaned back against his desk and folded his arms. Roland carefully and deliberately sat himself down on a chair in front of this desk and Mansfield wandered over and pretended interest in the bulging bookshelves.

'Do sit down, Mr Coates. I know this is your office, but you're making me nervous. Now, as I was saying, Lucy Hanson is — '

'Lucy is one of my students,' he interrupted, flinging himself down in his own chair.

'I believe you live at the same address?'

'All right, Inspector, she's my mistress!' His dark eyes glittered maliciously at Roland, who kept his face blank.

'Don't the college authorities frown on that sort of thing?'

'This is not a school. It's an institute of learning that caters for adults above the age of consent.'

'Quite. It must be quite a boost to one's ego — to have a bimbo.'

'Lucy is a highly intelligent young woman, not a page three sex object!' That had rattled him, Roland thought.

'It was you who brought up the sex angle,' he said coldly. 'You do remember the little contretemps of yesterday afternoon?'

'Are you accusing me of stealing that painting?'

'No, Mr Coates, I'm questioning you in connection with two suspicious deaths.'

The lecturer glared at him and a little tick jumped in his cheek close to his swarthy sideburns.

'I'm used to being harassed by the fuzz, but this time I think you've gone a little too far!'

'Have we, sir? Then perhaps you'll tell us where you were on the 1st and 2nd April — to clear the air.'

'How can I be expected to remember what I did so long ago?'

'A few weeks? It was Easter Monday and Tuesday.'

'Easter?' He gave a nasty grin. 'I seem to recall that we spent most of Easter Monday in bed, Inspector, and on the Tuesday ... I believe we went for a drive in Lucy's car.'

'Which took you to Monkbeggars Hall? Oh yes, we saw you there, Mr Coates.'

'There's no rule that says a girl can't visit her grandmother, is there?'

'No indeed, I'm sure Mrs Calder-Brown made you welcome. Actually, it's the night of the 1st to 2nd April in which we are interested, but I expect you were, er ... busy then too?'

'I was with Lucy. You'll have to take my word for it, there's no way you'll prove otherwise.'

'I see. Perhaps we'll be luckier with the other date: the 15th April. That was a Monday too.'

'On Mondays I don't have my first lecture until eleven o'clock so I usually spend the early part of the morning marking essays. I presume that was what I was doing on the 15th.'

'Would that be here or at home?'

'Either. I really can't remember but I'm sure someone here will have seen me arrive and be able to tell you.'

Lydia Cordingley was killed before midday, so he could have done it, Roland thought. His alibis were no more satisfactory than Hugh Calder-Brown's.

'Well, I think that'll be all for now, Mr Coates. Can you think of anything else, Sergeant?'

'I think we've covered everything, sir,' said Mansfield solemnly, snapping shut his notebook and restoring his pen to his breast pocket.

'I suppose you're going to pester Miss Hanson now?' Coates spoke belligerently.

'I don't think there's any need, not for the time being anyway — I'm sure you've been telling us the truth. Good afternoon, Mr Coates, enjoy the rest of your lunch hour.'

143

If looks could kill we'd both be dead by now, Mansfield thought as they walked back along the corridor. And he hasn't even slammed the door behind us — I find that somehow ominous!

Chapter Eight

'I want you and Mansfield in on this.' Bob Lacey thrust out his lower lip and flipped his pen against it. 'It's going to be a big operation run in conjunction with Customs, the tip-off came from them.'

'But I'm up to my eyes in my own case,' Roland protested. 'Surely that takes priority?' Then, as the superintendent made no reply, 'You're not taking me off it!'

'Keep your cool, James, I'm of the opinion that this ties in with your investigation. Your chappie got himself topped on the ferry and now the action is back there in the port area.'

'What about Lydia Cordingley and the painting?'

'Forget all this arty-farty business and concentrate on the facts.'

'Lydia Cordingley *was* killed by the same person.' Roland was trying hard to keep his temper under control.

'You have convinced yourself of this.'

'You read the pathologist's report!'

'A probability, a strong probability, but no absolute proof. A different weapon was used, a different setting; it's impossible to be a hundred per cent certain and don't forget – someone could have cashed in on the publicity that was given to the first murder and deliberately tried to make it look as if the same hand was behind it.' Roland gave up. 'And where exactly is this stake-out to be? You can't cover the whole dock complex – you'd need an army.'

'I'm briefing the team later on, but take a look at this.' He heaved himself out of his chair and stumped over to the row of filing cabinets along the wall. He extracted a roll of paper from the mass of documents littering the tops and spread it out on his desk.

'Here we are: a plan of the docks. We think the action is going to be concentrated in this area here.' His podgy finger indicated a point on the map. 'It's at the back of the complex away from the main activity, behind the bonded warehouses in the part where the containers are stockpiled. That's the old gasometer and as you can see, the river bends round there to an old disused jetty: it was the original quay when Felstone was just a fishing port.'

'And just what are you expecting?'

'It's a scam to knock off a small fortune. That area is a treasure-trove, James! Those containers are stuffed with consumer goods; there's a consignment of electrical goods from Japan, a fortune in computer components; a shipment of liquor from Holland awaiting haulage – advocaat, cherry brandy, genever. You name it, it's there.'

'And this tip-off is genuine?'

'The duty boys think so. They're playing it close to their chest – you can't blame them, we'd do the same in the circumstances – but they think there's some big illegal operation planned for tonight and as it seems to be stuff going out instead of coming in they've alerted us.'

'How can they be sure this is where the action is going to be?' Roland looked closely at the section of the map that Lacey had indicated.

'They aren't saying but it's been corroborated by the Dock Security Police. They've reported some suspicious happenings in that area over the past few weeks. We had to bring them in on this – it's on their patch after all – and apparently there's been the odd occasion when someone's been seen snooping around where they had no right to be, and one of the guard dogs nearly caught an intruder near the perimeter fence the other day.'

'Nearly caught? I thought those dogs were lethal!'

'There were some red faces over the episode. The dog appears to have been bamboozled in some way – I don't know the details. Well, there you have it.' Lacey rolled up the map and nodded at his detective inspector. 'I want everyone

146

to report here at 16.00 hours for the official briefing. You'll be given your positions and put in the picture to the best of my ability.'

'Are you in on this, sir?'

'Wouldn't miss it. This is the big one, James. Perhaps if we pull this one off it will distract the public from your singular failure to make any progress in the "April Fool Murders"!'

Roland spent the rest of the morning in his office, trying to catch up with his paperwork, and it was there that Mansfield found him a couple of hours later. He poked his head round the door.

'Glad I caught you,' he said. 'I've had something passed on to me from downstairs.'

'Something to help us in our inquiry?'

'No, nothing like that. There was a fracas this morning down in the new shopping precinct. Some boys were fooling around on skateboards and an old lady got knocked down.'

'Why weren't they at school?'

'Playing hookey. The old girl wasn't badly hurt, just shocked and bruised, but the police were called.'

'So? What is this — Get James Roland Day? First of all we're going to be pulled in for a stake-out at the docks tonight, and now you tell me the uniformed branch need my help to deal with a bunch of hooligans? What's it got to do with me?'

'I've been tipped the wink — Simon Dalton was one of the boys.'

'Hell!'

'I thought you'd like to know — have a word on the quiet with him.'

'Yes, thanks. Little devil, he doesn't realise it's his mother he's hurting most when he tries to embarrass me.'

'You think he's deliberately trying to vex you?'

'I'm afraid so. His big aim in life at the moment is to cause a rift between Ginny and me and what better way than to behave in a manner that calls down the attention of the force on his activities?'

'They can be right little sods at that age. I remember when

147

Gavin was fourteen he was caught smoking in the bicycle sheds at school — nearly set them on fire.'

'At least he was your son. You had the parental power to deal with him. I'm treading on eggshells with young Simon. I've got no legal authority over him and he knows it and plays on it.'

'You'll have to come down hard on him, you know, James. It's what he needs and probably what he'd welcome; he needs a father's firm hand. This behaviour could well be a call for help.'

'Since when have you been an expert in adolescent psychology? Still, you're probably right, only I have to be careful. In this respect I feel I'm walking a tightrope — Christ! The clichés! I sound like the old man. I don't want to alienate Ginny.'

'My heart bleeds for you — there, you've got me doing it now! Anyway, what's all this about tonight?'

'I hope you hadn't got anything planned for tonight, like bed and sleep?' Roland got to his feet. 'Let's go along to the canteen and get a bite and I'll bend your ear.'

Why shouldn't I? Ginny Dalton thought defensively, putting down the phone and finishing the dregs of her coffee. I'm free, white and over twenty-one, and James and I haven't even got an unofficial understanding; there's absolutely no reason why I shouldn't accept a date with another man. Why should I sit at home night after night waiting for the phone to ring and hoping it will be Detective Inspector James bloody Roland managing to spare me an hour and tucking me in between his other, more important engagements?

She went over to the sink and rinsed out her mug. As she dried it and hung the threadbare tea towel back on the radiator, she went over the phone conversation in which she had just taken part. How strange, but how typical of Hugh Calder-Brown to call her at just the time when she had a free period and was alone in the staff room. He had assumed an intimacy that had surely never existed between them. But it had been flattering, and she had agreed to go with him to the lecture that evening, a lecture sponsored by the local Book League at which a well-known art historian was to give a talk on the publication of art books. Hugh was a smooth talker and so confident of never being refused that she found herself agreeing to whatever he proposed.

'And why not?' she said out loud, rummaging in her handbag for her lipstick. 'I'm going, and I'm going to enjoy myself!'

'Good for you, Ginny!' Duncan Bird, the senior PE instructor kicked the door shut behind him and dropped his loaded holdall on the nearest chair. 'But you know what they say? Talking to yourself and all that ...'

'Aren't you supposed to be taking the third-formers for a cross-country this morning?'

'It's been cancelled. The Head's in a real sweat — he's got half a dozen third-year boys on the carpet in his study. I don't know what they've been up to but the police are involved.'

'Police?'

'Don't get excited. They're in uniform, it's not your tall, dark, handsome git. I tell you who is in there, though — your Simon.'

'Oh, dear,' said Ginny Dalton.

Celia Calder-Brown stood in the doorway, her hand on the light switch, and gazed at the wall opposite. The oblong where the picture had hung was a much paler colour than the surrounding panelling and wires sprouted from the wood. She sighed. She didn't care that the picture had been a copy, she didn't care about the small fortune that had gone missing; she just wanted the painting back, here on the wall where it had always hung.

What would Walter have said? He had always been fascinated by it, bewitched even, so much so that she had almost felt jealous; but he had used to tease her, tell her that he had two Celias, one in his bedroom and one in his dressing-room, and wasn't he a lucky man? She sighed again and, snapping off the light, closed the door and went back downstairs. Her footsteps echoed in the vastness of the great hall as she crossed it and for the first time she felt lonely and dwarfed by her surroundings. The Hall was meant to house a large community of people, an extended family, as it did on the days of the historical re-creations;

not one elderly, frail female who rattled around in it like a pea in a pottle.

The restoration of the Hall had been a dream fulfilled, but was that dream now crumbling? She told herself not to be so fanciful and lit a cigarette, gulping the smoke down into her lungs and trying not to cough. It was ridiculous when you sat down and really thought about it; one old woman in a house this size. The upkeep was enormous, she couldn't afford it and the family weren't interested in the carrying-on of a tradition. The family ... Smoke dribbled from her nostrils and she tapped the plume of greying ash from the end of her cigarette. Was the family unity crumbling too, falling apart at the seams?

Marian and Nigel were quite content with the home farm, had no hankerings after the grandeur of Monkbeggars Hall, but Nigel, unless she was very much mistaken, was plunging deeper and deeper into financial difficulties. It was that racehorse. Who would have thought a man as respectable and reliable as he would, in advanced middle age, kick over the traces and get involved in the racing world and all the chicanery that it implied? And it wasn't just his racehorse on which the money was going. Then there was Hugh ...

He had made her a promise, but was he keeping it? She had a horrible feeling that he was not, that he had only made it to keep her quiet; he of the golden tongue who had always been able to sweet-talk her. Even as a child he had had the ability to talk himself out of any unpleasant situation. Marian had accused her of favouring him. She had always strenuously denied this, but was it true? One shouldn't have favourites among one's children and she had tried to be fair, but Hugh had always been able to wrap her round his little finger, to charm her so that she forgot his faults. And Marian ... Marian hadn't been charming and had never learned to cajole prettily. She had whined and sulked and been an awkward, ungainly child. Yet she was the one who had taken after Walter in looks; but whereas Walter had been dark and attractive with warm brown eyes and a burly physique, in Marian that plumpness had turned to fat, her rosy cheeks had coarsened over the years and haughtiness looked out of those brown eyes, so like her father's and yet so different.

As for Lucy ... Lucy was everything her mother would never be, but had she swung too far in the other direction? She had encouraged Lucy to break free and espouse those radical causes, not because she herself supported them, God forbid, but rather to tease and annoy her dutiful daughter, which was naughty and looked as if it might now rebound on her own head. Lucy had got herself involved with this Richard Coates and she wasn't sure if he was to be trusted. He professed contempt and dislike, not for her personally – or so she was led to believe – but for all that she and her class stood for. But she had the uncomfortable feeling that he would only too willingly accept any largesse that came his way from the system that he purported to despise. Was she defaming him or was her intuition correct and he was using her and Lucy as a means to his own ends?

She stubbed out her cigarette and went in search of her housekeeper to discuss shopping lists. Hatty was rude to her, not at all respectful, but she could be trusted; you knew where you were with Hatty. Surely she knew her own family? She was letting her imagination run away with her but the events of yesterday had disturbed her deeply and sown the first seeds of doubt. Was everything as it appeared or was there something evil and corrupt touching on her world and threatening to engulf everything she held dear?

She gave herself a mental shake and banished these thoughts to the back of her mind. Should they have lamb for dinner, or would a nice piece of turbot or halibut make a change?

The rain started at eleven thirty. At first it was a light drizzle, sifting down like a damp cloak upon the concealed watchers; then the wind got up and the drizzle changed to an icy downpour, driving into every gap and trickling down the faces and into collars, boots and shoes. With the rising wind the noise level crescendoed; timbers creaked, metal shutters screeched and an empty cardboard carton hurtling backwards and forwards in a narrow alleyway made an incredible racket.

If it had to be a night like this at least the din was a plus, Roland thought, huddling behind a stack of crates and trying to turn up his collar still further. You could stand out in the open and beat a drum and no one would hear; on the other hand, it provided a cover under which the rustlers could operate without fear of being overheard. They would all need to be extra vigilant. This part of the docks was ill-lit compared with the working zone nearer the quayside where the fork-lift trucks zoomed between the gantries and cranes and the business of loading and unloading was concentrated. Single arc lights at either end of the container park illuminated this area but behind him the bank of warehouses and sheds loomed darkly.

Lacey had said these contained nothing of importance; some were derelict and surplus grain was stored in others. The old road from the disused jetty ran past them to a gate in the perimeter fence. This gate, never used nowadays, was sagging and rusty with neglect, and he was convinced that this was the point through which the loot would be removed. They must have transport standing by and he had arranged for police vehicles to wait under cover nearby, ready to move in and set up a roadblock when the word was given. Roland squinted down at the luminous dial of his watch: just after midnight, the witching hour. The night was a torrent of noise but was anything actually going to happen? The Super was convinced the tip-off was genuine and that a criminal conspiracy was going to be buttoned up that night. Roland was willing to go along with him on this; he just didn't see how the murder of John Hargreaves and subsequent events fitted in with it. He was cold and wet and thought longingly of whisky, Ginny Dalton and bed, in that order.

Alan Scopes, crouched at the side of the container park, felt his earlier euphoria slipping away as the wind buffeted his back and the rain ran down his face blurring his vision and stinging his eyelids. It had been by sheer chance that he had hit on the exact night. We'll act on your tip-off, his superiors had agreed, but you must pin your informant down to an actual date. And how to do that without alerting Netty that her hints were falling on all too fertile ground? But by sheer chance he had found out; his luck was unbelievable. There was a disco on this evening at the Dock Social Club, which he had thought she would be eager to attend. His invitation had been received enthusiastically but when she had heard

152

the date she had turned him down regretfully but firmly. Any night but this one, she had said, excitement glinting in her eyes; this was *the* night, but she had said too much already and he mustn't press her further. He had no need to. Tonight's date had fitted the criteria she had mentioned earlier: no moon and a midnight tide.

Now doubts were seeping in with the damp and cold. Supposing it was all moonshine? Maybe she had been teasing him and had really been referring to a student rag or some such event, and he had read far more into her hints than she had meant? With the full force of Customs and Excise and the local police backing his hunch, he suddenly felt horribly vulnerable. Suppose it was all a mistake — where would that leave him? Bang would go any thoughts of promotion; it didn't bear thinking about. On the other hand, what about Netty? He didn't like to contemplate the thought of her being involved in criminal activities; he had become more involved with her than he had ever intended. What had started out as a harmless flirtation, deliberately cultivated to further his professional ambitions, had developed into something far more serious. In the long hours of the cold, dark night he had plenty of time in which to review his part in the operation and his deliberations brought him no comfort. He was on the horns of a dilemma: if tonight's proceedings resulted in a victory for the forces of law and order it would advance his career but he would lose Netty; if the whole thing was a misconstruction of facts on his part, he would be castigated by his superiors but might still have a chance with her.

He fumbled for his handkerchief and dabbed at his face and hands. How the hell had he got himself into this situation?

Patrick Mansfield shifted his weight and cautiously stamped his left foot, which had developed cramp. At least this time he had drawn the cushy one, he was under cover while most of his colleagues were braving the full force of the elements. The derelict hut at the head of the old jetty where he was positioned was riddled with holes and cracks through which the wind snaked in icy draughts but at least he was dry — comparatively. Actually the wind was dropping, had lessened considerably over the last fifteen minutes or so. The slap and surge of the turbulent water against the ancient timbers had dropped to a slurp and the door and window frames were creaking now rather than rattling in fury as they had done earlier.

He wasn't going to complain about the post he had been given, but from there he could see very little of what was going on in the dock complex; in fact, he could see Hantwich across the estuary far better. He gazed out through the cracked glass over the black water to where Felstone's sister port straddled the opposite shore. Over to the left he could just make out the flashing light of the Man Ledge buoy that marked the edge of the shipping channel, and to his right, much closer inshore, the tall mast of one of the Thames barges, silhouetted against the same pink glow that illuminated Hantwich. Even further to his right, almost out of vision, was a huddle of riding lights where another group of Thames barges rode at anchor.

Beautiful craft, he thought, the last remainder of the age of sail long since departed from these busy shipping lanes. At one time they had been a familiar sight plying their trade along the east coast estuaries, carrying their heads of red-brown sail proudly; now the last vessels, restored and renovated by dedicated craftsmen, were only to be seen on high days and holidays such as the series of barge races taking place that week.

Jean had wanted to see these. Last year, when they had seen the pictures of the event in the press, she had expressed a wish to be a spectator next time and he had promised her that he would make the effort to get time off and take her. He could see little possibility of fulfilling this promise the way things were at the moment. While he was kept busy helping to keep the big police machine on the road, she held the fort at home, acting as both mother and father when the occasion demanded.

He glanced at his watch: twelve forty-five. Both Jean and Jane should be in bed and sound asleep, or so he hoped, but this had been the evening of the disco that Jane had begged to attend. They had given their permission grudgingly, persuaded by her plea that all her friends were going and assured that there was safety in numbers and that she was being brought home afterwards by another parent. He sighed. He knew he was almost paranoid about his daughter's safety but he knew only too well, from a professional point of view, the terrible things that could happen to a teenage girl nowadays. He and Jean discussed it interminably, had arguments and even rows, Jean surprisingly being less worried about it than he. They had to give Jane a certain amount of freedom at her age; after all, next year she would have left school and gone out to work or on to college; but how much and when was a vexed subject.

He reluctantly came out of his reverie and centred his attention once more on the scene outside. It was surely darker than it had been earlier? A black mass seemed to fill the window aperture. He strained his eyes and shock ran through him. The black mass resolved itself as an upside-down triangle of canvas. The Thames barge, sailing under topsail only, was almost alongside the jetty; he could hear the creak of her timbers and the wash creaming in her wake.

He ducked out of sight and spoke urgently into his radio.

'I'm sorry, Ginny, not exactly a scintillating evening.' Hugh Calder-Brown turned ruefully to his companion as he helped her into her coat in the foyer of the conference room of the Excelsior Hotel.

'What he had to say was quite interesting, he just went on rather,' said Ginny Dalton diplomatically.

'He's a pompous old fart.'

'You have a way with words.' She was aware that Hugh's upper-middle-class ringing tones had caused heads to turn in their direction.

'His essays and written dissertations are a marvel of brevity and wit.'

'Obviously the pen is mightier than the word in this case; all right, I know it's a bad pun.'

'Can it really only be nine thirty?' He checked his watch. 'I feel as if we've been in there hours. Ah, well, the night is young; where shall we go now?'

'But Hugh – '

'But me no buts, woman, and don't tell me that you have to get home because of that son of yours.'

'Simon is staying the night with a friend.' She regretted the words as soon as uttered.

'There you are, I have a proposition. I was going to suggest supper at Gino's but I've got a better idea. Come back to my place; I'll make a pot of this marvellous new blend of coffee I've obtained and knock up a snack — and I've got something to show you.'

'Etchings?'

'Don't insult us both. This is not a pass — I really have got something in which I think you'll be interested: the whole eight volumes of Morris' *British Birds*. I picked them up in a sale a few weeks ago and they are fascinating, both from an artistic and a conservationist point of view.'

'Do you know, I'm seriously tempted, Hugh.'

'The numbers of birds in it that are now extinct or no longer British residents is quite staggering.' He tempted her further. 'And most of them decimated by the very naturalists who recorded them.'

'I know, the Victorian naturalist and his collecting mania. The whole concept is quite horrific to us now. OK, you've won. I must see these masterpieces, but I'm not staying long; a quick coffee and I'll cast my eye over your new baby.'

'We may as well leave the car here; it's such a nuisance manoeuvring it in and out of the stable-yard. I'll run you back later, is that all right?'

'Yes, I could do with stretching my legs and it's a fine evening, thought I believe rain is forecast for later.'

As they walked the short distance to Goths Yard, Ginny Dalton caught sight of their reflection in a shop window. What was she doing, accepting an invitation to visit a man's flat late in the evening? And a man such as Hugh Calder-Brown who had a certain reputation with women? A rather disquieting frisson ran through her and she told herself not to be so ridiculous. She was no naive teenager being lured by a middle-aged lecher; she was a sane, level-headed widow quite capable of looking after herself and she knew how to handle the likes of Hugh Calder-Brown.

Karen Belstone, the ex-Mrs James Roland, saw them as they turned into Goths Yard. She was taking a short cut home from the bus station to her flat. She had been on evening duty at Woodford library and as her car was on the blink she had been forced to rely on public transport. She noticed Hugh first and was about to call out to him when she recognised the woman with him. She pulled up short and watched with narrowed eyes as they crossed the cobbled yard talking animatedly, Hugh's arm tucked under his companion's.

What was Hugh doing with James' new girlfriend? Hugh was a casual friend, she didn't take someone like Hugh seriously. He fluttered from flower to flower like the proverbial butterfly, spreading his charm and sexual favours among a wide coterie of female admirers, but the schoolmarm — what was her name, Ginny? — was another matter altogether. Karen felt a spurt of jealousy curl through her. The apricot-haired woman had stolen James and was now involved with another of her escorts. No, that wasn't fair; she had left James long before Ginny came on the scene — the worst day's work she had ever done and something she now bitterly regretted. Perhaps the affair between James and Ginny was not as serious as she had feared; it surely couldn't be if she was also swanning around with Hugh Calder-Brown?

She watched in disbelief as Hugh unlocked his shop door and the two disappeared inside. Almost ten o'clock and he was taking her up to his flat; there was only one possible interpretation to be put on that action. I wonder if James knows, she thought, and a little calculating smile hovered on her lips.

Unaware that she had been seen and recognised, Ginny followed Hugh Calder-Brown through the dim recesses of the bookshop.

'Can you see OK? I don't want to put on the shop lights.'

'Just about. I didn't realise it was such a labyrinth in here. How do you ever find anything?'

'Everything has its place. Here we are.' They had reached the back of the ground floor and he switched on a light that illuminated the staircase. He bounded agilely up this and unlocked the door at the top. Ginny followed him more sedately, wrinkling her nose.

157

'Why do old books always smell so fusty?'

The door opened onto a small hallway off which led several rooms. The door facing them was wide open and Ginny thinking this was where she was meant to go, moved towards it. Hugh leapt in front of her and slammed the door with alacrity.

'Not that one – this is my sitting-room.' He led the way into a low-ceilinged room lined with bookshelves.

'This is my private collection. Make yourself at home and I'll put on the coffee.' He disappeared through another door, which she presumed led to the kitchen, and she sat down in a leather-upholstered chair and looked around her. It was a typical bachelor pad, untidy but comfortable. There were two other armchairs and a sofa all upholstered in leather, a pile of newspapers and magazines on the floor and what looked like an extremely sophisticated hi-fi system at one end of the room.

'Damn!' Calder-Brown popped back into the room. 'I've left the milk downstairs. There's a sink and gas ring in a cubbyhole at the back of the shop where I make myself a drink during the day. I'll just pop down and get it.'

'May I use your loo?'

'Second door on the right.'

He clattered down the stairs and she went out into the hall. The second door on the right was next to the one he had slammed – that must have been the bedroom. She wondered why he had been so keen to prevent her from seeing inside. He's probably got articles of feminine wear lying around or other evidence of his sexual activities, she thought. On an impulse she pushed open the door and looked inside. A street lamp outside the window shone in through the undrawn curtains, giving enough light to see by. She had expected to find a frilly nightdress lying on the bed or female toiletries or make-up on the dressing-table, but the room was singularly free of any such thing. Instead there was a curious smell, not a woman's perfume but something more elusive and tantalising. She had smelled that smell before but couldn't remember when or where.

She advanced into the room and looked around her. The carpet was of such thick pile it was like walking across a lawn that needed cutting. A heavy bedspread patterned in a vivid Aztec design covered the bed and the headboard was decorated with strange, geometrical carvings. On the bedside table stood an ashtray containing a half-smoked cigarette. I didn't know that Hugh smoked, she thought, gazing at it; it looked hand-rolled too. On an impulse she picked it up and something clicked in her memory. She was back at art college, back in her bohemian late teens. They had used to gather, she and her fellow students, in someone's bedsitter where they would squat on the floor, discussing art and setting the world to rights. The atmosphere had reeked of the cheap red wine they drank and the reefer that was passed from hand to hand for anyone who wished to take a drag. That was it – pot. She sniffed gingerly at the limp object in her hand and knew that her memory had not played her false, Hugh was into cannabis; who would have thought it?

The sound of footsteps down below made her start guiltily. She dropped it back into the ashtray, slipped out of the room and bolted herself in the bathroom, flushing the toilet and running the tap.

'They're over there.' He gestured to a pile of books on the coffee table near the window as he went towards the kitchen, clutching a milk bottle and a bag of sugar. 'The Morrises.' Ginny knelt on the floor and examined them, and then moved on to the books in the bookshelves. They all seemed to be on the subject of natural history, the majority about butterflies, moths and other insects, and most of them looked very old and valuable.

'Interesting?' He dumped the loaded tray on a table and poured coffee into what Ginny was sure were two genuine Clarice Cliff cups and saucers.

'Very.' She tore her gaze reluctantly from the Art Deco china. 'But I'm surprised at your choice of subject. You're not into conservation or nature study, are you? It just doesn't seem your scene.'

'What do you think would be more appropriate – erotica?'

'Uh-huh.'

'You'd be surprised at what I've seen along those lines in the course of my travels. And guess who were the most avid consumers – the Victorians again.'

159

'The old double standards. Morally upright Papa, the model of virtue, ruling his wife and family with a rod of iron and getting up to all sorts of things on the side.'

'Just so.' He looked as her slyly. 'If you're interested in that sort of thing I can put you on to – '

'Oh, I'm not,' she cut in hurriedly. 'And you haven't told me why you collect books on butterflies?'

'My great-great-grandfather was a well-known entomologist. He had this quite famous collection of butterflies and moths and many contemporary books on the subject. When he died his collection was split up and sold, ditto the library, but some of the books were passed on through the family. Look at these two.' He pulled two volumes from the shelves and showed them to her. 'Wakefield's *Insects,* first published in 1816, and Newman's *The Natural History of British Butterflies and Moths:* they've got some of the old boy's sale catalogues pasted inside the covers. Anyway, I thought it would be rather fun to try and get his collection of titles together again, and that's what started me off.'

'You're a man of many parts, Hugh.' Ginny finished her coffee and held out her cup for a refill. 'This is certainly delicious coffee, did you get it locally?'

'No, it came from Brussels.'

'Since when has Belgium been renowned for its coffee?'

'There's a little shop that specialises in unusual blends. I got it at the same time as I picked up the Morrises. There was an antiquarian book fair in Brussels a short while ago.'

'I seem to remember reading something about it in the *Guardian*. Easter weekend, wasn't it?'

'No, I was in bed with 'flu over Easter so it certainly wasn't then, it must have been the week before.'

'Are you going to keep the books?'

'Regretfully no, my finances wouldn't stand for it and I had a prospective customer in mind when I bought them. He'll pay handsomely for the set and it will release some of my capital.'

He got to his feet and went over to his hi-fi equipment. Ginny watched as he selected a record and put it on the turntable. His black rollneck sweater and dark trousers emphasised his pallor and the fair hair that flopped over

160

his forehead reminded her of Laurence Olivier's Hamlet and a photograph she had once seen of Rupert Brooke. The dark circles under his eyes and the hooded eyes themselves gave him a look that was both decadent and sensual. Was he a drugger? She stood up.

'I really must go, Hugh.'

'Relax, the night is young.'

'It's considerably older than when you said that before,' she retorted.

'Listen to this,' he commanded, and dropped the arm onto the record.

She sat down, expecting to hear the strains of something romantic, and was startled when the harsh, abrasive tones of the Ebony Concerto tore round the room.

'Do you know it?'

'Yes. Stravinsky.'

'It's the original Woody Herman recording. Exciting, isn't it?'

'Very. Classical jazz at its best. I didn't know you enjoyed this sort of music, Hugh.'

'There's a lot you don't know about me, Ginny. Such as the fact that I find you very attractive and I want to go to bed with you.' He was suddenly looming over her and those delicate, white hands showed surprising strength as he caressed her neck and shoulders and nibbled her ear.

'Stop it, Hugh.' She tried to push him away. 'I made it quite clear that there was nothing doing – '

'But you didn't mean it, did you? You know you want it – why pretend.'

'I'm not pretending. Is this where I'm supposed to pay for the coffee?'

That pulled him up. 'That's unworthy of you, Ginny. Don't be so uptight. You're wound up like a top – you need a smoke to relax you.'

'I don't smoke.'

'Don't be so naive, dear. You're a big girl now. I'm not talking about ciggies.'

So it *was* true. 'No, Hugh, no to everything. You promised to behave ...'

'OK, have it your own way.' He had left her side as suddenly

161

as he had come. 'Never let it be said that I force my attentions where they're not wanted. I suppose I've blown it now?'

'How do you mean?'

'You'll be reporting me to your dick for offering you a reefer.'

'I'm not sure that I understand . . .'

'The excellent Detective Inspector Roland − he is your friend, isn't he?'

'Who told you that?'

'A little bird. I suppose *he* is satisfying your needs?'

'Don't be offensive! How do *you* know him?'

'Hasn't he told you? I appear to figure on his list of suspects for the April Fool Murders.'

'What?'

'Mother's Dutch masterpiece has gone missing and for some extraordinary reason he's trying to connect that with those two poor unfortunate people who were murdered.'

Several things slotted into place in Ginny's brain, the photos of the Ter Borch painting that James had shown her; the realisation that, of course, Hugh was the son of the owner of Monkbeggars Hall; the knowledge that the two victims were connected by links with the art world. She stared at him in amazement.

'But that's absurd!'

'I'm glad you think so. Perhaps you could put in a good word for me.'

'James doesn't discuss his cases with me.'

'Doesn't he? That's a shame. I'd like to know just what he thinks he's got on me.'

He walked over to the window and tweaked aside the curtain.

'The wind's getting up, it's blowing up to rain.' He turned back to face her. 'Am I forgiven?'

'If you promise to run me home immediately.'

'I'm a good loser, but it was worth a try, wasn't it? And you know you were expecting it.'

The message went round the compound, easing tension and stirring the adrenalin. It wasn't a wild-goose chase; the tip-off had been genuine and this was for real. Roland eased

162

his cramped joints and stared intently in the direction of the river. It was far too dark to make out anything, as he reminded himself, there were buildings between him and the water, but he kept his gaze riveted on that point all the same. So, instead of the lorries that Lacey had predicted, the gang were using a Thames barge to get away their haul: quite ingenious. With the largest gathering of barges to be seen for many years on the river, the presence of one near Felstone Docks would go unremarked and he knew just how much these boats could carry. He had gone over one that had been open to the public at Maldon a few years ago. The hold was vast and could easily accommodate 150 tons of cargo and more.

Bob Lacey cleared his throat and snapped into his UHF radio:

'Mansfield, *what* is happening your end?'

'They've got the hatches open. They seem to be unloading something.' His voice was distorted and static crackled over the air.

'What is it?'

'It looks like pallets or something similar.'

'How many men?'

'I can only make out two.'

'Are you sure?'

'I can't see very well. I'm looking through a crack in the wall and it's very dark. I daren't use the window in case I'm spotted.'

'What are they doing with them?'

'They've disappeared, must have gone below. No, they're on the jettty ... they've got these pallets stacked up. Wait, they're moving off with them. Hell! I can't see. I think they've gone round the back of the old gasometer. Do you want me to follow?'

'No, stay where you are. They've probably left someone on board as a guard. Keep watch on the barge. We'll take over now.'

Lacey craned forward and glared into the night; he could detect no movement but he knew that they were there. Very soon they would walk unawares into his trap; he felt good, the long vigil was nearly over. He spoke once more to his hidden listeners:

'Our quarry is here. They're approaching from the right, coming from behind the old gasometer. Don't anybody make a move until I give the signal. I want them in front of us, actually tackling the containers, before we close in — is that understood?'

The arc lights shone down harshly on the rows of containers. Roland thought that they looked like Lego, giant building bricks neartly arrayed in lines. There was no sign of any human presence and the wind had dropped, resulting in a lull in the background noise. If they were coming from the direction of the gasometer they should be on the scene any minute now; he braced himself for action. There was nothing to be seen but he thought he could hear a hissing sound that at first he put down to a fresh flurry of wind disturbing the water. This was odd, it seemed to be coming from behind him, not over to the right where the river lay. He stiffened and strained his ears. Was he imagining the unfamiliar noise that reminded him of skis skimming over the piste?

He straightened up warily and looked round the compound. None of the other hidden watchers appeared to have heard the noise; nothing moved, no human shadows darted among the containers and no further instructions came from Bob Lacey. He must be imagining it, but even as he thought this, over to the far left where a dog handler and his animal were positioned, came a muffled whine that was cut short and then the sound of scuffling. Pandemonium broke loose. There was the sound of pounding feet and Lacey's voice roared over the air waves:

'We've blown it — they've seen us! Don't let them get away!'

Roland charged out of his hiding place and ran after the line of figures disappearing behind one of the old warehouses. Hell! The gang had got nowhere near the containers, they had been alerted to the police presence when they had hardly got on the scene.

He sped round the corner and almost fell over the low, oblong object lying in his path. It was shaped like a child's toboggan, though much larger, and he caught it a glancing blow with his foot and as it shot sideways with a sibilant whirr, he recognised the sound he had heard. Ahead of him

164

he could see bodies locked in combat, the grunts and thuds of infighting.

He lunged after a figure that broke away from the struggle and darted towards a pile of crates. His tackle brought them both down among the crashing, splintering cases. His opponent was much smaller than he and Roland soon had the upper hand. He dragged him to his feet and snatched off the balaclava mask. Lucy Hanson's distorted features glared back at him.

Roland was so astonished that he almost relinquished his hold. The Super had been right after all! She swore and kicked at his legs. He tightened his grip and frogmarched her back towards the compound, where her fellow conspirators had all been overcome and unmasked. Among them was the swarthy, bearded visage of Richard Coates.

As Lacey's voice boomed out, arresting them on suspicion of burglary, it was overlaid by another, spitting hate and defiance in shrill tones. There was a second young woman among those rounded up. She jerked herself free of restraint and confronted one of the Customs officers who had been in on the surveillance.

'Pig! You f-----g pig!

Chapter Nine

'The grain mountain! Ethiopia! Robin Hood! It's like something out of a second-rate TV thriller!'

The action had switched to Felstone Police station and Bob Lacey was pacing the floor.

'Were they after the goodies in the container park? No, sir, they were only "redirecting the grain mountain at Felstone Docks to Ethiopia", quote, unquote! "A mission of mercy" as the good reverend put it!'

'They've admitted it?'

'The ringleader, Richard Coates, is singing dumb, but most of them were only too eager to explain – boast about it. They're proud of their plot and sick with disappointment that it went wrong.'

'What went wrong our end? I take it the wheel came off?' Mansfield, from his hide-out in the hut, had missed the first part of the action.

'You could say; we nearly lost them. That damn dog ...'

'It was hardly his fault, sir.' The dog handler spoke up. 'We were concentrating on the containers in front of us and he was trying to draw our attention to what was going on at our backs at the warehouses. It didn't make much difference – they were coming up behind us and we'd have been spotted anyway a few seconds later.'

'Hmn. It could prove a costly mistake. Come into my office, Roland, we've got a lot to discuss.'

Bob Lacey eased his bulk onto the desktop and Roland had visions of the whole structure collapsing under his weight. His senior officer crumpled up the sheet of paper lying on the blotting pad, flicked it into his wastepaper basket and pouted down at his empty hands.

'If only we hadn't blown it. If we could have caught them actually removing the stuff ...'

'But surely that makes no difference now they've admitted it? You *are* going to charge them?'

'It's not as straightforward as that.'

'Why not? It looks perfectly straightforward to me! We caught them in possession of tools − they were "equipped to steal", you can get them on that. And they've admitted they intended removing the grain from the warehouse and transporting it to Africa. They'd got those wheeled sledges to carry the stuff to the barge and there are two converted trucks standing by on the other side to continue the journey. What more evidence do you need?'

'Cool it, James. You've seen who we've got in here − they're not criminals. We've netted some very important personages, a well-known priest, someone who was high up in the diplomatic service before he retired, a representative from one of the leading international charities.'

'And someone who has form as a forger; not to mention Richard Coates.'

'I'd be quite happy to put your Richard Coates away for a stretch, but we've got to tread carefully. How can we charge them if there is no complainant?'

'No complainant? What do you mean?'

'Just what I say. Who owns that grain mountain? The dock company? The government? The EEC? We're into deep water here and I don't intend navigating it on my own. I'm bringing the chief constable in on this. I shall be informing him of the situation as soon as it's a reasonable enough hour to rouse him from his bed.'

'And in the meantime?' Roland's voice was deceptively soft.

'We grill them. You don't think I've gone soft, do you?'

'I wondered if you had forgotten that it was your idea that this operation tonight tied in with my investigation?'

'As a matter of interest, just how *do* you fit this in with your case?'

'It's obvious, isn't it? This conspiracy cost money, a great deal of money, and I'm willing to bet that money came from the sale of the stolen picture.'

'You may have a job proving it.'

'We've got Richard Coates down below. You've read my report, he's already under suspicion because of his connections with the granddaughter of the family — also in custody at the moment. It's just too much of a coincidence to believe he had nothing to do with the murders and the theft of the painting.'

'You know the rules of the game, James. We can only hold him for twenty-four hours without charging him and I'm not sure we've got enough evidence to charge him with anything.'

'That's not quite true, sir. *You* have the authority to detain him for thirty-six hours and we can get a magistrate's warrant to hold him for a further sixty hours if necessary.'

'Don't try and pressure me. And there's another aspect to this case, they're going to have public opinion on their side. Have you thought of that? A great many people will wish that they had succeeded in their conspiracy. Anyway, you heard what I said — the CC is brought into the picture at the crack of dawn. Until then Coates is all yours!'

Several hours later Roland was finding it increasingly difficult to keep a grip on reality and his temper. The man sitting opposite him — 'lounging' would be a more appropriate term — was cool and insolent and showed no sign of weariness although he had had an even more active night. Richard Coates was adept at dealing with cross-examinations, he had handled enough of them in earlier brushes with athority. He should have been a lawyer, a barrister, Roland thought, his talents were wasted as a lecturer. The detective ran his fingers through his hair and leaned forward across the table.

'Mr Coates, you're wasting your time as well as mine. We know what the set-up was tonight, you and your accomplices planned to break into the warehouse containing the surplus grain. You intended to bag up this grain, carry it on custom-built sledges to the barge, sail across to Belgium, where you had two trucks standing by, and transport it to Africa. Is that not so?'

'Well done! If you know all this, why are you still persecuting me?'

'Supposing I tell you that I'm not concerned with the relocation of the grain and its ultimate destination. What I *am* interested in is the financing of this operation.'

'You're losing your touch, Inspector. Don't tell me you haven't discovered that also.'

'I should like to hear your version.'

'It won't differ from my esteemed colleagues'. We started a charity subscription. It's amazing how people will dip into their pockets for a cause like aid for the starving thousands in Ethiopia – it assuages their conscience.'

'I don't think I quite believe you.'

'You mean that you don't agree that people are prepared to part with their money rather than actually do something about the problem?'

'I don't think, Coates, that that was how you acquired your financial backing.'

'It was *Mr* Coates before – are we getting ratty, Detective Inspector?'

'I suggest that the money for this venture came from the sale of Mrs Calder-Brown's painting, which you stole at the time that it was being cleaned by Lydia Cordingley, having arranged for a copy – which she painted – to be substituted in its place.'

'Fascinating, Inspector. Do go on.'

'This copy hung in Monkbeggars Hall and would probably still be there today, undetected, if Mrs Calder-Brown hadn't decided to loan it to the Langdale Galley for an exhibition. You knew that the moment an expert set eyes on it your switch would be discovered so John Hargreaves had to be killed to prevent exposure. Likewise, you murdered Lydia Cordingley to stop her speaking out and incriminating you.'

'What an incredible imagination you have! I really must congratulate you. But aren't we wasting the rate-payers' money? You haven't an atom of proof, and *I* suggest that you're concocting these fantasies to cover up for your inefficiency.'

'Mr Coates, by your own admission you have no alibis for the times of the two murders. And now we find that you have been in possession of enough money to finance this conspiracy. In my place, wouldn't you be suspicious?'

'But I've told you, we set up a charity subscription. Miss Hanson coordinated it; she has the entrée into many influential circles through her parents and she persuaded a great many people to give donations.'

'Donations to what, exactly? How did you manage to bamboozle these good people – who, I believe, are a section of the population you profess to despise – into supporting your felony?'

'They gave money towards buying and equipping a relief truck to carry aid to Ethiopia. It's all kosher, Inspector. We had donations from across the country and also from left-wing movements and many of the charitable organisations.'

'I'm sure you did. You probably acquired several hundreds of pounds this way, but your project cost thousands. What do you say to that, Mr Coates?'

'You've heard my story and I'm sticking to it. You can't prove me wrong.'

'I shouldn't be so sure about that.'

Roland stared with narrowed eyes at the man who sat there so confidently, glib answers rolling from his tongue, and felt a great desire to rattle him and puncture his confidence. He tried a shot in the dark.

'Supposing I tell you that you were seen on the *Mercia* ferry on the night that John Hargreaves was murdered?'

'Who told you that? It's a lie!'

He had provoked him. Richard Coates' face went a deeper red and there was a nasty glint in his eyes. But Roland didn't know whether he was reacting with anger or fear.

'You don't expect me to divulge my source of information?'

'You've got it in for me, haven't you? You'd like to pin something on me and get me out of your hair. It's police harassment.'

'Far from harassing you, I can't seem to get away from you; I fall over you at every turn. I am reminded of the nursery rhyme "Mary Had a Little Lamb"; you, of course, being the lamb, and Miss Hanson, Mary.'

'What do you mean?'

'How does it go? "And everywhere that Mary went the lamb was sure to go." I pay a visit to Mrs Calder-Brown and bump into you at Monkbeggars Hall; I speak to Miss Hanson at the historical recreation and you pop up at her shoulder; I follow a tip-off about an illegal operation at Felstone Docks and, lo and behold, who turns up? You and Miss Hanson.'

'How *did* you find out?'

'You were betrayed, Mr Coates. So much for the loyalty of your fellow conspirators.'

Roland relinquished the role of interrogator to Mansfield and, after sending Evans for coffee, went outside to get a brief breath of fresh air. The early morning sky was a pearly haze shot through with pink and gold. Soon the sun would break through; already the dawn chorus was belling away, the secret choristers tucked away in hidden enclaves of greenery among the urban sprawl of the town. A muted ship's siren in the distance reminded him that the dock's timetable related to tides rather than the passage of night and day, and that he also had more to do before the chief constable was informed of the night's happenings. He tipped his head back, drew in deep lungfuls of air, and winced as the first rays of sun struck the flagstaff on the roof and were reflected directly into his eyes. He went back inside to interview Lucy Hanson.

Lucy Hanson and Annette Shaw, the other young woman arrested, were being held in the same detention cell because the sudden influx of detainees had filled the station's jail. The custody officer jerked his head in the direction of the cells and grinned.

'No need to question them. Just step nearer and get an earful of that — they've been going at each other hammer and tongs. If we don't soon split them up someone's going to get hurt.'

'What's the trouble?'

'The dark-haired one, Lucy Hanson, is accusing the other one of betraying them.'

'This should be interesting; when thieves fall out ... A useful angle to follow up, and she's the one I want to question. Get her into an interview room and I'll be with you shortly.'

Roland collected WPC Judy Crane and the two of them went into the interview room where Lucy Hanson sat glowering darkly at the young policeman by the door. Roland dismissed him with a nod, indicated that his female colleague should efface herself in the background, seated himself at the table opposite his prisoner and leaned forward to flick on the tape recorder.

'Well, well, Lucy, what a to-do! All that plotting and planning gone to pot because of a weak link in your chain.'

She refused to acknowledge his presence but concentrated ferociously on a spot on the wall equidistant between the policewoman and herself.

'Your boyfriend's not very happy about it. I think he blames you for the debacle.'

That caught her on the raw and she flashed him a smouldering glance. 'It had nothing to do with me!'

'No? She's a friend of yours, a contemporary; I think he regrets ever letting you irresponsible young women in on the scheme in the first place.'

'It was my idea!'

'Well then, perhaps you can fill me in on some details.'

'I have nothing to say.'

'That's a pity. Your fellow conspirators are falling over themselves to put me in the picture. They seem to think that they were contributing to a noble and worthy cause.'

'So it is!'

'Theft? Illegal trespass? Damaging property?'

'That grain belongs rightfully to no one — it's an embarrassment! And it's rotting! Soon it'll be no good to anyone and now it could save hundreds of lives. Haven't you seen those pictures of little Ethiopian kids with stick legs and distended bellies, dying like flies? Doesn't it mean anything to you?' She was practically crying with anger and frustration.

Roland had to admit a grudging sympathy with her anguish. Whatever motives activated Richard Coates, there was no

172

denying Lucy's; she really was out to save lives. He leaned across the table and spoke softly and confidentially.

'Supposing I tell you that your cause has my sympathy; that your motives can be applauded and I'm almost sorry you did not succeed?'

'Don't think you can disarm me by sweet-talking; I'm not a fool.'

'Let me put it another way: I'm not interested in the rights and wrongs of what you were attempting to do, the ethics and possible charges facing you. All I'm interested in at present is how the scheme was financed.'

'I'm sure you've already been told.'

'You persuaded people to donate to your "charity" thinking they were helping to equip a relief truck for Ethiopia.'

'They were!'

'You have records of these transactions?'

'Yes. At least, some of them,' she muttered stubbornly.

'You probably pulled in several hundred in this way, but this little operation cost far more than that: the equipment, the boat, the adapted trucks ...'

'Then where do you think we got it from?' she flashed.

'The sale of your grandmother's painting?'

She looked incredulous for a few seconds and then gave a defiant laugh.

'That's good, that really is! Do you know, I wanted to steal the picture? But there was no way it could be done.'

'Except in the way it was done. A copy substituted when it was sent to be cleaned and that copy hung on the wall at Monkbeggars Hall until it was removed during the fire scare at the last historical re-creation.'

'You really believe that?'

'It's a fact, a proven fact.'

'Well, it had nothing to do with me. I wish we *had* thought of it — it would have saved a great deal of hard graft.'

'Aren't you forgetting the two people who were killed to prevent the substitution coming to light?'

'I had nothing to do with it. You must believe me!'

'It's not just you I'm referring to; another name keeps cropping up in my inquiries — that of Richard Coates.'

173

'Rick had nothing to do with it either! You can't pin it on him!'

'I'm willing to give you the benefit of the doubt for now and to believe that you were ignorant of the fact that he was using you — '

'That's not true! You're making all this up. You have no proof!'

'Mr Coates was on the *Mercia* ferry the night that John Hargreaves was murdered.'

'He's admitted it? To you?' She gave herself away in her surprise.

'Thank you for corroborating it, Miss Hanson.'

'It was sheer coincidence that he happened to be on the ferry that night. It had nothing to do with the murder.'

'No? Then what was he doing?'

'He'd been over to Belgium fixing up about the trucks in Blankenberge and he took the opportunity, on the way back, to check out dock security.'

'That's what he told you? Dear me, things look very black against Mr Coates.'

'You're trying to trip me up! We had nothing to do with those murders and you can't prove otherwise! In fact, you can't charge us at all. We were picked up before we actually did anything.'

'I shouldn't be too sure of that, Miss Hanson. For starters, there is the little matter of a couple of hundred sacks and a stapling machine. I wonder if your father will press charges.'

Roland went up to the canteen intending to snatch a quick snack before interrogating Richard Coates again. He had barely sat down when DC Evans came in search of him.

'The Super wants you in his office — at once.'

'Hell! No peace for the wicked.' Roland looked down at his plate, where the grease was already congealing and the fried egg glared balefully up at him from a nest of curling rashers and baked beans.

'You look undernourished, Evans. Could you manage to consume this?'

Evans admitted that he could do it justice and slid into

174

his superior's place. Roland went down to Lacey's office.

'Ah, James, I thought we had lost you.' Lacey was pacing the floor looking as ill at ease and embarrassed as Roland had ever seen him.

'You didn't look far. I've been questioning our detainees right up to ten minutes ago.'

'I hope you made good use of it. They're being released.'

'Wh-a-at?'

'We haven't enough evidence to make any charges stick.'

'I can't believe I'm hearing this!' Roland fingered the stubble on his chin and glared at his chief. 'We can get them on any number of charges – Christ! They've admitted it!'

'Admitted WHAT? Some crack-brained, ill-conceived scheme that had no hope of succeeding? They were playing at Robin Hood – it wouldn't stand up in a court of law.'

'That's nonsense and you know it – '

'James,' Lacey cut in ominously, 'I'm not asking your opinion, I'm telling you.'

'But why?'

'There will be no complainant, for one thing.'

'You've seen the chief constable,' said Roland accusingly, running his fingers through his hair and wishing his eyes didn't feel like grit trays. 'I suppose one of his friends is involved?'

'Cool it, James. I don't have to tell you this, but for your ears only, the Home Office is involved.' Bob Lacey gazed at his irate officer inscrutably and laid a finger against his nose.

For a few seconds the two men's eyes locked. Then Roland blundered over to the window and stared out unseeingly, his shoulders hunched, his hands thrust deep into his pockets.

'Coates has just admitted that he was on the *Mercia* the night that John Hargreaves was murdered,' he threw over his shoulder.

'As were seven hundred other people; you'll have to do better than that.'

Roland swung round. 'I intend going through those charitable donations that he alleges financed the operation with a toothcomb. I'm sure we'll find a big discrepancy between what they actually received and what this little venture cost them.'

'If you come up with new evidence he can be picked up again. In the meantime, it'll be another thirty minutes or so before the CC arrives in person. I can give you that.'

'What's the point?' said Roland bitterly. 'Our anarchist friend will soon be killing himself laughing; I might do something I should regret.'

The sunshine nearly blinded Roland as he left the building and walked towards the car park. He felt angry and frustrated and, he realised as his stomach gave a hollow gurgle, very hungry; it was a long while since he had eaten. He couldn't face going back to the canteen and the comments of his colleagues; on the other hand, he didn't think his own home held much in the way of food. He had been far too busy recently to think of such a mundane thing as shopping for provisions. This was when he needed a good woman. His thoughts immediately flashed to Ginny and he glanced at his watch. Not quite eight o'clock. She would still be at home, breakfast on the table. He made a decision, and got into his car and manoeuvred through the early morning traffic in the direction of Croxton.

Although it was only four miles from Felstone, Croxton had retained its village identity, unlike Wallingford, the village where Mansfield lived, which lay between them and was rapidly being absorbed by the encroaching suburbs of the town. Croxton was sprawling and untidy and could never be called pretty, but it contained some charming old buildings and a Norman church that was mentioned in all the guidebooks on the area.

Ginny Dalton lived in an old brick and tile cottage in Duck Lane surrounded by a garden where nature seemed to have got out of control. This impression was created more by design than neglect. Ginny was an ardent conservationist and had worked hard to achieve her wildlife garden. Roland was reminded of this as he got out of the car and opened the garden gate. The yellowing foliage of long-dead daffodils straggled over long grass under the ancient apple trees. He thought of the neatly knotted clumps of bulbs that marched in rigid order across the flowerbeds in Mansfield's garden and decided that Ginny's approach was far better.

A cuckoo called from the nearby woods, mocking him with its metallic notes, and a blackbird, disturbed by his footsteps, flew up onto an overhead branch, flicked its tail and proclaimed his presence to the world. Ginny looked concerned as she opened the door to him.

'James! You look awful — are you all right?'

'I haven't had any sleep for over forty-eight hours. I've come to throw myself on your mercy and beg breakfast.'

'But of course! Come in and I'll get you some. Is anything the matter?'

'You could say. I feel like throwing in the towel, resigning from the force.'

'Are you serious? Or is it just that you're tired and hungry?'

'A combination of both. It's at times like this that I wonder how I ever conceived of the force being an attractive career.

'It does sound serious. Will it help to talk?'

'I must confide in someone. But don't let on what I'm going to tell you or I won't have to do the resigning myself.'

'Let's get some food inside you first. What do you fancy?'

'Anything that's going. Don't make a fuss.'

He lolled back in a chair and watched her busying herself in the kitchen. He wouldn't get a fry-up here, that was certain, but what she did provide — orange juice, muesli, scrambled egg and granary bread — more than made up for it.

'Where's Simon?'

'On his paper round.'

'Of course.' A thought struck him. 'Did you know he's been in trouble with the police?'

Ginny stared at him. 'Were you the one who arrested him?'

'Don't be ridiculous. He wasn't arrested, just served up to your Head to deal with. It had nothing to do with me, but you can be sure that I was told.'

'I'm sorry, James. I didn't mean to insinuate ...'

'Would it help if I had a word with him?'

177

'I honestly don't know.' She sighed and picked up the coffee pot. 'But you didn't come here to talk about Simon, did you?'

He gave her a brief outline of the previous night's happenings as he sipped his second cup of coffee. She listened wide-eyed. When he ground to a halt, she asked almost regretfully:

'So they nearly got away with it?'

'No way. We had the whole place staked out. If we hadn't blown our cover too early, we'd have caught them in the act. As it is, they're getting off scot-free.'

'But they failed in what they set out to do ...'

Something in her tone alerted him. 'You sound as if you're disappointed that they didn't succeed.'

She faced him, arms akimbo and her odd eyes, one hazel and one blue, fixed on him accusingly. 'Yes, I reckon I am. I wish they had brought it off. I think it was a marvellous idea and it's a great shame you prevented them from succeeding.'

'Oh, hell, I might have known you'd be on their side. Ginny, you can't take the law into your own hands even if you think you've got right on your side. This was a criminal conspiracy.'

'I don't see it like that.'

'Listen.' He tried to stifle his exasperation. 'Forget the ethics of the thing – there's more involved. Their ringleader is one of the chief suspects in my murder case.'

'Is that a fact? And is there a connection between the two?'

'There has to be. I've told you too much already, I may as well go the whole hog and fill you in with all the facts.'

In a few succinct sentences he told her about his theory that the two murders were committed to prevent the exposure of the Ter Borch painting at Monkbeggars Hall as a copy.

'You mean you really think that two people were killed because of a painting?'

'You yourself told me it would be worth a small fortune.'

'Well yes. So you think that this Richard Coates could be the culprit?'

'He's certainly near the top of my list and he's admitted

178

that he was on the *Mercia* ferry that night, but it could be someone known only to Lydia Cordingley who I have yet to come across. Of course, all the members of Mrs Calder-Brown's family figure on the list too; I wonder how many of them I shall discover regularly trip across from Felstone to the Continent.'

'Well, Hugh does, but he certainly didn't make the crossing Easter weekend.'

'Hugh? Do you mean Hugh Calder-Brown?' Roland snapped, suddenly wide awake.

'Yes.'

'You know him?'

'Yes, he's an old acquaintance of mine.'

'You never told me!'

'You never asked.'

They stared at each other across a sudden chasm of mis-understanding. Ginny attempted to bridge it.

'Look, James, this is ridiculous. I've known Hugh a long time and we occasionally go out together.'

'And when was the last time that this happened?' Roland asked ominously.

'Actually it was yesterday evening. We went to a lecture given by the Book League. Hugh knew that I'd be interested in the subject and he kindly invited me to join him.' And, as Roland said nothing: 'I do have a life of my own, you know, James; you don't surely expect me to sit at home every night twiddling my thumbs while you charge about on police business without sparing me a thought.'

'You're a free woman, Ginny. I'm just astonished that you've never mentioned him before.'

'I suppose I never thought him important enough. After all, I'm sure you haven't told me about all your casual friends. Not that I wish to know,' she hastened to add, remembering his previous reputation with women, 'but trust is the name of the game . . .'

'Oh, hell, Ginny! I'm not trying to pick a quarrel. Look, let's start again. Do you mind telling me what you meant when you said Calder-Brown hadn't been on the high seas over the Easter weekend?'

'You don't really suspect him of being involved in your murder inquiry, do you?'

'He's a prominent member of that family,' said Roland carefully. 'He's involved in that he figures largely in the scenario. I can't just ignore him, but perhaps what you're going to tell me will help to clear him from my inquiries.'

'He happened to mention that he'd been to an important book fair in Brussels the weekend before Easter and had picked up a bug there that had laid him low over the holiday weekend.'

This tallied with what Calder-Brown had himself told Roland.

'He told you this yesterday evening?'

'Yes, it just came up casually while ... while we were talking.' Ginny changed her mind at the last moment about telling him that Hugh had shown her some of the books that he had bought in Belgium. Now was when she should tell him about her visit to his flat, but she funked it, telling herself that it had been quite innocent and of no importance.

For his part, James was listening to her incredulously. While he had spent an evening in discomfort, exposed to the elements at Felstone Docks, she had been entertained by one of his chief suspects.

'What do you know of his financial standing?'

'James!' she protested.

'I need to know. If you can tell me it'll save poking around among his other friends. It's all the same in the long run — we'll get the information we're seeking — but you can save me valuable time.'

'I wouldn't call him well off but he's not impoverished either. He moans about having to sell books he would like to keep in his collection but I think he's reasonably prosperous.'

She remembered the drugs. Drugs cost money ...

She almost spoke out, then checked as she realised that she couldn't tell James about her suspicions without revealing that she had been in his flat and in his bedroom to boot.

'Yes?' Roland noticed that she hesitated.

'Nothing. It's difficult to tell from appearances; if he were up to his eyes in debt I don't imagine he would advertise it.'

180

'No. I suppose he's in line to inherit Monkbeggars Hall? I don't think he's on very good terms with any of his family but presumably it's entailed.'

'I wouldn't know, but I should think it would be a millstone round his neck; think about death duties − no, they're not called that nowadays are they?'

'And the picture would be part of the inheritance.'

'Which you say has already been stolen?'

'Yes, it doesn't add up, does it? Why go to all the trouble of flogging the picture when it's going to fall into your lap in a few years' time anyway − unless you had suffered a severe cash crisis? On the other hand, I suppose Mrs Calder-Brown could leave the picture to whom she chooses; there's the daughter to consider and also her granddaughter Lucy, who, by the way, is cohabiting with our Richard Coates.'

'James, I know you have to entertain these suspicions, but you're talking about a friend of mine. Believe me, Hugh could never have murdered those two people. He's the sort of person who would faint at the sight of blood. I can imagine him coming to grief at the hands of a betrayed husband or boyfriend, but he's the type to quietly efface himself at the first sign of any trouble or unpleasantness.'

There was the sound of whistling outside the back door and a crash as a bicycle was leaned against a wall.

'Simon's back.' Ginny glanced at the clock. 'I must get going. Are you on your way home or have you got to go back to the station?'

'I've been told to take a couple of hours off.' Roland got to his feet and picked up his jacket. 'Thanks for the breakfast.'

'You don't have to go just because I have to rush off. Stay here and make yourself another coffee and help yourself to the bathroom; have a shower and a shave. I presume I can trust you to lock up safely when you go?' She grinned at him. He swept her into his arms and buried his face in her mass of hair.

'Isn't it a bit early for that sort of thing?' said a disgusted voice. They moved apart guiltily as Simon burst into the room.

'You've taken a long while this morning,' said his mother. 'You'd better get a move on.'

'I'm hungry, is there anything else to eat?'

She indicated the table. He flung himself onto a stool and upended the empty muesli packet over a bowl.

'Someone's finished it!' he protested, staring fixedly at Roland.

'There's a packet of cornflakes in the pantry.' Ginny picked up the dirty crockery and dumped it in the sink. 'I'm just going to get ready.' She made for the stairs and called down from halfway up, 'When you've done Simon, open the garage doors.'

'I'll do that.' Roland was glad of the opportunity to escape Simon's accusing eyes. He knew he should say something to him about his escapade in the shopping precinct but now was neither the time nor place, not while he was functioning under par and the boy in such a belligerent mood.

A short while later mother and son were on their way to school and Roland went back into the house. The cat appeared from nowhere and wound her way between his legs miaowing piteously.

'I'm quite sure your mistress wouldn't have gone off without feeding you,' he addressed her sternly. 'You're trying it on.' Faience continued to yowl and weave herself in and out, conveying that she couldn't possibly last the day unless he took pity on her. He succumbed and, finding an opened tin of cat food in the fridge, spooned some of it into a bowl. He eyed the dirty pans and dishes in the sink. He ought to do the washing-up, it was the least he could do, but first he must have forty winks. He subsided onto the sofa and closed his eyes.

It was not long enough even with his legs hanging over the arm; he was uncomfortable and yet too lazy to move. He thought of Ginny's bed upstairs, probably still warm from her body and scented with the perfume she used, and he drifted off into a sleep populated with erotic dreams. At some point he was aware of a weight on his chest and a rumbling purr.

'A video's been handed in which I think you lot will be interested in.'

Mansfield took the package from the desk sergeant and raised his eyebrows questioningly.

'Home movies 1990 style,' the uniformed officer continued, 'filmed aboard the *Mercia* ferry the night your stiff got his comeuppance.'

'I don't believe it! You're putting me on.'

'It's for real, but don't get excited, they didn't catch the murder on tape. Some young tearaways were celebrating a twenty-first birthday on the crossing and one of them attempted to film the party.'

'So why has it taken so long to reach us?'

'I gather they were on a right old bender and your amateur film buff was so tanked up the resulting footage is one unholy muddle. Apparently he nearly scrubbed it but on running it through again recently thinks he may have unintentionally captured the murdered man on film.'

'Then we'd better have a dekko.'

While Evans was setting it up, Mansfield went in search of Roland. He drew a blank and was preparing to run the video through in front of the rest of the team when Roland walked in.

'Where have you been? I put out a call for you but you weren't answering and you weren't at home.'

'I'm here now. What have you got for me? You sound like the cat that's swallowed the canary.'

Mansfield explained and was gratified to see the excitement that flashed across his superior's face.

'Don't say we've got our break at last. OK, let her roll.'

'Hell! I feel seasick just watching this,' Mansfield grumbled a little later as they strained to make some sense of the images flickering across the screen. The footage so far had consisted mainly of what looked like a lot of drunken yobs, lurching and tilting across the screen in distorted close-ups.

'It was a very rough night, let's give them the benefit of the doubt.'

'We're wasting our time. No wonder he didn't want to bring it to our attention.'

'Hang on, it's getting better, he's widening his scope.'

The camera zoomed round the bar area, flashing from one group of people to another. They saw, fleetingly, a couple stretched out on a seat, the woman with tightly closed eyes resting her head on her man's shoulder; a family group where

183

a toddler was being sick over his father's knee; a cluster of middle-aged men attempting to down their drinks with sickly smiles on their faces; and two elderly women huddled in a corner, trying to ignore the mayhem around them. There was a sudden kaleidoscope of whirling shapes as if the cameraman had spun round in a circle and then he focused shakily on a section of seating alongside the wall opposite the bar.

'Hold it! There, look!'

A pale, middle-aged man leaned forward to speak to someone out of sight, a glass clutched in a shaking hand.

'That's him, isn't it?'

'Yes! He looks hardly any better than he did after he was skewered!'

'Run it through again.'

They watched closely as John Hargreaves leaned forward again to speak to his hidden companion. Just as this figure was about to be revealed the camera darted away and zoomed in on the barman.

'Hell, just our luck! If only the camera had stayed with him for a few more seconds!'

'At least we know that he was with someone or had struck up an acquaintance with someone on board. And, as that person has never come forward, we must assume it was the murderer.'

'Do we have any idea at what time during the crossing this was filmed?'

'I doubt he could tell day from night, the state he was in.'

The camera was panning in again on the birthday celebrants. As a bleary, inanely grinning, bespectacled face flashed across the screen for the umpteenth time, Mansfield swore he would remember it to his dying day.

'Wait! That man in the background, going through the door. Go back!'

The sequence was run through again and Roland exclaimed in triumph, 'I'm not imagining things, am I? Is that who I think it is?'

'Nigel Hanson! It's Nigel Hanson!' said Mansfield in astonishment.

Chapter Ten

'Evans, *you* checked his alibi with his fancy bit!'

William Evans flushed to the roots of his carroty hair and turned a look of outraged innocence on his chief.

'Olive Durrant. She corroborated his statement, they spent Easter weekend together.'

'Yes, Evans, but where?'

'I don't know, sir. She didn't say.'

'And you didn't ask her?'

'I caught up with her during opening hours. She was behind the bar of the Laurel Bush — that's the pub where she lives and works. It was very busy, she didn't have much time to chat.'

'*She* didn't have much time? May I remind you, Evans, that you *are* a police officer, though I despair of ever making a detective out of you. What information did you manage to glean, between pints?'

'She admitted that she was a close friend of Nigel Hanson and that they had spent the weekend together, unbeknown to his wife,' said Evans stubbornly.

'And would you care to furnish us with a description of the lady?'

'She's a bit long in the tooth.' Evans spoke as if no one over the age of thirty should be indulging in sexual activity, and Roland looked at him suspiciously. 'But she's quite attractive in a rather flamboyant sort of way; vivacious and with an answer for everything.'

Your typical barmaid, Mansfield thought, and just the sort that Hanson would go for; the complete opposite of his wife.

'Well, it sounds as if she's been perjuring herself for him. I wonder how she'll talk herself out of this. Come on.' Roland got to his feet.

'We're going to see her now?'

'No, we'll tackle Nigel Hanson first. Mansfield and I will go together. You can accompany us in an official car.'

'Are you getting a warrant?' asked the young detective constable.

'Don't be imbecilic,' Roland snapped. 'I'm not going to arrest him – *yet*. Just going to scare the arse off him.'

They met Nigel Hanson on the approach road to the home farm at Barndon. As they turned in through the entrance he swung in behind them from the opposite direction in his Range-Rover. Roland stopped the car and he had perforce to draw in as well. He stuck his head out of the window looking alarmed, but when he saw who was in the anonymous car blocking his way his alarm turned to irritation.

'Inspector – er – Mansfield. You got me worried for a moment. I thought something was wrong.' He indicated the panda car driven by Evans that had pulled in behind him.

'Detective Inspector *Roland* and this is Detective *Sergeant* Mansfield,' said Roland pleasantly, 'We have a few more questions to put to you. Shall we go up to the house?'

'What do you want now? I've told you all I know.'

'I don't think that's strictly true, sir. Of course, if you prefer to come down to the station . . .?'

Hanson looked worried again. 'Come along to the office. But would you mind not driving right into the yard? I don't want my wife alarmed.'

He's a cool customer, Roland thought, or else he's even more frightened of his wife than he is of complicity in a murder case.

The three policemen parked at the top of the driveway and followed Hanson into the farm office. He flung himself down in the chair behind his desk and grimaced at them.

'Well, what do you want to know?'

'I asked you before, Mr Hanson, how you had spent the Easter weekend.'

'Yes, and I told you that I had spent it in the company of my lady friend – and I know that you checked with her,' he added.

'I think perhaps the wrong question was asked, or, should I say, we didn't ask the right one. Where were you over Easter?'

'But I've told you, I was with Mrs Durrant.'

'Where?'

'In Newmarket, where my wife thought I was.'

Roland sighed. 'Mr Hanson, you're lying. Please don't waste any more of my time. I ask you again, where were you?'

'What's the point of repeating myself if you won't believe what I'm saying? Where do you think I was?'

'On the *Mercia* ferry making the crossing from Zeebrugge to Felstone on Easter Monday.' Hanson gasped and flushed a mottled puce colour but still tried to bluster. 'This is preposterous. Whoever told you that is lying!'

'The camera doesn't lie. You were captured on film.'

He collapsed like a pricked balloon, his confidence fled, and said in a hoarse whisper, 'It isn't true ...'

'It is true, Mr Hanson. A fellow passenger was making a video of the journey and you were caught on film. What have you to say to that?'

'All right, Inspector, I *was* on the *Merica* – but there's no reason why I shouldn't have been there.' He had a minor flash of defiance. 'I took Olive to Bruges for the weekend. I can give you the name of the hotel, I'm sure they'll verify it. You can check up on me.'

'Oh, I shall, sir. But it's not the time you spent in Bruges that I'm interested in; it's the return crossing when John Hargreaves was murdered.'

'I know nothing about that! You can't pin that on me!'

'Have I suggested that? I want to know if you saw or heard anything suspicious.'

Hanson was somewhat mollified. 'We spent all night in our cabin. It was a very rough crossing.'

'Was it booked in your name?'

There had certainly been no cabin booked in the name of Hanson or they would have picked it up before.

'No. Mr and Mrs George White.'

'I see. And you spent the entire journey in this cabin?'

'Well, I may have made a short sortie out at some point. I believe I went to the bar to get a glass of soda water for Olive, she felt very ill. Well, I must have done, mustn't I, if somebody filmed me?'

'But that was all?'

'Yes — and you can't prove otherwise.'

Mansfield took over the questioning. 'Mr Hanson, did you recognise any of your fellow passengers?'

'No, of course — ' He checked himself as if some memory were stirring, then shook his head. 'No, the ship was full and we were glad that we'd got a cabin. We were trying to avoid people and, as I said, Olive was feeling poorly.'

'You weren't affected by the bad weather?'

'I wasn't feeling too good, I can assure you. Whoever killed that man must have had strong sea legs.' He leaned back in his chair, confidence returning with every minute. 'Is there anything else you want to know, Inspector? I'm a busy man.'

'Just a few more points. Why didn't you tell us you were on the *Mercia* that night?'

'Would you have in my place?' Hanson tried a man-to-man act. 'I didn't want anyone to know about my dirty weekend and when I knew you were trying to connect up that murder with the family I suppose I panicked.'

'Very foolish of you. It was bound to come out and for us to find out as we have has made us more suspicious.'

'I was hoping no one would ever have to know.'

'How does the quotation go? 'Oh what a tangled web we weave when first we practise to deceive.'' Remember that, Mr Hanson. Now, to change the subject, I should like the names and addresses of the two people with whom you share your racehorse.'

Hanson looked outraged. 'What have they got to do with it? You're harassing innocent people! Anyway, they know about Olive.'

'If you are innocent, Mr Hanson, I'm sure that you'll welcome the opportunity of helping us to eliminate you from our inquiries.'

He gave them the information grudgingly. 'Is that all?'

'Are you a betting man?'

He looked flustered. 'I have the odd flutter.'

'Would you mind giving me the name of your bookie?'

'I don't have one. I place the odd bet on the course, that sort of thing.'

'Really?' Roland left him in no doubt that he disbelieved him, but he did not press the point. He got to his feet. 'I should like you to come to the station and see this video.'

'What, now?'

'Just a formality, sir. I don't want you thinking we're manufacturing evidence.'

'I'm willing to take your word for it,' he said eagerly. 'I know you have to do your job.'

'I think it would be in both our interests for you to see this video. DC Evans will drive you across and bring you back.'

'But my wife ... what's she going to say?'

'Do you have to account to your wife for every minute of your day?'

'No, of course not. All right then, but it had better not take long.'

Roland watched impassively while Hanson was driven away by Evans, and then turned to his sergeant. 'And now we'll hie over to Newmarket and Mrs Olive Durrant before he has a chance to phone her and fix an alibi.'

'I wondered why you insisted on Evans coming in a second car.'

'There's method in my madness, Patrick my friend. Let's be on our way. Rather than double back on our tracks we'll drive cross-country and pick up the A45 farther along.'

The gales of the previous night had blown themselves out completely. The sky was a clear cerulean blue scribbled on by vapour trails from an unseen plane and the strong acid greens and citrus yellows of the burgeoning trees and hedgerows hurt the eyes. They drove down country lanes so narrow that two vehicles could not pass and followed twisting roads up and down through the heart of the country.

'Whoever says Suffolk is flat doesn't know what he or she is talking about,' said Roland, negotiating a hidden dip

189

in the road and a hump-backed bridge shrouded in willow fronds.

'Do you think he's our man?'

'If he is we're going to have one hell of a job proving it.'

'Did you get the impression that he did see someone he knew that night?'

'It could have been Richard Coates, though if he had seen him I should have thought that he'd have been only to glad to drop him in it; there can't be much love lost between them.'

'Maybe they're in it together?'

'I suppose it's possible but I can't see the connection.'

'Maybe the entire family is in cahoots together.'

'Not Mrs Calder-Brown. She must have thought the picture hanging on her walls was genuine or she'd never have agreed to loan it to the Langdale Gallery.'

'That's true.'

By this time they were crossing the rolling Newmarket Downs. The rich grassland stretched as far as the eye could see, broken every so often by a stud farm, the buildings pristine and prosperous-looking, their acres enclosed by neat wooden railings.

'They remind me of a toy farmyard that I had as a boy,' said Roland. 'My father made it himself. He bought the animals, of course, but he made the farm buildings and painted a large board to represent different types of fields and knocked up a wooden fence to go round it.'

'They're certainly an improvement on your barbed-wire strands. I wonder if Hanson keeps his racehorse at a place like these?'

'I shouldn't think so. I'd have thought these owners were in a much higher income bracket.'

'Maybe that's why he needed a hundred grand.'

'He had a motive and he certainly had the opportunity to commit the first murder, but how to get any concrete evidence is another matter. And how does Coates fit into the scene? He had a motive too and was also there. I can't believe his conspiracy had nothing to do with our case. And

190

then there's Calder-Brown; I certainly haven't crossed him off our list of suspects.'

'I wonder what this Olive Durrant will have to say for herself.'

'We'll soon find out, we must be nearly there. What's the time? Nearly twelve thirty. I tell you what we'll do, we'll have a pub lunch in the Laurel Bush and size up the lady before we talk to her.'

The Laurel Bush was an old pub with pink-washed walls and a thatched roof. An annexe had been built onto one side but it blended in well with the original; cartwheels were propped up against the walls and there was a large tub on either side of the main door planted with what Roland took to be laurel bushes. There was a garden at the back containing bench-and-table sets, swings and a see-saw, and the courtyard was set out with tables and chairs. There were several customers availing themselves of these, enjoying the spring sunshine as they sipped their drinks.

The two men had to duck to avoid low beams as they stepped inside and the sudden gloom after the brilliant light outside made them blink. There was a menu chalked up on a blackboard near the bar; a young woman presided behind this bar and another one was clearing dirty crockery from an empty table near the window. Surely neither of these two was Olive Durrant? Roland thought. They looked far too young. It would be just their luck if she were off duty that day. They placed their order and went over to the seat by the window. The pub was popular and doing a good midday trade. Mansfield slipped off his jacket and went to get their pints.

'I tried to get a look inside the kitchen door,' he said, carefully setting the glasses down on the table. 'It sounds as if there are several people working in there. Is our dame likely to be preparing the food?'

'I shouldn't have thought so, but who knows, if they're busy. She's supposed to be the landlord's niece, she probably doesn't work regular hours.'

They settled down to wait for their food and Mansfield had time to smoke a pipe before its arrival. Just as the young woman serving it was bringing their cutlery over to the table, the door leading to the garden opened and an older woman swept in.

'Number fourteen haven't had their tartar sauce, Katy,' she said to the assistant, 'and number nine want coffee.' Her gaze swept round the room, checking that everything was under control. 'I'll take over in here while you see to outside.'

'This looks like our Mrs Durrant. We're in luck after all.'

'Not bad, is she?' Mansfield breathed in appreciation.

Olive Durrant was older than they had expected her to be; not much younger than Hanson, Roland reckoned, but she was a handsome woman. Her titian hair owed more to the bottle than to nature but she had kept her figure and was dressed soberly and neatly in a grey suit with a white frilly blouse. Not the brassy type that Evans had given him to believe, but as she walked close to their table he could see that she had been heavy-handed with the make-up. She was wearing several rings on her wedding finger and he caught a whiff of expensive perfume as she passed.

'Well, I can't say I blame him,' said Mansfield, tucking into his steak pie. 'She's clearly an improvement on his missus as far as looks go. I wonder what she sees in him.'

'A gentleman farmer with interests in the racing world? She probably thinks he's a good catch?'

'Do you think she knows that he's married?'

'I shouldn't think there are any flies on her, she looks a woman of the world.'

They observed her closely as they ate their meal and she must have had her eye on them because she came over as soon as they had laid aside their plates.

'I hope everything was to your satisfaction? Do you wish to order desserts?'

'No thank you, but we'd like a few words with you; Mrs Durrant, isn't it? We're police officers.' He showed her his ID card but she barely glanced at it.

'What's the old fool done now? I suppose he's got the dates mixed up for the licence extensions?'

'This has nothing to do with the pub.'

'Sorry. My uncle's getting a bit forgetful in his old age;

192

but I mustn't tell *you* that, must I, or you'll revoke his licence? Well, what can I do for you, gentlemen?'

'Is there somewhere more private than this where we can talk?'

She looked at him shrewdly. 'You'd better come through to our private parlour.'

She had a few words with the young woman behind the bar and then led the way through a door at the back of the counter into a small, comfortably furnished room. She indicated the armchairs and sat herself down gracefully on the sofa, stretching her legs out so that they appeared to their best advantage, encased in sheer black tights and high-heeled black patent shoes.

'Well, what is this all about?'

'One of my officers interviewed you recently about events that took place over Easter weekend.'

For a few seconds she looked blank, then her face cleared. 'A young ginger-haired lad. My, but he had a strong Welsh accent.'

She herself spoke with a pleasant Norfolk burr. Whatever chicanery Hanson was involved in, Olive Durrant knew nothing about it. She showed no apprehension, only mild curiosity.

'I told him that I'd spent the weekend with Nigel Hanson. I am not ashamed of it, officer; we're adult people and what we do is of no concern to anyone else.'

His wife wouldn't agree with that, Roland thought. Out loud he said, 'I don't believe you told him that you spent the weekend in Bruges?'

'No, I don't believe I did. Is that important?'

'I understand you had a bad crossing on the way back?'

'You can say that again! I was as sick as the proverbial toad. Not very romantic at all, I'm afraid.'

'And was Mr Hanson similarly affected?'

'No, Nigel is made of sterner stuff. He spent half the night running round after me.'

'Oh?'

'He had this idea that if I could only eat or drink something I should feel better, but I couldn't keep anything down. I just wanted to die, believe me.'

193

Roland did. In her artless, casual way she had blown Hanson's alibi wide open. He shifted ground. 'Tell me, Mrs Durrant, did you spend the entire weekend in each other's company?'

'What do you mean?'

'Could Mr Hanson have had a meeting with someone in Bruges in which you were not concerned?'

'No, of course not. He hasn't told you otherwise, has he?'

Roland said nothing.

A frown puckered her smooth forehead. 'Nigel's not in any serious trouble, is he?'

'Just routine enquiries, ma'am.'

'Well, I can assure you, when I'm around he doesn't have time for anyone else.'

Roland could well believe this. 'Thank you, Mrs Durrant, you've corroborated our evidence. Just one thing, do you know anything about this racehorse Mr Hanson part owns?'

'Blue Boy?' He'll never get his money back on him. They're like schoolboys, playing at racing.' She smiled reminiscently. 'But I suppose it's a harmless hobby.'

'A very expensive one, I should have thought.'

'Yes, I never did know where the cash came from. His wife keeps him on a very tight financial rein; he never has much to throw away on me.'

I wonder what Hanson would say if he knew how she had damned him, Roland thought, as they took their leave and drove back to Felstone.

The next morning Roland held a briefing in his office. After getting back to Felstone the previous day he had sent Mansfield home for a well-earned rest and had himself left a short while later. He had felt that there was nothing further they could do that day and he had not wanted to hang around the station where the empty cells mocked him, reminding him of the important suspect who had, for the time being anyway, slipped out of his reach.

'I can't believe,' said Roland, regarding his colleagues ranged on the other side of his desk, 'that Nigel Hanson would be so involved in the racing world as to buy himself into a racehorse syndicate if he were not a betting man. I want you, Evans, to check out all the betting shops in the area to see if he does have an account or is known; that means at Newmarket and Woodford as well as here in Felstone. If that draws a blank you'll have to start on the bookies. There's racing tomorrow at Newmarket. I want to know what sort of money is slipping through his fingers, whether he's in debt – you know the sort of thing. Take Pomroy with you.' He nodded at the young constable who was on secondment to the CID. 'Mansfield, I want you to check out his two racing partners. Try and do it tactfully, but I want to know how much he had to put up for his gee-gee and just when this transaction took place. Have a good sniff around; are his co-owners crooked or just businessmen looking for a little excitement or trying to work a tax fiddle? And have they bought a pig in a poke and are pouring money away on a nonstarter?'

'You don't want to do this yourself?' Mansfield asked, surprised at the extent of his senior's delegation. Roland usually liked to keep all important leads firmly in his own hands.

'I've been thinking about this carefully and I think it's got to be tackled from a different angle. We have two suspects who we know had the opportunity and motives to kill John Hargreaves, but at the moment I can't see how we're ever going to get enough evidence to pin it on either of them. So I'm going to concentrate on the second murder. I think the answer may lie with Lydia Cordingley. If we can just find something to tie her in with one of them, then we'll really be getting somewhere. And if our murderer is unknown to us but was connected with her – well, we haven't tried hard enough to suss it out from that viewpoint. I'm going to dig into things that end.'

After his colleagues had left, Roland reflected on how little they had been able to turn up concerning Lydia Cordingley's life style. Like John Hargreaves, she had been a solitary person, living on her own and apparently not involved in any social circle. If the evidence was to be believed she had had, at some time, a lover, but whether this affair had been going on at the time of her murder or whether the murderer had been her lover they did not know. As no one had come forward to admit to having been her intimate friend, Roland was inclined to believe the latter, but there could be some perfectly innocent explanation; the man could be married or naturally reticent about the limelight and suspicion that would inevitably fall on him.

He sifted through the reports of the house-to-hourse inquiry that had been carried out in the Helsby district. No one had remembered seeing a vehicle parked regularly in the vicinity of her cottage, but as it was so far off the beaten track, at least a mile and a half from the village, this was not surprising. She had bought some of her supplies at the local shop but had used her specially adapted car to bulk-buy at the supermarket in the nearest town and to obtain the materials necessary to her professional work.

An enigma, and yet ... Roland frowned. She hadn't known that she was going to die, she had been struck down during the course of a normal day, so there must have been evidence lying around to give a clue to her private life. Had they overlooked anything? If she had had a regular lover there must surely have been some trace of his presence in the place? It was time he had another poke round her cottage.

He went out to his car and drove to Helsby.

Lucy Hanson scowled down at the sheet of paper on which she was compiling a list of the people who had contributed to their project and the amounts given. She had kept records of a sort but the catalogue was by no means complete. The money had come in from so many different sources and much of it by the efforts of others. So far she had accounted for over £400 but she had realised, as she had sat down to do her sums, that she had really no idea how much the operation had actually cost. As the money had come in, in dribs and drabs, it had been passed on to Rick, who had always been complaining that there was not enough cash in hand to do this and that.

She sighed and scribbled down another donation as it came to mind. She knew that the police would follow up their demand to see the accounts. That damned inspector, so arrogant and sarcastic, determined to catch them out.

Why, oh, why had they been so unlucky? All those months of planning and perfecting the scheme, everything worked out to the last little detail, nothing left to chance — and then the police had actually been waiting for them! Going over it in her mind, she could cry with disappointment and frustration. And she would bear the bruises of that short scuffle for many a week. They had been rounded up like criminals and herded off to the police station ... and she had been put in a cell with Netty!

For a few minutes she gave her imagination full rein, thinking of all the things she would like to do to Netty. And to make matters worse, she knew that the blame, as that copper had suggested, would be laid at her door; she had recruited Netty. The only thing that had kept her sane during that long night had been the thought that something might be salvaged from the situation; the resulting publicity would surely rock the Establishment. The press would pounce on the story and scream it out in headlines an inch high and she was sure that they would get massive support from the public — possibly enough to twist the arm of authority and get the grain released for humanitarian purposes. But then, after hours of questioning, they had suddenly been released, bundled out of the back door, as it were. The whole thing stank. They were too much of an embarrassment and pressure had been applied from above to hush the whole thing up — that was obvious.

Lucy threw the pen down on the table and mooched round the room. After their release she had wanted to proclaim their situation to the world, had tried to insist that the media be alerted, but Rick had pulled the plug on that. He had explained that if there was a cover-up going on the press would be nobbled anyway and it was in their best interests to keep quiet. Whose best interests? said a nasty little voice insider her brain and a voice replied 'Rick's'. In her thoughts she raced to his defence. It was only natural that if the police were trying to link him with those dreadful murders he would wish to lie low. They hadn't an atom of proof, it was just that they had no leads at all and had picked on Rick because he had happened to be on the *Mercia* ferry that night.

What actually had happened that night? Rick had been

remarkably reticent about it. He was a very evasive character, you never knew what was going on behind that mask that he presented to the world. She realised that she really knew very little about him. She had been flattered when he had taken up with her and kidded herself that they met on an equal footing, but had he really been manipulating her, as that bloody policeman had suggested?

This was crazy, she told herself angrily. It was playing into the hands of the fuzz. They were hoping to drive a wedge between them and start up nasty suspicions like hares. Rick was a fine man, he cared about his less fortunate fellow humans.

The wardrobe door was ajar and as she paced the floor she caught her wrist on its edge. She winced and slammed it shut with her knee. There was a thud and the door shot open again as a large bundle of clothes that had been wedged precariously on a shelf fell to the floor. They were the costumes that she and Rick used for the historical re-creations. Muttering under her breath, she bent down and gathered them up. She started to shake them out and refold them. There was a clatter as she held up Rick's ragged shirt and jerkin and a dagger that had been tucked inside fell to the floor.

She picked it up and examined it. It was old and discoloured but wickedly sharp; had it come from the kitchens of Monkbeggars Hall? She tried to remember whether she had seen it on Rick's person during the last re-creation; he had certainly had an axe about him. A knife such as this had been used to kill those two murder victims. She stared at it mesmerised, trying to quell the horrible suspicions that suddenly rose to mind.

A voice from behind her startled her so much that the dagger slipped from her nerveless fingers and thudded against the wardrobe door.

'Just what do you think you're doing with that?'

She spun round and when she saw the figure so dangerously still, menace glittering in his dark eyes, she gasped and croaked:

'Rick! I didn't hear you come in . . .'

Chapter Eleven

Lydia Cordingley's cottage could in no way be called pictur-
esque, Roland decided as he parked the car outside the gate
and advanced up the path. It had once been two dwellings,
labourers' tied cottages dating from the turn of the century,
and they had been knocked into one with little care for the
aesthetic appearance. One of the front entrances had been
bricked up and no attempt made to conceal this fact; the
outline of the doorway was clearly visible and the bricks
used did not match the rest of the house. It had a slate roof,
unusual in this part of Suffolk, and the old bumby, which
had housed the sole sanitary arrangements for the labourer
and his extended family, still stood at the bottom of the
garden, leaning at a dangerous angle, its green-mossed door
rotted and sagging. The modern studio clapped onto the side
of the cottage looked totally out of place.

Roland surveyed the garden. An attempt had been made
to cultivate the part nearest the building; there was a patch
of lawn and several flowerbeds where the burgeoning herbaceous plants vied for space with the dying spring bulbs,
but the vegetable plot was neglected and overgrown, apart
from a row of purple sprouting broccoli that was bolting
into yellow flower. From this standpoint he could appreciate
just how isolated the cottage was. It lay in a hollow, and
the hill sloping away in the direction of the village and the
thicket of trees curving round the other side of the property
effectively hid it from view. She could have entertained half
the neighbourhood, Roland thought, and no one would have
been any the wiser.

Once inside, he poked around trying to find some trace of her unknown lover, with singular lack of success. She had kept scrupulous accounts of her business transactions. Every restoration she had carried out had been noted in meticulous detail and they had followed up each and every one. None of her clients had had any cause for complaint; the work had been carried out competently and returned safely. No other copies hung in place of originals on the walls of unsuspecting people's homes; the Ter Borch painting appeared to be the only copy she had ever done. And why had she done that?

Someone must have had a hold over her, and who better than her mysterious lover? She had been a plain, crippled woman in her forties who could not ever have had many admirers, just the sort to be swept off her feet by a plausible rogue. She had probably been grateful to him for his attentions and could have been persuaded to almost anything to hold on to this attachment. Oh yes, Roland thought, it was easy to work out these theories but it brought him no nearer to finding out who this person was; she had left no clues to her private life.

Her bedroom had revealed a wardrobe of neat, unfussy clothes, functional rather than decorative; there had been no glamorous undies, no hidden taste for the exotic, and her reading matter had been very run-of-the-mill, a couple of romances by a popular exponent of the genre, a spy thriller and several armchair travel books. She had also had a collection of art books, both technical and decorative, and he ran his eye over these as he scanned the bookshelves. Next to them, on top of a china cabinet, was a photograph of two people whom he assumed to be the dead woman's parents. Apparently they had been killed in a plane crash when she was in her early teens. She had no brothers or sisters or any other relations as far as they had been able to ascertain.

She must have led a lonely life, he mused, with only the dog for company. A photograph of this dog stood beside the other one; a black, tan and white Jack Russell, its head cocked jauntily to one side, its jaws held half open so that it looked as if it were smiling. The dog ... Roland stared at the photograph thoughtfully. Had they overlooked something there? He had been told that it had been put down because of its appalling injuries, but they had never followed this up. An idea glimmered at the back of his mind and he let himself out of the cottage and went in search of PC Morton, the local bobby.

'Yes, Paul Bulstrode sent for the vet as soon as he saw him. The poor little bugger had been clobbered so hard that he was partly paralysed, had literally dragged himself over there on two legs.'

'That's the farmer, her nearest neighbour?'

'Yes, at Manor Farm, you passed it on the way here, sir.'

Stephen Morton had been having his elevenses when Roland called at the police house and he had been invited in to share this snack. Mrs Morton, young and newly wed, had been flustered at the prospect of a CID inspector entering her kitchen, but Morton was a phlegmatic man, at ease with everyone and not bothered by the hierarchy of the force. He carefully selected a second biscuit and pushed the plate towards Roland, who asked:

'What time was this?'

'It turned up just after the evening milking session. He thought it had been injured in a road accident. He called the vet and while they were waiting for him to arrive his wife tried to phone Miss Cordingley but, of course, there was no reply.'

'Who is the local vet?'

'A Gregory Daniels. Has his surgery at Woodford. He's in partnership with two other chaps.'

'Did you see the dog?'

'Not till after it had been put down. After Daniels had put it out of its misery he realised that its injuries hadn't been caused by a vehicle. They couldn't raise Miss Cordingley on the phone and they began to get alarmed. I happened to be passing by just as they set out to go over to her house — and you know the rest.'

'I must speak with this Gregory Daniels. Where is he likely to be at this time of day?'

'You may catch him at his surgery.' Morton consulted his watch. 'Unless he's on call and out on an emergency. Shall I give him a buzz, sir?'

While Morton was phoning, Roland tried to draw out his wife on the subject of local gossip. It transpired that Lynn Morton worked part-time in the local newsagent's and was aptly placed to hear any rumours going the rounds. She admitted that the whole district had been set on its ear by the murder.

'Nothing like this has ever happened here before,' she blurted out. 'The worst Stephen has had to deal with has been traffic incidents and the time old Mrs Potter was found dead in her house – she'd had a fall and died of hypothermia ...' She faltered to a halt, wondering whether her remarks were selling her husband short.

Roland tried to ease her embarrassment by changing the subject. 'Did you know Lydia Cordingley at all?'

'I'd seen her about, but she didn't mix much with the village folk, she kept herself to herself.'

Now, where had he heard that phrase recently? Roland thought and remembered that the same words had been said of John Hargreaves. Two people of similar character and both killed by the same person.

Morton came back into the room.

'He's out on his rounds at the moment and his receptionist is not sure where he can be contacted, but he'll be back for afternoon surgery at three o'clock. You should catch him then if you call in just before it starts.'

Roland made a note of the vet's address and thanked Lynn Morton for the coffee.

'By the way, has there been much panic among the villagers since the local incident room was dismantled? Are they frightened that the murderer may strike again?'

'There was concern at first, as you know from the reports, sir, but now the general opinion seems to be that it was someone she knew, a private dispute that got out of hand.'

'I think general opinion may be right, for once.'

The waiting room was austere and clinical. Rows of chairs lined two of the white walls and a notice board on the wall near the surgery door advertised local pet shows, kennels, catteries and all manner of veterinary treatment. There was a pervading smell of antiseptic and ether, so strong that Roland felt his

202

nostrils pricking as he sat awaiting the vet's return. He had been told by the receptionist on arrival that Gregory Daniels was out on an emergency case over on a farm near Croxton and she couldn't say how long he was likely to be.

By the time the vet returned, the waiting room was filling up, a couple of retrievers, kept on a tight rein by their respective owners, crouched on the floor and regarded each other warily; a young mongrel puppy yapped and trembled on its owner's lap; and from a cat basket came the occasional piercing yowl of a protesting Siamese that set the dogs whining and produced an echoing cry from somewhere in the depths of the building.

A door slammed and Roland heard the murmur of voices and the gushing of a tap. He got up and went through the door marked SURGERY, shutting it firmly behind him. A large, untidy-looking man, whose fair hair was standing on end, was sluicing his hands and arms at the sink in the corner and looked up in surprise.

'Detective Inspector Roland, Felstone CID.' Roland showed him his ID card.

'Jenny said the police wanted a word with me. I hadn't realised it was the CID. Is it important – can it wait?' He indicated the waiting room with a nod of his head.

'I'm a busy man, too. I need some information and it is urgent.'

'Will it take long?'

Roland made no reply.

'Oh, well . . . ' He crossed the room and poked his head through the other doorway. 'Jenny, try and get hold of Keith to cover for me here. I don't know how long this is going to take.' He turned back to Roland. 'You'd better come into the office.' He led the way through and slumped into a chair.

Roland saw how weary he looked. 'A difficult case?'

'You could say. A valuable mare in foal decided to present us with a breech birth. Very tricky for a while, but mother and baby are now doing fine.' He gave a tired smile and Roland realised that he was younger than he had at first thought. 'At least she timed it well; these things usually happen in the small hours.' He ran his fingers through his hair, leaving a cockatoolike crest. 'Now, what can I do for you?'

203

'I want you to cast your mind back to the day you were called out to Manor Farm at Helsby — a badly injured Jack Russell.'

'Oh, that?' An alert look came over the vet's face. 'A nasty business; any idea yet who did her in?'

'We're following up several leads. I understand you were called out to see the dog and it had to be put down?'

'Yes to both your questions. I could tell from my preliminary examination that there was no hope for him, I didn't need an X-ray.' At Roland's look of enquiry he continued, 'He'd had a hefty blow behind the thorax which had dislocated the spine, I could feel the vertebrae out of position. From there back everything was put out of action except his respiratory system. His bladder and back legs weren't functioning — he couldn't have crawled, but somehow he dragged himself on his forelegs over to Manor Farm. He must have been in agony. A plucky little dog, devoted to his mistress.'

'PC Morton tells me that you thought at first that he had been involved in a road accident?'

'Yes, that's the usual cause when an animal has injuries such as that. But after I'd put him out of his misery I examined him more carefully and realised that this wasn't the case here.'

'How do you mean?'

'There were no traces of road burn. When a dog is a victim of a road accident you find the nails are scagged — they're rough and jagged where they've dug into the road and there is what wc call road burn of the skin and hair. This wasn't so here. And there was blood on his shoulder and collar that hadn't come from him — he had no open wounds. So I began to suspect that he had been attacked and the injuries inflicted by human agency.'

'Are you telling me that he got a nip at his assailant?' Roland couldn't keep the excitement out of his voice.

'More than a nip.' Gregory Daniels looked at him quizzically. 'If the dog had given him a nip it wouldn't have bled straight away — there's always a time lapse, about a minute and a half. So his blood wouldn't have got onto the dog's fur. It's my belief that the dog tried to defend itself; got its teeth into its assailant and hung on. That would account for its injuries.'

'In what way?'

'You'd have expected the dog to meet its attacker head on, in which case he would have been struck around the head and mask, but if he got his teeth into – say – the chappie's ankle or leg and wouldn't let go, then that makes sense of the fact that he was hit crossways on the spine.'

'Why didn't he finish him off?'

'Probably thought he had. The dog would have been knocked unconscious and was possibly out for as much as twenty minutes.'

'So the dog got a mouthful of blood?'

'There was none left round the jaw because obviously he had salivated and washed it away, but there was blood on the fur of the left shoulder and on the collar. I tell you what, Inspector, your murderer will be marked. Nasty things, dog bites. I should be surprised if he didn't have to have medical attention. More often than not these wounds fester.'

Roland racked his brains. None of their suspects or the people they had interviewed so far had had an obvious injury; he had noticed no bandages or sticking plaster. But if the wound had been in the leg rather than the hand, it was easily hidden.

'Why didn't we learn of this earlier?'

'Nobody asked. I didn't realise it was significant.'

Roland cursed inwardly. He had slipped up there. They had been so engrossed in Lydia Cordingley's murder that they hadn't given the dog another thought, apart from noting that by its heroic action it had brought her death to their attention much sooner than her killer intended.

'And now for the million-dollar question: what do you do with the bodies of animals you've put down if they're not claimed by their owners?'

'Until quite recently they were put in black plastic bags and dumped on the tip.'

'You're not serious!'

'It's the council's responsibility, not ours. But now they usually go to a pets' crematorium in Norfolk.'

'Cremated?' Roland groaned.

The vet leaned back. He was enjoying himself now.

'Don't worry, inspector, that wasn't so in this instance. Bulstrode said he'd bury him on the farm. He has a sort of pets' cemetery in his orchard.'

'Then there will have to be an exhumation. What are the chances of finding something after this time lapse?'

It's not all that long. You should still be able to find traces of blood; of course, it's been unseasonably hot weather.'

'If he was put in a plastic sack, that will have accelerated putrification,' Roland mused out loud.

'He won't have buried him in plastic − what do you think fertilises his fruit trees? He probably wrapped him in sacking or put him in a paper potato sack.'

'Good. First thing tomorrow we'll have him up. I should like you to be present.'

'What are you hoping to achieve? Even if you manage to get a sample of that blood, how is that going to help you?'

'I'm surprised at you asking that, Mr Daniels, you being a scientific man. What I'm talking about is DNA fingerprinting. Even with only a minute sample of blood we can get a genetic fingerprint that is unique to its owner, in this case, the murderer.'

'What are you doing?'

Rick lounged against the bed watching her, arms akimbo, seemingly relaxed, but Lucy could feel the tension emanating from him; he was wound up like a top.

'I'm ... I'm tidying up.' She got a grip on herself. 'There are far too many clothes in this wardrobe, the door won't shut.'

'So what are you throwing away?'

'I'm not throwing anything away, just trying to sort things out.'

He took the jerkin from her. 'Do you think these will be wanted any more?'

'Why not?'

'Will your family be staging any more historical re-creations? After the trouble at the last one and the interest the Bill are taking in us all, I should have thought that your grandmother would cancel them for the time being.'

'It would kill her to do that. She pretends they're only put on to make money to help cover the running costs of the Hall, but she's really into it all and I think she loves the opportunity to show off the place to a wide audience.'

Lucy chattered brightly to cover her embarrassment but was aware that he was still regarding her oddly. What was wrong? This was Rick, her lover and fellow conspirator; why was she suddenly overcome with fear and suspicion? Out of the corner of her eye she could see the dagger protruding from under the bottom of the wardrobe. Unable to stop herself, she picked it up.

'Where did this come from?'

'The kitchens at Monkbeggars Hall – where else? There's a positive arsenal of knives lying around there.'

He plucked it out of her grasp and handled it carelessly, tossing it lightly from one hand to another, then he looked up and caught her frozen gaze.

'What's the matter? You look as if you've seen a ghost.'

'I . . . Be careful, Rick, it's very sharp.'

'So it is. One could do a deal of damage with a weapon like this.'

She gave a startled gasp. A look of malicious glee spread over his face.

'Why, Lucy, I do believe you think I knifed those two murder victims. You really think I'm capable of that!' He grapped hold of her in a sudden, violent movement and rammed her against his chest so hard that she cried out. 'What a charming display of trust! And do you think I'm now going to run you through?' He took her silence for affirmation and his voice throbbed with excitement and provocation. 'You really do, don't you?'

She felt the cold metal against her neck, tingling as gently as a caress, and his voice thick with emotion in her ear:

'Oh yes, my witch bitch. I *am* going to stab you . . . over and over again . . . but not with this.' The dagger clattered to the floor. 'I've got a better weapon.' His hands tore at her clothing. She moaned and shuddered and pressed herself against him. He dragged her over to the bed and threw her down. 'You must be punished. How shall I punish you? Like this? And this? And this?'

207

'Oh, please, Rick ... please ...'

Later, as they lay in a tangle of exhausted limbs, she murmured, 'What would mother say if she could see me now?'

'She'd probably be envious. What a time to call up your mother!'

'I'm frightened, Rick. All this business with the police ...'

'They've cancelled the rap, there's nothing to worry about.'

'I don't mean that.' She struggled up on one elbow. 'There's this horrible atmosphere of suspicion; it's touching everything, even us.'

'You're letting your imagination run away with you. Stop worrying.'

'No, it's real.' She hesitated and looked down at him, searching his face warily. 'Rick, what *did* you do that – '

'Shut up, woman!' He pulled her down on top of him. 'We've more important things to think about.' He stopped her mouth with a kiss and as his beard bruised her skin and his fingers started their insistent exploration she responded and gave herself up to his embrace.

Later, as she lay sleeping, he picked up the dagger and hid it in his briefcase.

Mansfield was pleased with his day's work checking out the racing fraternity at Newmarket. As he reported back to Roland, it couldn't have been easier. He had contrived to fall into conversation with Hanson's partners, having had them pointed out to him, and by some devious questioning and professed interest in owning a racehorse he had managed to extract the information they needed.

'They bought this racehorse at the Newmarket October sales four years ago when it was a yearling colt and it cost them £75,000. For the first three months it cost about two and a half grand and then, from January when it became an official two-year-old, it went into training.

'You managed to get all that out of them without revealing who you were?'

'Yes, it was a doddle. They were quite happy to boast about

the money they've spent on their hobby. Anyway, this horse is kept at Thacker's yard in Newmarket and runs them up a little annual bill of £12,000 for upkeep, which includes vets' bills, travel, jockeys and so on.'

'So, Hanson would have had to pay out £25,000 initially and dig into his pockets for a sum of £4,000 annually. It's all beginning to add up. Though he had to find the purchase money three years before the picture was switched.'

'Perhaps he had run up such bed debts that he was desperate to get his hands on a large sum.'

'Yes. Evans, how did you get on with the bookmakers?'

'He hasn't got an account with any of the local bookies.'

'No?'

'He did have, but he's been blacklisted, they think he's a bad bet.'

'Is that meant to be a pun?'

'He had an account originally with Salters here in Felstone but he couldn't settle up his debts so they wouldn't let him go on laying bets through them. When something like this happens word gets round to the other bookmakers in the area that a certain person is a bad risk. I was told that there used to be an organisation called the Turf Guardian Society which kept records of customers and he was on their blacklist, but it folded up about eighteen months ago.'

'Yes, I'd heard of it. What about bookies on the course?'

'That's more difficult to follow up. If you want to bet at the races you have to put up the cash there and then, no running-up of accounts. I asked around and although nothing was actually said I got the old nudge-nudge, wink-wink treatment – he's known, all right.'

Roland put them all in the picture about his day's investigations and the results.

'I haven't been able to get hold of Bulstrode yet. There's been no reply each time I've tried to contact him over the phone, but I'll try and raise him later this evening. He can hardly object and if he does it's just too bad. We'll get out there first thing in the morning and Daniels, the vet, is joining us.'

'I thought you had to get a coroner's order for an exhumation?'

'Christ, Pomroy! This is a dog we're talking about, not a human stiff.' Roland gathered his papers together. 'You've all done well today. We're getting together a nice little dossier on Hanson; things are beginning to look very black for him. Get your reports down in writing and then shove off home.'

'We've got to write it up now?' Evans was aggrieved.

'But of course, while it's all fresh in your minds. I don't trust your memory, Evans. I want facts, not vague recollections.'

Roland himself stayed on catching up with his paperwork long after his colleagues had left the station, and he drove home as the sun was going down in a blaze of colour over the river. A bank of luminous cloud, its underbelly limned with pure gold, divided the evening sky; below, the lambent glow was shot with streaks of crimson, coral and chrome; above, a single star sparked in the deepening blue bowl of the heavens. He tried to remember what star it was that shone so brightly in that quarter of the sky at this time of year but his memory failed him.

He let himself into his house, heated up a frozen meal in the microwave and as he ate it he scanned the evening newpaper. There was still no mention of the dock escapade. He smiled cynically and tried the Bulstrode number again. This time he got the farmer and made arrangements for the following morning. As he put down the phone, the front doorbell rang. Against all reason his immediate thought was that it was Ginny. He opened the door in pleasant anticipation and was astounded to find Karen standing on his doorstep.

'Hello, James. I'm obviously not the person you were expecting.'

'Karen! Why are you here?'

'Not a very nice welcome. Aren't you going to ask me in?'

'What do you want?' He moved back.

She took this as an invitation and stepped inside, brushing past him. 'I *do* know the way, I used to live here, remember?' She walked into the sitting room and looked round critically. 'You've not altered much.'

Roland shrugged. 'There didn't seem any point. I'm here very little.'

'And is that because the police force are still claiming

90 per cent of your time or are you shacking up with the girlfriend – or shouldn't I ask?'

He kept his annoyance in check. 'I was just going to make coffee, will you have some?'

'I'd rather have something stronger.'

'Whisky?'

'Yes please. Just a little water, you know how I like it.'

She sat down on the sofa and watched him as he poured out two whiskies and added water to hers and ginger to his. She gestured that he join her and he reluctantly sat beside her. She clinked her glass against his. 'To old times, James. They weren't all bad.'

'You still haven't told me why you're here.'

'Do I have to have a reason? I was passing by and I saw the light and decided on the spur of the moment to drop in.'

'You acting on a whim? I don't believe you, Karen.'

'How long has it been?'

'Since you left me? Six years.'

'You're a hard, unforgiving man, James, you always were; the professional policeman. You never could leave it behind, could you?'

'Have you come here just to discuss my faults? I thought we'd gone over that ground enough times in the old days.'

'No, it's not your faults I want to talk about, it's mine. Have you forgiven me?'

'Forgiven you, Karen? Forgiven you for what?'

'For walking out on you, being unfaithful; I know that I hurt you badly.'

'Yes, you did at the time, but it was a long time ago, that's all water under the bridge now.'

'Especially as you've got a new woman.'

'Karen!' he said warningly.

'Have you really forgotten all the good times we had? It was good in bed, wasn't it?'

She had slid along the sofa towards him. Suddenly her arms were round his neck and she was clinging to him and pressing her lips against his. For a few shocking seconds he felt himself responding, then revulsion set in and he pushed her away.

'It's over, Karen, it's been over a long while. Don't try and resurrect a ghost.'

211

'You're lying, James. You still feel something, you know you do!' She held his gaze, there was excitement lurking in the depths of her dark eyes and something else, was it desire? He thought how many times he had gone through this scene in his imagination since they had parted; how he had fantasised about her coming back and begging him, just like this, to take her back and make love to her. She was his for the asking and it was too late. He felt nothing, nothing at all, nothing except embarrassment at her self-abasement. He made a movement of distaste.

'I think you'd better go.'

She saw his gesture and her passion turned to anger. She wanted to hurt him, to make him feel as rejected as she did.

'I suppose you're getting enough from *her*!'

'Karen!'

'Well, I hope she satisfies you because you don't satisfy her!'

'What are you talking about?'

'She spreads her favours, James, she shares herself out.'

'You lying bitch! You think everyone is as promiscuous as yourself!'

'That's good, coming from you of all people. Do you really want to know why I'm here? I came to warn you, James, to try and prevent you from getting hurt. I must have been mad!' She gulped the remains of her whisky and banged the glass down on the table. 'I'm going! Don't bother to see me out.' She made for the door.

'Oh no you don't!' He grabbed hold of her arm and swung her round to face him. 'You're not going until you tell me exactly what you mean by making insinuations like that!'

She pulled herself free and shrugged. 'All right, if you insist. Your beloved Ginny Dalton is going round with a certain person who has a very unsavoury reputation with women.'

Roland relaxed. 'Do you mean Hugh Calder-Brown? I know Ginny is a friend of his.'

'Do you, And do you also know that she visits his flat late at night? All right, James!' She gasped as he made a threatening gesture towards her. 'There's no need to take it out on me. Ask her if you don't believe me.'

He restrained himself with an effort, determined that he was not going to give her the satisfaction of knowing how much she had jolted him.

'You're a troublemaker, Karen. What Ginny does is her business, not yours — or is she queering your patch? How well do *you* know Calder-Brown?'

'Oh, I know Hugh, I admit it,' she said mockingly, 'but it's past tense. He's out of my league, I don't move in those circles.'

'What circles?'

She looked at him, half triumphant, half afraid. 'Drugs.'

'Drugs?' he snapped. 'What do you mean?'

'Nothing.' She faltered, alarmed by his reaction. 'It's just a rumour I've heard.'

'You're not holding out on me now. What are you talking about — cannabis? LSD?'

'Forget it, it's probably not true.'

'Answer me! Is it hash?'

She shook her head.

'We're not talking about the hard stuff, are we?' he demanded.

'I've said too much already. Look, leave it alone — '

'You're asking *me,* a policeman, to forget what you've just said? You're telling me exactly what you mean or, so help me God, I'll run you in on suspicion of — '

'James, don't be crazy! It's nothing to do with me! I just heard this gossip at a party. Coke was mentioned.'

'Cocaine?'

She gulped and nodded.

'Who told you?'

'I honestly don't know. You know how it is at parties, someone had had too much to drink and was talking unwisely. I'm sure it was just scandal-mongering.'

'Yet you believed it — why?'

'Why?'

'You must have had a reason for believing a scandalous whisper about a friend of yours, by someone in their cups.'

'God, James, I wouldn't like to be grilled by you for real. You make me feel that I'm in the dock.'

'I'm sorry,' he said more gently. 'But I can't just leave it, surely you can see that?'

She paced the floor, biting her lips, then stopped and spoke in a low voice.

'You won't like this, James, but here goes. I've slept with Hugh — just once, but it was quite something . . . too much so. He was insatiable, wound up to such a sexual pitch that there was no satisfying him. He was . . . too much for me. I flatter myself that I can bring a man to the boil but this was unnatural and I felt that his sexual arousal had nothing to do with me.'

'He was psyched up?'

'I think so.' She caught the expression on his face and said heatedly, 'There's no need to look at me like that, you did ask!'

'Yes, I did, didn't I? You're a slut, Karen.'

'I don't sleep around, James, I'm a one-man woman.'

'And who's the current lucky man?'

'There isn't one, that's why — ' She bit off what she had been going to say, but he finished it for her.

'That's why you're trying to make it with me again? Sorry, but nothing doing. It's over, finished, done with.'

'Yes, I can see that now. I really loved you, James, I should never have left you, but we all do things we regret. As they say, I've made my bed and now I've got to lie on it.' She picked up her handbag and moved towards the door. 'Well, I wish you joy of her, James, but I don't think it'll work out; you're no better at picking them than I am.'

She went out, closing the front door behind her, and he sat motionless for a long while. Then he poured himself another whisky and drank it neat. As a policeman he should concentrate on what Karen had told him about Calder-Brown and the probability that he was involved with the drugs scene; it opened up a whole new area of inquiry. But all he could think about was her remark that Ginny visited his flat late at night.

Karen had been trying to make trouble between them, it had been said in spite, but he didn't think she had been deliberately lying. He groaned and looked with longing at the whisky bottle. There was one way of finding out, wasn't

214

there, as she had suggested? He pushed his glass aside and slammed out of the house.

Simon answered the door. He was dressed in outdoor clothes and Roland said, without any preliminaries: 'You're going out? Good, I want to talk to your mother.'

He strode through the hall and the boy stared after him, affronted. Ginny was ironing in the kitchen and she looked up surprised but pleased as he burst into the room.

'James! You're making a habit of these unexpected visits – but it's lovely to see you,' and, as he said nothing, 'Something's happened – there's something *really* wrong this time, isn't there?' She moved to put her arms round him but he stepped aside and very deliberately closed the door.

'Simon's just going out,' she said, puzzled.

'Yes, I told him to keep out of the way.'

That surprised her even more. James usually handled Simon very tactfully.

'This case you're working on – isn't it going well?'

'You could put it that way.' His light-grey eyes, such a contrast to his black unruly hair, were chips of ice. 'Why did you lie to me?'

'Lie to you? What are you talking about?'

'About Hugh Calder-Brown. Why did you tell me that he was just a casual acquaintance when I have it on good authority that you visit his flat late at night?'

She gasped and the colour crept up her face. 'And may I ask who this good authority is?'

'Is it surprising that you were seen if you make a habit of it? Goths Yard is rather a public place.'

There was the sound of movement in the hall and Ginny whipped open the kitchen door.

'Simon – I thought you'd gone out.'

'I forgot the book I wanted to show Andrew.'

'Well, hurry and get it.'

'I don't think I'll go this evening after all, it's getting late.'

'You can't let Andrew down if he's expecting you. It'll do you good to have a break from your homework, but make sure your back light is working.'

215

Roland heard the boy go out and then the sound of him cycling down the path. Ginny came back into the room. She had worked herself up into a fine temper. Her normally pale skin was rosily flushed and her hair seemed to catch light from her anger and blazed incandescently round her neck and shoulders like a fiery nimbus.

'So, someone drops a malicious word in your ear and I am condemned out of hand. You don't choose to hear my version of the truth — you'd rather believe what someone else has told you!'

'So you don't deny it?'

'Why should I? I've done nothing to be ashamed of.'

'Let's get this straight. You won't sleep with me but you visit another man's flat at night. You can hardly expect me not to draw the obvious inference.'

'You think I've slept with him?' Her voice was ominously quiet.

'Well, have you?'

She launched herself at him and delivered a stinging slap on his left cheek. So sudden was the attack that he was taken unawares. He stumbled back and cracked his head on the edge of the dresser. She stepped back aghast. He rubbed his head and tried to speak placatorily.

'I'm sorry, Ginny. I really am — I'm not thinking clearly. It's just that the man has such a bad reputation, what with women and now drugs.'

'Drugs? You know about the drugs?'

His head snapped up. 'I don't believe it. For Christ's sake, Ginny! Are you telling me you know about his drug-taking and yet you still — '

'James, it was only pot. I suppose as a policeman you have to come down hard on that sort of thing, but a lot of people smoke. When I was at college there was plenty of experimentation with soft drugs — don't look like that, I never tried it — and I recognised the smell in his flat. It is rather distinctive.'

'Could you bear to explain your . . . your relationship with Calder-Brown?'

'So you can judge me?'

'Hell, Ginny, I've said I'm sorry. I know you haven't slept

216

with him — I must have been mad to accuse you. It's just that I'm so crazy about you, I love you so much that I'm quite unbalanced about everything ...'

She reached out and touched his face. 'Do you know, this is the first time that you've mentioned love.'

'Don't be ridiculous, I'm always telling you — '

'That you want me? That you lust after me? Yes, but that's not quite the same thing.'

'Ginny, how could you have thought ...? Oh, hell, I took it for granted that you knew and hoped that you felt the same way. I love you, woman, do you understand? I love you and I want to make an honest woman of you — there, how's that? I've proposed in a trite cliché!'

'Oh, James ...'

'Don't say anything now.' He was suddenly afraid that she would turn him down out of hand. There was always Simon to consider and their courtship had had a very chequered course.

'I'm not asking because I'm checking up on you. I shan't mention it again. But from a professional point of view I must know.'

So she told him about her visit to the flat and how and what she had discovered in Hugh's bedroom, skating over his attempt to seduce her. Roland listened intently and when she had finished he asked carefully:

'Are you sure it was pot?'

'I'm pretty sure it was a reefer, it was hand-rolled and lying in the ashtray half smoked, but I suppose I could have been mistaken. Maybe I'm doing him a grave injustice.'

'I don't think so. In fact, I have reason to believe he could be into the hard stuff.'

'Hugh?' She was horrified.

'Is that so impossible to believe?'

She considered. 'No ... I suppose it is possible. He has big mood swings. Sometimes he's very low and irritable and at other times he seems to be on a high — really hyped up.' She looked at him thoughtfully. 'Do you know, we've had lectures on drug abuse at school to instruct us teachers what to look out for — all the tell-tale signs of drug-taking that could manifest themselves in our pupils — and now that you've drawn my attention to it I believe Hugh Calder-Brown could be displaying classic symptoms. So it's not pot?'

'The two often go together. Did he really offer you a smoke?'

'Yes.' She looked unhappy. 'Are you going to arrest him?'

'Not at this stage. If he's got the stuff lying around in his flat we could possibly bust him and get enough evidence to stick but I'm interested in him for far more serious crimes.'

She suddenly remembered the murder case. 'Oh no ... not Hugh?'

'Ginny, I have no evidence, but if he's on the hard stuff, well, drugs cost money. It gives him a motive for needing the sort of money that painting could have fetched. He's not the only one, though; I can build up a good case against at least two other suspects but I haven't any proof. Not yet, but tomorrow I may strike lucky.'

She looked at him enquiringly but he shook his head.

'No, I'm not saying anything further. Try and forget what I've told you, and now I'm going in case I forget myself.'

'You want to stay ...'

'Yes, and I know this is not the time or place. I can wait. When you're ready to commit yourself, just say the word.'

'Oh, James, thank you for being so understanding.' She reached up and kissed him.

Some minutes later he reluctantly broke away from her embrace. 'Unhand me, woman, or I shall really forget my good intentions.'

As they parted in the doorway, she remembered something.

'Who did tell you they'd seen me go into Hugh's flat?'

'There's always someone who's envious of other people's happiness and has to try and destroy it. Don't worry about it, it isn't important.'

He drove back to Felstone in deep thought. After all these weeks he had at last picked up information that could definitely tie Calder-Brown in with his case. Both Ginny's and Karen's descriptions of his behaviour pointed to his being under the influence of drugs. Cocaine made its victims excitable and edgy and was supposed to enhance their sexual prowess, at least in the early stages of addiction. Calder-Brown would be spending far more money on supplies than he earned from his bookshop — was that money coming from the sale of his mother's painting? And if so, had he murdered John Hargreaves and Lydia Cordingley to cover his tracks?

His alibis for the times of the two murders had been very ambiguous, probably deliberately so, Roland thought. Was he tomorrow going to get the evidence that would enable him to point the finger at Calder-Brown or one of the other two suspects? Everything now centred on whether he could get a sample of the murderer's blood from the mortal remains of a pet dog who had died defending his mistress but might yet lead the police to her killer.

Chapter Twelve

Manor Farm was a mixed arable and dairy farm and Mansfield was pleased to see that it was farmed along traditional lines. There were hens scratching in the yard and the cattle were out at pasture; none of your battery units or veal-forcing sheds here.

Paul Bulstrode, a raw-boned, grizzled man in his late sixties, was waiting for them when they drove into the yard the next morning, and with him was Gregory Daniels. Roland explained briefly to the farmer what they were hoping to achieve, and the latter said gruffly:

'Well, let's get on with it. I haven't told the missus, she were fond of that little old dorg and I don't want to upset her. She's out at the moment visiting our daughter.'

He produced a couple of spades and took them up a rutted path past the barn to the orchard. Mansfield noted again that this was definitely an olde-worlde orchard, looking like the reproduction of a Victorian painting that featured on a current calendar hanging in his kitchen; not cost-effective at all. The apple trees were old and gnarled and could have done with a good hard pruning but they were covered in blossom and the ground beneath them was knee-deep in bluebells. Where the trees thinned out towards the hedge separating the orchard from a field of winter barley, the lush grass was colonised by buttercups and dandelions.

'Here you are.' Bulstrode led them through the trees to a little clearing dominated by an even more ancient pear tree that had been propped up so many times during its life cycle with stakes, which had themselves weathered, that it was difficult to tell which was trunk and which was prop. Beneath this tree markers were sticking out of the grass, some of them like miniature gravestones.

'We used to bury the children's pets here when they were young. That's the one you want.' He pointed to a small area of disturbed ground that bore a short wooden stave on which a name had been written. 'The missus did that. Well, I'll leave you to it.' He walked off and Mansfield squinted at the grave.

'HOGARTH,' he read out loud. 'That's a funny name for a dog.'

'Hogarth was an eighteenth-century artist,' said Roland. 'He specialised in charting the downhill path of the human race.'

'Well, this one's mistress certainly met a nasty end.'

Mansfield felt his guts twist as the spade measured the first spit. This, if they were honest, was surely the task that all policeman most dreaded, the exhumation. Fortunately it was a rare occurrence and not everyone was similarly affected, he suddenly remembered. At the last exhumation he had attended, in the churchyard of the little village of Birnham, Brasnett, the pathologist, had positively revelled in it all. There was no comparison to be made with today's proceedings, the unearthing of a dog's body. Exhumations usually took place at the dead of night to avoid publicity. It was always dark and cold and they worked by the light of lamps that threw monstrous shadows on the screens erected around the grave.

Today the sun was high in the sky, bright shafts of sunshine struck through the overhead branches and shimmered in fragmented pools of light on the disturbed ground, and not far away a blackbird whistled to his mate enthusiastically, but the smell was the same, the sickly-sweet carrion smell.

'Is this what you're looking for?' Bulstrode burst onto the scene, waving something in his hand. 'I just remembered that I took it off.'

'Is that the dog's collar?' Roland asked.

'Yes, I hung it up in the old stable, thought it might come in useful one day.'

Roland met Mansfield's eye across the opened grave.

'Thank you, Mr Bulstrode.' He carefully accepted the collar held out to him and examined it closely. Near the buckle were easily discernible rusty brown encrustations. Euphoria surged through him. They had got their vital clue. 'OK, put him back, we've got what we want.'

The collar was sealed in a plastic bag and labelled, and Evans was once more dispatched to the forensic laboratory at Aldermaston.

'Make sure they realise that it's a murder inquiry and ask them to give it top priority — and also tell them that I hope to follow it up with three other samples for comparison.'

'Are we going to ask our suspects to give blood samples?'

'No, Evans, we have to be far more subtle that that."

'How are we going to get samples?' Mansfield asked when Evans was out of earshot.

'We're going to have to do some ingenious thinking.'

'We can't do it officially?'

'You know as well as I do that, as the rules stand, you have to get consent from both the suspect and the superintendent, and the super has to be satisfied that it's a serious offence and there's a high possibility that it will prove or disprove the case.'

'Surely this is serious enough — two murders!'

'If we had just one suspect it would be plain sailing, but three? He's not going to buy that. Besides, if we do it officially we'll let our guilty man know that we're on to him and I don't want him scarpering before we've got the proof. You know how long Forensics take over something like this. We've got to get our heads together over this one.'

'Well, at least we got the collar, that's a lucky break.'

'I'm losing my touch. We ought to have checked that the collar had been removed before the dog was buried. We should have realised that a provident farmer was likely to do just that if the vet hadn't already done so.'

He swung on his heel and walked back to the car.

'Come on, Patrick, things are looking up. I think the end is in sight.'

Celia Calder-Brown was in the garden when they arrived at Monkbeggars Hall. Roland had intended driving on to the farm and interviewing Nigel Hanson first, but when he saw her white curls bobbing up among the plants and shrubs in the herbaceous border, he changed his mind. She was dressed in a purple tracksuit and her feet were encased in green wellies. Not the green wellies of the county set, but bright-green, shiny boots with little protruberances at the front, painted to resemble eyes, giving the boots the appearance of frogs. They were like the wellies young children revelled in, thought Roland; correction, they *were* children's boots, she had such tiny feet.

She waved a trowel at them and got to her feet when she saw them get out of the car.

'Inspector, Sergeant – have you got any news?'

'We're still following up several leads, ma'am, and there are a couple of points I'd like to check with you.

'Ah, there's Nigel, I wonder what he wants.' Celia Calder-Brown was distracted by the sight of her son-in-law approaching from the opposite direction.

Nigel Hanson had been on his way to the piggery but when he recognised the two police officers he changed course and stumped towards them, alarmed by their presence. He tried to take a short cut and ploughed through a corner of the shrubbery, getting entangled in a rose bush. He jerked his arm free to the sound of ripping cloth and demanded pugnaciously:

'What is it now? Haven't you got anything better to do than harassing innocent people?'

'Now, Nigel, don't be silly. The inspector is only doing his duty. Don't you want him to get it cleared up?'

Nigel looked as if it was the last thing he desired. He glowered at the two detectives.

Celia Calder-Brown remarked,

'You've torn the sleeve of your jacket.'

'Hardly surprising, the state of that jungle.' He jerked his head behind him. 'You want to get those brambles rooted out.'

'That's not a bramble, that's my Burnett rose,' said his mother-in-law indignantly. 'You've cut your hand, too.'

Hanson dabbed ineffectively at the gash.

'You are up to date with your anti-tetanus injections, aren't you? This is the worst area in the country.'

'Don't fuss, Mother-in-law,' he cut in. 'I want to know why these gentlemen are here.'

'Just checking up on a couple of things,' said Mansfield. 'That's a nasty scratch, sir, You want to get it seen to or it may go septic.' He stared at the blood trickling down Hanson's palm and couldn't believe their luck.

'Yes, Nigel, go up to the house and get Hatty to bandage it for you.'

'There's no need for that. We always keep a first-aid kit in the car − required equipment. Now it can be put to use.'

Mansfield persuaded the man over to the car, where he mopped up the blood with a pad of cotton wool and applied a sticking plaster. Hanson muttered his thanks. As he turned back to the other two, Mansfield quickly and surreptitiously sealed the soiled cotton wool in a plastic bag.

'Do you want to see me?' Hanson demanded of Roland.

'I don't think that'll be necessary now. I'm sure Mrs Calder-Brown can help us, and I know that you're a busy man.'

This threw Nigel Hanson. The last thing he wanted was to leave the two men with his mother-in-law. He was afraid that they would tell her of his extramarital relations or reveal some even more damming evidence about his activities. He tried to bluster his way out of the situation.

'I'm quite capable of dealing with my own affairs, Nigel,' she said tartly. 'If the inspector wants to question you further he knows where to find you. We'll go up to the house,' she said to Roland and Mansfield, 'and take coffee.'

Thus dismissed, Hanson had no option but to continue on his way, which he did with a bad grace.

Seated once more in Celia Calder-Brown's sitting-room sipping coffee, Roland pondered on his next move. It was with a sense of déjà-vu that he watched his hostess broach a new packet of cigarettes, light up and inhale deeply. Smoke dribbled from her nostrils and she coughed harshly.

'Well, Inspector, what do you want to know? I take it as read that you haven't found the painting, but surely by now you've eliminated the family from your inquiries?'

Roland ignored this. 'I know that I asked you this before, Mrs Calder-Brown, but can you please check your memory carefully, are you sure that you didn't tell anyone about your intention to loan the painting to the Langdale Gallery?'

'I'm quite positive that I mentioned it to no one.'

'Not to your children? Surely that would have been the natural thing to do?'

'I hadn't seen Hugh, so there was no way I could have told him, and I made a point of not telling Marian until all the arrangements should be complete because she fusses so.'

'What about your granddaughter Lucy?'

'No, I hadn't seen Lucy either for some weeks. Look, Inspector, I made the decision to lend the painting and I didn't see that it was any business of the rest of the family.'

'What about your housekeeper?'

'Hatty? She knew that I was expecting a caller the morning that John Hargreaves was due to call, but she didn't know who it was or why. You're surely not suspecting Hatty?

'No, of course not, you've just confirmed my conclusions on this point. We can now concentrate on a different angle.'

'Was there anything else you wanted to know?' Celia Calser-Brown got to her feet, signifying the interview was over.

'There was just one thing, but it's a private matter, nothing to do with my investigations, and I hardly like to ask you ...'

'Whatever it is, man, do speak up!'

'Well, it's like this, ma'am. My fiancée, who is a teacher, is bringing over a party of children to take part in your next historical re-creation and she is very worried about the costumes, especially the boys' headgear. I wondered if we might just look at some of the costumes? You do keep the family ones here, I suppose?'

Mansfield goggled at his chief. They had agreed on this course of action before the visit but this bit about Ginny Dalton being his fiancée – this was news indeed, wait till he told Jean! But perhaps Roland was making it up as he went along to make his proposition sound more feasible? Mansfield was aware that his colleague was eyeing him coldly while putting his case sweetly to Celia Calder-Brown, and he made his face go blank.

'Well, yes,' she replied. 'But Hugh's is the only male costume, the others are mine, my daughter's and my grand-daughter's.'

'They were all so charming and authentic, I should really like to see them again, and I'm sure that I can pick up a few tips to help my friend.'

'They should be authentic, they were copied from a con-temporary picture. Certainly you may look at them if you really want to. They're kept in a spare room in the east wing.'

As she led them to this room she kept up a running com-mentary on the design of the costumes, the yardage needed, and the difficulties of utilising the modern man-made fabrics so that they resembled the original Tudor materials. Roland tried to look knowledgeable and inserted the odd yes and no into the conversation when needed.

The room was also used as a props store. There were a couple of spinning wheels, cushions of lace bobbins, many different-shaped rush baskets containing dried herbs and seedheads, and an outsize dark oak cradle in one corner that looked large enough to house a sow and her litter, let along a baby. The costumes were hanging in built-in wardrobe cupboards. Celia Calder-Brown opened the doors and indicated the clothes inside, plucking a black velvet cap off a shelf and handing it to him.

'I really don't think this is going to be of much help. This is the only cap we have here and it belongs to my son, who takes part as one of the gentry. The caps your schoolboys need to wear must be much simpler − I presume they are acting as scholars in the schoolroom?'

'I imagine so.' Roland pretended interest in the rest of the costumes, then looked casually down at the cap he was holding.

'Is it all right if Sergeant Mansfield does a rough sketch of this ma'am? I'm sure it would be a great help.'

'Yes, I don't see why not.' Celia Calder-Brown was sur-prised but not suspicious.

'Here you are, Sergeant.' Roland handed him the cap. 'We'll leave you to get on with it. I've just seen something out of that window about which I must ask Mrs Calder-Brown.'

He drew the elderly woman out of the room and pointed through the window of the corridor. This window overlooked the moat and part of the kitchen garden beyond. 'Those plaited skips under that wall — are they really beehives?'

'Oh yes, and they've got colonies of bees in them ...'

As they conversed, the woman's attention on the conical beehives outside, Mansfield quickly moved out of sight behind the door and examined the cap carefully; several blonde hairs glinted in the black velvet of the inside of the cap. Expertly, Mansfield removed these with a pair of tweezers and sealed them inside another plastic bag, which he stowed away in his pocket. He then joined the others in the corridor.

'Did you manage it?' Roland asked.

'I think I got what you want. Do you want to see the sketch?'

For a few seconds Roland grinned at him maliciously, then he said, 'You can show it to me later. We really mustn't take up any more of Mrs Calder-Brown's time. You have been most helpful, ma'am. My fiancée will appreciate this.'

Later, in the car, Roland turned gleefully to his companion.

'Well done, Patrick! Two down and one to go. I didn't believe we could be so lucky.'

'I only hope we've got some follicle left on those hairs. It's difficult to tell with only the naked eye.'

'We must keep our fingers crossed.'

A couple of phone calls to the college procured the information that Richard Coates was lecturing and that Lucy Hanson was away sick with a cold.

'I really do believe the gods are smiling on us at last.'

'Yes, but how the hell do we get this one?'

'We'll have to play it by ear.' Roland tore his gaze away from the Croxton signpost and headed back to Felstone. 'Make an excuse to use the bathroom and poke around and see if you can come up with something.'

'More hairs?'

'It's a possibility, if he leaves his brush and comb lying around, or there's his shaving tackle — no, he's got a beard, that's no go. Most people keep their dirty-linen basket in the

227

bathroom. You might strike lucky and find dirty sheets with seminal fluid on them.'

'Or I might not,' Mansfield growled. 'Isn't this rather iffy? The powers that be are not going to be very happy about our methods. Is it going to stand up in a court of law?'

'If we can match up DNA prints it is irrefutable evidence, we'll get a confession.'

They cruised along the road looking for the number they wanted. The houses were mostly semidetached villas, many of them with ornate galleries or balconies running round the upper storey. They had been built when Felstone was enjoying its heyday as an Edwardian watering place, and both between the wars and after the Second World War they were the home ground of the seaside landlady. But the trade in B and B had declined in recent years and many of them were now divided into flats or bedsitters, providing homes for permanent residents as well as student digs.

'There we are – number 34.' Mansfield pointed out the house. 'Maybe she'll be in bed if she's ill.'

'Or maybe she's skiving. There's one way of finding out.'

She was such a long while answering the doorbell that the two men nearly gave up, but just as they were on the point of turning away there was the sound of someone fumbling with the lock and the door opened. Lucy Hanson was fully dressed, in her usual nigrescent tones, and she blinked her black-ringed eyes in the sunshine, looking dazed.

'Ah, Miss Hanson, I was afraid we might be getting you out of bed. The college authorities told us you were ill.'

'I have a . . . a migraine.' She scowled at them. Roland could see that the bright light was making her flinch and he thought she really was suffering . 'What do you want?'

'The answers to a few questions. Shall we go inside?'

'No, you haven't got a warrant.'

'I don't need a warrant for questioning, but if you prefer to stand bawling on the doorstep so that all the neighbours can hear, that's up to you.'

'All right, come upstairs – but I know my rights!'

'I'm sure you do, Miss Hanson.'

They followed her up the stairs, aware of the pungent

smell of curry and garlic that pervaded the house; the room into which she took them still reeked of yesterday's Indian takeaway. Lucy Hanson was not a homemaker, Roland decided, looking about him, not a domestic bird at all. You couldn't go so far as to say that she and Richard Coates lived in squalor but it wasn't far off. No attempt had been made to create a comfortable environment. The place was furnished anonymously and there were no personal touches apart from a sick-looking pot plant on the table and a large, crudely painted picture on the wall which appeared to represent some protest march. The room certainly hadn't seen duster or hoover that week.

Lucy Hanson perched on one of the uncomfortable-looking stools that stood round the table and the two men took this as an invitation to do likewise.

'We've been released without being charged, you can't pick me up again.'

'Unless we're in possession of new evidence,' Roland agreed. 'We're not here to arrest you, just to check over some of the points in your statement.'

'I have nothing more to say.'

Roland ignored this. 'There's the little matter of the amount of money you received in charitable donations. I advised you to make a list.'

'I have done,' she admitted grudgingly, 'but it's not complete. I was more concerned with the end results than producing a balance sheet.'

She went into the next room and came back clutching a sheaf of grubby papers which she slammed down in front of Roland.

He made a point of perusing these carefully and called Mansfield's attention to one item listed. Mansfield leaned across the table and in so doing knocked aside the pot plant. He grabbed at it but somehow his hands slipped and it crashed to the floor, strewing soil and desiccated leaves across the sisal matting.

'Sorry, Miss, very careless of me.' Mansfield plunged off his stool and started to gather up handfuls of potting compost and stuff them back into the pot, which fortunately hadn't shattered. 'If I could have a brush and dustpan?'

229

'I'll do it later.' Lucy Hanson looked distressed. Roland reckoned she was near to tears. 'Leave it alone − I'll see to it when you're gone.'

'There, I've put most of it back.' Mansfield rocked back on his heels. 'It looks rather sorry for itself. They want feeding, you know, you mustn't neglect this sort of plant.'

The girl snatched it from him.

Mansfield lumbered to his feet, waving this dirty hands. 'Could I just use your bathroom to wash my hands?'

She pointed to a door across the landing. Mansfield thanked her and went through, shutting the door behind him. He looked round in disbelief. The bathroom windowsill, the washbasin and the floor underneath it were littered with crumpled, blood-stained tissues. A disposable razor lay on the edge of the basin and there was a tide mark round the inside of soapy scum mixed with short, bristly black hairs. It was a gift, Mansfield thought, an utter gift. Once more he busied himself with tweezers and plastic bags and, for good measure, also removed two longer black hairs clinging to the bath edge, though he was certain that these belonged to the girl.

Lucy Hanson, he reflected as he turned on the tap and rinsed his hands, had probably never down a hand's turn at housework while living at home and had seen no reason to rectify this state of affairs after setting up on her own. He wiped his hands with distaste on the grimy towel and returned to the other room.

'It looks as if someone has tried to cut their throat in there,' he remarked jocularly. The girl flushed.

'Rick nicked himself shaving and I haven't had the time to clear it up yet.'

'Don't tell me that Mr Coates has shaved off his beard?'

'No, but he has to keep it trimmed into shape. Anyway, what's it to do with you?'

You'd be surprised, my girl, Mansfield thought. Roland gathered up the lists she had given him.

'I'll keep these, but I suggest you check your memory further. These accounts are not going to help you at all.'

'Well, we didn't get the money knocking off Gran's painting!' she flashed.

230

'Ah, yes, the picture; did you know that your grandmother was going to loan the painting out for an exhibition? Had she told you?'

'It was news to me.'

'I see. And what about when the painting was sent to be cleaned? Did you know about that?'

Lucy Hanson looked at him suspiciously. 'I really can't remember.'

'Well, that'll be all for now. I hope your migraine goes.' Roland got to his feet and moved towards the door.

'Rick won't be very pleased when he knows that you've been grilling me behind his back.'

'Is he your keeper? I thought you were an independent, liberated young woman, Miss Hanson.'

'I am,' she snapped, 'and you're wasting your time trying to pin it on him. There's no way he could have committed those ghastly murders. He's against all taking of life on principle.'

'Well, you know him better than I.' The shaft went home and she flushed. 'I hope he appreciates your confidence.'

As they drove back to the station, Mansfield told his colleague about the state of the bathroom and how easily he had acquired a sample of Richard Coates' blood.

'This certainly hasn't been a wasted day. All we've got to do now is contain our impatience until the results come back. Did you get the same impression as me about Lucy Hanson?'

'She was edgy, almost as if she's beginning to have doubts about the boyfriend.'

'I thought the same. I wonder why.'

Roland spent the next few days catching up on his paperwork. He also had to attend court to give evidence in a complicated case of embezzlement on which he had worked earlier. Later in the week there was an emergency at Felstone Docks. A container had sprung a leak and dangerous chemicals were seeping into the compound. The dock complex was sealed off and the nearby houses were evacuated until the firemen had dispersed the poisonous fumes and cleaned up the area.

After this, a break-in at a nearby hypermarket, in which

231

the nightwatchman was badly beaten up and nearly died, involved most of the workforce. Mansfield, who had been hoping for a lull before their case broke, grumbled and made excuses to his wife, who sighed, tackled the task of cutting the lawn herself, and faced her various fund-raising committees in her usual role of grass widow.

At the forensic laboratory at Aldermaston complicated, time-consuming tests were being carried out on the samples supplied by Felstone CID; back home, Roland tried to concentrate on the work in hand and not dwell on the possible results. He knew there was no way the process could be hurried. By the end of the week he might know which, if any, of his suspects was the guilty man; until then the ball was still in play.

'Simon, do you still miss your father badly?'

It was Saturday morning. Simon had finished his paper round and was now tackling his second breakfast. He finished crunching his piece of toast and scooped up a dribble of marmalade from his plate with a finger before answering warily:

'Yes.'

'So do I,' said Ginny, resting both her elbows on the table and preparing to tackle a difficult subject.

'No you don't, you've forgotten him!'

'I haven't!' she exclaimed in distress. 'Simon, how could you say that? Your father and I were very happy together, we had a very good marriage but ... but it was cut short, unfairly short. He wouldn't have wanted us to mourn for ever.'

The boy stared down at his empty plate. Ginny tried again.

'Don't you see, he wouldn't have wanted us to go on being unhappy, he wasn't like that. He would have wanted us to get on with our lives. You mean more to me than anyone or anything, surely you know that? But in a few years' time you'll have left home and be carving out your own niche. That's how it should be − but I ... I have to think of the future too. You wouldn't want me to be alone and unhappy for the rest of my life, would you?'

'Which one is it going to be?' He was brutal in his youthful way. 'They're all after you, it's disgusting!' His voice rose and cracked and dropped a couple of octaves. Normally she would have teased him about this but now she was aghast. He had obviously heard the altercation between her and James last week about Hugh Calder-Brown and had read far too much into it.

'Simon! You're being ridiculous! It's not like that at all.'

'Yes it is! You want another husband but I don't want another father! I'm never going to leave you! I'm going to stay and look after you for always — we don't need anybody else!'

He got up and rushed out of the room, leaving his mother staring after him in dismay.

Oh, God, I made a pig's ear of that, she thought as she heard him banging out of the house. What do I do now? Teenage girls were supposed to be difficult to deal with but they had nothing on adolescent boys.

She gathered together the breakfast things and started to wash up. Simon had probably gone down the lane to his friend's home. She hoped that when he had calmed down he'd think over what she had said and be in a more receptive mood. Surely once he had got used to the idea he would accept James as a substitute father?

Simon had not gone to see his friend. He grabbed his bicycle from where it leaned against the shed and cycled speedily off towards Felstone. He was angry with himself for betraying his emotions and sick to think that his mother wanted to put someone else in his father's place. He couldn't understand how she could be so disloyal to his father's memory. He felt as if his little world was breaking up around him and re-forming in a pattern that was both unfamiliar and unwelcome.

He pedalled furiously, nipping dangerously in and out of the inside of vehicles stopped at traffic lights. As he reached the centre of town, he hit the kerb and buckled his front wheel and the chain came off. Half sobbing with exhaustion and emotion, he dragged the bike across the pavements and slung it into a passageway between two shops. The crenellated archway that led into Goths Yard was just ahead. He wandered through and slumped down on the coping bordering the fountain.

It was still early morning and the Saturday shopping crowds had not yet amassed. He kicked fretfully at the stonework and a loose piece broke off and shied across the paving. He fought back the tears and stared at the shopfronts through a shimmering veil. The name of Hugh Calder-Brown advanced and retreated in a wavering pattern above the door of the shop in the corner. He knuckled his eyes and scowled, taking in the plate-glass window and book display inside. His swinging foot brushed against the broken stone and he bent down and picked it up. There was no one about. He drew back his arm and hurled the missile at the shop front.

The result was quite electrifying. The glass cracked from top to bottom in a zigzag like a streak of lightning and the crack sounded like a thunderclap. For a few seconds it hung in a myriad of fractured, crazed pieces, a crystalline spider's web, then it imploded, scattering books and showering them with jagged fragments. Simon was horrified. He backed away and, turning, bolted back the way he had come. He ran into a policeman's arms.

'And what have you been up to, my lad?'

'I saw him do it, officer!' an elderly voice screeched from behind him. 'It was definitely him!'

Chapter Thirteen

Celia Calder-Brown gnawed at her bottom lip and stared unseeingly out of her bedroom window. Roland would have been shocked if he could have seen her; in the last week she had aged twenty years in appearance, changing from a sprightly, vivacious wrinkly to a very old lady. Even her curls drooped and her movements were disjointed and slow.

Ever since the inspector had last visited her and asked to see the historical costumes, she had been turning over in her mind the questions he had put to her. He had asked her again whether she had told anyone about her plan to loan out the Ter Borch painting and she had answered him truthfully in the negative. She was sure that she had mentioned it to no one, no one had been told of her intentions, and yet that day, the day John Hargreaves had been killed, Hugh had turned up on her doorstep and had argued with her about the foolishness of lending out the picture. *How had he known?*

She lit a cigarette and dragged at it deeply then stood motionless, the smoke curling up from her fingers, the ash drooping in a grey arc, as she tried to recall everything that had happened that day. It had been the day after the storm and she had stood at the window just as she was standing now, looking out over the destruction in the park, torn, flattened daffodils and the tree limbs wrenched from their parent trees and littering the ground as far as the eye could see. She had been awaiting the arrival of John Hargreaves but instead Hugh had blown in, in a quite neurotic state, hellbent on trouble. He had argued and cajoled and when she had remained adamant, telling him that it was none of his business, he had stormed off again, deliberately aiming his car at a branch that lay at the side of the drive. She heard again the cracks like pistol shots as it shattered beneath his wheel, and she shuddered.

That was the day that Inspector Roland and his sergeant had first appeared on the scene. Wait a minute. She brightened at a sudden memory. The two detectives had spoken to Hugh, the inspector had said so; they must have told Hugh about the painting. Then she remembered that they had met Hugh as he was leaving, and her hopes crumpled. She must have mentioned it casually to Hatty or one of the cleaning ladies from the village and the word had got about ... but she knew that she hadn't.

She came to a sudden decision and, stubbing out the unfinished cigarette, she went in search of Jack Hatfield, who acted as her chauffeur when the occasion arose. She ran him to ground in the greenhouses where he was stringing up tomato plants. The pungent smell of bruised shoots hung heavily in the humid air and made her recoil as she pushed open the door. He straightened up and rubbed his yellow-stained hands down his dungarees.

'Is anything wrong, ma'am? You look a bit peaky.'

'I want you to drive me to Hugh's shop in Felstone.'

'What, this morning?'

'Yes.'

'Later on?' he suggested hopefully.

'No, now – I want to leave immediately.'

Now that she had made up her mind she could brook no delay. She wanted to get over there as soon as possible, hear his explanation ... He must have an explanation.

'You don't look at all well. I think you ought to leave it till another day.'

'I'm the one who gives the orders around here,' she said with a flash of her old imperiousness. 'I shall be ready in fifteen minutes and I expect you to be waiting with the car outside the porch.'

The call came through as Ginny Dalton was carrying out her weekly house-clean. She listened with growing anxiety as the duty inspector at Felstone police headquarters explained that

236

her son Simon had been caught committing criminal damage in the town centre and was being held, prior to questioning, in the station to await the arrival of his parent. In her agitation she forgot to ask just what he had done and spent the short journey from Croxton turning over in her mind the most alarming possibilities.

The boy sat scuffling his heels and refused to look at her when she was shown in.

'Simon — what have you done?'

'He threw a stone through a shop window,' said the duty inspector, eyeing Ginny with interest.

'But surely there's been some mistake — '

'He was caught in the act, ma'am. Someone saw him do it.'

But *why,* Simon?'

The boy muttered something inaudible, and Ginny appealed to the policeman.

'I'm sure it was an accident, he didn't mean to do it. I will pay for the damage.'

'It's not as simple as that, Mrs Dalton. This is not the first time Simon has been in trouble. He was one of the ringleaders of a disturbance in the new shopping precinct recently in which an old lady was hurt.'

'So what will happen now?'

'He could be let off with a caution, but as it is his second offence ...'

The boy didn't look like your usual hooligan, the policeman had to admit, more like a mixed-up adolescent with an outsize chip on his shoulder. Another victim of a one-parent family. 'We have to ask ourselves,' he continued, 'why he did it. The usual reason for hefting a brick through a window is to remove some of the contents therein.'

'Simon didn't *steal* anything?' She was horrified, and the boy's head shot up.

'No, but he caused a lot of damage; if the owner decides to press charges it'll be out of my hands.'

'Where did it happen? Which shop?'

'The antiquarian bookshop in Goths Yard. It belongs to a Mr Calder-Brown.'

237

This time Simon did meet his mother's eye, then he flushed and looked down again.

'Yes, I know the place,' said Ginny faintly.

When mother and son left the station a short while later, Simon still had the threat of a charge of criminal damage hanging over him. He had been castigated by both his mother and the inspector and was in a very subdued state of mind. Ginny frogmarched him down the main street, ominously silent.

'Where are we going?' he presently asked tentatively.

'*You*,' said his mother, 'are going to wait in the library. You will sit down and read a book and not *move* till I get back — is that understood?'

'What are you going to do?'

'*I* am going to try and repair some of the damage. I don't suppose I shall be successful, the road to hell is paved with good intentions, but at least I'll have tried.'

She ushered him up the steps of the central library and only when she was sure that he was safely incarcerated with reading matter did she turn back and make for Goths Yard.

In another part of the station, Roland, totally unaware of the scene that had just taken place between the Daltons, *mère et fils,* and a uniformed colleague, flung open the door of the CID general office and beckoned out Mansfield.

'We've got the gen from Forensics, it's just come through.'

'And ...?' For once Mansfield couldn't read his chief. Roland looked neither satisfied nor disappointed, just keyed up as he paced his office floor.

'The two blood samples from Hanson and Coates were negative.'

'So it *was* Mr Double-barrelled after all?'

'Don't jump the gun, Patrick. It's not as simple as that. The specimen hairs we sent them had no cell tissue attached. They couldn't get a DNA print.'

'But if the other two are now in the clear, it only leaves him. It's a matter of elimination.'

'Unless, as I've feared all along, our murderer is someone known only to Lydia Cordingley, who we've yet to identify.'

'You don't really believe that, do you?'

238

'If it is we've wasted an awful lot of time and effort on the wrong trail.'

'Can't we get the authority, now that he's our only remaining suspect, to take an official blood sample?'

'The trouble is we've got absolutely nothing on him. If we could only break his alibi ...' Roland rumpled his hair. 'We've only got his word that he was ill in bed over Easter and stocktaking alone in his shop on the other Monday. We're going to go over his statement again and see if we can spot any discrepancy we may have overlooked before.'

The two men studied the case notes. Mansfield carefully filled his pipe and tamped down the tobacco.

'He was ill because of a bug he picked up at the anti-quarian book fair in Brussels the weekend before, or so he said.' Mansfield struck a match and sucked furiously at what Roland called his substitute dummy. 'Are we sure there *was* a book fair on then?'

His colleague looked at him with narrowed eyes. 'There's one way of finding out.'

A little while later another telex was winging its way from Felstone CID to its counterpart in Brussels.

'You can stop here,' said Celia Calder-Brown, seeing a gap in the traffic. 'I'll walk the rest of the way, it's not far.'

'How long will you be? Do you want me to try and park nearby?'

'No, you go on to the garden centre and find out about those new varieties of lily. You can pick me up outside the entrance to Goths Yard in an hour's time.'

She got out of the car and walked slowly up the street, pausing every so often to get her breath back. She wished she didn't feel so wretched; now, when she needed all her strength and wits about her, all she wanted to do was to relinquish the reins and slip into the torpor of old age which, up till now, she had so strongly resisted. She turned the corner of the yard and took a grip on herself. Hugh was her only, much-loved son; how could she, his mother, suspect him of these nameless iniquities?

He was in the window of the shop, trying to patch up a gaping hole in the glass with a sheet of cardboard. She stood watching him. There was something uncoordinated about his jerky movements and he plucked continuously at his nose. A dreadful weight settled in the pit of her stomach. He looked up and saw her standing there.

'Mother! To what do I owe the honour of this visit?' He spoke through the hole in the glass.

'What's happened? Have you been burgled?'

'No, just vandalism, nothing's been taken. Why didn't you let me know you were coming?'

He scrambled down and opened the door for her. She walked inside and looked at him, unable to speak.

'Mother, what's the matter? Are you all right?'

She took a deep breath. 'You lied to me, Hugh.'

'What are you talking about?' His eyes darted behind her, round the shop, looking everywhere but at her. He licked his lips.

'You made me a promise – you haven't kept it. I don't think you had any intention of keeping it.'

'I don't know what you're talking about.'

'Yes you do. You promised me that you were going to kick the habit, get help – and I believed you. I don't think you've even tried! You're still on drugs!'

'You'd better come upstairs to the flat.'

He flicked the placard on the door to read **CLOSED** and plunged ahead of her through the shop. She followed more slowly, labouring up the stairs. He faced her, arms akimbo, in the living-room and moved to attack.

'I'm not an addict, Mother. You read too many of the wrong sort of newspapers. I just indulge from time to time; it's a pleasurable feeling – like you get from all those cigarettes you smoke. There's no harm in it.'

'You can't stop. What's that if it's not addiction? And where is the money coming from?'

'From my business.' He gestured down below. 'I'm doing nicely, thank you.'

'Is that why you're selling off your private collection? Oh yes – ' as he looked startled – 'I've heard all about that, you're disposing of it as fast as you can find a buyer. I suppose the other money is running out?'

'What other money?' His voice was cold and thin.

240

'The money from the sale of my painting.'

His hand jerked involuntarily and a pile of cassettes crashed to the floor. He ignored them and thumped on the table.

'Now I know that you're off your rocker! You're losing your touch, mother − it's called senile dementia.'

'Are you denying it?'

'Denying it? It's all that bloody policeman's fault! Just because I admitted that I put you on to Lydia Cordingley when you were looking for someone to clean the picture, he thinks that I fixed the whole thing. And you believe him! You believe him in preference to your own son − how's that for trust?' His eyes glittered feverishly as he threw himself about the room.

Celia Calder-Brown gave a little moan and slid down onto a chair. 'Hugh, how did you know that John Hargreaves was visiting me that day?'

'Which day?'

'The Tuesday after Easter Monday when you came storming over to the Hall and tried to persuade me not to lend the painting to the Langdale Gallery.'

'I don't know. You'd mentioned your plan, word had got around and I . . . I thought it was a very unwise decision.'

'I told no one about my decision to lend out the painting. I deliberately kept it to myself. How did you know?'

Her son looked at her wildly, trying to subdue his shaking hands.

'The only way you could have known,' his mother continued forcing each word out slowly as if the task were almost beyond her, 'was by hearing about it from John Hargreaves.'

Hugh said nothing and she stared at him in horror.

'You killed him, didn't you, Hugh? You killed him and that poor woman, too!'

There was the sound of movement on the stairs. Galvanised into action, he pushed past her and flung open the door.

Roland got the answer to his telex almost immediately. The antiquarian book fair had taken place in Brussels over Easter weekend, ending at 16.00 hours on Easter Monday.

'He lied to us!' Mansfield was jubilant. 'If he went to the

book fair he was over there during the relevant weekend. What's the betting he came back on the *Mercia* the night that John Hargreaves was killed?'

'Right. We've got a good case now for pulling him in for further questioning and demanding a blood sample. Is Lacey in?'

The superintendent was not. He was over in the west of the county discussing tactics with an ex-colleague who now headed another force. He was due back later that morning.

'By the time we get Calder-Brown here he should be back.'

'Do you want me to pick him up?'

'No, I've got a better idea. We'll phone him and ask him to step down here to confirm something in his statement. We'll make it sound like a routine matter and lull his suspicions and while he's here you, Patrick, will have a little poke around on his premises. Are you game?'

'You bet. And I've got the perfect excuse: some yobbo chucked a brick through his shop window this morning — had you heard?'

'No. Why wasn't I told?' Roland asked sharply.

'It's only just been passed on to me by one of the lads downstairs. Still, it gives me a good reason for having a look around. I presume you'll clear it with uniformed?'

'Afterwards, Pat, afterwards. In the meantime, see what you can pick up.'

'What am I after — drugs? Something to tie him in with Lydia Cordingley?'

'Anything that'll give us enough evidence to hold him.'

Roland reached over and picked up the phone.

Ginny fetched up outside the bookshop. She stared at the smashed shopfront in dismay. It would cost a small fortune to replace the window; Hugh would have every right to be hopping mad. Could she persuade him not to press charges, to allow her to pay for the damage and not insist that Simon be punished? The placard on the door said **CLOSED,** and she pressed her face against the glass and tried to see into the shop. There was a dim light filtering through from the rear of the building; it looked as if Hugh were in his flat. She tried the door. The handle turned and she stepped inside.

It was dark in the interior after the brilliant sunshine outside, and she walked cautiously past the book stacks towards the back of the shop. She could hear the murmur of voices coming down from his flat. Blast! He had company. She moved closer and now she could make out some of the words. She caught the word 'policeman' and comprehension flooded in. The police were with him, probably collecting evidence that would damn Simon. She must put her suggestion and plea to him now, before it was too late.

She started up the stairs, wondering what was the best approach. Hugh Calder-Brown's angry voice echoed down the stairwell. Puzzled at his furious tones, she pricked up her ears. His visitor was a woman, not a policeman. She was sure that she knew the voice and had heard it before somewhere, but she couldn't place it. As she listened, the sense of what she was hearing penetrated her understanding and she clung to the banister, reeling with horror.

It was Hugh's mother up there with him and she was accusing him of murder. It was unbelievable! But even as the words sunk in she remembered James' warnings and hints. He had suspected Hugh all along, and now it looked as if he had been right. She rammed her fist against her mouth and tried to move backwards down the stairs, but her foot slipped and she blundered against the wall.

The half-closed door through which she had heard the exchange was flung open and a shaft of light struck across the staircase, pinning her as if in a spotlight. Hugh stood at the top looking down at her and a variety of emotions chased across his face before he spoke.

'Ginny! Have you come to join us?'

He moved down the stairs towards her, scuttling like a black spider. She cringed back, unable to speak, as he grabbed her arm and yanked her up, across the landing and into the room.

'We have a visitor, Mother!'

He released Ginny so suddenly that she slammed against the table and cried out in pain. Celia Calder-Brown was slumped on a chair opposite, one hand clamped to her chest, her lips mauve as the sweater she was wearing.

'Well, has the cat got your tongue?' he demanded of Ginny. 'I presume you heard our little conversation? Well, you know what they say of eavesdroppers ...'

'Hugh ...' she gasped.

'Mother worked it all out for herself – isn't she clever?' His mother gave a little moan. 'Cleverer than your dick – he's still blundering around in the dark. What a pity you won't be able to tell him!'

He suddenly lunged across the room and pulled open the sideboard drawer, rifling wildly through the contents. When he spun round again there was a knife in his hand, a carving knife with a bone handle. Ginny was transfixed, her lower limbs turned to lead, heavy, immobile. He was going to kill her and all she could think about was Simon waiting for her in the library. What would he do when she didn't turn up?

'Hugh, don't be crazy! Give me the knife!' Celia Calder-Brown swayed to her feet, a trace of her former authority echoing in her voice.

'Get out of the way, Mother!'

She ignored him and stepped forward holding out her hand, then she gave a little cry and crumpled to the floor, clutching her chest.

Her action released Ginny from her state of petrification. She darted forward and plunged to her knees beside the woman. Celia Calder-Brown lay like a discarded rag-doll, white and limp. There was not a vestige of life about her.

'She's dead! You've killed her!' Ginny whispered, looking across at the son.

'It's spared me from committing matricide,' he snarled, but his hands trembled and his face seemed to fall in. He stared at his mother's body with wild, dilated eyes and spoke in disjointed tones. 'She deserved it ... always ordered me around ... Hugh, do this! Hugh, don't do that! She always interfered ... wouldn't leave me alone ...'

The knife, in his shaking hands, rattled against the tabletop and he seemed to fall apart. A thread of hope curled through Ginny. If she could just edge out of the room and slam the door on him she might even now escape. She got slowly to her feet and took a step backwards. Immediately he was on

244

the alert, his head came up and the arm holding the knife lifted threateningly.

'Don't go, Ginny. You can't leave me, too.' He spoke almost crooningly and somehow that was more frightening than everything that had gone before. He stepped towards her. At that moment the phone shrilled on the bureau beside her.

So electrifying was it that she nearly screamed. She shrank back and stared at it, mesmerised. Across the room, Hugh twitched and shook and regarded it as if it were a snake. The ringing seemed to go on and on. Just when Ginny thought she could bear it no longer, he shouted:

'Answer it!'

She gaped at him. He gestured to the phone. 'Answer it — but be careful what you say, or else . . .' He brandished the knife.

She reached out and picked up the receiver. With her eyes fixed on him she licked her lips and croaked:

'Hello?'

Roland dialled Calder-Brown's number and waited. He looked across at Mansfield and shrugged. 'Damn, he must be out.' Just as he was about to ring off, he heard the click as someone picked up the receiver at the other end.

As Mansfield was to say afterwards, never had he seen such an expression of horror and disbelief on anyone's face as that which settled on his chief's when he heard the voice coming over the line. Roland, the tough, hard-boiled policeman, who never showed his feelings and never let his emotions get in the way of his work looked stricken. In a voice that his colleague had never heard before, Roland spoke:

'Hello? Is that Felstone 221385?'

There was a gasp down the line and then a faint voice said:

'Yes . . .'

'Ginny, is that *you*? Is Calder-Brown there?'

'Yes . . .'

'Is anything wrong?'

'Yes.'

'What's happened? Can you tell me?'

'No, I'm afraid you can't speak to Mr Calder-Brown. His mother has died.'

'Died? Was it an accident?'

'No. I'm afraid I can't say.'

'Ginny, are you in danger? Is he armed?'

'Yes. You'll have to try next week, the shop is closed now.'

The receiver was replaced at the other end but Roland refused to believe that he had been cut off. He jiggled the recall button and repeated her name over and over in a hoarse voice. Then he flung the phone down and turned to Mansfield, who had caught most of the dialogue from the other end.

'He's got Ginny there. Did you hear that?'

'But how ...?'

'In Christ's mame, I don't know what she's doing there! But Mrs Calder-Brown is dead. It sounds as if he's killed her and he's threatening Ginny.'

'You mean he's holding her hostage?'

'He's got her there and he's armed! What's to stop him carving her up like the other two who got in his way?'

Seeing that his chief was incapable of action, Mansfield sprang into breach.

'I'll put out the alert. We'll get everyone in on this, surround the building, get the shooters – '

'No! We haven't got time. If we raise a siege he'll just drop her. He's got nothing to lose.'

'But ...'

'He doesn't know that we know. That's the only thing in our favour. Thank God she kept her wits about her!'

Roland raged round the office, holding his head in his hands. 'Think! I've got to think! Oh, Christ!' He blundered into a chair and kicked it savagely out of the way. 'We've got to trick him, that's the only way. Take him unawares. How?' He fetched up against the filing cabinet and gave it a slap with his open hand. 'Wait a minute ...'

Mansfield watched his chief, afraid to open his mouth. He felt that he could see the cogs clicking round in Roland's brain, the thought processes in action.

'I want two uniformed constables – who's on this morning? Are Jones and Pendle around?'

'They were in the canteen a short while ago.'

'Get them. And Evans and Pomroy. Where the hell is Evans!'

A few minutes later Roland was outlining his plan to them, working it out as he went along.

'Evans, you investigated his premises. Is there a back entrance?'

'There's a fire escape that leads up from the stableyard to the kitchen of his flat. There's no door but I think you can get in through the kitchen window – it's a large casement.'

'Good' His glance took in Pomroy who, he was thankful to see, was casually dressed in jeans, T-shirt and trainers. 'Pomroy, can you lose a few years?'

'Eh?'

'I'll explain as we go. Let's get the hell out of here!'

It was a crazy plan, Mansfield thought, as the cars screeched to a halt not far from Goths Yard and the men tumbled out to take up their allotted roles; crazy, unorthodox and not the way the police machine operated at all, but because it was so bizarre it might just work. It had to, hadn't it? Ginny Dalton was in there and if it didn't succeed Roland would be headed for a padded cell.

'Who was it?'

'I don't know. One of your customers.' Ginny clenched her teeth to stop them from chattering like castanets.

'What did he want?'

'He didn't say. I told him to come back ... to come back another time – you heard me.'

'You're a quick thinker, Ginny. She would have approved of you.' He looked over at his mother's body, which lay like a discarded life-sized doll. 'Mother's dead!' There was hysteria in his voice and he gabbled on: 'I didn't kill her, did I? I didn't kill her?'

He's mad, Ginny thought, crouched against the sideboard. Or was he under the influence of drugs? She felt her own grip on reality was slipping. That had been James on the phone, hadn't it? Or was she also cracking up, hallucinating? No, it had been James, unbelievable though it was, and he *knew,* he would come for her. But even as she thought this she knew it was impossible. Long before James could get here she would be dead, butchered like his other victims, unless she could stall him.

'No, Hugh, she's had a heart attack. We may be able to save her. We must get a doctor.'

'No! No doctor, no one. She's dead ... like the others.' He plucked fretfully at his lips.

'Hugh, we must try! She must be got to hospital.'

'No, she has to die, she knows too much.' His gaze switched to her and his eyes narrowed. 'You know too much. You, too ... you'll tell them ...'

He advanced on her and she shrunk back, trying not to show how afraid she was.

'No I won't, Hugh, I'm your friend.'

'My friend ...' He reached out and clasped her limp hand. 'Yes, you're my friend, you're not like the others.'

'What others?'

His face contorted. 'That interfering old fool! He was going to spoil everything. And her − she couldn't get enough ... wanted to marry me! Said she'd tell everyone if I didn't marry her! I had to stop her, hadn't I? She asked for it. You do understand, don't you Ginny?'

'Yes, I understand.' She forced herself to grasp his hand but she felt so sick she thought she was going to retch. 'It's over now, Hugh. You must go away and forget it.'

'Go away? Yes, I hate this place! The narrow-minded people, so parochial, so prejudiced! But you're different, Ginny. You'll come with me, won't you? We'll go away.'

'Where to?'

'I don't know ... Where shall we go? Where would you like to go? France?'

'France? Paris?'

'Paris − yes, Paris! The city of lovers! You feel the same way too, don't you, Ginny? I've always fancied you ...'

He crushed her to him and she tired not to recoil, conscious of the knife in his right hand laying coldly against her shoulder.

'You must pack, Hugh. I'll help you. Where are your cases?'

'My cases?'

'Are they in your bedroom? Lets go and find them.'

'No! You're spying on me! You mustn't go in there . . . but I must. You'll wait for me, won't you? No, I don't trust you.' He muttered incoherently and his eyes darted round the room.

'Hugh, I think you should rest first, you're tired.'

'No, I'll be fine soon. Come on.' He pulled her out onto the landing and kicked open the bathroom door. 'You stay in there, Ginny!' He gave her a push and she fell into the room. 'Stay there and wait for me. Don't move! If you move I shall have to kill you!'

'What are you going to do?'

'Get ready. You won't move, Ginny, will you? Promise me?'

'I'll . . . I'll do what you say.'

He slammed the door on her and she heard him stumble into the bedroom. Shaking all over, she clamped her arms round her body to try and stop the trembling and quell the hysteria rising in her throat. She had a respite, she must make good use of it. She must lock the door, barricade herself in until help arrived. But the bolt on the door was broken and the only piece of furniture was a small, cork-topped stool. The window? She was quickly disillusioned on that point, the window was only a small aperture with a fanlight at the top. There was no way she could get through that even if she could manage to break the glass without being heard. Besides, she was on an upstairs floor, there would be a long drop.

What was he doing? Why had he thrust her in here? Was he even now preparing to kill her − arming himself with gloves and cloths to mop up the spilt blood, *her* blood? Where was James? Please God, James, come soon, she prayed. Then fresh horror hit her. Hugh had the knife but James wouldn't be armed, policemen weren't in this country. He'd walk in here unprepared and Hugh would attack him. Hugh wasn't much taller than she and thin with it, but he seemed to possess a superhuman strength, as she knew to her cost. The odds would be stacked against James. No! Please don't let him come! What was Hugh doing?

She put her ear to the door. She could hear nothing. She gently turned the handle and eased it open a fraction. She

249

could see or hear nothing. Very, very carefully she pushed the door open still further and peeped out. The bedroom door was ajar and she could see part of the room reflected in the dressing-table mirror opposite. He was bent over the bedside cabinet. Even as she strained to see what he was doing, he straightened up and seemed to look straight at her through the mirror. She pushed the door shut and reeled back against the wall.

She could hear his footfalls, he was coming back. She must find a weapon! She looked wildly round the bathroom for something with which to defend herself. There must be a razor ... a razor blade. Instead she saw an electric razor coiled in its case on the shelf. She moaned and flung open the cabinet above the washbasin. It contained the usual assortment of aftershave, deodorants and medicinal aids. At the back was a large bottle of mouthwash. If she wielded it by the neck it would make a passable weapon. Grabbing it, she knocked down a bottle of aspirin. It crashed into the basin, making what seemed to her a deafening noise.

Clutching the bottle, she faced the door and watched it open. He wasn't holding the knife. That was the first thing she registered. Yet he seemed somehow larger, more confident and relaxed than the neurotic creature who had pushed her in there a short while before.

'What have you got there, Ginny?'

This was when she should have sprung at him and smashed the bottle over his head. But she couldn't do it, she couldn't move. He reached out and plucked the bottle from her nerveless hands.

'That was naughty, I trusted you. Was I wrong? Have I made a mistake?'

'I'm sorry, Hugh. I thought you'd gone and left me ...'

'You're coming with me, Ginny. You and I are going to start a new life, remember?'

He was actually smiling at her; there was euphoria in his voice and his face was flushed. As he pulled her tightly to him, she noticed that the irises of his eyes were almost swallowed up by the distended pupils and there were faint traces of powder round his nostrils. Then she understood, he had just had a fix. That was what he had been doing

250

in the bedroom – snorting his coke. Where did that leave her? He was no longer paranoid as he had been earlier but he was just as dangerous because he was now in charge, hyped up and unstoppable. His mouth sought hers, his dry lips crushed hers as if he were sucking out her very essence and his hard member pressed against her.

She felt all control going. He was going to rape her and she was powerless to resist, he was possessed of an overwhelming strength. She wrenched her lips free. He grabbed her hair and forced her head back again, muttering thickly:

'Ginny ...'

'Not now, Hugh. We haven't got time. Later ... later when we can relax ...'

'No, now.' He started to pull her towards the bedroom. Suddenly he pushed her away and she staggered back against the door jamb.

'What was that?'

'What?'

'Listen!'

She heard it then. Raised voices coming from outside the shop down below, and the sounds of a scuffle.

'What's going on?' He was immediately suspicious. Grabbing her hand, he pulled her to the top of the stairs. 'Can you see what is happening?'

She descended a few steps and crouched to look through the banisters so that she could see the front of the shop. Through the jagged glass she caught glimpses of two uniformed policemen who appeared to be struggling with a youth.

'It's the police!' A frisson of hope and fear shot through her.

'The police!' He joined her on the stairs, cruelly grasping her shoulders. 'What's happening?'

A black-clothed arm loomed into view through the heavily patterned glass door panels and hammered on the knocker.

'Mr Calder-Brown, sir? We've caught him – the hooligan who broke your window.'

The voice boomed through the broken window and echoed along the length of the shop, resounding off bookcases and fitments. Ginny felt she really had flipped. Simon had broken that window and the police had caught him.

251

'Mr Calder-Brown — are you there?'

'Go away!' Ginny's captor spoke in a low voice. 'You blundering fools!'

The door opened and the two policemen stepped inside, propelling the youth, who kicked out, trying to escape.

'If we could just have a few words, sir, and you would see if you can identify this yobbo?' one of them called out as they advanced farther into the shop.

'Come on, get back!' Hugh Calder-Brown ordered, dragging at Ginny.

'Hugh, you'll have to go down and speak to them,' she whispered.

'Are you crazy?'

'They know you're here. They're going to come up into the flat and find your mother's body.'

'Bloody hell! All right. But you stay here, Ginny. You're not to move from this spot — do you understand?'

She nodded weakly. He dropped his hold of her and started down the stairs.

She heard him walking through the shop and then the murmur of voices. She couldn't imagine what had happened, but it was a miracle, it had given her the chance to escape. She slipped down the stairs and felt her way to the back of the shop. The walls were lined with bookshelves and she could just make out the darker oblong of the door. She pushed it open and found herself in a sort of cubbyhole kitchen. There was a sink beneath the tiny window and a gas ring on the worktop. There was no back door. She looked round wildly. The only exit was through the front door near where Hugh was arguing with the policemen.

She nearly cried out with despair and frustration, then common sense came to her rescue. what was there to stop her from running out there and telling them everything? Hugh couldn't harm her in front of two officers of the law. She would be safe and she could shop him at the same time. She moved forwards. At that moment she heard the shop door slam and Hugh was hurrying back.

'That's got rid of them — interfering fools. As if I care who heaved that brick through the window.' He projected his voice up the stairs to where he had left her. 'Ginny?' She heard him bounding up the stairs. 'Ginny? Where are you?'

She cringed behind a bookcase and he started to swear. 'You bitch! Where have you gone? I shan't let you go!'

She heard a scrape and a metallic click and knew that he and the knife were reunited. Then he bounded back down the stairs and started to run up and down the narrow aisles between the book stacks, searching for her.

'Ginny? You won't escape me this time, you cheating bitch! I'm going to kill you!'

She shrank back and heard him pass across a little way in front of her. She caught a glimpse of him silhouetted against the window and saw the knife in his hand.

'Where are you? You can't get away!'

He was coming nearer. She knew that she had to move but she was rooted to the spot, frozen with terror. She could hear his breath, the ragged, exultant panting, coming closer and closer and she willed herself to dash in the opposite direction down the nearest gangway. He immediately heard her, turned round and stormed after her. She rounded a corner and crashed into a display unit and a shower of volumes scattered in her wake.

Behind her he stumbled over the fallen books, swearing and cursing her, and then he was hot on her heels again. Up and down the dimly lit aisles she fled with him in pursuit and somehow she found herself once more at the back of the building with her escape route cut off. She could no longer hear him. The silence was deafening. She looked round desperately, fumbling her way from shelf to shelf. Was he even now creeping up on her, knife raised, about to give her the *coup de grâce*?

Her hands encountered the kitchenette door, which swung inwards, and she stumbled backwards.

Arms reached out and grabbed her in a vicelike grip and her erupting scream was cut off by a hand clamped hard across her mouth.

Chapter Fourteen

She blacked out for a few seconds, spiralling down into darkness, and as she fought her way back to consciousness she was dimly aware that the arms that had imprisoned her were now supportive and a voice was whispering urgently in her ear.

'Ginny, are you all right?'

'James!'

'Ssh! Don't say a word. You're safe now.'

'Oh, my God! James! I th-thought ...'

'Ssh. I've got to go now. Stay here and don't move.'

The same words but how different! She slumped back against the worktop, drained of emotion, unable to believe that the nightmare was over.

It took three men to overpower Hugh Calder-Brown, and Mansfield received a nasty gash in the upper arm. The bracelets were finally snapped on and, leaving the prisoner in the hands of the sergeant and Evans, Roland went back to Ginny. She fell into his arms, shaking like a leaf; reaction had set in and she was half laughing and half crying.

'Steady on, my love. Did he hurt you?'

'N-no. But ...'

'He's under arrest. He'll never harm anyone again. Do you understand, Ginny? It's all over.'

'What will happen to him?'

'Don't worry about that. I'll call up reinforcements and get him taken away. You won't have to see him again. And I must get Patrick to hospital – he got stabbed in the arm.'

'Patrick Mansfield? Is it bad?'

'Not serious, but he'll need some stiches.'

'James, I don't understand how you got here. Those uniformed policemen and that youth ...'

'Later, I'll explain everything later. Can you bear to wait upstairs in the flat for the moment?'

'There's a body up there. His mother.'

'Sweet Jesus, I hadn't realised ...'

At that moment a stentorian voice boomed round the building:

'We have the place surrounded. Drop your weapon and come out with your hands above your head and you will not be harmed.'

'James?' Ginny squeaked, clutching his arm in alarm.

'Don't worry.' A wry grin passed over his face. 'That's the back-up team. I rather think I may also be under arrest soon.'

If Superintendent Bob Lacey was astounded to see a posse of plain-clothes officers answer his call over the megaphone, he covered up well. Hugh Calder-Brown was bundled into a van and taken to the station to be charged; the men covering the building were withdrawn; and Lacey, after a quick look upstairs at the body of Celia Calder-Brown, gathered Roland's team together round the desk in the shop.

'You too, Mrs Dalton. Have you recovered enough to answer some questions?'

Ginny replied weakly that she had and Lacey waved her to a chair, eyeing her speculatively. So this was James' fancy bit, and a bit of all right too. James knew how to pick them, but he had nearly lost this one. Lacey allowed his righteous anger full rein and, lowering himself onto the other chair, thumped the desk and sent a pile of books tumbling to the floor.

'I don't normally castigate an officer in front of his subordinates but you were all in on this and I want to express my extreme displeasure. What you did, Inspector, was criminally rash. There is a procedure for this sort of thing, but you took the law into your own hands – '

'There wasn't time, sir.'

'As I said, a correct procedure to deal with the situation.'

'If we had mounted a siege, he would only have used Mrs Dalton as a hostage and when her use was over her life wouldn't have been worth a sou. I had to work quickly, do something before it was too late.'

'So, just what did you do? No — ' as Roland made to speak — 'we'll hear Mrs Dalton's story first. How did you come to get involved in this case?'

Ginny flashed a nervous look at Roland, received an encouraging smile, swallowed and started to speak:

'It was my son who threw that brick through the shop window. He was picked up by the police and I was asked to go down to the station. I was afraid he was going to be charged and I thought that maybe if I tackled Hu — Mr Calder-Brown and asked him not to press on with — '

'You knew Calder-Brown?'

'He was a ... a casual friend.'

Lacey gave her a thoughtful look but said nothing, and she stumbled on: 'I walked in here and I could hear voices coming from his flat. I recognised his and I thought at first that he was talking to a policeman, then I realised ...'

Slowing and painfully she explained what had happened, finishing with the chase through the dimly lit shop and her rescue by James Roland.

'A very nasty experience, ma'am, but you behaved well under the circumstances, didn't lose your head — unlike some people around here.' He threw Roland a malicious look. 'Perhaps we can now hear Inspector Roland's version of what happened?'

'When I realised that Mrs Dalton was here with Calder-Brown and in terrible danger, I knew time was critical,' said Roland crisply. 'I commandeered constables Jones and Pendle and used them with Pomroy to set up a little diversion. Pomroy pretended to be the youth who broke the window and they manhandled him and dragged him in here and persuaded Calder-Brown to come down and talk to them.'

'Three of my officers *play-acting*!' said Lacey in disgust.

'While he was downstairs, Mansfield, Evans and myself entered the flat upstairs via the fire escape and kitchen casement. It was a nasty surprise to discover that Mrs Dalton was not there. I managed to get down the stairs and hid myself in that little kitchenette place at the back before he returned. Mansfield and Evans hid themselves in the bedroom. You know the rest. He was stalking her round this shop, in and out of the bookcases, and as soon as I had managed to snatch her out of the way we jumped him. He put up quite a fight — he was high as a kite.'

'He'd just had a fix,' Ginny put in.

'Had he indeed?' said Lacey.

'Coke,' said Roland, 'he was a cocaine addict. Of course we overpowered him and Mansfield got pricked.'

'Want to get that seen to,' said Lacey, heaving himself to his feet.

'It's nothing,' said Mansfield, who had wound a tea towel round his upper arm.

'You go straight to Casualty — and that's an order! As for you, Roland, I should throw the book at you.' He paused and turned his attention to Ginny. 'I suppose all I can say, Mrs Dalton, is — all's well that ends well. You realise that you'll be a key witness when the case comes to court?'

'Yes,' said Ginny unhappily. On hearing James relate what had happened she had relived the events of the past hour and she felt sick and faint.

'James, make the lady a cup of tea and look after her,' Lacey commanded. As he saw the look of recoil and distaste that passed across her face, he added, 'Better still, take her across the yard and treat her at the café.'

A little while later Roland and Ginny were sitting at a table at the back of the restaurant in Goths Yard. Ginny was looking better, her colour had returned and she managed to drink a second cup of tea without her teeth chattering against the rim.

'Try and forget it for now,' Roland urged, laying his hand over hers and wishing he could take her in his arms and kiss away her fears there and then. 'It was a terrible experience but it's all over now.'

'I shall never be able to forget it. It was horrible, James! He was completely psychotic, changing from one second to the nest. I didn't know whether he was going to jump me or stab me, and when his mother collapsed — '

'Now, stop it. You must try not to think about it. It's over and you mustn't let your mind dwell on it. Think instead of the future, you've got me and Simon – '

'Simon! Oh, my God!'

Ginny clapped her hand over her mouth and Roland felt a fresh surge of apprehension.

'What's the matter?'

'I told him to wait for me in the library, not to move until I got back.'

Roland grinned. 'Well, we'd better go and get him, hadn't we?'

'Are you telling me that it was sheer chance, Calder-Brown meeting up with John Hargreaves on the *Mercia* that night?' Superintendent Lacey demanded, looking at the men lined up in front of his desk, this time in his own office. Roland was presenting his case and, as Lacey put it, 'tying up loose ends' and 'putting him in the picture'.

'Yes. Calder-Brown was coming back from the book fair in Brussels and he just happened to get talking to Hargreaves at the start of the crossing. I suppose as casual acquaintances they exchanged facts about their professions. Calder-Brown must have been completely poleaxed when Hargreaves told him the reason for his trip on the Continent and his prospective visit to Monkbeggars Hall. He had had no idea that his mother was thinking of loaning out the Ter Borch painting to the gallery.'

'Did Hargreaves realise who Calder-Brown was?' Lacey asked, steepling his fingers so that his hands looked even more like bunches of bananas, and resting his chin on them.

'No. From what I've gathered from his disjointed ramblings since, he didn't reveal his connection with Celia Calder-Brown. Hargreaves had no idea that he was talking to the son. Anyway, Calder-Brown knew that the game was up; he had exchanged a copy for the painting and sold off the original when it had been sent to be cleaned – more of that later – and he knew that the minute Hargreaves set eyes on it his substitution would be discovered. He had to be silenced and he immediately set up a plan to do just that.'

'But you don't scrub somebody out just because they get in

your way – not unless you're stark, raving bonkers! They'll get him off on a plea of insanity.'

'He was unbalanced at the time all right, suffering from withdrawal symptoms. He was hooked on cocaine – that was why he'd lifted the painting in the first place, to finance his little pastime – but he was shrewed enough to realise that he couldn't indulge his craving while on his jaunts to the Continent, it was too risky to carry supplies. So there he was, unstable and agitated, and Hargreaves' revelations were enough to tip him over into a state of real paranoia. He grasped the first opportunity and Hargreaves played into his hands by admitting that he was a terrible sailor and was already feeling very ill and that he had booked a double-berthed cabin. It happened just as Mansfield and myself had conjectured earlier: he told Hargreaves that he had some marvellous seasickness pills and offered to give him one; he also told him that he had not been able to get a cabin. So what does Hargreaves do? He takes pity on him, invites him to use the other bunk in his cabin and accepts one of the pills that Calder-Brown presses on him, which is actually a very strong sleeping pill.

'While Hargreaves is in a drugged sleep, Calder-Brown somehow gets hold of the souvenir paperknife and attacks him. He strikes the first blow in the dark, misses a vital organ and his victim comes to and tries to defend himself. This so unbalances Calder-Brown that he goes berserk – you know the result. Afterwards, he takes off his outer clothing, which is soaked with blood, rifles through the dead man's possessions and removes means of identification which, together with the bloodstained clothes and dagger, he throws down the maw of the ship's "muncher". When the ship docks he locks the cabin door behind him, walks off the ship in the company of the other foot passenagers, and picks up his car, which he has left in the car park at Felstone Docks.'

Roland leaned back and snapped his fingers. 'And he got away with it. It was so outrageous that it succeeded, although so many things could have gone wrong. For one thing, my two other suspects were also on the ferry that night – Nigel Hanson and Richard Coates – and yet none of them set eyes on the others. It was such a coincidence that at one time I thought they were all in it together, especially as I knew that Hanson and Coates had needed, in the near past, to get their hands on a large sum of money.'

'Did you suspect Calder-Brown right from the start?' asked Evans.

'Only in so much as once I knew about the business with the painting I thought it must have been someone connected with the family. Hanson and Coates were far more in the running until the last little drama. Hanson was up to his eyes in debt, what with his racehorse, his gambling debts and his mistress, and I knew that Coates had somehow managed to finance his proposed "famine relief" operation. Well, to get back to the sequence of events, Calder-Brown immediately drove over to Monkbeggars Hall to find out just what his mother was up to. We bumped into him, almost literally, as he was leaving; he was in a furious temper. Apparently his mother had known for some time about his drug-taking, which was why they were alienated. He tried to persuade her not to go ahead with the loan of the painting but she was adamant. He now had to make further plans to prevent discovery and work out a way of persuading Lydia Cordingley to keep her mouth shut.'

'Yes, what was the tie-up with her in the first place?' Lacey eyed his inspector shrewdly.

'He'd met her at some function. I don't know whether even then, at the first meeting, he had some notion of setting up the fraud, or whether he couldn't resist adding her to his conquests − every female was fair game to him. Anyway, he seduced her and I should imagine she was an easy victim, a lonely, plain, partially crippled woman who couldn't have had much going for her in that line before. She became besotted with him and willingly agreed to copy the picture. But she tried to cover herself, in case there was any trouble later, by signing the copy, photographing everything and lodging these photographs with her bank. He probably slept with her enough to keep her sweet and she, poor woman, thought she was the only one in his life.'

'You sound as if you were a fly on the wall.'

'We knew that she had a lover, we found contraceptives beside her bed; it was my fear that this unknown boyfriend might be someone unknown to us, with no connection with Monkbeggars Hall, who had set the whole thing up; but he's confessed. Even now he can't resist boasting about his sexual prowess.' Roland's voice was tinged with disgust and Lacey had difficulty from chipping in with a remark about Roland's own reputation in that field.

'He now got to work,' Roland continued, 'planning how he was going to remove the fake picture from Monkbeggars Hall without drawing suspicion on himself. He decided the perfect opportunity could be arranged during one of the historical re-creations, when the place would be crawling with visitors and participants, and he healed the rift with his mother to make sure that he would be there, taking part. It was sheer coincidence again that Mansfield and I should happen to be there on the occasion he chose. He started the fire, making sure that it activated the alarm, and afterwards, before it was reset, he removed the painting from the wall.'

'Just a minute. Lydia Cordingley was killed before the picture snatch at Monkbeggars Hall.'

'I was coming to that. He knew that once the theft of the painting was made public, Lydia Cordingley could point the finger at him, so he had to make sure she didn't blab. I think he quite honestly thought he could do this by sweet talk and promises. He went over to her cottage early on the Monday morning and explained that he was going to have to "steal" the picture hanging in the Hall to prevent the substitution being discovered. He expected, in return for a little amour, that she would be won over, but she turned the tables on him and tried to blackmail him: he must marry her or she would tell all.'

'Did she know that he had killed Hargreaves?' Lacey interrupted.

'No, the question didn't arise. She would have known nothing about Hargreaves' proposed visit to the Hall. Anyway, as I was saying, Calder-Brown thought she was joking, but when she insisted he became incensed and went berserk again. He snatched up a kitchen knife and butchered her. I think by this time he was actually enjoying the act of killing, it gave him a wonderful sense of power and of being in command. However, he had forgotten about the dog, who

261

went for him. He exchanged the knife for a heavy-bottomed frying pan and tried to bash the dog over the head but it got its teeth into his ankle and hung on − he still has a scar on his leg from this attack − so he struck it across the back, fracturing its spine, and when the dog fainted he thought he had killed it.

'He then takes off the bloodstained boiler suit − which he had worn as a precaution, though how he explained this away I really don't know − and puts it in a plastic sack. He wipes his fingerprints off everything he has touched, pockets the murder weapon, picks up the sack and walks out. He had previously left his car some way from the cottage, tucked away out of sight down a country lane, and he makes his way back to it by a devious cross-country route, unseen by anyone. He drives back to Felstone, sees all the refuse sacks outside the shops awaiting collection, and deposits his sack on a doorstep − a bad mistake, as he chose the wrong door − goes back to his place and carries on as usual.'

'When did you start suspecting him?'

'Although he figured on my list all along, we couldn't pin a possible motive on him until we heard a little whisper about drugs. I then checked and discovered that the book fair actually took place over the Easter holiday, so I wondered if he had been on the *Mercia* that Easter Monday night. We had failed to get a DNA print, but I reckoned that by now I had got an excuse to pull him in to check his alibis and ask for a blood sample. I rang his shop and that triggered off the drama.'

'I don't understand all this business with his mother,' Lacey grumbled.

'He made another mistake early in the proceedings, and that was what caused the showdown between himself and his mother. As I've said, when he left the ferry that morning he drove straight to Monkbeggars Hall and started haranguing her about the foolishness of loaning out the painting. Afterwards she remembered that she had told no one of this plan and the only way he could have known was from John Hargreaves himself. She brooded over this, becoming more and more suspicious and unhappy, and finally decided to have it out with him.'

'Has he confessed all this?'

'He didn't have to. Mrs Dalton overheard the exchange between them when she arrived at his flat. His mother confronted him with the truth and at the same time he realised that Mrs Dalton had learned the true facts. By this time he was in an advanced state of paranoia. He threatened Mrs Dalton with a knife; his mother tried to intervene and collapsed with a heart attack. Whether he would have killed her we shall never know. Apparently she had a bad heart — she was a heavy smoker — and could have popped off at any time.'

'Well, we found cocaine in his flat and cannabis,' said Lacey, 'but that aspect of the case must be kept under wraps for the time being while we follow it up; I think we're going to uncover a nice little racket which could lead us to some of the big boys.'

'Coke and pot seems a funny combination,' said Mansfield, fingering his pipe but not daring to light up in Lacey's office. 'Polyabuse usually involves coke and heroin or coke and one of the barbiturates.'

'I think the pot was kept for his visitors,' said Roland. 'He offered a reefer as other people might offer a beer or a coffee. It gave him a buzz to flout the law, he was contemptuous of normal conventions.'

'A nasty piece of work,' said Lacey, gathering up his papers to indicate that the meeting was over. 'But he won't be up to any more tricks for a very long time. We've got enough evidence to put him away for a good stretch. By the way, Pomroy, is there any truth in the rumour that I've heard?'

'Sir?'

'That you're applying for a scholarship to RADA?'

'He acted on my orders and put in a very good performance just when it was needed,' said Roland. 'He certainly fooled Calder-Brown.'

'Yes, I was coming to that,' said Lacey ominously. 'Stay behind, will you, Roland? I have words for your ears only.'

After the others had gone, Lacey rounded on his inspector.

'You may feel that you have cause for congratulations over solving this case but it's not going to look so good down in

263

writing. Supposing it had gone wrong? I can't understand why it didn't go wrong — how you got away with it. Your methods of working have been suspect to say the least — very unorthodox.'

'There's been an awful lot of unorthodox policing around here just lately.' Roland held his chief's eye and the latter gave way first.

'All right, James, but what are you going to do about Mrs Dalton?'

'Do?'

'For God's sake, marry the woman and get her out of my hair. I'm fed up with Ginny Dalton figuring in all the murder cases on my patch. Marry her and keep that boy of hers under control!'

'It's not as simple as that, sir.'

'It seems perfectly simple to me. If someone doesn't come down hard on him soon, he's going to end up in really bad trouble. You don't want that and I'm sure his mother doesn't want that. Discipline is what he needs so make sure he gets some, right?'

'Is that advice or an order?'

'When have I ever interfered in my men's private lives?' Lacey's rhetorical question made the other man wince. 'Just remember it would be easier for me to overlook his latest little misdoing if I knew there was no chance of it recurring.'

'I get the message, sir.'

The waves surged up the shingle bank and gurgled away in scummy foam; the pebbles gleamed tawny, amber, butterscotch and slate as they lay exposed between each breaker. Overhead the seagulls dipped and screamed as Ginny Dalton and James Roland crunched along the beach. The sun was dazzling but it was very windy. The scarf that Ginny had knotted round her head had slipped onto her shoulders and her hair streamed out behind her like an apricot banner. She pointed over the water.

'Look at those terns, James, aren't they graceful?'

'They look like seagulls to me.'

'No, over there to the right. They're much more streamlined and slender than the gulls. Take a look through the glasses.'

She handed him the binoculars. He swung them up and focused out to sea.

'Can you see them?'

'Uhmm.' He swept the horizon.

'What are you looking at now?'

'That ship out there, I think it's the ferry.'

'The *Mercia*?'

'No, it will be her sister ship the *Bernicia* at this time of the day, though they're almost identical.'

'Except that the *Bernicia* didn't have a murder committed on it.' She shivered.

'Are you still worried about the trial?'

'No. Yes ... It's just the thought of having to come face to face with Hugh Calder-Brown again. Oh, James, it was so awful! I shall never forget the way − '

'Stop it. It's all over and you've got to try and put it behind you. I know it's difficult to do that with the ordeal of the trial to come still hanging over you, but it's really only a formality. He's as guilty as hell and he'll get what he deserves.' He sought to distract her. 'What are those plants over there growing out of the shingle? The ones that look like giant cabbages in bloom?'

'Sea kale. Quite showy, aren't they? The bluish spiky ones are sea holly and that mass of small white flowers creeping over the stones is sea campion.'

'Amazing, all those different plants flourishing on shingle beaches, what with the wind and salt and what have you.'

'Don't forget this is a nature reserve. They're protected and woe betide anyone who's caught picking or disturbing them.'

'Come on, race you to the sea.'

He caught hold of her hand and they plunged down the slope through the high-tide line of decaying seaweed, bleached shells and shipping detritus, to the water's edge where spent waves nibbled at their feet. Across the water a ship's hooter boomed out and, even as they watched, the *Bernicia* ferry altered course and swung round almost broadside to them as she negotiated the narrow shipping channel leading into the estuary. Roland looked down at the woman beside him, who was watching the ship's progress with a perplexed look on her face.

'What's the matter now? There's something still worrying you?'

'Not really, it's just that ... When Simon had to give evidence in that other case, you said at the time that it would be out of order for us to meet until it was all over. Does that mean that I'm not going to see you for a long while?'

'Well − ' Roland feigned indifference − 'there is one way round it.'

'And what is that?'

'I could hardly be prevented from communicating with my wife.'

'Oh!' Ginny assimilated this. 'Are you asking ... ?'

'Let's go.' He turned and loped up the beach. Ginny stumbled after him, her eyes stinging from the salt wind and her hair whipping across her face.

'What's the hurry? Where are we going?'

He waited until she caught up with him and then said firmly:

'We're going home to tell Simon that he's getting a new father.'

You have been reading a novel published by Piatkus Books. We hope you have enjoyed it and that you would like to read more of our titles. Please ask for them in your local library or bookshop.

If you would like to be put on our mailing list to receive details of new publications, please send a large stamped addressed envelope (UK only) to:

Piatkus Books, 5 Windmill Street
London W1P 1HF

PIATKUS

The sign of a good book